Nobody's Hero

NOBODY'S HERO
a novel
PAUL HEMPHILL

RIVER CITY PUBLISHING
Montgomery, Alabama

Printed in the United States.
Text designed by Lissa Monroe.

Library of Congress Cataloging-in-Publication Data:

Hemphill, Paul, 1936-
Nobody's hero : a novel / by Paul Hemphill.
p. cm.
ISBN 1-57966-029-0 (alk. paper)
1. African American football players—Fiction. 2. Quarterback
(Football)—Fiction. 3. Radio broadcasters—Fiction. 4. Football
coaches—Fiction. 5. Male friendship—Fiction. 6. Southern
States—Fiction. 7. Race relations—Fiction. 8. College
sports—Fiction. I. Title.
PS3558.E4793 N63 2002
813'.54—dc21
2002004586

River City publishes fiction, nonfiction, poetry, art, and children's books by
distinguished authors and artists in our region and nationwide. Visit our web
site at www.rivercitypublishing.com.

For Susan, again,

whence cometh all good things.

♟

And in memory of Bobby Hannah,

Ramblin' Man.

Other books by Paul Hemphill

FICTION
King of the Road
The Sixkiller Chronicles
Long Gone

NONFICTION
The Ballad of Little River
Wheels
The Heart of the Game
Leaving Birmingham
Me and the Boy
Too Old to Cry
The Good Old Boys
The Nashville Sound

COLLABORATIONS
Climbing Jacob's Ladder (with Jock M. Smith)
Mayor (with Ivan Allen, Jr.)

AUTHOR'S NOTE

Atlantans, noting what might appear to be errors in geography here and there, are advised that this is purely a work of fiction.

Smart lad, to slip betimes away
From fields where glory does not stay
And early though the laurel grows
It withers quicker than the rose.
                    —A. E. Housman
                    "To an Athlete Dying Young"

Gadabout Billy Ray ("The Gunslinger") Hunsinger has
landed on his feet again, this time hosting "Jock Talk"
on tiny WWJD in Austell (AM 1690), where he will
ruminate Sundays 10–midnight. . . .

                    —Item in the Atlanta *Journal-
                    Constitution*'s "Peachtree Parade"

ONE

L ong shadows, brown grass, wispy cirrus clouds drifting across a high blue sky. Warring armies parry and thrust. On a scoreboard rising high above one end zone: N ALA ST 34, BAMA 40, fourth quarter, 1:31 to go, visitors with the ball. Cheerleaders in pleated skirts, turtlenecks, and ponytails, flashing pom-pons and megaphones. A stunned crowd, on its feet, craning necks, gawking at a bad wreck. On the sidelines, shirtsleeves rolled to his elbows, God in a hound's-tooth hat, Bear Bryant points and shouts at players wheezing now, hands on their knees, trying to catch a breath before the next onslaught. All eyes on a stranger in town, No. 13, HUNSINGER across the back of his jersey, a rawboned cowboy, reloading.

Voiceover. "The Gunslinger's about to ruin the Bear's day, sports fans. Can you believe this? Little pissant school's about to mess up homecoming at Tuscaloosa. David and Goliath, the Gunslinger and the Bear. Okay, here we go. Ball at midfield, the Gun's standing all alone in shotgun again, Patton on the battlefield, looking cool, pointing to his troops." . . . *Bing-bing-bing.* A bullet over the middle for eleven yards, first down. A flare pass for six more, out of bounds to stop the clock. *Wham*: a rifle shot deep and over the middle, two defensive backs colliding in pursuit of a nifty little receiver who lands on his head with the ball at the Alabama twenty.

Timeout. Fifty-six seconds left, Bryant slamming his hat to the ground, and then . . .

"Ah, *shit!*" The screen, set on a tripod at one end of the pool table, now emits a blinding white glare. There is the acrid smell of melting celluloid as the film flops wildly on the reel of the projector, whirring at the other end of the table. Muttering, chomping his unlit cigar, kneading his bare toes into the shag carpet to soothe his athlete's foot, he rises from his director's chair—GUNSLINGER lettered across the back—to address the problem. When he yanks the chain to turn on the green lampshade centered over the pool table, the kids blink and raise the backs of their hands to their eyes.

Nine o'clock on a Saturday morning in the Atlanta suburbs, early summer of 1985, and what are they to make of this old honkie? Barefooted, wearing cutoffs, shirtless, hasn't shaved, having beer for breakfast. They've seen him on television, before he got fired, wearing a pale blue shirt and tie and navy blazer, but not like this. Where's Mrs. Hunsinger, anyway? There are five of them, two boys and three girls, neat kids with bright ebony faces, brownish nappy hair arranged in Afros and cornrows and dreadlocks, wearing starched blue jeans and identical T-shirts proclaiming "Dixie = Slavery," and they are wondering if this is some kind of practical joke. Or a test, maybe, to see if they're ready for prime time. Jackie Robinson had to go through the same thing, they've heard from their parents, but they thought all of that was pre-history.

From where he stands now, on the other side of the pool table from where the kids are scrunched together on a ratty plaid Early American sofa, they look like a row of prairie dogs who have poked their heads out to see if the coast is clear. He says, "What do you think, sports fans?"

They are struck silent until the tall, handsome boy, the one wearing a white baseball cap with a black "X" on the crown, figures somebody ought to say something, anything, no matter what. "So what happened?"

"Film broke," he says. "Damned thing's older'n dirt. It's more Scotch tape than film now."

"No, sir. I mean, who won?"

"Well, that's a long story, pardner." He guzzles the last swig of a Budweiser, crushes the can with one hand, flips it toward a tall plastic garbage pail in the corner of the room. "Scared the hell out of the Bear, anyway."

A pretty girl in a massive Afro, big as a beach ball, like one of those Black Panthers from the 'sixties—Angela Davis?—brightens when she remembers something. "Bear *Bryant?* Wasn't he the famous football coach at Alabama?"

"Bingo. The one and only."

The boy, Malcolm X, clears his throat. "Was that you? Number thirteen?"

"You got it." Fussing with the broken ends of film, fumbling for the roll of tape, he looks around and sees blank eyes, uncomprehending. "'Hunsinger the Gunslinger.'"

"You must have been good."

"'Good'? You saw the film. Gunslinger right, Gunslinger left, Gunslinger short, Gunslinger deep. We had this one play—pardon my French—but we had this one play. Called it 'Niggers Go Long.'" The kids flinch and recoil at hearing the word, but he plunges ahead without noticing. "Flooded the secondary. Receivers all over the place. Hell, couldn't nobody stop it, not even the Bear."

Compared to this, farting in church would have been nothing. Time stops. The kids are stunned, looking around for Mrs. Hunsinger, wondering what the ground rules are when you're in another man's house. "Sir . . ." one of them begins.

"Aw, hell, it's just a figure of speech."

"But—"

"Nothing personal, understand."

"Yeah, but—"

"Hell, we didn't even have black players then. Come on, where's your sense of humor?"

Malcolm X isn't buying. Wordlessly, with all of the dignity he can muster, he eases up from the sofa, for an instant glaring as though he might go one-on-one with this old fart, and takes the first step of what he intends to be a righteous grand exit when he stops in his tracks upon seeing that Ginny Hunsinger has heard the whole thing. She is standing in the doorway to the den, tight-lipped and frowning. She cuts a look at her husband and says, "Outside, kids." Stumbling over each other, they can't leave fast enough.

...

A man's home is his castle, right? Some men, the ones whose favorite class in high school was Shop, build elaborate workshops crammed with all of the latest woodworking gadgets and thingamajigs—jigsaws, planers, sanders, dados, lathes, whining contraptions that can do anything with a piece of wood—where they spend their nights and weekends happily turning out tables and chairs and sconces and birdhouses and fanciful mailboxes for wives who really wish they would quit. Others, the more studious types, make of their spare rooms a cool inner sanctum of soft lights, brooding bookcases, deep leather chairs, hidden stereo speakers, a globe, Atlases, maybe an aquarium, where they can escape to the life of the mind, listening to Bach, reading the masters, contemplating. Still others, Ozzie & Harriet, create a Family Room, replete with a big television set rigged with a VCR, mom-and-dad chairs, boxes full of toys for all the kids, hooked rugs, a circular table for the weekend games of Scrabble and Monopoly, and over there in the corner a cozy little wicker bed for the cocker spaniel.

But this, now, this retreat to which William Raymond Hunsinger has been repairing ever since his retirement from football ten years ago, is something else indeed. Above the doorway where Ginny now stands— seething, hands on hips, in battle mode—there is one of those bronze historical markers with the legend THE GUN ROOM, which needs no explanation to those who enter, and the room is many things at once: a shrine, a saloon, a pool hall, a snack bar, a locker room. It was a thing of beauty when he had it converted from a two-car garage, and his buddies couldn't believe their eyes when they came by to check it out. Jukebox, giant television screen, pool table, leather recliners, popcorn machine, refrigerator, wet bar, framed headlines and eight-by-tens; even, as a bow to his wife, pennants and pom-pons and megaphones once waved by Ginny during her college days. There is a wall clock reading No Drinking 'til Five, with the numeral 5 at every hour. Against one wall, the *pièce de résistance*, there are five glass-fronted trophy cabinets in a row, holding helmets and jerseys and various pieces of equipment, everything but jockstraps and dirty socks, from each team he ever played for, from city playgrounds to the pros. He had gotten the idea from a visit to the College Football Hall of Fame in South Bend, Indiana, where he found his name in a forlorn cubicle dedicated to Small Colleges.

In the beginning he would spend hours in this room; whole weekends, in fact, if there was some good football on the tube. He could while away those hours in the company of pals from the old days, or, more often than not in recent years, all alone in his reverie: shooting pool, playing the jukebox, watching football, polishing the cabinets, dusting off his scrapbooks, phoning friends who seldom return his calls anymore, simply daydreaming, or hauling out the old-fashioned projector and the bulky reel of film that might be the only vivid record of that great day in the fall of 1965 when he nearly brought down the Bear and the Alabama Crimson Tide all by himself. Ginny has been putting up with it because it beats the alternatives: the bars and the women and what she calls, with some bitter detachment, his *pied-à-terre* downtown.

Lately, though, the room has taken on the feel of one of those dank antique shops on the edge of town; junk stores, really, where cobwebs cling to rusty Pure Oil signs and gas-station tea glasses and busted piano stools that nobody wants anymore. He hasn't dusted or vacuumed or polished in months; has done little more than empty the ashtrays and toss out the beer cans and whiskey bottles when they fill the trash barrel; hasn't bothered to replace the glass in one of the trophy cabinets that he smashed with an errant cue stick one night while playing eight-ball with "my ol' buddy Jim Beam," as he is fond of saying; has gotten bored with the room, in fact, and doesn't exactly know why.

...

In spite of all the horror stories Ginny has told him over the years about growing up Catholic, he has to admit that the nuns must have done more things right than wrong with her. It's the only way he can explain her sticking with something she believes in, her loyalty, her devotion to duty, a tenacity that would give a bulldog pause. She is no more an intellectual than he, but she managed to graduate summa cum laude out of the fear that some nun, somewhere, might be keeping score. She can forgive anybody for anything, it seems, as long as they're trying. To her, marriage is for better or for worse, hell or high water, and he can be thankful for that. He knows nobody who has more loyal friends than the former Virginia Sue Bradford of Decatur, an orderly staid old neighborhood of tree-lined streets and churches and mom-and-pop businesses some five miles east of downtown Atlanta.

Just don't cross her. When her childhood priest said he wouldn't christen their daughter, Maggie, unless Ginny returned to the church, she fired off a blistering letter to say he had reminded her of "why I left the goddamned church in the first place." When Maggie's godmother married a man whom she, Ginny, personally despised, she promptly "fired" her and never spoke to her again. When their bank was caught red-lining black neighborhoods, making it virtually impossible for the homeowners there to get loans, she made a fuss and switched banks. When an Exxon tanker spilled oil in Alaska, she mailed them her credit card, chopped into a zillion pieces, and switched to Texaco. She quit going to her favorite restaurant when it was slapped with a class-action suit by homosexual waiters.

Now, from the looks of it, he's next. Buying time, girding himself, he opens the curtains that cover the sliding glass doors and gazes at the backyard, something else that has gone to hell during his malaise: the fallen limb he has been promising to haul away since the ice storm in January, the tire swing hanging from a limb of the big oak tree that hasn't been used in five years now, the riot of weeds and hedges and fence-climbing Carolina jasmine untrimmed since last summer, the sad little grotto at the base of the oak now overrun with lichen and moss and ivy.

Sensing that she has finished shepherding the five kids out of the room and is back now, dug in and waiting, he figures he might as well get in the first word.

"Malcolm X," he says, turning to confront her. "Let me guess. Your star running back, your token."

"Tennis, actually," she says.

He snickers. "Tennis. They're good at *tennis*?"

"As in Arthur Ashe. Also editor of the paper, National Honor Society, president of the student body."

"Sounds like a credit to his race."

"You have no idea."

He moves to the pool table, picks up the loose ends of the film, ponders how much more splicing it can take. He keeps promising himself he'll take it somewhere and get it copied to videotape, preserve it forever, so he can play it on the VCR. He says, "You're gonna get your ass fired, you know."

"At least it'll be for a good cause."

"Christ, Gin. School's out and it's Saturday morning. It's like the tree falling in the forest. You'll be picketing for yourselves."

"It's a teachers' work day, so all the ones who need to hear what we've got to say should be there," she says. "Anyway, here's an irony for you. WSB's sending a crew out to tape it for the news tonight. You've had your say, now I get mine. The Hunsingers, at war."

"I bet they love that."

"You do understand irony, then."

"I still say you could lose your job over this. What's your principal think?"

"Forget all of this." She sinks into the sofa, manages a glimmer of smile, pats the cushion beside her. "Come sit. I've only got a minute."

He doesn't budge. "Don't let me keep you."

"Billy, Billy." Exasperated, sighing, she can see that nothing has changed since the night before. "Your performance this morning just about nails it. You can keep saying 'the whiskey did it' all you want, but you still don't get it. These are just kids, hon, standing up for what's right, and you're stuck somewhere in the 'sixties. This isn't easy for them. They could go along and take the easy way, but they won't."

"Aw, hell, babe, I was just kidding around with 'em. You know me well enough to know that."

"But *they* don't, and that's the point. How *dare* you?"

"Anybody comes into my house, they play by my rules."

"That's *disgusting*." She throws up her hands, slaps them on her knees, rises from the sofa. "I can't help you anymore, Billy. You're on your own. Whatever it takes, do it. Go get yourself fixed."

"Lawd, Miss Scarlett, don't throw me in that brierpatch."

"Whatever." She's in the same tight jeans, sandals, and T-shirt the kids are wearing. Forty-two years old, but you'd never know it. Still pretty after all these years, with the same wide blue eyes and blonde hair now showing only a faint streak of gray. "Be gone when I get back. I mean it."

...

Thus banished, alone in a room that now seems childish to him, he absently rolls the cue ball into a corner pocket, then relights the cigar stub with his Zippo. He gives a moment's thought to checking on the goldfish in the pond out back, thinks better of it when Ginny yells upstairs for Maggie to hurry up—"Two-minute drill!"—then takes another beer from the refrigerator, cracks it open, and heads for the stoop at the front door.

All of the kids have brought their own cars, little 'teen deathtraps, bleached Datsuns and Dodge Darts with bald tires and dragging mufflers and sprung bumpers, in order to create the illusion of a large rally. The cars, sprayed with slogans protesting the playing of "Dixie" by the Lee High Rebels band, sit in the circular gravel driveway. When they fire up, all at once, it sounds like the prelude to a stock-car race.

Clattering down the stairs from her bedroom, dressed in her cheerleader's outfit, Maggie nearly knocks him down in her rush to catch up.

Ginny is already in the red Chevy Blazer, at the head of the caravan, exhorting her to get a move on.

"How's about a hug for the old man?" he says.

Practically a clone of her mother at this age, which is seventeen, Maggie stops and turns, walks back toward him. "Oh, hi, Daddy." She seems tentative, not sure how to handle all of this, and he can't say he blames her. "I'm running late," she says. "Sorry."

"I'm sorry, too, Mags. About the whole thing."

"You gonna be okay?"

"Aw, hell, it's just a little road trip, kid. Unauthorized vacation."

"You'll be at The Ranch?"

"Same-old. Home away from home."

"Call me, okay?"

"Come to town, I'll spring for onion rings at Manuel's."

"Deal."

A beer in one hand, cigar in the other, he wraps his arms around her and holds her tight, lifting her off the ground. She breaks away, can't hold eye contact, says, "I gotta run. Love you, Daddy."

"Same here, babe."

Then she is gone, jumping into the Blazer with her mother, who cranks the engine, yells out the window to remind the others to turn on their headlights, and the caravan slowly crunches away. Standing alone on the stoop, old before his time, he waves to his wife and his daughter. What he gets in return are the wide-eyed stares of the five black kids from the cars following in their wake.

TWO

As with most practical matters in his life, he owes his financial stability to Ginny. It now pains him to admit that he might be doing heavy lifting just to pay his bar tab if she hadn't insisted on managing the bonus he got for signing his first pro contract. With the Green Bay Packers' money, a not inconsiderable amount for a bad-kneed quarterback from a Division II school—the son of a house painter and a piano teacher at that—she saw that they bought the house in Crestwood and two adjacent cinderblock duplexes in a seedy in-town neighborhood known as Little Five Points. This was in the mid-sixties, just before Atlanta real estate would take off, when the pooh-bahs at City Hall had only begun their bleating about how Atlanta was on its way to joining the company of the world's great cities. *That'll be the day*, Billy Ray recalls thinking at the time, having grown up in an Atlanta that was hardly more urbane than Birmingham and Chattanooga, but within five years Ginny's investments had doubled.

During his playing days, they had always come home to Atlanta during the off-season. Ginny would take jobs as a substitute teacher or as a private tutor, while Billy Ray picked up parttime work selling cars or doing sports commentary on radio; anything that didn't interfere with his holding forth at Manuel's Tavern during the day and cruising the disco clubs and strip joints at night. Their home was the place in Crestwood, which was quickly becoming the hottest suburban neighborhood in the metro area, but Billy Ray held a special affinity for the two ratty duplexes. Over the years he had rented three of the units to a succession of hippies who insisted on calling themselves "artists"—painters, sculptors, writers, magicians, Tarot-card readers, jugglers, actors, guitar-pickers—while holding open the other, a cramped little two-bedroom affair like all of the rest, for his own devices. He called it The Ranch, and Ginny, for obvious reasons, didn't much care for it.

Such debauchery! "See you at The Ranch" came to be known as an invitation not to be taken lightly. It could be issued at any time, day or night, answered by just about anyone within earshot, and the impromptu parties that ensued became legendary. Revelers appeared from all over—"bunnies" from the downtown Playboy Club, jocks and ex-jocks, carpenters and plumbers and electricians being paid in services rather than cash, sports-writers blackmailed into secrecy—to drink from the fully stocked bar, listen to loud music, play Ping-Pong, argue sports, arm-wrestle, shoot baskets in the grassless backyard, watch sports on a giant television set, ultimately to have sex on the jumble of futons, cots, and sleeping bags in the back bed-room, the "bunkroom." The place "sleeps twelve, fucks four," Billy Ray liked to say back then.

In this malaise that has swept over him in the past five years, Billy Ray has been spending more time alone in The Gun Room back home than whooping it up at The Ranch. For one thing, he has gotten older, no thanks to the boozing and the pounding he took as a player; for another, something he doesn't like to admit, his circle of friends seems to have shrunk. (Drowsily watching a documentary about Scott and Zelda Fitzgerald one night at home, beside Ginny, he bolted wide awake when he heard a drunk-en Zelda say, "Does it occur to you that people no longer find us amusing?") He settles these days for banking the monthly rent checks drifting in, more or less on time, from the cluster of self-employed artistes, referring to him-self as a slumlord before someone else does. For a year now, in fact, he has been renting out the fourth unit, The Ranch, to a dippy sculptor and artist who goes by the name of Rima the Bird-Girl.

...

It's only fifteen miles from Crestwood to The Ranch, but even late on a Saturday morning it takes him forty-five minutes to make it through the Atlanta traffic, clogged on a weekend with shoppers and tourists and eighteen-wheelers blowing through town. He's still driving the '62 Chevy station wagon they bought from a used-car lot when Maggie was born—*Rosinante*, Ginny christened it, for Don Quixote's faithful steed—and it has served him well, particularly during those wee hours when he would be weaving his way homeward, confident that no cop was likely to pull over a man in a clunky station wagon laden with evidence of proud fatherhood: infant car seats, a playpen and other baby stuff, decals reading Crestwood Elementary PTA, Baby on Board, My Child Is an Honor Student at Robert E. Lee High. Even though he couldn't help himself, buying a vanity tag reading GUN, not once has he been stopped for driving under the influence.

Soon after passing through the street circus that Little Five Points has become, a jangle of strolling teeny-boppers and long-haired skateboarders and homeless drunks and guitar-strumming acid heads, he bumps the curb and parks haphazardly in the dirt yard fronting the duplexes. He has to unload what little he tossed into the wagon, mostly clothes and booze, and he's got to find a way to get Rima out of there with as little fuss as possible.

"Well, you really screwed up this time, didn't you?" He hears her, but can't find her.

"A little bird told me to do it."

"A 'Fal-*coon*,' maybe. What the hell were you thinking?"

"It seemed like a good idea at the time."

"Obviously, WSB didn't think so."

He sees her now, curled up like a baby in the front-porch swing, barefooted, cooling off in front of a fan she has dragged from inside. Her hair is dyed pink this month. She is drying it and brushing it out, making no attempt to conceal the fact that she is wearing only a pair of ragged bib overalls cut off at the crotch, and when she sees him trying to catch a glimpse of her breasts jiggling beneath the straps with each brushstroke she says, "Think Lady Godiva."

"She a stripper I don't know about?" Billy Ray steps onto the porch, sets down the case of Jim Beam he has brought from the wagon, and motions for her to move over on the swing. She's crazy as a loon, probably broke her parents' hearts, but he kind of likes her because she's smart and sassy and won't take any crap from anybody. She's from Valdosta, down on the Florida line, a banker's daughter, graduate of Agnes Scott, the prim women's college in Decatur. In due time she discovered there wasn't much of a market for a double-major in Art History and Buddhist Philosophy, so here she is, living the Bohemian life.

"You get my message?" he says.

"Your old lady finally did it, hunh?"

"How would you know that?"

"A wagon full of clothes on hangers says it all."

"Well, we just need a little time to think."

"What's to think about, stud? You're a drunk, you blew off your job, so she kicked your ass out."

"If I wanted to catch hell, I'd'a stayed home." As hot as the day is, here in the city, the fan feels like an ocean breeze. From inside comes the sound of Janis Joplin wailing about Bobby McGee. They watch a bluejay come squawking out of a bent oak tree, dive-bombing a mangy orange cat. Finally, he tells her, "Like I said in my message, I need the place."

"Hey, whoa, bubba. That's not in the contract."

"Being three months behind in rent is."

"How 'bout, 'It's in the mail'?"

"Yeah, sure. And you're Michelangelo in drag."

"Well, I thought maybe we could work something out." This time, still brushing out her hair, she lifts a thick strand and holds it out long enough for him see an ample breast. "I could go for a hundred bucks on the street, you know. I figure a busy weekend in the sack, we'd be even."

"It'll never happen, sweetheart. Business and pleasure, and so forth. I'm in enough trouble already, anyway. I don't need to be screwing somebody half my age."

"Is that why we never got it on? I never got that figured out. We're a pair, you and me. Art meets brawn. The odd couple. Nobody else'll have us. See what I mean? We could make beautiful music together."

"Well, I ain't no Hubert Hubert."

"I declare, the man's been reading again. It's Humbert Humbert, by the way, but I'm impressed."

"They'd put that pervert under the jail these days."

"Yeah, but you've got to admit he and Lolita had a good ol' time together while it lasted."

"Reckon so." Billy Ray looks her over, tries to imagine the two of them in bed, quickly reminds himself that this is no way to start over, if that's what this exercise is all about. He heaves himself off the swing. "Guess I better go in and check out the damages."

...

Rima's thing, her trademark, is to paint and sculpt flying genitals in their myriad stages of development: flaccid, awakening, erect, coupled, spent. Gay men are paying big money these days for her glazed statues of erect penises, some of them three feet tall, with purple heads and blue veins and the wings of angels, perfect for the foyer. Lesbians have been coming from as far away as Macon to buy her delicate little ceramic ashtrays and soap dishes and even Christmas tree ornaments of winged vulvas, always painted blush pink, and she can't turn them out fast enough. The Atlanta newspapers and *Atlanta* magazine try to pretend she doesn't exist, but she is a star to *Queer* and *Our Thing*, two of the latest tabloids appealing to the city's growing homosexual population. Billy Ray still carries one of her business cards in his billfold: *Rima the Bird-Girl: Intimate Statuary.*

She holds the screen door open while he enters the front room with the case of bourbon, and he freezes at the sight. Her side of The Ranch looks like a foundry, or a storage room in the rear of a hardware store, maybe the art room of a kindergarten where kids have been allowed to express themselves without supervision. The Ping-Pong table has been turned on its side to become an easel, propped up on two dinette chairs from the kitchen, covered with a canvas upon which Rima has been sketching an orgy in charcoal. The floor is covered with old copies of *Hotlanta,* a tabloid alternative newspaper, as protection from the dust and spatterings of a madwoman. He sees and smells piles of dirty rags, reeking of mineral spirits; discarded coffee cans and mayonnaise jars holding varnish, turpentine, paint brushes, glazes; one cardboard box holding a mountain of crushed beer cans; another overflowing with crumpled sheets from a sketch pad, ideas that didn't work. Mangled and spent squeeze-tubes of paint lie where they landed. The fireplace bulges with twenty-five-pound plastic bags of fresh clay.

"What the hell?" he says, setting down the case of booze. "You've wrecked the place."

"Oh, right," she says, "like it used to be something out of *GQ* or *Playboy.* 'Bachelor Pad of the Month.'"

"Look at this crap."

The tour continues. In the kitchen: beer and Vienna sausages sharing refrigerator space with more jars and cans holding brushes and rags soaking in acrid chemicals, dinette table crowded with figurines taken from the kiln to cool, white sink now irredeemably coated with oils of many colors, oven a holding area for works awaiting glaze, upon each stovetop burner a cookpot containing goo he doesn't want to know about. In the bathroom: cotton shower curtain used as a hand towel, tub and sink smeared with a rainbow pattern of oils and paints, same for the toilet. One bedroom, obviously her living quarters, holds a salvaged iron bed, and the big television set and stereo, and hundreds of her wrinkled paperback books stacked on the floor; the other, pristine when compared to the rest of the place, is more or less a gallery with scores of finished products displayed on laundry tables lining the walls. Out back, on the covered landing, there squats a metal contraption that looks like a barbecue smoker but turns out to be her kiln.

...

Back on the front-porch swing, she holding a bottle of Dixie beer, he a Flintstones jelly glass brimming with warm Jim Beam, they rock gently in front of the fan. Rima waves theatrically at a maroon Cadillac Coupe de Ville slowly cruising past, Mom and Dad and two little kids gawking through rolled-up tinted windows, tourists from the suburbs checking out the freaks. He has a fleeting thought of Ginny and Maggie, but it passes.

"So," he says, "how're we gonna work this out? I need the place. You're in it. You owe me."

"The eagle's about to scream, stud. No kidding."

"I can't believe people buy that crap."

"Would you believe two thousand dollars for one piece?"

"A *real* dick, in working order, won't fetch two thousand bucks."

"As we say in Valdosta, *au contraire*. That one on the mantel above the fireplace? Three pieces in bas relief? Hinged together? Eve going down on Adam. It's called a triptych. That means 'three' to you. I call it 'Eden Redux.'"

"Lord help us."

"A couple from Crestwood's bought it. They ought to be here with the cash any day now. Be a hell of a note, wouldn't it, if they turned out to be neighbors of yours."

"If they don't show up in the next fifteen minutes it'll be too late, babe. I'm talking now. This minute. I'm a runaway husband on the loose."

They haggle. It's obvious to both that it would take a month to clean up Rima's mess, even if that were remotely possible. It's then that she tells him what she had promised not to reveal until they've had time to clear town: Walter and Robbie, the gay couple on the other side of this duplex, have split for a fresh start in New Orleans, skipped out on the rent, bye-bye, gone-gone, adios. They've left behind what heavy pieces of furniture they had. Bingo! Clean as a pin, ready for occupancy.

"I don't know," says Billy Ray. "God knows what's gone on in that place."

"Now, now," Rima tells him. "Love is where you find it, don't you think? It's a good thing they missed this dump in its heyday. Boys and girls in bed together. Whoever heard of such?"

"Okay, okay." It's been a long day and he needs a place to alight. He'll work things out with Rima later. He's stuck with her, for the time being, and he has the nagging thought that he may never get rid of her. "For starters, I want my television back."

...

By late afternoon, the vacated apartment is more or less habitable. He and Rima have moved the big television set from her side of the duplex into the front room of the other. A run to a thrift store in Little Five Points has netted him a clock radio, some pots and pans and other stuff for the kitchen, toilet paper and shower curtains for the bathroom, fresh sheets and pillowcases for the ghastly cream-colored French Provincial bed the boys left behind. He has stocked the pantry with cereal and canned soups and stews, and the refrigerator with beer and frozen dinners, from a quick pass through the IGA Headliner on Moreland Avenue.

Groggy, sweaty, hung over, he awakens on the overstuffed sofa in the living room to the sounds of WSB-TV's six o'clock news. There is the usual rundown of mayhem in the city—fires, rapes, killings, traffic accidents, drug busts—and he's nursing his hangover with a beer, abiding the weather update until the sports comes on, when he sees a perky female reporter standing on the front steps of Robert E. Lee High. ". . . The protest was organized by Virginia Hunsinger, a teacher at Lee High," she is saying, and soon the screen is filled with a closeup of Ginny.

She is grim, tight-lipped, pissed, a look he has seen a lot of lately. "It's about respect and common decency," she says. "The Civil War ended a long time ago. All these kids ask is to be left alone so they can follow their dreams. For them to hear that song at every football game is degrading. . . ."

A cheer goes up from the knot of teenagers around her, and when the camera pulls back he sees Maggie, shaking a pom-pon with one hand and holding Malcolm X around the waist with the other. Back to the studio.

Sirens wail, cats yowl, dogs bark as night falls over the city. For dinner, he eats Dinty Moore Beef Stew straight from the can and washes it down with a beer while sitting in the swing of the porch that he shares with Rima. Classical music floats from the stereo, *his* stereo, inside her apartment, but he can hardly hear it for the jangle across the way. The two lesbian psychics in 405-C are having at it, cursing and throwing dishes at each other; the boys in 405-D are entertaining a half-dozen college students, boys and girls in T-shirts and cutoffs, all of them playing grab-ass around a galvanized tub full of beer while ribs sizzle on a Hibachi.

"Ta-*daaa!*" The screen door flies open to reveal Rima, dressed like a gypsy: flowery floor-length skirt, breasts bulging from a halter top, bells on her sandals, a yellow rose stuck in her pink hair.

"There a carnival in town?"

"A bunch of us are off to see Blondie."

"That ol' broad at the Clermont?"

"One and only. Wanna come?"

Fat, cackling, ageless, high camp now, Blondie has become an institution at the decadent resident hotel on Ponce de Leon. Her grand finale each night is to crush a beer can between her breasts. Billy Ray says, "I don't think so."

"Hey, you old fart, it's Saturday night. What're you gonna do, sit here and play with yourself?"

"I've got a new gig on radio, starting tomorrow night. Better get my beauty rest."

"You? A job?"

"Man can't live on interest and late rent payments alone."

"Whatever. Don't wait up for me, dear."

"Yeah. And you don't take any wooden ones."

She bounds off the porch, bells jingling as she trots across the yard to her pickup, vanity tag reading BIRDGIRL, fires it up in a billow of black smoke, bumps off the curb, and roars away into the night. Slumping into his new digs, he ponders waiting up for the eleven o'clock news to find out if he saw what he thinks he saw.

THREE

R adio station WWJD was born in failure and has stayed that way. It was started up in 1964 by a gaggle of patriotic and religious zealots who hoped to help Barry Goldwater, the conservative Arizona senator, take the White House out of the hands of those Godless forked-tongued Democrats. During that summer and fall, the fare on the little 5,000-watt station was relentlessly Christian and fire-breathing Republican, a grab bag of evangelists, gospel singers, syndicated conservative pundits like Paul Harvey, canned campaign rhetoric from Goldwater headquarters, even a weekly show hosted by Lester Maddox, the Georgia governor-to-be, best known for chasing black protesters away from his fried-chicken emporium with an axe handle. When Goldwater was roundly defeated that November, those few people who even knew there ever *was* a WWJD—stuck out there as it was on the far right end of the AM dial at 1690 with the Spanish-language stations—assumed the operation would die as abruptly as it had been assembled.

Not so. The original owners bailed out immediately, secure only in the knowledge that they had created a catchy Christian motto with their call letters (WWJD, for "What Would Jesus Do?"), and in the ensuing years the station got passed around like an unwanted orphan. Under a series of backers, who bought it for reasons ranging from simple ego to being a tax write-off, WWJD has changed its format nearly every six months in its hapless attempts to catch the ears of the public; any public. At one time or another, it has featured rock-'n'-roll, rhythm-'n'-blues, country, all-talk, all-sports, all-Christian, once even making a stab at becoming "the homemaker's friend" with eighteen solid hours of news about cooking, cleaning, entertaining, and parenting, between reruns of such old-timey comedies as "Fibber McGee and Molly." Alas, nothing has worked.

But where there's a broadcasting license and a place on the dial there is always hope, and that seems to be about the only bright spot for the latest owner, one Broadus Delany Spotswood, Jr. Built like a bowling ball, right up to his shiny bald head, B. D. has been a force in the earth-moving business since getting in at the beginning of the interstate-highway development period in and around Atlanta. He knows nothing about the radio business, being a graduate in Civil Engineering from Auburn in the 'sixties, but in his search for some measure of fame he has set his heart on becoming known as a communications mogul. Even he admits he hasn't made much progress toward that end in the six months he has run WWJD—it still serves up a smorgasbord, from dawn to midnight, of high school sports and preachers and all sorts of music, plus any non-controversial chatter he can get cheap—but he's been thinking lately of going back to all-sports.

This, of course, is where Billy Ray comes in. B. D. has been a devout fan ever since he, a rabid Auburn man, heard the radio broadcast of that game when the Gunslinger nearly upset Alabama, Auburn's hated cross-state rival, that day in Tuscaloosa. He is, in fact, one of those fans who won't go away; a man who has been sending birthday cakes to Billy Ray every year on the anniversary of that great game, the sixteenth day of October, even when the Gun was living and playing in Canada; who has a huge grainy blowup of the Bear angrily slamming his hound's-tooth hat to the ground at Denny Stadium; who once waited at the bar at Manuel's for three hours in hopes of catching his hero coming through the door; whose dream it is to get a guided tour, by Billy Ray himself, of The Gun Room he's read so much about, maybe even be invited to shoot some eight-ball with the Gun on his famous pool table.

Not one to turn aside adulation, Billy Ray nevertheless has never quite understood B. D. Spotswood's devotion, bordering on madness, and tries to shake him at every opportunity. Now, though, he seems to be stuck with him. B. D. called the house right after the misfortune at WSB, begging Billy Ray to hear him out, making an outrageous offer for him to host a Sunday night sports call-in show on WWJD. "Hey, Gun, you can say anything you want to on my station," he promised. "We believe in free speech around WWJD." Sensing that he was likely to be headed out the door of his home at any moment—given Ginny's reaction to his latest adventure—Billy Ray had no recourse but to accept the man's offer. After all, he has convinced himself, his audience awaits. And bills must be paid.

...

He's supposed to meet B. D. at the station at eight o'clock Sunday night so they can go over things before his debut, but finding the place might be a problem. WWJD is located where it's always been, on the Bankhead Highway west of downtown Atlanta, old U.S. 78, the road to Birmingham before it was preempted by I-20. "You can't hardly miss it," B. D. said. "Just look for the busted angel and the tower." The directions, Billy Ray is finding out, are easier given than followed.

Chewing on his cigar, leaning forward on the steering wheel of the Chevy wagon, squinting as he drives straight into the setting sun, he sees the sad remains of a white working-class civilization in its fitful decline. Bud's While-U-Wait Mufflers. Pit Stop Grill. Madam Olga's House of Palmistry. Bernice's Hairstyles. Bubba's Beer Shack. Hub Cap Heaven. Doggy-Do-Rite Obedience School. Tire recappers, used-car lots, camper-body emporiums, drive-in hamburger joints, pawn brokers, gun shops, cut-rate gas stations, auto mechanics; they're all here in a woebegone strip connecting the abandoned roadside towns of Austell and Villa Rica. He is thinking about wheeling into Jo-Jo's Suds for a beer and directions when he finally sees it: a bent metal tower rising through the dusk, sort of an Erector Set version of the Eiffel Tower, with the big block letters WWJD hanging to it more or less vertically.

The station is housed in a low-slung cinderblock building, spray-painted in a heavenly pale-blue and cloudy-white, with the wings of angels sprouting from the roof on either side, a touch left over from the station's beginnings as "The Voice of God in Greater Austell." At some point in time the wings either crumbled or were vandalized, for now their tips dangle and shift in the light breeze, held up only by the bent and rusted wires that once held them together. On one side of the station is Miss Piggy's BBQ, housed in a single-wide trailer encased in a pink adobe shell shaped like a pig; on the other is The Still, in another trailer, this one topped by a fanciful plastic moonshine jug ten feet tall, held in place by guy wires.

He bumps off the highway and onto the gravel lot fronting the station. Parked at the base of a flagpole that holds the American flag and the stars-and-bars of the Confederacy, each of them faded and streaked by the elements, are a beat-up Ford pickup and a classic white Cadillac, both caked with dust. He rolls into the space between them, reaches into the back seat for his Packers baseball cap, and takes a deep breath. *Another opening, another show.* He has barely hit the gravel with his booted left foot when he hears a man's voice yelp: "There's my man!" Waddling toward him, all pink skin and pearly teeth, in a wrinkled seersucker suit and Panama hat, is B. D. Spotswood himself.

"Mister Spotswood, I presume."

"Aw, hell, Gun, make it 'B. D.' if you don't mind."

"Okay," says Billy Ray. "'Gun' and 'B. D.' How's that?"

"We gon' be a great pair, you 'n' me."

"We'll see how it goes, pardner."

B. D. has grabbed Billy Ray's hand with both of his and is vigorously shaking it. Trying to divert the man's attention, as much as anything, Billy Ray points with his free hand to the roof of the building and says, "What's the deal with the wings?"

"Aw, the boys that built the place figured they needed something special to make 'em stand out. A whatchamacallit, a logo, if you get my drift. Pretty damned tacky, if you ask me, but I ain't gon' be the one to test the Lord by taking 'em down. What we need's a good lightnin' bolt to finish the work. That might tell us God don't like 'em, neither." B. D. finally gets the message that Billy Ray would like his hand back, lets go, and invites him into the station. "I swear, this is about the second-greatest day of my life," he says, leading the way, reaching up to wrap a pudgy hand around Billy Ray's shoulder. "Me and you, we're about to make some history, Gun." With the porcine B. D. in his ill-fitting seersucker suit and Panama hat, Billy Ray towering a foot taller in his jeans and cowboy boots and Green Bay cap, they resemble the old comic-strip characters Mutt and Jeff.

...

If it's possible, the inside of the station appears less promising than the outside. The place looks like one of those machine-gun nests the Germans left behind at Omaha Beach following D-Day: a pillbox, a bunker, a drab windowless redoubt whence a man might hole up and fight his last battle. Painted a pale schoolhouse green, illuminated by bluish fluorescent tubes that buzz and flicker at will, floored with black-and-white linoleum squares, it makes your heart sink just to walk through the front door and look at it. To the right is a little reception area, nothing but a torn yard-sale sofa and two mismatched chairs gathered around a low table laden with souvenir ashtrays, old magazines, and Styrofoam cups holding the moldy remains of days-old coffee. Straight ahead is a Coke machine, a water fountain, a tall wire trash bin overflowing with crumpled balls of paper, and a narrow plywood unisex restroom barely larger than a telephone booth. To the left, at the deeper end of the building, where B. D. is now leading Billy Ray, there are two cramped glass cubicles, beyond which there is a plywood partition with a hollow door marked "Private."

The only sound is the muted singing of Hovie Lister and the Statesmen Quartet, this being the Sunday Night Gospel Hour at WWJD. Perched morosely on a stool at the controls in the engineer's booth, elevated slightly higher than the other glass cubicle, is a sullen-looking young man in his early twenties, woefully thin, decked out in a ponytail and earrings and wire-frame glasses. He is wearing headphones, nodding his head to the music, chomping away at a barbecue sandwich brought over from Miss Piggy's. B. D. waves at him, gets a nod in return, and leads Billy Ray over for an introduction.

"Gun, this here's Wally Medders. Call him 'Spider' for obvious reasons. Spider, meet Billy Ray Hunsinger."

The young man rises halfway from his stool, wiping his lips and hands with a paper napkin, extends a greasy handshake. "Nice to meet you," he says. "Old jock, right?"

"Spider here's studying to be a pharmacist," says B. D. "Over at Kennesaw College."

"Drug-pusher, right?" says Billy Ray, returning the insult. The boy shrugs, rolls his eyes, sits back down to his dinner.

"Okay." B. D. clears his throat. "Spider's your engineer. Any problems you get, he'll take care of 'em. He's got enough taped commercials and stuff to last from here 'til Labor Day. Need to pee, just give him a signal. Phone lines go cold, he'll cover. You get tired of runimatin' and need some time to—"

"Say what?"

"*Roonimatin'*. You know, thinkin' out loud. That's what the show's all about."

"He means 'ruminating,'" Spider says to Billy Ray.

"What I said. *Runimatin'*. Anyways, come on in the office here, Gun, so we can talk."

...

Billy Ray has had a couple of weeks now to ponder the meaning of what happened to him that night on WSB-TV, and he's still in what the shrinks call denial. For two years he'd had a gig every Sunday night on WSB, the dominant television station in Atlanta, doing a three-minute commentary inside a show called "The Locker Room" that followed the late news. Basically, he was paid to run off at the mouth—*runimate*—on any sports subject of his choosing: inflated baseball salaries, stupid mascots, college recruiting scandals, artificial turf versus natural grass, pre-game prayers, women's basketball, and the like. "Just be yourself, Gun," was the station manager's only advice, and that he had done with great gusto. "Baseball hasn't been the same since they quit breaking their cigars when they slid into third base," he once remarked. "Puck-off time's seven o'clock," he said of a National Hockey League game. He got into some trouble when he pondered whether the Georgia women's basketball team, the Lady Dogs, shouldn't be called the Bitches, but charmed his way out of it. He dearly loved stock-car racing and pro wrestling, ridiculed tennis and golf ("Meanwhile, in Augusta, the trust-fund babies . . ."). He was a handful, but he knew what his bosses knew: that "Billy Ray's Corner" had been primarily responsible for a steady rise in their Sunday-night ratings since its inception. Love him or hate him, just don't ignore him. Getting paid to do what he'd been doing for years as the center of attention at the big round table up front at Manuel's was, to him, a dream job, if not an out-and-out scam.

He still doesn't know what hit him. So what if he'd spent a little time with his muse, Jim Beam, during the long hot summer's day; that was nothing new. So what if he'd said what he'd heard a hundred times, at Manuel's and the liquor store and on the streets, about the predominantly black Atlanta Falcons football team; it was just a good-natured comment, all in fun. At any rate, summing up that night's commentary with a few words about the Falcons' prospects for the coming season, he had referred to them as the "Fal-*coons*." Hell, all of the old boys he knew said it all the time. Some of his best friends from the pro football days were black, weren't they? And hadn't "Niggers Go Long" actually been in the playbook at Green Bay, at the suggestion of a hot-shot black receiver, eager to fit in, a rookie out of Florida A&M? So what's the fuss?

Even while he was unhooking the microphone clipped to his blue blazer and dismounting from the stool, he heard not the usual whoops and laughter from the cameramen, among his steadfast fans, but, rather, the mad ringing of telephones. He saw the director, up in the glass booth overlooking the studio, slam his clipboard to the floor. As he walked toward the exit, heading toward his office, he saw his buddies diverting their eyes. There was a present awaiting him a few minutes later when he arrived at his desk after a stop at the john: the near-empty fifth of whiskey, which somebody had fished from the bottom drawer, now resting like a paperweight on a memo from the show's producer. There were two words, hastily scribbled with a red grease pencil. "You're Fired."

...

Now, two weeks later, he finds himself sitting in a busted web-and-aluminum lawn chair across the desk from B. D. Spotswood, erstwhile radio magnate, as they talk about the new show's format and matters of technology. "If this thing works, Gun, I'll be replacing that danged alunimun chair." *Al-u-ni-mun.* "Yessiree. It's gon' be gen-u-*wine* black leather, from here on out. Anyways, reckon you might have some questions."

"So all I gotta do is just sit and talk for two hours?" Billy Ray says.

"That's it. Up to you if you want to talk about WSB. I never liked the *aggorant* bastards, anyways."

"Who do you figure's listening?

"Don't really know, to tell the truth. Over the years, WWJD's changed clothes more'n a stripper. We got coloreds that think it's still James Brown, good old boys searching for Hank Williams, homemakers wanting to learn how to cook asparagus. I'm gon' spring some money for one o' them audience sur-views once you get started."

Billy Ray looks around the sad office, its stained plywood walls decorated, if that's the word, with Auburn mementos and souvenir silver shovels representing ground-breakings; its grimy linoleum floor littered with stacks of newspapers and trade magazines; B. D.'s desk a jumble of tapes and press releases and unopened mail. He winces now to recall the broken angel wings outside on the forlorn Bankhead Highway, a long way from the staid white-columned fortress of WSB on Peachtree Street, and the general seed-iness he encountered upon entering the building. He leans sideways to knead his jock itch, the curse of his life, then looks B. D. square in the eye. "I don't know about this deal," he says.

B. D. Spotswood won't be denied. "If it's about money . . ."

"Aw, naw. Five hundred bucks a night's about twice what I was getting over there. What I'm wondering is . . . Well, hell, it don't seem like your sig-nal would go much beyond Metropolitan Austell, if you don't mind my say-ing."

"Nosir. No . . . *sir!* Got that worked out, first thing. Turned that *tran-spitter* around, aimed it on downtown Atlanta like them damned Yankees did their guns, took care of that real quick. Right about now, when these little ol' pissant day stations go off the air"—looking at his watch, seeing it is nine o'clock already—"hell, we get right into Atlanta like we was a local station. Yessir. We're playing with the big boys now. Look out, Atlanta."

They seem to be grandiose plans, indeed, and Billy Ray knows he is in no position to negotiate. He'll play it as it lays, give it a shot, see how it goes. It beats not working at all, which hasn't helped his spirits of late. Loony as this fellow B. D. seems, not to mention the snarly hippie engineer, Spider, he's being given a blank check, handed the ball, invited to make up the plays as he goes along. It'll be called "Jock Talk with Billy Ray Hunsinger," ten-to-midnight Sundays, open-mike, let 'er rip.

"Lookie here, now, Gun"—B. D. takes another glance at his watch—"hate to miss your very first show, but I gotta run. My mama's waiting up for me, still pissed I didn't make *community* with her this morning. You know how them Cacklicks are. Gon' cost me supper at a fancy restaurant."

"So it's me and Spider."

"Don't worry. I'll be listening in to see how it goes, but I figure y'all can take care of things."

"Just give the ball to Gun, right?"

"You got it." B. D. frowns, searching his mind. "Oh, yeah," he says. "You might want to steer things around politics and religion, *contraservial* stuff like that. We ain't got one o' them time-delay gizmos yet, so you might oughta cut 'em off if they get to cussin'. Last thing I need's trouble about my license. People want football, Gun,"—*FUH-baw*—"so let's give it to 'em, okay?" B. D. suddenly kicks back his chair, shuffles out in front of the desk, goes into a rigid crouch to emulate a quarterback going under center to take the snap. "Hut!-hut!-hut!!!" he shouts. "*FUH-baw*, Gun. *FUH-baw*." And then he's out of there, like a receiver hauling ass on a post pattern.

...

Billy Ray follows him to the door, watches the Cadillac throw up a roostertail as B. D. hurtles out of the lot onto the Bankhead Highway; choked, even at this hour, with lumbering church buses and frisky pickups and belching eighteen-wheelers. He crunches across the gravel lot to Miss Piggy's BBQ, crowded with teenaged boys ogling pony-tailed girls, buffing the new paint jobs on their hotrods, showing off new tattoos—apparently, it's the place for teenagers to hang out in Austell on a Sunday night—orders a barbecue and fries and a tall Coke with lots of ice, then returns to his faithful wagon, *Rosinante*, parked below flags now drooping in the hot windless sky. Opening the rear gate, he rummages through a box holding dusty plastic toys that have been there since Maggie was a toddler, fishes out a fresh fifth of Jim Beam, locks up, and trudges back into the station.

He has always felt like an admiral at the bridge of a battleship in these studios, surrounded as he is by a console of luminous dials and toggle switches and mysterious knobs, a silver boom mike on a flexible crane neck, a telephone with a half-dozen pushbuttons that can light up and blink, a set of headphones so you can keep your hands free while conversing. Sunk deep in a cushy executive's swivel chair that enables him to roll free in the slot of a U-shaped counter, punching this button or that one, free to grimace or shoot a bird or make a face at the unseen voice on the other side of the phone, under the benevolent gaze of an engineer in the sound booth opposite, he is the center of attention, the star of the show, the commander-in-chief, the engine that drives the machine. He feels the same God-like power that he did when he was the Gunslinger, under center, checking out the defense, deciding which of his receivers he would bless this time with a bullet on the numbers.

"Ol' B. D.'s something, ain't he?" Billy Ray is saying to Spider.

"He's one for the *becord rooks*, all right." Spider's demeanor toward Billy Ray has changed dramatically since the moment Gun came back with dinner, uncorked the Jim Beam, and gulped three times straight from the bottle.

"Hope he don't screw up my paycheck like he does the English language."

"You should've been here the night he decided to sing the 'Star-Spangled Banner' to go off the air. *A capella*."

"You're kidding me. *Nobody* can sing that damned thing."

"I kid you not. Said, 'Now, I'd like to honor our forecestors by singing the "Star-Studded Anthem," archipelago.'"

"*Archipelago?*" Billy Ray, in the midst of taking another swig when Spider recounts the story, spews whiskey all over the console. "How'd he do?"

"Started out fine." Spider sings in falsetto, "'Ooh, saay, can you seeeee . . .' Then he got lost. 'Purple mountains' ma-jes-teeee . . .' Good thing I'd already shut down the phone lines."

They're still yukking it up when Spider checks the clock. Three minutes 'til ten. They've already been over the routine, the phone lines and the cues and the commercial breaks, and what little else Billy Ray needs to know, so now he's on his own. Soon Spider is in his booth, counting down the seconds—four, three, two, one—then stabbing his index finger at Billy Ray, mouthing the word "go." Showtime.

...

41

Howdy and a good evening to you, sports fans. It's the Gunslinger here, Billy Ray Hunsinger, talking sports with y'all over WWJD in beautiful downtown Austell, Georgia. Ain't nobody here but me and my engineer Spider and my good buddy Jim Beam. We're gonna be here 'til midnight, taking your calls and talking football or whatever comes to mind. All you got to do is give us a call at—where's that number at, Spider?—here we go, write this down. It's Ask Jock, that's A-S-K J-O-C-K, two-seven-five, five-six-two-five. Got that? We'll be right back, folks. Gotta pay some bills . . .

...

Hell, this deal just might work out. While Spider slaps on some commercial tapes, for dog food and used cars and an outlet store, Billy Ray pours some more bourbon into his tall cup of Coke and ice. The thought is crossing his mind that he might wind up sitting here for the full two hours, talking to himself, when he sees one of the buttons on the phone blinking red. A caller! He can't wait for the commercials to end.

...

Hey, there, Gun, ol' buddy.

Yo.

I bet you don't know who this is.

What the hell kinda—Excuse me, folks. Naw, 'fraid you got me there. You're gonna have to give me a clue.

Tuscaloosa. October the sixteenth, nineteen damned sixty-five.

I'm gonna have to ask you to watch your language there, friend. Boss's orders. Plus, I gotta eat.

Sorry, Gun. Anyhoooo. That date ring a bell in that ol' hard head o' yours?

Wait a minute. This ain't, aw, shoot, gimme a second. Is this ol' Peahead? North Alabama State Catamounts, nineteen sixty-five?

The one and only.

42

Bobby Gillespie. You old dog. Folks, this old boy saved my life that day we almost beat Bama and the Bear. He could block an Allied Freight Line truck, fully loaded. Didn't see you at the reunion last spring, Peahead.

Me and the wife was sick, both of us. Heard about your little adventure, though.

Well, that's another story for another time. Not much I can say that wasn't in the Birmingham paper. What're you up to these days, anyhow, buddy?

Sanitation engineer, Gun. Over in Villa Rica.

That's a fancy word for garbage collector, ain't it?

If you want to put it that way.

I'm sorry to hear 'bout that, Peahead.

Aw, it ain't so bad, Gun. Sometimes they let me drive. . . .

...

This is great! Billy Ray is having the time of his life. He eats up nine minutes with Peahead Gillespie, the center on that great team, just carrying on about the old days and how the others are doing now. Then comes another of his old teammates, Stork Sims, his ace receiver, now a postman, and they cover another eleven minutes discussing how they almost made a believer out of Bear Bryant that day by totalling 521 yards passing. There is even a call from the enemy, a fellow identifying himself as Ben Burns, "Scottie" Burns, who had been in the stands with the Alabama band on that long-ago October afternoon and recalls it as the "highlight of my four years at the Capstone, if you throw out the drinking." He plays it straight when there is another call, this from B. D. Spotswood, thinly disguising his voice and identifying himself only as "an Auburn fan" wanting to know how it looks this year for the Tigers, saying how much he loves the show, especially Billy Ray's "runimations" on the game.

When they reach the end of the first hour, that's it, only those four calls, and that's fine by Billy Ray. He'd just as well rock back and forth in the swivel chair, sip whiskey, tell his stories, make monkey faces at Spider through their respective studio windows, rather than be interrupted by God-knows-who on the phone lines. At eleven o'clock, time for Spider to plug in to the network for ten minutes of news, sports, and weather, then to strip and read some copy off the Georgia Network News wire, Billy Ray takes the bottle outside for some fresh air. Except for an occasional police cruiser and a Greyhound and a Peterbilt trudging along under the sliver of a new moon, the Bankhead Highway is virtually empty now, reminding him of his lonely winters in the Canadian Rockies.

So far, so good, he's thinking. Piece of cake. Settling into his chair after the break, forty-five minutes to go, feeling good, deciding to talk a little about the flap at WSB, he signs on again. "Give us a call at A-S-K J-O-C-K, that's two-seven-five, five-six-two-five," he says, hoping nobody will. He's doing a dance step around the issue, explaining as how he didn't mean any-thing personal by saying "Fal-*coons*," and going into some detail about how it was a black player, after all, who had come up with the description, "Niggers Go Long," for one of their favorite pass routes during his days with the Green Bay Packers, when the red pushbuttons on his phone begin blink-ing like Christmas-tree lights.

...

Line One. You're on the air.

So there you are. Thought you'd been lynched, bubba.

Who'm I talking to?

What do you care? I'm just another nigger to you.

Hold on there, just hold on. We can't be using that kind of language here.

You honkie motherfucker—

That's it, pal. Line Two. The Gun speaking. Who we got?

You don't know yo' ass from a goalpost, you—

Lookie here, sports fans, I've told you about the cussing. Let's every-body calm down, now, just calm down. Line Three, we're talking football.

Brother Hunsinger?

This is Billy Ray Hunsinger.

It's a pleasure to speak to you, sir.

Who've we got here?

This is the Reverend T. Vivian Beaumont of the First Calvary AME Revival Assembly on Moreland Avenue.

Yes, sir, preacher. Got the football fever, do you? Won't be long now, you know, before the boys start bustin' heads.

Well, sir, first of all I want to apologize for some of the brothers. I'm sure they know better than to use that kind of language.

Thanks, Rev. That okay, to call you Rev?

Long as I might refer to you as Brother Gun.

I been called worse.

As have I, sir.

So what's on your mind, Rev?

Well, sir, I've got a little riddle for you.

This is different. Go ahead, Rev, what you got?

I was wondering if you know the difference between the N-C-A-A and the N-A-A-C-P.

Sure, I do, Rev, and I've got a good story about that.

I'm sure you do. You're a wonderful storyteller. But I've come to you this evening—

Back in the 'fifties when Auburn kept getting in trouble with the N-C-A-A for buying players, they had this colored boy who was kinda like a mascot. LEE-roy. Must've been eighty years old. Anyway, he goes up to Shug Jordan one day when they'd just learned Auburn had gotten another two years of no bowl games, and he says, Coach, I just can't figure out this En Double-A Cee Pee. First, they're wantin' to make us to go to school with white folks, next thing you know they're puttin' us on prohibition.

I fail to see the humor in that, Brother Gun.

Naw, see, he just couldn't get 'em straight. The En-Cees and the Double-As, and then that Pee thrown in.

What you fail to understand, sir, is that these are racist comments. For one thing, how can you refer to an eighty-year-old man as a boy?

Oh, come on, Rev—

That is most demeaning, sir, to a very large segment of our population.

I don't see why you people—

That, too, Brother Gun. You people. Who are you people?

Well, you know. Y'all. Black folks. But, hey, I don't mean anything by that. They're just words. You know what they say. Sticks and stones might break my bones, but words ain't never gonna bother me.

You're good, Brother Gun. Now I've forgotten my riddle.

I think it was, What's the difference between the NCAA and the NAACP?

That's right. Do you know the answer?

Well, let's see. You've got the National Collegiate Athletic Association, and the National Association for the Advancement of Colored People. Hunh. I don't know. You got me.

There's not a bit of difference in them, Brother Gun.

I don't follow you, Rev.

They're both for helping the less fortunate to realize their dreams.

Whoa, wait up a minute, Rev. That's a bit of a stretch, don't you think? One of 'em's about football, and the other one's about, you know, something else.

No, sir, not quite. They both stand for the same thing: opportunity. Now that the NAACP's done its job, don't you see, the NCAA can get on with its job. What I'm saying is, no matter the race or creed or color, the Lord loves 'em like Coach Jake Gaither used to say down at Florida A&M: agile, mobile, and hostile. Understand what I'm saying?

I heard that one, but—Hunh?

And about that sticks and stones business. Looks to me like you would've learned by now that words can harm you.

But I've tried to explain all of that.

I know, Brother Gun, and I commend you for that. It's gon' be nice, working with you.

Hey, wait just a minute here, Rev.

You have a good evening, now, sir.

...

Angry callers are lighting up the switchboard again, some laughing and others wanting a piece of either Billy Ray or the preacher, all of them spouting blue streaks of profanity, demanding to be heard. With a full twenty minutes to go, Spider simply shuts down the phone lines, scrawling a note and waving it at Billy Ray—TECHNICAL DIFFICULTIES!!!—who fans himself, greatly relieved, and rambles on about the particular difficulties of playing in snowstorms in the Canadian Football League until he runs out of steam and finally collapses across the finish line.

At midnight, following the last strains of the National Anthem, he and Spider are finishing off the fifth of Jim Beam while sprawled over the torn sofa near the front door of the studio. The phones are still ringing, but they can forget that now. Other than their voices, the only other sounds come from faulty plumbing and the flickering fluorescent tubes.

"God *damn*," says Billy Ray.

"Man, B. D. better get that time-delay fast, before the FCC gets here."

"I thought you were gonna be screening the calls."

"These guys were too quick for me, Gun."

"You mean you couldn't just *feel* it coming? Guy comes on and the first thing he says is 'honkie motherfucker'?"

"Hey," Spider says, "they all sounded like preachers when *I* talked to 'em. That one told me he was a huge fan of yours. Talked real calm and respectable. Wadn't much I could do—"

Suddenly the door flies open, freezing Spider in mid-sentence. It is B. D., in his Teddy-bear pajamas and a purple velour robe, sweating and flailing his arms and sputtering, Elmer Fudd on a rant. "*FUH-baw*, Gun, I said *FUH-baw*, hot dammit! How'm I gon' get to be a radio *magnet* if you ain't talkin' *FUH-baw*? Hanh? I'm bumfuzzled, boys, utterly complexed. Spider, I'll deal with you later. Gun, me 'n' you got some serious runimatin' to do."

FOUR

She's a trouper, this Rima. The best he can recall, his troubles began when he turned right instead of left out of the station parking lot, headed for Birmingham rather than downtown Atlanta. He was drunk, very drunk, with a serious need to relieve himself, and he knew better than to stop at a gas station or any other public place in his condition. Seeing a weedy gravel road coming up, he took it. Suddenly, in his headlights, he saw a barricade of oil drums announcing the road's end, hit the brakes, left the road, and wound up in the ditch. That was at two o'clock, somewhere in the wilds near Villa Rica, not a soul in sight. From there he walked back to a convenience store he had seen, closed for the night, and called her from a pay phone. He went back to the wagon and was asleep at the wheel, aching and bleeding and snoring, when she finally found him at dawn on this morning after his very first show on WWJD.

"What year is this crate, anyway?"

"A 'sixty-two. Best Chevy ever made."

"You might qualify for an antique tag, you know."

"Me, or the wagon? You need any help?"

"I can handle it. Here, catch. Hair of the dog." Rima has found a warm beer and tosses it to Billy Ray, who is sitting on the grass embankment, still trying to staunch the bleeding with an oily rag dipped into the tepid water

49

of the sewage ditch. "Christamitey, stud, you going on a safari? Booze, sleeping bag, tent, spare tire, flashlight, jug of water, antifreeze, oil, can of gas, transmission fluid, old *Playboy,* sweatshirts, Big Wheels, football without any air in it, portable radio. Everything but rope."

"Well, you never know what might come up."

"You do now, sport."

Rima is on her knees, rummaging through the back end of Billy Ray's station wagon, which is stuck nose-down in the mud where it landed sometime around two o'clock in the morning. *Rosinante* ought to be okay, she thinks, if he can live with a little cockeyed alignment.

The only thing that seems broken is his nose, which slammed against the steering wheel when he lost control and wound up in the ditch. If Ginny wants an irony, he's thinking—getting a whiff of the urine that has darkened the crotch of his jeans—how about this: I went looking for a place to relieve himself, left the road, wrecked, peed all over myself in the excitement. Through a grove of scraggly pines he hears the *stickety-stickety* of traffic moving on the Bankhead Highway, less than a hundred yards away, a caravan of pickups and panel trucks and neat little compacts taking people to their jobs in the city.

"Aha! El ropo." Rima wiggles backwards out of the wagon, dragging a coil of rope with her, stands for a moment to get the kinks out of her back and neck, then begins to lash the rope to the rear bumper of the station wagon. "Ever tell you about my rodeo-groupie days?" she says, looping the other end around the bumper of her pickup and then deftly cinching the ropes into a square knot. Though not a bit surprised, Billy Ray says nothing; he just wants to go home. "You betcha, bub, them was the days. Yippie-ki-yi-yo and a big howdy, ma'am. What say let's take this dogie home, pard-ner."

Billy Ray tries to stand, loses his balance, and pitches forward into the ditch with a mighty splash. At least she has the decency not to laugh. "How we gonna do this?" he says, getting up.

"What's this *we* shit, Kimo-Sabe? Just stand back, if you can manage to stand, and leave it to me." She slips into the cab of her pickup, a four-wheel-drive Ford, and shoves the stick into its lowest gear. Engine grinding, wheels spinning, grass and gravel flying, smoke belching, the truck eases onto the narrow gravel road, finally pulling the wagon out of the muck. "Take 'em to Missouri, boys!" Billy Ray flips the empty beer into the ditch, gets behind the wheel, fires the engine, and soon finds himself following Rima home like a found calf. Bloody, bowed, and broken.

...

He remembers that she wouldn't let him go to sleep until she re-set the nose; made him lie back in Walter and Robbie's garish bed, straddled him, took a hold, and popped it back into place. Now, late in the afternoon, he lies there, staring at the ceiling, attuned to every bone in his body. He hasn't felt like this since the day his offensive line at Calgary, feeling underappreciated, conspired to let the Edmonton Eskimos bury him under a blitz to teach him a lesson in humility. He's had plenty of hangovers in his time, but nothing like this, and the worst part is that he can't think of a single good thing he's done in his life, only the bad, and, God knows, there's been plenty of that lately.

He recalls Guntersville in the spring, twentieth reunion of that great Catamount team, full house in the stands at North Alabama State, laughing at the sight of him, sprawled on the cinder track and trying to get on his feet. His first DUI, his first night in jail, made bearable when his fellow revelers recognize him and he spends the evening entertaining the troops with football stories. Maggie, his sunshine, pulling back from him these days, like he had a contagious disease. Same deal with the guys on the floor at WSB-TV that night, who wouldn't even make eye contact as he stumbled to his office to find he'd been canned. Five black kids, walking out on him in his own house. Ginny, before tossing him out: "I'm giving you a long leash, ace, but not so you can pull crap like this." And now this: a butt-kicking to beat all butt-kickings, from this fat little turd who runs a jackleg radio station in the boonies.

For nearly two hours he'd had no choice but to sit and take it while B. D. Spotswood, in his robe and pajamas, raved on about personal responsibilities and obligations to the people out there in radio-land and his own disappointment in how Billy Ray had let him down. Hands clenched behind his back, pacing back and forth in his bedroom slippers, in full rage, B. D.'s performance would put Vince Lombardi to shame. "Hot dangit, Gun, this is embarrassing! Where's your sense of disrespect? I'm gon' be a laughing-stock to all my friends after this stunt you just pulled!"

If this isn't rock bottom, having to endure a tongue-lashing from a bumbling idiot like this, Billy Ray doesn't want to hear what is. The fifth of whiskey he drank during the evening, with only a little help from that pony-tailed hippie engineer, Spider, hasn't dulled him to the point that he can't recall B. D.'s ultimatum: "You've got one more show to redempt yourself, or you're out! Keep this up, and there won't be no more sacrificial birthday cakes for you, buddy-boy!"

Funny, though, that what really gnaws at him is the lecture he got from that preacher, what's-his-name, the one who must be with the NAACP. A girl's name. Vivian? If the man was mad he didn't show it, and that was the unnerving part. He can deal with a shouter like B. D., the way he learned as a player to shut out hostile crowds and maniacal coach-es, but he doesn't know how to respond to someone who calmly points out your shortcomings, one by one, like a teacher explaining why you're currently failing math but can pull out of it if you do this and this and that. "God put us here together not to fall but to rise, Mister *Hunsucker* . . . We can debate, but not deflate, celebrate rather than denigrate, get along instead of tag along." The man rips him apart, leaves him bleeding, then calls him "sir," wishes him a good evening, and hangs up. A smiling assassin.

...

By mid-afternoon, having slept off the booze, he is out in the yard hosing down the wagon and assessing the damage. From the looks of it, he's lucky to be alive. Clumps of grass and mud are stuck to the front bumper and grill and undercarriage. His own blood has dried on the steering wheel and dashboard. The rear bumper, nearly pulled loose during Rima's salvage operation, will have to be jury-rigged with a coat hanger. While straightening out the driver's-side mirror he sees his reflection: the bridge of his nose is plastered with tape, there's a Band-Aid strapped across his forehead, and he has two black eyes. She's right about the antique tag, he's thinking, one for him and one for his horse.

Here she comes now, barefooted, wearing cutoff jeans and a pink halter top to match her dyed hair, looking a little worse for the wear herself from lack of sleep. She might as well be going to the beach, loaded down as she is with a webbed aluminum chaise lounge, a towel the size of a bedspread, a six-pack of Budweiser, a tube of sunblock, a newspaper. She spreads the towel on the bare ground, pops open the chaise lounge, smiles faintly through her giant sunglasses, sits down, and opens a beer. "Help yourself," she says.

"No, thanks."

"Be good for your health."

"You're kidding, right?"

"'Faded Jock Turns over New Leaf'?"

"He's giving it some thought."

Rima settles into the chaise, takes a sip of beer, pushes the halter down just short of revealing her nipples, then throws her head back to take in the sun. Billy Ray, barefooted and wearing only a fresh pair of jeans, cuts off the hose at the nozzle and walks around the wagon. He unlocks the tailgate and sits on it.

"Time to review your performance," she says.

"So now you're an entertainment critic."

"Rima's a lot of things, in case you hadn't noticed." She begins lathering her shoulders, neck, arms, and legs with the sunblock. "*Artiste*, social critic, tow-truck operator, wrangler, all-around good ol' gal." When a teenaged boy cruising past in his pickup hits the horn and whistles at her, she shoots him the bird. "Saint Rima, the Bird-Girl."

Billy Ray says, "I'd just as well not talk about the show."

"Too late, sport." She pulls out the Living section of that afternoon's Atlanta *Journal*, opens to the TV-Radio page, and begins to read. "Says right here, and I quote, 'Lively Night at Radio WWJD.' That's the only good part, the headline. Wait'll you get a load of this. 'Billy Ray Hunsinger, a/k/a the "Gunslinger," took some incoming fire Sunday night in his debut as host of "Jock Talk" . . .'"

"Lemme see that thing." He snatches the paper from her and scans the story. "In an obscenity-filled exchange with several black callers . . . Hunsinger, obviously on the defensive . . . Station owner B. D. Spotswood, expressing concerns about possible FCC sanctions, would say only that the show has 'a few ripples [*sic*] to iron out' . . . Hunsinger was calmly lectured by the Rev. T. Vivian Beaumont, a respected black pastor and veteran of the Civil Rights protests during the 1960s . . ." Billy Ray was unavailable for comment, the story went on, and "his estranged wife, Virginia Bradford Hunsinger, said she had no idea of his where-abouts. 'Billy's been under a lot of pressure lately,' said Mrs. Hunsinger . . ."

Billy Ray slams the newspaper to the ground. "His 'estranged' wife? Hell, I ain't been gone but two days."

"You got to admit she was nice about it, though, bubba. Think what she could've said. 'I don't know where the sonofabitch is, and I don't care.' The lady had a hell of an opening, but wouldn't bite."

"Yeah, but 'estranged'? It ain't like that at all."

"Wonder where the reporter got that?"

...

They watch bumblebees buzzing around a hummock of clover, the only greenery in a yard that turns to mud after the briefest of showers; they listen while the bluejays resume their squawking at the cats foraging through the neighborhood; gaze upward to see jet contrails crisscrossing in the cloudless cobalt sky. Idly scanning the two duplexes and the crumbling old frame houses up and down the street of this neighborhood where he grew up in the 'forties and 'fifties, when it was a lively town unto itself, where fathers returned from their factory jobs at day's end for meat-loaf suppers with their aproned wives and snot-nosed kids, he can see that the place is going downhill fast. Not that he can complain out loud, understand, seeing as how as a slumlord he's become a part of the problem, but still . . .

"Everything's changed," he says, almost wistfully.

"Right. 'Now, back when I was a lad . . .'"

"Naw, I'm being serious now. I was born two blocks from here. The daddies worked, the mamas stayed home, the kids played in the streets, and nobody ever got divorced that I know about. A kid could walk or ride a bike to everything he needed. School, church, drugstore, picture show, it was all right here. You could take a city bus to watch the Atlanta Crackers play baseball at old Ponce de Leon Park, or to see Georgia Tech football at Grant Field, maybe catch a movie at the Fox where they've got these stars in the ceiling. Now look. Christ, they've even changed the name of my old high school. Used to be Forrest High, now it's McGill."

"It's a sign of the times, bubba," Rima says. "Forrest was named for the Confederate general who gave us the Ku Klux Klan. McGill is for Ralph McGill, the editor, who had the novel idea that lynching was bad for black folks' health. I'm not but thirty, but I know that much."

"I understand the high school's all-black now."

"All-black and all-poor. I do some teaching there."

"You? A teacher?"

"Well, you know, art classes. All the school money's going to the suburbs now. They'll hire anybody these days, sweetie, even Rima. Place is going to shut down after this year, be turned into a warehouse or lofts or something."

"No wonder we don't have reunions there anymore."

"Speaking of which." Rima wrestles with the catch on the chaise lounge, turning it into a cot, and turns over onto her stomach. "What was that business about your 'adventure' up at the ol' alma mater? The one your first caller mentioned."

"It ain't worth talking about."

"Must be, if the Birmingham paper got a hold of it."

"You know how newspapers are. They got it all twisted up and blown out of proportion." He's willing to lay out some basic facts. During halftime of the annual spring football game at North Alabama State in Guntersville, with about 5,000 fans in the stands, the great Catamounts team of 'sixty-five was being honored. Two dozen of the players, the ones still alive and ambulatory, were being chauffeured around the track in the back seats of vintage 'sixties convertibles. The biggest cheers went up for Billy Ray, the team's small-college All-America quarterback, riding in a burgundy Mercury alongside Ginny, who had been North Alabama's head cheerleader that season. "I stood up to acknowledge the cheers, you know, and I sorta lost my balance there for a second or two."

"You fell on your ass."

"To tell the truth, I think the driver must've goosed it or something. But, yeah, I guess you could say that."

"Drunk as a skunk, right?"

"Oh, there'd been some cocktails at lunch. You know how these reunions go."

"Let me get the picture," she says. "You got drunk, you fell off the car, and you got a standing ovation. Am I right?"

"Well, it wasn't *exactly* like that." By this time, Rima is trying to sit up but she's laughing so hard that she can't. Billy Ray reddens, tries to put a spin on it, but makes it worse. "You had to be there."

"'Had to be there.' Oh, God, I'm gonna die!"

Billy Ray looks hurt. "I mean, there were extenuating circumstances."

"'Extenuating circumstances.' Take me now, Lord, I'm finished down here!"

"It was a long drive back home, I tell you."

"'A long drive home.'"

"Ginny never could drive, especially when she's talking at the same time."

...

In that heat, with no air conditioning, they decide to dine *al fresco* that evening. Dinner is hamburgers, burned to a crisp on the rusty cooker beside Rima's kiln on the rear landing of the duplex, served up on a card table they've hauled to the front porch. She complements the burgers, hard as hockey pucks, with some canned pork-and-beans and potato chips. She even sticks birthday candles in a menorah she salvaged from somewhere so they can dine by candlelight. That's the "William Tell Overture" on the stereo, she says, with the Lone Ranger hot on his trail. She has a beer. He opts for a Coke.

They devour the meal in less than ten minutes. When they're done, she goes inside, changes the music to Edith Piaf, then returns to the porch and sits on the swing. "Along about now," she says, "I'd be looking for some payback. Now *you* owe *me,* bubba. Big-time."

"Well, I appreciate what you've done. I could've gotten killed out there this morning. I know that. Thanks."

"That's all? 'Thanks'? Then I lay on this four-star dinner for you, candlelight and music and the works? 'Thanks'? A girl expects more than that."

"Come on, we've been over that. You 'n' me'll never work."

She nods and winks, inviting him to join her on the swing. "If you don't mind my asking, stud, are you getting any *strange* these days?"

He can't believe he's blushing. "Not really."

"Just curious, you understand. What does 'not really' mean?"

"It's been a while, is all." Still sitting at the card table, he coughs and begins to stack the paper plates and napkins. "It's probably been a couple of years, before you moved in. I picked up this young 'un at a disco, brought her here, had her going pretty good. I'm ready and she's ready, you know . . ."

"I'm familiar with the process, yes. Go on."

"I don't know what got into me, but while we're rassling I say something about the day they shot Kennedy and she sits up in bed and says, 'Shot Kennedy? What'd *she* ever do to hurt anybody?'"

57

"No! Poor baby."

"Me, or her? Anyway, that's when I figured I'm getting too old for that stuff." He moves across the porch and joins her on the swing. "I'm getting too old for a lot of things these days.'"

"Sounds to me like we've got a classic case of the old mid-life crisis here." Before he can react, Rima has thrown her arm around his shoulder and pulled him toward her, nuzzling his head to her breast. She begins curling the hair at his neck with her fingers. He feels like a little boy in his mother's arms. Soon she is cooing to him. "It might be time for you to start figuring out what you're going to be when you grow up. Don't you think?"

FIVE

A couple of days later, he has no idea where he is, or why. This stuff is getting old. Stirring awake, eyes out of focus, head pounding, stomach feeling as though someone had hammered it with a mallet, he peeks from beneath sweaty sheets. Harsh light slants through Venetian blinds, giving no indication of whether it's daybreak or sundown. The tip of his right index finger is patched with a tiny Band-Aid, there's a molded plastic splint taped over his nose, and he finds that he is wearing a loose-fitting gown he has never seen before. The room, or what he can make of it when it stops spinning, appears to be painted a pale green. Everything smells of laundry soap and disinfectant. A chirpy female voice keeps paging people. He thinks it might be the green room in Purgatory, where guests bide their time until St. Peter shows up for the pre-interview.

When he begins to make out the large form of someone standing at the end of the bed, a ruddy man wearing a wry grin and an Alabama baseball cap, he figures it's worse than he expected. This isn't St. Peter. It's Bear Bryant, still pissed after all of these years, come to cash in his chips.

"You know," the man says. "I've got to start jogging or something. I'm not getting any exercise since I quit having seizures."

"Is that what happened to me?"

"A *grand mal*. 'The Gun' never was the type to do anything halfway."

"Where am I?" Billy Ray says. "And who the hell are you?"

"Grady Hospital. Me, I'm the ghost of whiskey past."

"No, really. I've seen you before."

"Not as much as I've seen you, I'm sure." He comes around to the side of the bed, pulls up a stool, makes himself at home. "Ben Burns. Call me Scottie. Alabama, 'sixty-five. Bryce Sanitarium, 'seventy-five. Recovering drunk, now and forever more."

"We know each other?"

"Oh, our paths have crossed. I've done some movies, plays, and stuff. You might've seen me on television. I'm the Roto-Rooter Man in the commercials."

"Maybe that's it. Our paths have crossed, you say."

Ben Burns says, "We go 'way back. I was there that day in Tuscaloosa."

"You played for the Bear?"

"Nah, I was in the Bama band. Guess that makes me an athletic supporter."

"Burns, you say. I've heard your name."

"I called your show the other night. Before the callers jumped you. Figured you'd need all the help you could get."

"That's right. The show. God." He feels he could use a drink, more than anything, but the odds seem long against that, seeing as how he's in a hospital. Drugs, they've got; whiskey, not a chance. "Fill me in," he says.

...

There had been many memorable moments in the long history of Manuel's Tavern, most of them involving disagreements about politics, but none so spectacular as what had transpired the day before. Billy Ray was working on his second day of sobriety when he walked into the place at high noon. His thinking was that he might give up the booze but he'd be damned if he'd give up the company of drinkers, so he had chosen the busiest time of day as a means of testing himself. The place was crawling with the usual crowd of politicians, reporters, plumbers, Emory professors, career drunks, and secretaries, and he was roundly hailed as he took his favorite seat at the round table nearest the front window. There was some discussion of his taped nose, bandaged forehead, and black eyes, a few hoots and talk of how the cold day in hell had finally arrived when they heard him order a glass of iced tea, but they soon got bored and left him alone in his agony.

The mere sight of the tiers of whiskey bottles lining the wall behind the bar, the way the sun filtered through the amber liquid in the decanters of Johnny Walker Red and Jack Daniel's, had him jumping out of his skin. But he persevered, hunkered down, tried to think pure thoughts, figuring if he could make it through lunch at Manuel's he'd be home free. He had knocked off a hamburger and was on his third glass of tea, trying to grin and bear it, feeling like some person he had never met before, when the lights went out.

"For the record," Ben Burns is saying, "you got a standing ovation."

"I must've passed out."

"No, it was more like a swan dive, actually. You dropped your tea and let out a Tarzan yell. *Aaiieeyaaahhheeee!* I was having lunch at the other end of the bar, and when I looked over there I saw you throwing out your arms and legs and going into spasms, like you'd heard the Lord. I've been there. I know. Reminded me of a Holy Roller I saw one time at a revival over in Cuba, Alabama. Then you pitched forward, over the table and onto the floor."

"It was that bad, huh?"

"Bad? If I were a judge, I'd give it a nine-eight for style. Throw in degree-of-difficulty, we're talking gold medal."

...

An intern appears. He wears a loose pale blue smock, opened in the front to reveal a silk paisley tie and a tan poplin suit. He is young, handsome, and black. After inspecting the chart that hangs at the foot of the bed, he nods to the two men, drags a stool to the side of the bed opposite Ben and proceeds to take Billy Ray's pulse.

"Vodka martini, rocks, twist," Billy Ray tells him. "Stir, don't shake. I hate it when it's bruised."

A glimmer of a smile. "I suspect you could use one about now."

"You don't know the half of it, doc."

"Oh, I do, I do." He leans over, pulls back Billy Ray's bruised eyelids, probes with a pinpoint flashlight. "That's not a bad job somebody did on the nose, by the way. I put the splint on to protect it." Then he asks him to sit on the edge of the bed, pull up the gown, and proceeds to tap just below the kneecap with a little rubber tomahawk. Nothing happens. The doctor notices the network of old scars on the gnarled knee, like a roadmap of West Virginia. "I can see you're no stranger to the knife."

"Oh, Christ, not again."

"Not to worry," the doctor tells him. With his chocolate skin, cropped Afro, and widow's peak, he reminds Billy Ray of Harry Belafonte. *Dayyy-O, da-da-day-O . . .* "Be a great step for mankind if a little surgery would cure alcoholism. Afraid we aren't there yet, though, Mister, ah, Hunsinger, is it?"

Billy Ray brightens. "That's right. Billy Ray Hunsinger." The name hanging in the air, echoing, he waits.

"I've heard that name somewhere."

"Yeah?"

The doctor doesn't bite. Instead, he reaches into a pocket of his smock and whips out a needle that looks to Billy Ray like something a veterinarian would use on a horse. "I want you to pull up your gown, roll over on your left side, and scrunch up in the fetal position. This might sting a little at first."

Billy Ray is terrified. "Hey, wait a minute. What the hell are you *doing?*"

"Just a little chunk's all I need."

"A *chunk?* Of what? Who *sent* you, anyway?" At that, Ben Burns begins laughing so hard that he can't stay on his stool; has to get on his feet and walk toward the window, where he bends over, hands on his knees, guffawing, trying to contain himself.

"Hunsinger," the doctor says as he drives the needle into the small of Billy Ray's back. "*Hunsinger . . .*" He probes, his eyes closed in concentration, feeling his way, then begins to twist the needle. "*HUN*-singer . . ." Finally he slowly withdraws the needle, swabs the pinhole with a wet cotton boll, then holds the glistening needle up to the light. "That's fine, thanks," he says. There is a sliver of skin on the ratcheted end of the needle.

"You gonna put it in a museum or something?"

"I hope not. We'll send it off to see how far gone the liver is. You can cover up now, Mister Hunsinger."

The doctor scrapes the specimen of skin into a glass vial, pockets the vial, and tosses the needle into a red container labeled SHARPS. He begins talking about how seizures happen, of how a pill called Dilantin can prevent it, of how he can't understand why a man can't just put in a day's work, relax with a glass of wine, eat dinner, and go to bed. "How much alcohol do you consume every day, anyway?"

"Oh, a couple of belts, I guess," Billy Ray tells him. "Maybe three. You know, when I'm under pressure."

A smile, a roll of the eyes. "Sure, right."

"Well, anyhow, I've got this behind me. Might as well be movin' on. Where's my clothes at?"

"Whoa. Not so fast. Let's see you hold out your hands." Billy Ray throws out his arms, straight from his body, and his hands are shaking like tuning forks. The doctor clucks his tongue and nods. "One more night, maybe two."

"Hey, doc, I'm a busy man. My public awaits."

"If that's the case, you don't want to embarrass 'em. Sorry."

The doctor turns, as though to leave, then suddenly snaps his fingers and faces Billy Ray. "Now I know. Hunsinger. That's the name of that teacher out there in Crestwood, isn't it, the one trying to make 'em stop playing 'Dixie' at football games. Am I right?"

"Yeah, yeah, yeah." Billy Ray is crestfallen. "She's my wife."

"Tough lady. You must be proud of her. Tell her to keep up the good work, okay?" He winks at Ben, then leaves the room.

...

Now that Ginny's name has come up, Billy Ray wonders why she isn't there. Instead, he's gotten a doctor from Timbuktu and this clown who played in the Bama band, for God's sake. Just when he needs her the most, there's no Ginny. She must be madder than he thought.

"She's a tough lady, all right," says Burns, back again at bedside.

"You know her?"

"We met. A long time ago."

"Funny, she never told me about you."

"Hey, Gun, you're in the book," says Burns. "It's pretty hard for you to hide in Atlanta, you know."

"You talked to her, then."

"The medics rolled you in and started working on you, and somebody at the desk stopped me. Figured I might be family, wanted to know about insurance. I looked up your number, got the house, and told her what had happened."

"And?"

"She gave me the insurance numbers."

"That's it? That's all?"

"She sends her best wishes for a speedy recovery. Said she would've sent flowers, but she was busy."

The way his stomach muscles are drawn up in knots, repositioning himself in the bed takes heroic measures. He manages it, though, with the help of Burns, who grabs him under the shoulders and hoists him. Reaching for the glass of water on the bedside table, Billy Ray tosses the straw aside and drains the glass in steady gulps, all the while keeping his eyes on this stranger. It's Thursday, the best he can reckon, and he's ticking off the list of people who have come into his life since he was kicked out of the house—*when?*—last weekend: B. D. Spotswood, Spider Medders, Rima the Bird-Girl, whom he had known previously only as a tenant, and now this fellow Ben Burns.

". . . So here it is, Christmas Eve, and it suddenly occurs to me that I haven't bought a single damned thing for Christmas. . . ." Back at bedside now, Burns has been rambling for at least ten minutes, regaling Billy Ray with stories from his drinking days. "I've been at Manuel's all day, having a hell of a time, but now it's midnight and the only place open in all of Atlanta is Plaza Drugs, right around the corner, We Never Close, place doesn't even have a lock and key. I back my car up to the front door, and twenty minutes later I walk out with Christmas for my wife and the kid. Chocolates, perfume, lipstick, plastic toys, a yo-yo, coloring books, magazines, hair dryer, you name it. It's two o'clock in the morning when I get home, singing 'Santa Claus Is Coming to Town,' and there's my wife in her robe, kneeling beside the tree, wrapping packages. 'Where'd all these presents come from?' I ask her. She says, 'You pulled the same shit last Christmas, Benny. This stuff's been in the attic all year. Merry goddamned Christmas.'"

"If you ain't drinking anymore," says Billy Ray, "how come you hang out at Manuel's?"

"Same reason you were there yesterday, probably. I like bars and the people in 'em. Manuel's is a safe-house, anyway. They love me like I was family. Hell, they'll eighty-six me if I even *look* like I want a drink."

"You seem awfully damned happy about it."

"What's the alternative, bubba?"

"Well, yeah, you've got a point." Billy Ray's stomach feels like a washboard. "Did I hear the doctor right? 'Alcoholism'?"

"What he said. Could be."

"I've just had some bad days lately, is all."

"Yeah, sure."

Billy Ray counts the ways: Catamount Days, WSB, a DUI and a night in jail, Ginny's ultimatum, the wild night at WWJD, the wreck, now this. "Looks like my ol' buddy Jim Beam's let me down this time. That's a pretty long streak of bad luck, if you ask me. It can't last forever."

Ben Burns lets the thought hover for a few seconds, then purses his lips. "You might think about trying AA. I've got a list of Atlanta chapters here—"

"Won't happen. You can forget about that right now, my friend. No. *Hell,* no."

Here comes another story. The guy's full of them. "This drunk goes to the doctor. Says, 'Things ain't going so good, doc. I can't eat. My wife and kids left me, parents disowned me, and my friends won't return calls. Lost my house, my car, my credit rating, my driver's license, my self-respect, my dog, my job, my health, and all my money. What can I do?' Doc says, 'You ever think about AA?' Guy says, 'Aw, hell, it ain't *that* bad.'"

"Hunh. Well, it ain't. Me, sitting in a room sharing stories with a bunch of drunks? No way."

"Suit yourself," says Burns. "All I can say is, it saved *my* ass. I was a drunk by the time I got to college. Wanted to be an actor, but I left my best stuff in every beer joint on the Bessemer Superhighway between Birmingham and Tuscaloosa, doing Shakespeare for a bunch of house-painters, roustabouts, and sawmill workers. I worked both sides of the wall in that town: graduated with a bachelor's degree from the university, and then got my master's from the state nuthouse. Now you're looking at the Roto-Rooter Man."

"AA saved you for *that*?"

"Yeah, but I'm a happy Roto-Rooter Man."

"That's a relief."

"The point is, I got everything back. You can do it, too, Gun, with or without AA. What you've got to do is find something to replace the stuff. Stand on your head, read Tarot cards, take up trout fishing, talk to telephone poles. Whatever it takes. You're sick, bubba."

...

Throughout another long night, he hardly sleeps. Sirens scream, patients moan, nurses shuffle in and out of the room, and it seems as though the doctors are playing hide-and-seek with the same perky receptionist who is paging them. *Doctor feye-yuv neye-yun three-yuh.* Sweating, moaning, tossing, he sees his life spinning in review and it isn't pretty: dizzying kaleidoscopic flashes of a world upside down—a car in free-fall, nameless faces pointing and laughing, a herd of elephants rampaging toward him, Ginny crying, pink-jowled B. D. Spotswood squealing like a stuck pig, African drumbeats as menacing black men corner him in a dark alley—and at three o'clock in the morning he's had enough. He eases out of the hospital bed, finds his clothes and puts them on, simply walks out of the place, hires a cab to take him to The Ranch. His pockets empty, he pounds on Rima's door until she comes to pay the driver.

SIX

T he weekend is spent tidying up the place, doing things he's never done before: sweeping, dusting, mopping, scrubbing toilets and sinks, moving furniture around to his liking, replacing some of the stuff Walter and Robbie took when they skipped out for New Orleans. With the back rent given him in cash by Rima, who finally got paid by the couple from Crestwood for her "Eden Redux" triptych while he was in the hospital (they turn out to be the Suttons, his next-door neighbors, co-chairs of the neighborhood garden club), he has bought a rug, towels, a couple of lamps, some flatware and plastic dishes and a cast-iron pot, a giant floor fan, a second-hand sofa for in front of the television set in the living room. He now has his own phone number, but the same Mickey Mouse telephone the boys left behind, and he calls and leaves the new number at the house, where he suspects Ginny is hiding behind the answering machine. The beer in the refrigerator he gives to Rima; what's left of the Jim Beam goes in the rear of the pantry, just in case.

With this pill, Dilantin, he figures he won't have to worry about another seizure; but, still, it'll take a while to wean his body away from running on whiskey. He can't imagine: nearly a fifth a day, over the past five years, and now it's out of his life. This must be like taking a baby off of mother's milk and putting it on formula. He walks softly now, no sudden moves, easy does it with this new body, and each afternoon since his return he coaxes Rima into strolling through the neighborhood like an old married couple. She's taking the whole thing well, it seems, cooling it with the wisecracks, even showing him some basic cookery. Often, each day, he has a vision of returning to the house in Crestwood and being welcomed home by Ginny and Maggie as though he never left, but he squashes it.

Well after dark on Sunday, refreshed and on a mission, he holds on tightly to the steering wheel as *Rosinante* wobbles along the Bankhead Highway. He is timing his arrival at the station to eliminate any chit-chat, hoping to walk through the door and go straight to the booth, ready to work. Sure enough, when he slows and turns onto the gravel driveway, he sees B. D.'s Cadillac and Spider's pickup parked beneath the flags. It's ten minutes before ten. He looks into the rear-view mirror, winces to see the black eyes and the contraption holding his nose in place, shrugs, dismounts, and strides to the front door. Drunk or sober, the place still looks like crap.

B. D. in billowing industrial-size jeans and an Auburn sweatshirt, Spider in khaki shorts and a tank top, the two stop talking the instant the door opens. Their eyes widen at the sight of his shiners and the nose. "Oh, hi there, Gun, me and—" B. D. begins, a bit too jovially, but Billy Ray cuts him off. "Later," he says, heading straight for the restroom in the corner to eat up more time. In the booth now, with two minutes 'til air time, Billy Ray is snuggling into his swivel chair and lighting his cigar and intently watching Spider in the control booth, like a man beginning a countdown at Canaveral, when B. D. pokes his head in.

"You okay, buddy?" he says. "The eyes—"

"Don't ask."

"Hope you'll be a little bit nicer tonight, Gun."

"I'm gonna love 'em to death, boss."

...

Before we start taking calls and talking football, there's some things I want to say. Ol' Billy Ray kinda got out of hand last week and he wants to clear the air. I ain't much for apologies, but some friends of mine say that might be in order. Call it what you want to, whatever makes you feel good, I don't care. Anyhow, here's the deal. I've been having some personal problems lately, like most everybody, and I reckon I let that get in my way. Line One, hold on for a minute, will you? . . . I mean, it ain't like I can change my ways overnight or anything. I yam what I yam what I yam, you know? But, hey, we all make mistakes. Me and you both. So I thought maybe we'd just sit back and take a deep breath and . . . All right, all right. Line One, what you got?

You still there, you damned motha—

See there? Now that's what I'm talking about. Here I am, promising to play it straight with y'all, and I'll be . . . dang . . . if this ain't what I get in return. This ain't easy to do, folks, so come on. Fair's fair, takes two to tango, and all of that. Line Two, talk to me.

Mister Hornblower?

Close, but no cigar.

Hunh? Y'all giving out cigars?

Just a figure of speech.

Ah-hanh. Figure of speech. That's what you said last week, you know? About that play y'all had. Niggers Go Long.

Well, let me say this about that—

Me and some o' the brothers was—

I was wrong to even bring it up. Dead wrong. Okay? See where I'm coming from tonight? I apologize for even—

You're welcome. That's all I wanted. Be talkin' to you.

Hello? Line Three? He's gone? Well, now. Here's that number again. Just dial ASK-JOCK, that's two-seven-five, five-six-two-five. It's Jock Talk with Billy Ray Hunsinger, every Sunday night from ten to midnight.

...

The first fifteen minutes are gone before he knows it. At the break, while Spider starts reading a news update off the Associated Press wire and

71

playing commercials, Billy Ray heads for the Coke machine in the lobby. B. D. is there waiting for him, his frame taking up the entire sofa.

"Got your work clothes on tonight, I see," says Billy Ray.

"Thought I might stick around, if you don't mind."

"It's your show. Where do you order your jeans from, anyway? Chattanooga Tent and Awning?"

"You aren't mad at me, are you, Gun?"

"Hey, I'm sorry, buddy. Mad at myself, more than anybody. Like I said, there's been some bad times."

"From the black eyes, looks like you had an *alteration* of some kind. Just wondering, understand."

"Took on a pine tree, is all."

"Hunh. Pine tree." B. D. is trying to make some sense of it all, but he can see that Billy Ray is dead serious and so he's not about to push him. "Say, now, Gun, Tech and Georgia'll be starting up practice before we know it. Hope you're gon' be talking some *FUH-baw* tonight."

"I will if they'll let me."

"*FUH-baw,* Gun, *FUH-baw.*"

...

Hey, Gun, how you doin' tonight?

Fair to partly cloudy. That you again, Peahead?

One and only. Say, lookie here now, Gun, I don't see no reason why you got to apologize to those folks. We didn't own no slaves. Wadn't around for the Civil War, neither. These coloreds have been gettin' all the breaks these days, anyways. I just hate to see you gravel like that.

It's gruh-vul, Peahead, and I'm not—

Well, excuse me. Hell, I was—

And watch your language. Anyway, like I was saying, I'm not groveling. I owed some apologies for letting things get out of hand last week, and so I gave 'em. You got a football question for me?

I'm thinkin', Gun.

72

Call me back when you got one, Peahead. Line Two, you're on the air.

Yea Alabama, drown 'em Tide.

Least you can do is sing it on key. Who's this, Paul Bryant Junior?

A secret admirer.

You sound like Scottie Burns to me. Looks like all the regulars are checking in. If we run out of time, maybe we can all take a cab and go to my place.

Hey, Gun, you got your friend Jim Beam there with you tonight?

Naw, left him at home. Bad influence.

When in doubt, kick 'em out.

That's real good, Scottie. Let me write that down. That all you learned in four years at Bama?

We learned how to whip North Alabama State's butt. ·

That mean we're finally gonna get around to talking football on this show?

Just kidding, Gun, just kidding. Talk to you later.

Who's next? Line Three, thanks for being patient.

See there, that doesn't hurt a bit, does it?

This the Rev?

T. Vivian Beaumont, sir, First Calvary AME Revival Assembly on Moreland Avenue. How are you this fine evening?

Fine, sir. Been thinking about you this week.

And I, you, sir. Looks like my prayers got answered.

Well, I don't know how much the Lord had to do with it, but you did get me to thinking about things. I'm much obliged to you.

The Lord works in mysterious ways, Mister Hucklefinn.

It's Hunsinger, sir.

Oh, I know that, sir. I was just trying to make a point. These European names give me trouble. Hun-Singer. Now, if I were the sort to judge a man by his name I'd be prejudiced against any person named Hun-Singer. Hun is for a person of German descent, don't you see, and we all remember the Holocaust. Now—

Excuse me, Rev, but I—

Please bear with me, sir.

But it's a sports show, Rev.

I'll be getting to that directly. Now. Put Hun and Singer together, and what you've got? Hun and Singer. A person who sings of the Huns. Understand what I'm saying?

Lord, Rev, I didn't name myself. I got that from my daddy. Born with it.

But see, suppose I don't know that. Suppose I'm a prejudiced person, quick to jump to conclusions, and when I hear the name Hun-Singer I make up my mind that this is a person who hates Jews.

Oh, come on, now.

You can't judge a book by its cover, Brother Gun. See where I'm coming from?

Yeah. From 'way out in left field. I don't know, Rev, that's a pretty good stretch.

The lesson to be learned here, sir, is that we are all innocent until proved guilty. Just because my skin is black doesn't mean that I'm poor and dumb and diseased. You see? Get my drift?

Well, sure. I mean—

And there's one other thing before I go. Remember that business about sticks and stones from last week, do you?

Sure. Sticks and stones might break my bones, but words don't bother me none, or something like that.

That's close enough. You see, Brother Gun, what happened here in the long sad history of the civil rights movement was that there was a time when sticks and stones was just the beginning of what was used to break our bones. There was some chains and guns thrown in there, too, if I remember my history correctly, followed in due time by the noose. Am I right about that?

Well, times change, Rev. Folks don't do that no more.

So then the white folks moved on to words. You following me, Brother Gun?

But I just got through apologizing, Rev.

Your apology is accepted, Brother Gun. But I just want to make sure that everybody out there, all of those fans of yours, those folks that look up to you, I want to make sure they understand. Those words, Brother Gun, those words can harm us.

Come on, Rev, gimme a break here.

A nigger ain't gon' go long or anywhere else, long as you don't address him properly.

Lord. Is that all, Rev? We need to be moving on here.

It's nice working with you, sir. I can tell you're a man with an open mind. You have a nice evening, now, you hear?

...

"That guy's dangerous, Gun. You better keep an eye on him." B. D. Spotswood is helping Spider pigeon-hole the tapes afterwards, still wondering if Billy Ray is ever going to get around to talking sports, and about all he can talk about is Rev. T. Vivian Beaumont's second straight appearance on the show. "He's a jailbird, you know."

"How so?"

"Oh, hell, everybody knows about that. Him and that Martin Lucifer King. He's got a criminal record a mile long." *Criminal.* "Starting riots, fighting with the police, stirring up things."

"Hell, B. D., I can't hardly cut off a preacher."

"*Some* preacher, if you ask me."

Billy Ray turns to Spider. "How about it, chief? I noticed you grinning while the Rev was talking."

"The man's one of my heroes," says Spider, glancing at B. D., delighted to see him wriggle and redden.

"He ever hurt anybody, like the boss here says?"

"Just the rednecks."

"And how do you define a 'redneck' these days, my man?" Billy Ray tosses a wink at Spider and gets one in return. B. D. has gone sullen now, turning his head back and forth as the two men pick up the banter, like he's watching a tennis match. "If I remember correctly, it once was a fine and noble thing, like a job description."

"Indeed, it was, Brother Gun," says Spider, returning the volley. "A farmer worked hard all day in the fields, beneath an unforgiving sun. Thus, he was said to have a red neck."

"But now the word has become a, ah . . . Help me out here, Spider, you're the intellectual."

"A 'pejorative' is the word you're seeking, I believe."

"Ah, yes. Thank you, professor."

"Glad to help."

"So now we have a whole new meaning of the word 'redneck.' Am I right?"

"You are correct, sir."

"And that is?"

"A Fascist pig who doesn't know his ass from a cow patty."

...

With B. D. standing in the parking lot, shaking his fist and shouting as he drives away in the wagon—"Hot dangit, Hunsinger, you're still on prohibition until you straighten up!"—Billy Ray feels energized as he turns left on the Bankhead Highway, the correct choice this time, and negotiates his way home through vacant streets. Things are happening. He doesn't fully grasp what those things are; but, hey, action is action.

Rima is waiting up for him when he arrives at The Ranch, curled up again in the front-porch swing, wearing Donald Duck pajamas, sipping a beer. "All hail," she says as he bounds onto the porch and joins her. "Mister Hucklefinn, is it?"

"Hush up and scoot over," he says. "I feel like a schoolboy."

"Adult education is more like it."

"So how'd it work out?"

"'Work out'? You make it sound like you had a game plan."

"Well, I did," Billy Ray says. "Sort of."

"Oh, right. You planned it so the preacher would make you eat dirt, in front of God and everybody. That's bullshit, and you know it."

"I've still got the job, ain't I?"

Rima says, "I've got to admit it was pretty good stuff, whether you meant for it to happen or not. There's so much crap on radio these days that it's a wonder anybody listens to any of it. Same songs over and over, right out of the can. Syndicated hucksters with their own agendas, right and left, mostly right. 'Better living through meatloaf.' This show, now, I hate to admit it, but I think you're onto something. The beauty of it is, you don't know what the hell you're doing. It's original, I can say that much."

"That's a compliment?"

"Best I can come up with, this time of day, bubba. Anyhow, I've got a suggestion. 'Jock Talk with Billy Ray Hunsinger' seems kinda dull, don't you think?"

"Ask me, it gets right to the point."

"Yeah, but you ought to elevate it, give it a higher tone, like they do on National Public Radio."

"I'm sure you have a better idea."

"Well, I do. How about 'Vox Jox'?"

"What the hell does that mean?"

"It's Bubba-Latin for 'Jock Talk.' 'V-O-X' for voice, 'J-O-X' for jocks. Vox Jox. Jock talk. Got it?"

"Nobody'd know what the hell we're talking about."

"Ah, well, it was just a thought. No charge for the consultation." Rima gets up from the swing. "By the way, check your messages. You had a call a while ago."

SEVEN

G inny's voice is on the answering machine. "The goldfish died," is all she said before hanging up. Sitting on his bed in the darkness, he figures that's just like her. It sounds like those coded messages the agents are always leaving in the World War II spy novels that make up the extent of his ventures into literature; or maybe one of those poems that he never could understand, the ones she used to read by the fire during the long snowy nights in Calgary, on the eastern slope of the Canadian Rockies, after they had made love on the bearskin rug. She's always been a big one for irony—that word again—and loves to tease him with it, knowing that he's the literal type who doesn't believe in anything he can't see or feel or hear. *The goldfish died.* His thinking is, if you don't feed 'em or keep the pond clean, that's what happens. Ginny, the poet, always trying to make something out of nothing.

The goldfish had been her idea in the first place. For an entire month, after it happened, he spent nearly every waking hour working on the grotto in the farthermost corner of the backyard, beneath the spreading oak: digging the hole, installing the plumbing, laying flagstone, erecting a trellis, planting Carolina jasmine, then buying two wrought-iron park benches and placing them face-to-face on either side of the pond. "Any memorial needs some life," Ginny had said, explaining the dozen goldfish she brought home from a pet store and ceremoniously slipped into the running waters. Then they gathered under the trellis for a sort of christening, he and Ginny and Maggie, and everything was calm and peaceful until Ginny began to recite a poem by some Brit—*Smart lad, to slip betimes away*—and that did it. Maggie burst into tears and ran into the house; he began to sob, himself; but Ginny simply got up, rubbed his neck, then walked away, never to return.

He has enough sense to know that if he could trace this malaise to its beginnings, it would be found at that precise moment; for it was there, alone beneath the trellis, feeding his misery with booze and black thoughts, that he began spending long stretches of his time. He could be found either there or in The Gun Room, when at home, and it was a measure of Ginny's feelings about his obsession with the grotto in the backyard that she had even begun to suggest that he go out with the boys—to Manuel's, to the clubs, to The Ranch—anywhere but the backyard. "It's over, Billy," she kept saying, but he wouldn't listen. And now there is only this cryptic message. *The goldfish died.* He concludes that the problem with messages, whether by mail or phone or answering machine, is that you can't tell whether they've been delivered with a smile or a frown.

It is another fitful night, fraught with dreams bordering on nightmares. In one, he gets the ball back for one more chance, two seconds left on the clock, and beats Bama with an electrifying eighty-yard strike to Stork Sims in the end zone. In another, playing in a blinding snowstorm at Saskatchewan, everybody is suddenly swallowed up and the world ends. He dreams of a sky full of clowns, like Mardi Gras, all of them laughing and pointing at him; of pretty young maidens, naked and young, dancing for him, unable to respond, now a broken old king whose gray beard reaches the floor; of him and Ginny and Maggie in the stands somewhere, giddy and on their feet, cheering, as a teenaged quarterback drives a team down the field; of ghosts ascending from a mangled automobile, one of them a goldfish wearing a football helmet.

...

Up early, just after dawn, he bends to his new regimen: pushups, situps, kneebends right there at bedside; then bacon and eggs cooked in the new cast-iron skillet Rima has blackened for him in the oven, washed down with some orange juice and milk; finally, out onto the porch to treat himself with coffee and a cigar (no more Lucky Strikes, thank you, just the cigars that he half-chews rather than smokes, anyway) while he skims through Rima's New York *Times*, delivered in the yard every morning, before she gets up. Bursting with new energy now that he isn't drinking away the hours, just as Scottie Burns predicted, he has been giving some thought to resurrecting the bare yard here at The Ranch with rye grass when the days begin to cool.

Thinking of the yard, he looks up from the *Times* and notices there is a strange car parked beside Rima's pickup, one that wasn't there when he rolled in from WWJD past midnight, a well-preserved old Karmann Ghia convertible with a white top and a chartreuse body. He's been so preoccupied with his own doings that he hasn't given much thought to the fact that Rima might have a life of her own beyond what she insists on calling her "art." She's a knockout, but he knows very little about her beyond the great body and the smart mouth and the college background that seems to have amounted to nothing. If she has boyfriends, or any friends at all, he hasn't seen them around. Whoever this is, he sneaked in after they said goodnight well past midnight. *Atta girl*, he thinks, giving the Ghia the once-over. There are two stickers on the bumper, one a pink triangle and the other a legend reading *Vegetarians Taste Better*, neither of them making any sense to him whatsoever.

He'll get back to Ginny later about the goldfish, or whatever it is she's really trying to tell him, because he's convinced himself that he has another busy day ahead of him. At a laundromat, in the company of lost teenagers and old women, he blows an hour-and-a-half watching his scant wardrobe of jeans and T-shirts and socks and underwear come clean. At Bud's body shop, he swaps a dozen bottles from his stash of Jim Beam for a quick fix on the wagon's front-end alignment. At Lorino's Grocery, across the street from his old school on Euclid Avenue, he loads up on more canned goods and cigars and the early street edition of that day's Atlanta *Journal*.

...

Noon finds him at Manuel's, sipping tea and perusing the sports section, when Scottie comes through the front door wearing tartan kilts, a brocaded vest, and a tam. The fellow seems to have attached himself to Billy Ray, like another of those fans he can't shake, and he may be as crazy as B. D. Spotswood. But *kilts*? Burns curtsies to acknowledge the hoots and whistles that greet him, and slides into the front booth across from Billy Ray.

"What's that crap the Scots eat?" Billy Ray says, "The pig guts stuffed in a kidney."

"Haggis," says Burns. "Food of the gods."

"The gods don't work here. Not in this kitchen. Is there a holiday I don't know about?"

"Nah, I'm taping a commercial today. MacGregor Dog Food."

"You just keep on lowering those expectations, don't you?"

"Hey, it pays the rent." Scottie hails one of the waiters. "Hey, Pat, what happened to the yuppie salads? The ones that lady cookbook writer suggested. I don't see 'em on the menu."

The waiter shrugs. "They lasted about a month. The regulars were going to boycott the place."

"Tea, and the burger, then," Scottie says.

"How do you want that cooked?"

"You gotta be kidding."

Scottie Burns has managed to insinuate himself into Billy Ray's life with little more than an introduction, like a fly at a picnic, and to see them together is to assume they are longtime friends. As far as the Gun knows, they have only the two things in common—both were at Denny Stadium in Tuscaloosa on the sixteenth day of October, 1965, and both no longer drink—but maybe that's enough. His circle of friends has shrunk to almost nothing over the past five years. Right now he can count them on one hand: Rima, B. D., Spider, and this failed middle-aged actor sitting at a neighborhood saloon in kilts. All of them certified nut cases.

"So," Scottie says. "How's it going? You staying busy? Golf? Fishing? I assume you've given up racing up and down the Bankhead Highway."

"Hey, I'm busy as a whore on payday." Billy Ray describes his morning, stretching a couple of errands into four hours of work, and how he has agreed to guard the cash register at Lorino's that afternoon while the old man visits his wife at the hospital. "Golf's out of the question, seeing as how when I was a kid they weren't in the habit of inviting the sons of house painters to the country club to knock balls around. Fishing, I'd fall asleep. Sunday nights, I'm busy. Otherwise, I'm free."

"I don't know what you're doing for entertainment these days, but you could do worse than go to some meetings with me."

"You call AA meetings entertainment?"

"Best show in town," Scottie says. "Completely unrehearsed. Last night there was this old boy, about seventy-five, who got up and started telling about the rose garden he planted when he announced he'd quit drinking. His wife was so happy that she told the family, 'Now, nobody's allowed in the rose garden. That's Paw-Paw's new hobby.' The old geezer had hooked up hoses, started fertilizing, and pretty soon those danged rose plants were taller than he was. Problem was, every afternoon when they called him to dinner they had to go out there and wake him up. Turns out he'd buried a fifty-gallon oak barrel out there, rigged it with a siphon, and filled the thing with a lifetime's supply of vodka."

"What happened to the rose garden?"

"Maw-Maw had it plowed under. Said she always thought roses were tacky, anyway."

...

Just before six o'clock, after napping away the afternoon at the apartment, he shows up at the grocery store. He has no idea exactly how old Frank and Teresa Lorino are these days, probably in their seventies, but they were living above their store when Billy Ray was a student at the school in its days as Forrest High. Football being the closest thing they could find to

European soccer when they migrated to Atlanta after the war, the Lorinos became devout fans of the Panthers, making all of the home games at Grady Stadium, and doted on Billy Ray and the other players in lieu of the children they never had. Then, as now, their store was a hangout where kids would load up on everything their parents had warned them against—comic books, candy bars, Nehis, smokes if they could filch them—before racing to beat the bell; the tide reversing seven hours later when school let out. The only changes, a quarter-of-a-century later, are that they have closed the soda fountain and the kids are black instead of white.

"Reporting for duty, Frankie," Billy Ray says when he enters. "So how's the bride?"

"Not so good, Billy, not so good. The diabetes keeps getting worse. They might take some toes tomorrow."

"Not to worry, old friend. They know what they're doing at Grady Hospital."

"That's good to hear. You know Grady? Football days, I bet."

"It's a long story." He looks around and sees that the place is nearly empty; wonders how they make a living in the summer when school is out; sees a video camera suspended from the ceiling in the rear of the store and points toward it. "Still stealing you blind, I see."

"Kids are kids, Billy. Still the same, except these are poorer than your bunch was."

He'll be gone for an hour, at most, the old man says, proceeding to give Billy Ray a quick run-through: here's a price list; no pistol for protection, only a button underneath the counter that you push to lock the doors in case of an emergency; the same old cash register held over from the 'sixties. No tabs for the kids, just the old women, he says. No lingering over the comic books, no eating or drinking in the store, only three kids allowed in the store at the same time, "just like the old days, Billy. Okay? I go now."

...

Perched on the stool behind the cash register, checking out the angles of the convex mirrors hanging from the ceiling, Billy Ray settles in. For the next forty-five minutes, ducking in from a sudden thunderstorm, there is a steady stream of customers—work-booted construction roustabouts buying six-packs for the ride home in their pickups *(ka-ching!),* barefooted children licking popsicles while their mother buys dinner from the shelves *(ka-ching!),* white teeny-boppers in sandals and beads trying to buy cigarettes with bogus ID cards *(No Sale!)*—and he is beginning to groove on this, thinking that maybe ol' Frank and Teresa Lorino do okay here, especially when school is in session and the volume of traffic quadruples, at least. A dime at a time can add up.

He is glancing at the Coke clock on the opposite wall, above the comics rack, ten minutes 'til seven, when he first sees the boy. He's tall and skinny, a lot like Billy Ray at eighteen, except for the coal-black skin, wearing sneakers and jeans and a mesh purple-and-gold McGill High baseball cap. He wears a long bulky suede coat, as well, like the Marlboro Man, and that alone sets off an alarm in Billy Ray's head. It's raining, sure, but the temperature's still in the eighties. That thing's meant for riding through a blizzard on a horse, rescuing strays on the High Plains, not for stopping at a mom-and-pop store in the middle of an Atlanta summer.

It must have a lot of inside pockets, too, because now Billy Ray can see by the mirrors on the ceiling that the kid is casually filling them with stuff from the shelves; helping himself to canned stew, crackers, and he can't tell what-all, like it's his own pantry. *Brazen little fucker.* Now Billy Ray can see that he's limping on his left leg, getting about with a cane. To the shock of a woman who has just brought a head of cabbage to the counter, Billy Ray lets out a shout: "Hey, *kid!"* The boy looks up, calmly, as if to say *Who, me?* It's unnerving, how cool he is. "Yeah, *you!"* Now, just as cooly, the boy begins to stroll toward the front door. "Hey! Somebody grab that kid there!"

The only other people in the store are the woman at the counter and an old black man using a walker to get around, engrossed in picking a perfect tomato from the vegetable bin near the glass double doors, seemingly unaware of anything else. Billy Ray's first instinct is to vault over the counter and tackle the kid, but then he thinks of his knees and does the sensible thing. The kid is reaching for one of the doors, about to push it open to make his escape, when Billy Ray fumbles for the button beneath the counter and hits it. *Click-click.* The boy pushes on the door, finds resistance, then whams it with the heel of his hand. "You ain't going nowhere, kid."

The kid still hasn't panicked. Instead, he slowly limps over to the shelves—it's more of a shuffle, really—and begins emptying the pockets of his great coat, putting the items back where he had gotten them. "Yeah, right," Billy Ray says. "I'm supposed to think you're straightening up the stock. Get your ass over here."

"Who are you, man?"

"I'm the cops, until they get here. Come on, move it."

"Where's Mister Lorino?"

"What's it to you, pal? I'm in charge here."

"But he—"

"Over here. Behind the counter. *Now!*"

Already, three more customers have gathered at the front doors, trying to enter. One of them, an older man, is banging on the doors with his fist. Another, a black teenager, sees what is happening inside and does a quick about-face and scurries away. The two other customers, trapped inside with Billy Ray and the boy, freeze and wait to see what will happen next.

"Don't be touchin' on me, man." Billy Ray has come out from around the counter and grabbed the boy by the elbow and is pulling him over to the beer cooler, next to the counter, where he intends to hold him under house arrest until he figures out what to do next. They are standing there, face to face, glowering at each other, when they hear more fierce pounding on the locked doors and both look up to see that this time it is Frankie Lorino, demanding to be let into his own store.

...

The old man has apologized to the two trapped customers, let them out, turned the sign around to read Closed, and re-locked the doors. Now, beneath the flickering glow of fluorescent lights, the two men and the boy, representing three distinctive generations and backgrounds, stand looking at each other.

"It's your ball now, Frankie," says Billy Ray. "I figured you ought to be the one that calls the cops."

"I don't think we'll have to do that, Billy."

"What? But we've got him red-handed. Two witnesses, plus the tape."

Lorino looks at the kid, who seems relieved to see him. "No more crutches, I see."

"No, sir. I'm getting there."

Billy Ray has been listening to this exchange in utter puzzlement. Lorino says, "You took things, son?"

"Yes, sir, I did."

"There you go," says Billy Ray. "Now you've got an admission from the punk."

"The usual?" Lorino asks the boy.

"Yes, sir." He cuts a look at Billy Ray. "He made me put it back."

"Your mama still sick?"

"Yes, sir."

"Get what you need, son," Lorino tells him. Still looking at the boy, Lorino says over his shoulder, "Billy, it's raining and his leg's bad. Can you take the boy home?"

Billy Ray can't believe this. "Take him home? Are you nuts? The kid comes in here and cleans out the shelves and you're gonna let him take it and go? What the hell kinda business are you running here? Christ, if the word gets out they'll help themselves to everything you've got. What're you, the Salvation Army?"

"It's okay, Billy. He's a good boy."

"Well, hell. This don't make any sense at all."

"Billy, Billy. Just this time. It isn't far."

...

Through the slanting rain, with darkness descending, Billy Ray nego-tiates the narrow streets of Little Five Points in his battered Chevy wagon. The boy is scrunched down in the front seat, holding the can between his knees, sullen, speaking only when giving directions to his house in a neigh-borhood known as Fatback. To get there, they pass through the restored Victorian mansions of Inman Park, home to white doctors and lawyers who have lately moved back into town to escape the distant suburbs, past Mercedeses and Volvos and Saabs, past old-fashioned front porches taste-fully appointed with wicker furniture and swings (chained and bolted to the floor, to be sure), past backyard swimming pools encircled by flagstone patios and gay cabanas.

The boy literally lives on the other side of the tracks. The two neigh-borhoods are separated by a corridor formed by DeKalb Avenue and a rail-road yard and MARTA, Metropolitan Atlanta Rapid Transit Authority, the city's commuter rail system. The neighborhoods share a stop on the MARTA line, and when a train stops to let off passengers, the whites walk one way to their cool mansions in Inman Park, the blacks the other way to their shanties in Fatback.

Not so much that he's curious about the kid but because silence makes him nervous, Billy Ray has been trying to get a conversation going. "You oughta be at home this time of day, anyway," he says. No response. "What's with the cane?" Nothing. "When's school start?" The kid stares straight ahead, shifting in the seat now and then, finding no good reason to answer. "You don't want to talk, it ain't no skin off my back."

"Left, under the tracks."

"Well, I'll be damned. He speaks. You got a name, boy?"

"I ain't no boy."

"You will be until you show me different."

"I ain't got to show you *nothin'*."

Billy Ray mimics him. "For a kid that just got free eats and a drive home in the rain, you're awfully damned *grateful*. Will that be smoking, or non-smoking, sir? Will this table be all right, sir? Our waitress will be right with you, sir."

"Leave me alone."

"Oh, well, now, he's a barrel of laughs, folks. He's gonna be our entertainment for the evening. Tell you what you need, kid, you need a good ass-kicking. I don't know what the hell kinda deal you've got going with old man Lorino, but it looks to me like a simple 'Thank you' might be in order somewhere in there."

"Mavis."

"Pardon?"

"Said my name's Mavis."

"That your last name, or the one your mama gave you?"

"What do you care?"

"Hey, *whooaaa*, back off. I'm just trying to carry on a conversation here, pal."

"You don't give a damn about me."

"That a fact? You have the right to remain silent, you know. But, then, you know the routine. Bet you've heard that one before."

...

Billy Ray has been around in his time, figures he has seen places like this, but usually it has been from a train or through his windshield while passing through. This is his town, isn't it, Atlanta? Now, having bumped through the tunnel beneath the MARTA tracks and the Southern Railway line, he sees a part of it he never knew existed. Fatback is a jangle of broken frame houses, of cars older than his, propped up on bricks and being cannibalized in streets glistening with broken glass, of overturned garbage cans being picked through by long-tailed mongrel dogs, of barefooted and half-naked black kids throwing mud balls at each other in pot-holed streets flooded by the thunderstorm, of old men passed out drunk on busted front-porch swings, of women in rocking chairs sitting beside their men, shelling peas or sewing, staring straight ahead.

When they reach a small house with a rusted tin roof and a front porch cluttered with discarded sofas and chairs and a doorless refrigerator, the kid abruptly raises his hand, signaling Billy Ray to stop. A woman about Billy Ray's age lies sprawled out at an odd angle on a rusty old glider—it looks like a seizure to him—while an older woman fans her with both hands and a man, obviously drunk, slaps her on the cheeks as though to revive her.

"Dammit, get away from her!" the kid yells.

"What's up?" says Billy Ray.

"Same old shit," the kid says.

"Somebody oughta call somebody or something."

"It's okay."

"You sure?" Billy Ray doesn't know what he should do, or even whether it's any of his business do to anything. "I mean, if there's something I can do—"

"I can handle this." The kid jiggles the busted car-door handle until it finally works, swings the door open, grabs the cane, gathers the tails of his great coat around him, and slides out of the wagon. He shouts to the man, still slapping the woman—"Dammit, that's my mama, you motherfucker!"—then slams the door closed behind him. "Thanks for the ride," he says. His pockets bulging, brandishing the cane like a shillelagh, the boy charges the house in full shriek.

EIGHT

In a simpler time, which is to say before school desegregation sent white folks scurrying to the distant suburbs during the 'seventies, Grady Stadium was one of the prime venues for high school football in Atlanta. Crowds of five thousand would fill the concrete grandstands every Friday night, double that if the game pitted two particularly bitter rivals, and the scene represented a slice of American life at its most robust and promising: young gladiators pushing each other up and down the field, perky cheerleaders shaking pom-pons and screaming encouragement from the sidelines—*Y'all yell, now!!*—proud parents in the stands, younger siblings more interested in chasing each other around the end zone than in following the game, college scouts with binoculars and stopwatches and clipboards earnestly focusing on the blue-chip prospects, even a clutch of gamblers huddled high on the top row of seats, old codgers so hooked they would bet on anything from whether the next play would be a run or a pass to whether the head majorette would drop her baton.

Grady was only two miles from dead-center downtown, and from a perch high in the stands one could see no evidence of the frenzied construction that was soon to come. The tallest building in Atlanta in those days was twenty-two stories high; the biggest sports shows in town were the minor-league Atlanta Crackers and the Georgia Tech Yellow Jackets; the hottest night-club act was Brother Dave Gardner's racist riffs between strippers in the basement lounge of the seedy Imperial Hotel. Only a handful of city fathers could predict what would follow toward the end of the decade: Atlanta's "solving" the crisis in desegregation, the arrival of major-league sports, the rise of a real big-city skyline, the blather from City Hall about a City Too Busy to Hate and a Next International City and blah-blah-blah. From within the confines of Grady Stadium, on a Friday night in the fall, this was still smalltown neighborhood America: Bass High versus Grady, Brown against Murphy, Forrest and Northside.

The single most distinctive feature of the stadium is the lighting that comes from a half-dozen cantilevered concrete standards, bent over the field like praying mantises, and it was under that glare that young Billy Ray Hunsinger glittered like a diamond on velvet. Scrawny, at six-three and only 165 pounds, already nicknamed "The Gunslinger" by some long-forgotten prep sportswriter, he was a teenaged god in 1961, his senior year, a bullet-throwing quarterback for the Forrest High Panthers, courted by teenaged Delilahs and college recruiters alike.

Except for the near-defeat of Alabama four years later, Billy Ray's greatest moment had come right here, at Grady Stadium on one of those crisp Friday nights under the lights. An overflow crowd had come from all over the city to take a gander at this phenomenal kid, the "Gunslinger," and he did not disappoint. It was one of those times when everything comes together—the weather, the crowd, the competition, the passer, the receivers, the sheer ebullience of it all—and even now, old sports fans in Atlanta still talk about his heroics that evening when Billy Ray lit up the skies. Back at the house in Crestwood, on the paneled walls of The Gun Room, he still has a framed enlargement of the lead paragraph of the story in the next morning's *Constitution,* written by Charlie Roberts, a balding cigar-chomping sportswriter who figured he had the best beat in town:

> Even the light standards at Grady Stadium craned their necks in disbelief last night as Forrest High's Billy Ray Hunsinger, a/k/a "The Gunslinger," passed for 510 yards and six touchdowns in a shocking upset. . . .

...

He has had the stadium to himself for most of the long summer—a very good thing, given his condition—and it seems as though this will never get easy at his age. Trudging around the cinder track at Grady in the middle of a breath-sucking afternoon in August, nearly a quarter of a century since his exploits on this very same field, he wonders if this is another of those psychedelic dreams he's been having lately. The damage wrought upon his body, most of it self-inflicted, has never been more evident. Strolling through the old neighborhood with Rima has been one thing, but this is quite another. This isn't "jogging," this is freaking *running,* made nearly unbearable by the years of smoking and boozing, of late nights in the clubs, of falling asleep in front of the television set, of too many hamburgers and French fries and pork chops.

Around and around the track he goes, a middle-aged man wearing cut-off jeans, cracked old Converse sneakers, a washed-out green-and-gold Green Bay T-shirt and a matching mesh Packers cap, wheezing and adjusting his soaked headband and wincing from the pain in his bad knee. He never could run, anyway, not since the surgery at the end of his high school career that destroyed his chances of going to a major college, but this is pure torture. The only thing different today is that his usual audience, pigeons wordlessly flitting about the light standards, has swollen considerably. Now he sees a band of ragamuffins going through their pre-season drills in the stifling heat and humidity. They wear helmets, cleats, shoulder pads, cotton shorts and mesh tops. From their purple-and-gold colors, he assumes they are the McGill High Panthers. They are scattered all over the field, its grass burned out from the summer's heat, one group going at half-speed in blocking drills, another running through offensive plays in slow-motion, a kicker working on field goals with a snapper and a holder and a ballboy to fetch and return his kicks.

He hears a voice over one of those battery-powered megaphones. "You oughta at least get out of the sun." He pays it no mind, figures a coach is advising his players, stumbles on. Then, moments later: "You're getting too old for this stuff." He stops this time, bends over to catch his breath, and sees a thick black man sitting beneath the canopy of a golf cart in the middle of the field. Judging from the man's age and girth, a silver whistle hanging around his neck on a shoestring, he has to be the coach. When Billy Ray points to his own chest—*Me?*—the man waves his hand, beckoning. "This ain't no time for heroes," he says into the megaphone, his voice echoing off the empty stands. The kids pause, anything for a break, idly curious about the exchange between these two old men, then return to their labors.

"I couldn't've said it better myself," Billy Ray says when he reaches the golf cart.

"It's too hot today even for these kids. Come aboard before you get heatstroke."

"Thanks." The coach scoots over to make room and Billy Ray slides onto the cushy seat. "Must be the only shade between here and Crestwood. How do you rate one of these carts, anyway? You gonna be playing some golf today, are you?"

"Coaches get *some* privileges, anyway."

"I wouldn't coach high school ball if they gave me a Cadillac."

"Don't worry. They won't."

Billy Ray scans the field, taking in the rag-tag groups of kids going through their routines. They are clearly flagging in the heat. "So who we got here?"

"Come on, you know who this is," the coach says. "It's your old school, gone colored on you."

"How would you know that?" Flapping his T-shirt to stir some air, Billy Ray takes a closer look at the man. He sees a frizzy gray head the size of a watermelon, rings of fat around his neck, a massive upper body turning to fat, a heart attack waiting to happen. "I know you from somewhere."

"Herman Graves. Blue-Gray Game, nineteen and 'sixty-five."

"Well, I'll be damned. Tank? That you? Tank Graves? Grambling, wasn't it?"

"That's right. One of Eddie Robinson's boys. We integrated Montgomery, you and me, right there in George Wallace's front yard."

...

Well, yes. That game, which usually begins at the ungodly hour of noon on Christmas Day in Montgomery, was the one that made it possible for Billy Ray to go higher than he had reckoned in the National Football League draft. One of the oldest of the post-season all-star games for graduating seniors, and thus an audition for the benefit of pro scouts, the Blue-Gray has always been for players from schools that, for one reason or another, aren't going to a bowl game; they've had a poor season, they're on probation, or they don't get invited because they're too small to bring a big crowd of fat-cat alumni. Still, knowing that over the years more NFL stars have come out of relatively unknown colleges than from big ones—the Tennessees and Nebraskas and Michigans—the scouts have always shown up in search of a diamond in the rough.

That's exactly how Billy Ray Hunsinger was regarded when the players reported for a week of practice leading up to the game: smart, a cannon for an arm, but slowed by a wrecked knee, and, except for that one game against Alabama, unproven against major opponents. He couldn't run, but he sure as hell could throw. Give him an offensive line, five large personal body-guards willing to give up their lives for him while he stood in the pocket looking for receivers, give him some gazelles who could go anywhere and catch anything, and he would beat you. That had been the recipe at little North Alabama State, up in the lake region at Guntersville, when the Catamounts regularly beat up on little schools like Troy and Chattanooga and Western Carolina, scoring more than fifty points in six of their ten games. And that was the recipe for the Gray squad in the Blue-Gray game.

"All right, give me ten good men and it'll be payback time for what Sherman and them did to Atlanta," Billy Ray had pronounced on the first day of practice, sounding like Muhammad Ali before a fight, and he was the main source of all news emanating from Montgomery for the rest of the week. The coaches, not particularly happy about being there during the holidays rather than having their own teams in a real bowl game, more or less stepped back and allowed him to hand-pick his offensive starters, his "ten good men"—the five bodyguards, the four gazelles, a squat fullback to run the ball now and then to keep the defense honest—and the game belonged to the Gunslinger. Never sacked, never intercepted, he completed twenty-four of twenty-eight passes, five of them for touchdowns, won the Most Valuable Player award, "kicked some Yankee butt," as he gleefully opined in the post-game interview, and was selected early in the second round by the Green Bay Packers.

Of larger note at the time was the fact that the Blue-Gray was integrated that year, with the inclusion of Herman "Tank" Graves and three other players from the all-black colleges of Grambling and Florida A&M, and now more than ever before Billy Ray wishes people remembered that as well as his performance. Maybe he and Herman didn't become bosom buddies that week—*okay?*—but, hey, when the Gunslinger was inspecting the meat, selecting his bodyguards, wasn't Tank the first offensive lineman he picked? Tank was a center, his snapper, and not once did any Blue defender, not a soul, manage to even get his hands up to block the Gun's view of the secondary. With all due respect for Bobby "Peahead" Gillespie, Billy Ray told the press, if he'd had five guys like Tank Graves blocking for him, why, hell, he'd be quarterbacking North Alabama State in a rematch with Alabama at the Sugar Bowl instead of defending the South's honor in front of 10,000 fans who'd rather be home sipping wine and basting turkey.

But then, as these things go, they went their separate ways. Billy Ray got his bonus money and put away a nest egg, wound up throwing only ninety-three passes during five seasons as a third-team quarterback at Green Bay, had some moments during five years with the Calgary Stampeders in the wild-and-hairy Canadian Football League, then got crippled by a blind-side tackle, and had to give it up at the age of thirty-two. Herman Graves, in the meantime, a mere toiler in the trenches, turned out to be too slow in a summer tryout with the Chicago Bears. He came back home to Atlanta, where he had attended one of the segregated high schools before going off to play for the famous Eddie Robinson at Grambling, to get married and begin having kids and coaching high school football.

...

"I'm sorry, Tank, but I just flat lost track of you."

"It's okay, Gun. A man has a way of disappearing when he goes to coaching high school. It was easy to keep up with you, though. Green Bay, Canada, then your broadcasting career. You've done pretty good for yourself."

"Yeah, right. Tell my wife." He would just as well not talk about it. "So how's it going?"

"The coaching? Hold on a minute." Graves puts the whistle to his mouth, blows three short bursts, and the players break up into different groups: passers and receivers and defensive backs in one, snappers and punters and returners in another, linemen queuing up in front of the one blocking sled to form a third. The change in routine seems to revive them. "You see that? Like clockwork. They're learning."

"That's pretty damned impressive. You blow a whistle and they jump."

"Discipline. You and me know that's a big part of it for any team. With these boys, it's a big step."

"Guess so." Given his recent track record on matters pertaining to race, Billy Ray figures he'd better lie low. "Being poor kids, and all."

"Aw, shoot, Gun, you can go ahead and say it. Poor *black* kids, right? No daddies to speak of, right? Nobody to answer to, right?" Billy Ray can't read the look on Graves's face, which is somewhere between a smile and a smirk. "Your show's on too late for me, but I hear stories."

"Well, hey, it ain't what you think. It was the whiskey talking."

"You say 'Fal-*coons*' around these kids, they'll whup the shit out of you, whether you're drinking or not. Don't even think about 'Niggers Go Long.'"

It's a grin, is what it is, and Billy Ray is greatly relieved. "Yassuh, boss."

"Any rate, there's some truth behind what most white folks think. We've got a sort of a Touchdown Club that meets every week to watch film, talk about the games and how the boys are doing. Lots of mamas in it, 'bout two dozen of 'em, but there ain't but six daddies that show up and most of the time they're drunk. That's why we call the club the Touchdown Mamas. What that makes me is these boys' coach, preacher, teacher, their truant officer, and their best buddy. The long and the short of it is, I'm the daddy they ain't got."

"But you're gonna tell me there's more."

"Damn right. They can be a bunch of mean little motherfuckers. You would be, too, if you grew up like this. They figure nobody cares about what happens to 'em, and they've got a point there. The trick is, you've got to *use* that. Turn it around. You've got to harness all that anger, don't you see, hitch 'em up like a mule to a plow, whack 'em on the butt, tell 'em 'giddy-up, let's go,' and if you hit 'em hard enough they'll turn out to be some kinda plowin' fools. Understand what I'm saying?"

"Sure," Billy Ray says. "Ol' Bear Bryant did the same thing everywhere he went."

"White boys, right?"

"In the beginning, anyway, before the blacks came along."

"*Hungry* white boys, Gun, hungry white *country* boys. Same difference. Poor is poor."

...

They turn their attention to the boys. It's none of his business, and he doesn't want to butt in, but it seems to Billy Ray that Herman Graves has a lot of them playing out of position: too many tall athletic kids are with the group of interior linemen, the punter looks more like a linebacker than anything, and hardly any of the receivers can catch anything thrown by the skinny quarterback. "If you don't mind my saying, it's a pretty scraggly-ass looking bunch you got here. It's gonna be a long season, don't you figure?"

"That ought to make me mad, hearing you say that, but I can't argue with you." Billy Ray hears a tired man talking, and Graves looks ten years older than his forty-two. "I might be getting too old for this stuff. We were out here at six this morning and came back at four in the afternoon, trying to miss the heat. The two-a-days are killing me and them both. We'll go to pads and one-a-days next week when school starts up. You'd think I could rest easy then, but that's when I have to start teaching two classes every morning before I can put on my coach's hat. Top of that, me and the wife still got four young-'uns at home and I got this little heart problem. If it ain't one thing, it's another. Like they say, there ain't no rest for the weary."

"A heart problem, you say."

"Wife can't cook anything without fatback in it."

"That why you've got the buggy?"

"Oh, I get around all right. Ain't a cripple yet. Next week when we put the pads on, I'm liable to pass a few licks with the boys. The cart came from the Touchdown Mamas. Little love offering. Keeps me out of the sun when I need to."

...

Out of one eye, Billy Ray has been watching the tall skinny kid, whom he presumes to be the Tank's starting quarterback, and he can't help but think of himself at that age: all arms and legs, limping slightly, armed with a rifle. The boy seems to thrive on dropping back, winding up, and throwing bullets, even though nobody can catch him. It pains Billy Ray just to watch.

Graves lets out one long piercing blast on his whistle, signifying the end of practice, and while most of the others drift off toward the fieldhouse beyond the end zone the kid implores three other boys to stay behind. Still wearing his helmet, with a pile of footballs gathered around his feet, he begins cutting loose in the direction of the others as though he were a catcher and they were shortstops. They are fifty yards downfield, about the distance from home plate to second base, and now he is on his *knees*, for Christ's sake, just showing off. All Billy Ray can think to say is, "*Goddamn*."

"Something, ain't it?" says Graves.

"Air mail. Don't even put a stamp on it."

"Maybe he ought to. Otherwise, it'll wind up in China. You never know where it's gon' land."

"If he toned it down he'd be dangerous."

"What I keep telling him. 'Mavis,' I say, 'maybe it'd help—'"

"Mavis."

"Jackson. Mavis Jackson. Anyway, I tell him he might try to complete one now and then, just to keep things interesting. 'Yes, sir, Coach, sure thing, Coach.' Then he goes back out and sees how hard he can throw it. What the hell. Kids these days don't listen like they used to. That, or I'm losing my touch."

There is little doubt in Billy Ray's mind that this is the same kid, the one he caught stealing at Lorino's Grocery back in June. He had all but forgotten about the episode, but how many tall, skinny black kids with a limp could there be in this neighborhood, anyway, with a name like that? "You never know, Tank. I was like that myself, in the beginning."

"You sure weren't by the time you got to the Blue-Gray. You had the touch, brother."

"Remember Coach Hyder? Frank Hyder?"

"Seen his name in the school record books, is all. When it was all-white."

"He coached when I was here. Hell, he's famous. I thought everybody knew about him."

"To white folks, maybe. When I was playing at Carver, the black school, we didn't even bother reading the sports pages. We were lucky if they printed the score."

This is news to Billy Ray, who couldn't wait to get up on Saturday mornings to read all about the Friday night games. "My daddy was a drunk and I was pissed off at everybody by the time I got to high school. Hell, I was throwing *at* my receivers, not to 'em, trying to see how many hands I could break. Coach Hyder took me in, kicked my butt until I got the hang of it, made me what I am. What I *was,* anyway."

"Like I was saying, there's that coaching for you."

"Reckon so." Now the kid takes the ball, steps back into an imaginary pocket, pumps once, then sails a rocket eighty yards on a line into the far end zone, letting the three receivers fight for it. The tallest of them rises above the others and pulls it in, slamming the ball to the ground in celebration, as if it were the first pass he's ever caught. The kid, Mavis, calmly walks away toward the fieldhouse, leaving them to gather up the footballs. "He even limps like I did, after I got hurt."

Herman says, "He got shot."

"Come again?"

"Took a bullet."

"You mean *really* shot. With a gun. What happened?"

"Wrong place, wrong time. There was some foolishness going on and he got caught in the middle of it. Caught a bullet in his butt."

"When? Where? What kind of 'foolishness'?"

"April Fool's Day, if you can believe it." Spring practice had just ended, says Herman, and the players were hanging out at a Dairy Queen when shots began to fly from a passing car. "Had one of those cheap little ol' things, small caliber, a Saturday Night Special, got him kinda low in the cheek. Ask me, the boy was lucky."

"Lucky, my ass."

Herman fails to catch the humor, goes on. "Bullet went in at an angle and caused a hairline fracture of the femur, the biggest bone you've got. We had to put a cast on it and then he was on crutches for six weeks. Biggest worry was that the hamstring would atrophy on him. Best thing we've got going for us is that the mama of one of the boys is a doctor at Grady and knows all about this stuff. Got to hand it to the boy. He's been doing leg-lifts and riding this old bicycle we've got ever since. Bone was healed by July. He's off his cane now, 'bout ready to go."

"Christ Almighty. And I thought I came by *mine* honestly. Don't guess he's much of a threat to run, then, hunh?"

"Oh, he can run when he has to. Leg-lifts, curls, range-of-motion stuff ought to get the hamstring back where it ought to be."

"They've got some of these Nautilus machines these days, you know. That ought to help speed things up."

"You gotta be kidding."

"You know, those exercise gizmos."

"I know what they are. You're out of touch, Gun. This is a poor-ass city high school on its last legs. Only gizmos we've got is our own sweat: pushups, situps, weights. We ain't even got real barbells. Might as well be the nineteen-thirties around here."

...

The quarterback and the other kids decide to call it a day and trudge toward the gym for their showers. With the sun settling over the stadium, and rush-hour traffic picking up on the surrounding streets, Herman and Billy Ray go quiet, enjoying the late afternoon. Twice, Herman starts to speak, stops himself, then goes ahead: "Seems to me you had a son that played, didn't you?"

"Me?"

"Out at Robert E. Lee."

"Naw." Billy Ray drops his head, looks the other way.

"I swear I thought I remembered talk about 'Gunslinger II' or something like that. Real good quarterback on his way up."

"He never played there."

"Look, I'm sorry," Tank says. "If you don't want to talk about it. . . ."

"Things just didn't work out, that's all."

"Guess I know about that, seeing as how not a one of mine played. Maybe they learned better from their daddies." Tank drops the subject, clears his throat, and turns the key to the cart, signaling the end to another long day. "Look here," he says as Billy Ray dismounts, "why don't you come around some day before practice? I'm in the gym after lunch."

"Well, I'm pretty busy these days, with the radio show and all."

"Just a thought. We got some catching-up to do, Gun. Been too long."

"If this jogging don't kill me, I'll be here most afternoons when it cools off."

"Come by the gym a little early one day and we'll sit out the heat together," Tank says. "Besides, I found something the other day that belongs to you."

NINE

Although hardly anybody seems to be listening to "Jock Talk with Billy Ray Hunsinger," as far as he can tell, he has nevertheless gotten to where he looks forward to doing the show. He had so distanced himself from his friends and even Ginny and Maggie during the bad times—*We are no longer amusing*—that it seemed like the only person interested in what Billy Ray Hunsinger had to say was Billy Ray himself. He knows now that Crestwood, where candor is to be avoided at all costs, has been a part of the problem. Living out there was Ginny's idea, from the very beginning, and he has always felt out of place among men who seem to count the days until Saturday when they can suit up and tackle the lawn and the hedges. The suburbs were never his idea of the real world.

Now, sober and back in town, however temporary his sobriety and exile might be, he finds that he enjoys being on familiar ground: the white-bread-and-peanut-butter days of his childhood. The neighborhood where he grew up has changed, sure, what with the blacks and gays and hippies and all who have moved in, but he is finding a certain comfort in the landmarks like Little Five Points and his old high school, and Grady Stadium and Lorino's Grocery and Manuel's Tavern, places he has begun to see every day in his perambulations. He has, in short, reconnected; with the world as he understands it, and with himself.

He has new friends, too, after wandering virtually alone for too long, and although they might have their faults and idiosyncracies they're anything but dull. Rima the Bird-Girl; what can you say about an Agnes Scott girl who has dumped everything for a career as a pornographic artist? Scottie Burns, now there's a guy who manages to make sobriety a grand adventure in itself. A buffoon like B. D. Spotswood, master of malaprops, would never find happiness in a place like Crestwood; and only God knows where Spider Medders, the career student, might wind up when it's over. Were an imposing black man such as Herman Graves to cruise through the white suburbs, looking for an address, he would likely be pulled over for DWB, Driving While Black.

And there's another thing he can accomplish with this gig on WWJD. During their lunch sessions at Manuel's, which has become a major part of Billy Ray's daily routine, Scottie Burns has told him of the AA way, not the least of which is to atone for one's sins by apologizing to everybody a person might have offended during the dark days. "Christ," Billy Ray remembers telling him, "there ain't that many days left in the world." Where would he begin? Sure, he could sit down and make out a list—those five black Lee High students from that Saturday morning at the house, the five thousand people in the stadium during Catamount Days at North Alabama State, the Atlanta Police Department, WSB-TV, the black players with the Atlanta Falcons—but he also knows that tracking down all of those people and begging their forgiveness not only would take forever but is just about the dumbest idea he's ever heard of. It would be embarrassing all the way around. The easier course would be to use the two hours he has every Sunday night on WWJD as a public forum, a means of making those atonements, so that's how he's been handling it.

Thus, the show has become his own means of catharsis; a psychiatrist's couch, a mother's bosom, a confessional booth, an AA meeting in its own right. The mandate handed him by B. D. Spotswood, to "runimate" on anything that comes to mind, especially *FUH-baw*, neatly dovetails with his own needs to talk his way back to sanity. Billy Ray, not one given to introspection and self-examination, would be the last to understand that he is becoming much like the writer or singer who practices his art not for fame or commercial success but for the primordial need to express himself; to say what's on his mind, damn the consequences, to open a vein and bleed, as Kris Kristofferson sings, "hopin' someone's gonna hear."

...

Let me get this right, Gun. What you're saying is, man-to-man coverage will beat the zone anytime. That right?

Naw, naw. What I'm saying is, man coverage is better'n zone if you got the horses for it.

Execution's everything, right?

Something like that.

Thanks, Gun. Think I've won my bet.

Ten percent's all I want, pal. Look here, folks, let's get off techniques and stuff for a while. What I was wanting to talk about, if you'll give me a chance, is how I ran into an old friend the other day. When I say ran into, I mean it. Gun's been doing some jogging lately, a fancy word for running, just trying to get the blood going, you know, and I came across this ol' boy I played with once, Tank Graves, Herman Graves, the coach at McGill High, what used to be Forrest High when I played there. Dang! It felt like a hundred and ten degrees on the field at Grady Stadium and there was ol' Tank out there coaching this sad little ol' bunch of boys, just some teenagers that's heard some rumors about blocking and tackling. The school's in its last year, the way I hear it, gonna be closed down, waiting for the other shoe to drop. Can you believe they ain't got but one blocking sled to work with? Tank's got one assistant coach, is all, and he's the wrestling coach, so those two, they've got to take care of everything. Anybody else worried about Tank not having anything to work with? Hell, no. Board of Education don't care much about McGill High, being in their last year, 'cause they're too busy looking out for those big fancy white schools out in the suburbs like Robert E. Lee and them. Tank ain't got but about thirty boys to choose from, can't hardly practice eleven-on-eleven when they go to pads. They're poor kids, what they call inner-city kids these days, not many daddies around to speak of, ain't got much going for 'em 'cept that it might be fun to knock somebody's head off if they get in the way. I was there watching 'em practice the other day and I couldn't help but notice this one kid, the quarterback, sort of reminded me of myself back at that age: big ol' skinny kid, no daddy to speak of, busted leg from where he got shot one time, just a poor black boy from off the streets, but that boy can flat throw bullets. Never knows where it's gonna go, get the women and children off the sidelines, but he's got a rifle on his shoulder. Anyway, me and Tank got to talking about football at that level—FUH-baw, you know—and it got me to thinking about when I was a kid that age, a snot-nosed little bugger with a chip on his shoulder, ready to fight anybody, anywhere, anytime. Guess I didn't realize at the time that my old man was taking it out on me what the Japs did to him over in Iwo Jima, and I was taking it out on anybody in my way what the old man was doing to me danged-near every night when I got home. That's probably why they had to kick me out of the gym or run me off the field every day. Live tackling drills was a piece of cake compared to what my ol' drunk daddy had waiting for me at home. Thanks a lot, Pop. . . . Line two, this better be good.

Yeah. Am I on?

Not for long.

Hunh?

What do you want?

Hell, if you're gon' be that way—

Adios, bubba. Truth is, and me and Tank were talking about this the other day, that deal at home between me and my old man turned out to be the thing that made it easy for the coaches by the time I showed up to play ball at Forrest High. Know what I mean? Things couldn't get no tougher, and I'll always think Coach Hyder knew that. Like Tank says, I needed me a daddy to make me do right and to pat me on the back when I did, and that's how Coach Hyder, Frank Hyder, that's how he went about coaching. I mean, he knew his X's and O's all right, like most coaches do, but he knew his boys, too, and that's what meant the most. We won us a lot of football games while I was there, and it got me off to college and then the pros, but forget about that for a minute. There wadn't no way for me to know it at the time, but I was learning some things from Coach Hyder that were gonna come in handy later on when I got out there in what they call the real world. One of 'em was patience, believing in yourself, hanging in there, never giving up the fight. I remember this one game against Murphy where it didn't matter what we did, we just couldn't catch up to 'em. We'd score, then they'd score, back and forth, like that all night. I got frustrated and called for a triple reverse, on my own, and we got nailed for about a thirty-yard loss. What the hell are you doing, son? Coach says when I come off the field, chewing me out in front of ten thousand people. We don't run, we throw. Find your power and use it, dance with the one that brung you. Throw, throw, throw. You're the Gunslinger, remember? Keep going at 'em, bam-bam-bam, they'll break. Well, he was right. Their asses got to dragging from chasing after receivers, and we won on a pass in the back of the end zone with ten seconds left. That was the last time I ever tried to be something I wasn't, like calling for a triple-reverse, I can tell you that right now. Dance with the One That Brung You. When the Going Gets Tough the Tough Get Going. Quitters Never Win, Winners Never Quit. Coach Hyder was a big one for putting these posters like that all over the locker room. We used to laugh at 'em behind his back, you know, but I guaran-dam-tee you we brought 'em with us to the fourth quarter. . . . Line one, talk to me.

Hey there, Gun.

Yo, bubba. What you got?

I was wondering if you ever did any coaching yourself?

None to speak of. Why?

Seems to me like you'd be pretty good at it.

Oh, I helped out the kid who was gonna replace me at North Alabama when I left. Showed some things to the rookie playing behind me at Calgary. There was another boy once, but I ain't gonna get into that. That's about it.

The way you're carrying on about what your old high school coach meant to you when you was a kid, sounds to me like you might be thinking about it.

Me? A coach? I ain't crazy.

It's your old school. Your old pal, whatshisname.

Whooaa, bubba. Forget about it.

But hey, Gun, you got all this knowledge about quarterbacking and all.

No way, my man. No way.

I was just thinking out loud.

Well, you better keep it to yourself. I'm in semi-retirement, don't you see? I ain't got the time, the patience or anything else it takes to wind up being no baby-sitter for a bunch of teenaged boys. I got a full plate in front of me, thank you very much. Like to live my life out in peace, if you don't mind. Let me get this other call, okay?

Mister Hunsinger?

Just call me Billy Ray.

All right, then. Thank you. Oh, Lord, I don't know how to say this.

Whatever's on your mind, ma'am. That's the rules around here.

Well, first of all, let me say that you have a very, a very interesting program. You seem to have a great deal of knowledge to impart. In your own way.

Uh-oh. Yes, ma'am?

Oh, my. Well. I'm a schoolteacher, you see. English. In Decatur. Now I don't know how many schoolchildren might be up at this time of night, listening to your show, but—

Maybe a lot more than you think, if I know kids these days.

Yes, sadly, you're probably correct. At any rate. Oh, Lord. If you don't mind my saying so, Mister, ah, Mister Hunsinger, it seems to me that you're, what I mean to say is, your grammar, your use of the language, is, well, it leaves much to be desired. In other words, to put it bluntly, I think you're a bad influence on children.

I been waitin' for that, I reckon.

Your grammar is atrocious, in fact. All of those double negatives. The word Ain't. It goes on and on. I'm sorry, but I—

Yes, ma'am. I don't mean to be a smartass about this, but it kinda reminds me of something the old pitcher Dizzy Dean said when a bunch of teachers in St. Louis tried to boycott his broadcasts of Cardinals games for the same reason. There's a lot o' folks that ain't sayin' ain't, that ain't eatin' is the way Diz put it.

Oooohhh. I could just—

Hello? Ma'am? Ah, well. Line two, get me off the hook here.

Aw, hell, Gun, don't let no schoolteacher get you down. I remember what ol' Merle Haggard said when somebody asked him how come he cut his records out there in California instead of doing it in Nashville. Says, It don't matter where you cut it at, it's what you put in the groove. Know what I mean? It don't matter how you say it, it's what you got to say. You keep it up, now, Gun, you hear?

The lady's probably right, you know, but I reckon it's too late. I mean, they taught a mean class in basket-weaving over at North Alabama.

What's a English teacher know, anyways, huh? Tell it like it is, Gun.

Well, I 'preciate that, pardner. Now where was I at? . . . I'm a little bit reluctant to talk about this, but—Hey, Teach, you still there? 'Reluctant'— well, anyway, there was this really bad thing that happened a few years ago and I don't think I could've made my way out of it if it hadn't been for some of the things I learned playing football. Just say somebody real close to me was gone and left a big hole in my life, okay, and I thought it was the end of the world when that happened. I flat lost it, couldn't do nothing, just sat around mopin' and cryin' all the time, no good for nobody, including myself. It took me a long time to get around to it, but one day not too long ago I started hearing Coach Hyder saying, Come on, Gun, it's always darkest before the dawn. It wasn't him because he's dead now, rest his soul, but it was like him talkin' to me, you know, preaching from the grave. Come on, Billy Ray, it ain't over 'til it's over. The fourth quarter is ours, son, let's pick 'em up and go. The man had lost his wife to cancer and wadn't doing so hot himself, but he was still fighting, still living, still smiling. Quitters never win, Go get 'em, Stop that damn raggedy-ass dragging, Let's go, boys, let's go, don't let the bastards wear you down . . .

. . .

B. D. Spotswood is still coming by the station before midnight most Sundays, just keeping an eye on his investment, and he is waiting in the little reception area when Billy Ray leaves the booth. From the looks of B. D.'s puffy red eyes and the bandanna in his hand, Gun can swear the old boy has been crying.

"That enough *FUH-baw* for you?" Billy Ray says after making a detour to the dispenser for a Dr. Pepper.

"That's great, Gun. Just great. Might explain some of the mail you been getting lately."

"Mail? Me?"

"Aw, it's just a few. Mostly women, which inclines me to think the Gun's still got his fastball, if you know what I mean."

"Probably crackpots like that teacher. Whatcha got?"

Reaching into the inside pocket of his bright orange Auburn blazer, B. D. hands over a passel of crinkled envelopes held together by a rubber band. There are about a dozen of them addressed in many fanciful variations of his name—*Hunslinger, Guncannon, Humdinger*—and Billy Ray settles into one of the mangy loveseats to go through them. Three or four of them aren't worth reading twice, diatribes about how he's being partial to the Georgia Bulldogs or the Georgia Tech Yellow Jackets. Another, from a preacher, takes him to task for cussing. There are a couple that he might take as mash notes, from a woman who says he reminds her of her father, another from an old flame who would like to meet him somewhere. Those he tosses into the wire trash bin.

There are two letters, though, that puzzle him. Neatly typed, on expensive linen stationery, they are from women whose return addresses he recognizes as being in Ansley Park, the exclusive old-money neighborhood of stately mansions close to downtown. Whether the women know each other he can't tell, but each is saying pretty much the same thing: they happened to be wandering across the radio dial late one night, came across his show, got hooked, and stayed up listening. "In spite of the subject matter," says one, "I find your candor refreshing."

Billy Ray tosses those, too, into the trash. If he can't even type, how can he respond? He's getting up from the sofa, draining the Dr. Pepper, when B. D. says, "Fan mail, huh?"

"Just some horny old broads."

"Rich ones, from the addresses."

"Why don't you just open 'em yourself, B. D.? Read 'em to me so my lips don't get tired."

"No need to get testy, Gun. I just like to know who's listening."

"Well, I told you," says Billy Ray. "Far as I can tell, it's some rich old ladies with too much time on their hands. While they're throwing tea parties, their husbands are out carrying on with their secretaries. Maybe they like it when I talk dirty. Who the hell knows?"

TEN

Bounding up the broad worn steps and through the main front doors of his old school, he can see that all memories of Forrest High seem to be gone without a trace. Once, the foyer was a shrine to Forrest Panthers football, past and present. The walls were ringed with framed photographs of the dozens of players who had made All-State over a period of half a century. The centerpiece of it all was a massive glass case holding five state championship trophies, wrinkled autographed footballs representing great moments in Forrest High history, letter sweaters and pennants from different eras, even bronze busts celebrating a half-dozen of the school's greatest players and coaches down through the years (one of them, young Billy Ray Hunsinger). The trophy case is still there, but now it is all McGill High: girls' basketball, track, one lonely football denoting a fourth-place finish in the state playoffs. There is an embroidered sampler proclaiming Purple Pride, a white megaphone with a menacing purple panther, and, on an easel, a copy of this fall's schedule, courtesy of Lorino's Grocery, with a photo of Head Coach Herman Graves. Forrest High has been consigned to oral history.

He is standing in his jeans, sneakers, and Calgary T-shirt, contemplating the forlorn trophy case, when he hears a police whistle. "Late again! Come on, babies, this train's leavin' the station!" He sees a large black woman in a massive salt-and-pepper Afro, new Reeboks beneath a billow-ing flowered dress the size of a tent, blowing the plastic whistle around her neck at teenaged boys in baggy jeans slouching toward their next classes. "Get those caps off! This ain't no pep rally. Come on, move it!" She stands in front of the glass doors marked Principal's Office like a prison matron, and just as he steps off in the direction of the gym she turns her eyes on him and stops him in his tracks.

"Can't y'all get nothing right?"

"Ma'am?"

"Ain't you the air conditioner?"

"No, ma'am, I'm just—"

"Can't hear you with that cigar in your mouth."

"Well, it ain't lit."

"That ain't no kind of image to be setting for these *chill-rens*." For an instant he imagines her blowing the whistle at full shrill, summoning a squad of Mau-Maus brandishing spears. "If you ain't the air conditioner, what you doing on school property?"

"I'm looking for Coach Graves."

"Oh. *Him*." She practically spits it out. "Follow me."

In the principal's office, scrunched in a student-sized desk he swears he remembers from his days in this very same room, he fills out a sheet as long as a Form 1040: name, age, address, phone, employer, Social Security num-ber, purpose of visit. He hears snippets of conversation as he scribbles— *Claims to know you . . . Hornblower . . . Cigar, baseball cap*—obviously on the phone with Herman. She grabs the completed form, tosses it on her desk without looking at it, then hands him a gummed white nametag reading VISITOR. "Straight down the hall and out back to the gym," she says. "And no stopping. These babies are here to study, not to lollygag with no for-eigners."

...

This is the first day of the last year in the school's existence, if he remembers Graves correctly, and the place has the feel of a graveyard left untended. Sidling down the wide hallways, familiar to him except that everything now seems so small, he sees battered lockers with sprung doors lining the walls, cobwebbed clocks that aren't running, clattering floor fans trying to do the job of air conditioners, and sawhorses blocking entry to the stairs leading to the building's second floor. Forrest High at its peak housed two thousand students, McGill High at its death barely four hundred, the custodial staff now down to a skeletal crew of caretakers. Only the whiff of chalk dust and disinfectant, and the drone of teachers' voices echoing in near-empty classrooms, are there to remind him that some things never change.

Once through the wide doors at the end of the main hallway, propped open to allow the hot air to circulate, he continues along the sheltered sidewalk leading to the gym. Somewhere at his feet there's a crudely scrawled heart holding his initials and those of a cheerleader, scratched with a stick one day when the cement was still wet—Debbie? Marilu? Jeannie?—but he'll play hell finding it beneath a layer of twenty-five years' worth of spray-painted graffiti. Looking to the right, in the distance beyond the graveled faculty parking lot, he can make out the lights of Grady Stadium gleaming in the early afternoon sun. To the left, still standing in a grove of oaks on a foundation of cinderblocks, is the Music Building, whence now emanates the jerky strains of the Mighty Marching Panthers band as they put together "Sweet Georgia Brown," section by section, horn by horn, stanza by stanza.

In the old gymnasium, where the collapsible seats have been rolled up and locked into place until basketball season, it's playtime. At the far end, a dozen girls wearing old-timey one-piece bloomers listlessly play at a game of volleyball in the stifling heat of late August, their darting brown eyes less on the ball than the boys at the other end. Near the entrance, where he now pauses, a half-dozen teenaged boys stripped down to their baggy shorts are squeaking back and forth in high-topped basketball shoes in a vigorous game of three-on-three. The ball breaks loose and he fetches it, thinking to

117

toss it back, but instead he bounces it a couple of times into the corner of the court and takes aim and lets fly with a two-handed set shot. "Air ball, air ball, air ball!!!" The hoots are still ringing in his ears when he walks the length of the floor and opens the big double doors at the other end, stenciled with the word Football.

...

Built sometime in the 1920's, the place now looks more like the floor of a musty flea-market warehouse than the dressing quarters of a high school football team. The steel lockers of Billy Ray's era have been replaced by jerry-built wooden stalls with nails to hold each player's gear. Brown water spots stain the dropped white ceiling, many of its tiles missing to reveal galvanized pipes and air-conditioning ducts leading to nowhere. As in the hallways of the school itself, floor fans stir the air. The whitewashed cinderblock walls have yellowed and streaked, cobwebs forming high in every corner. The "training bike" is a rusty old Schwinn, its naked wheel rims raised off of the curled linoleum floor by an ingenuous contraption involving cinderblocks and two-by-fours. The "weights" aren't barbells at all, but rather lead pipes laden at each end with tin cans full of concrete.

The coaches' office is partitioned off in one corner of the room at the far end, alongside the showers, the door marked Coach Graves torn from its hinges and propped against the wall. Walking past wooden benches and wrestling mats and an industrial-sized washer-and-dryer combination, stepping around laundry carts and wire bins holding footballs and helmets and shoulder pads, he follows the sounds emanating from the office: fluttered snoring, another whirring fan, organ music, tinny television voices.

Herman Graves is sprawled out on a narrow cot in the office, a sleek black cat perched on his belly, while an afternoon soap opera—*As the World Turns*, maybe?—spins in an uncontrollable vertical roll on an old black-and-white Zenith. Herman wears a pair of faded purple cotton shorts and a gold T-shirt emblazoned with McGill Football Staff. He jerks awake, sending the cat flying, when Billy Ray raps his knuckles on the doorjamb.

"You go down in a hurry," Billy Ray says. "Wadn't five minutes ago the warden was talking to you."

Herman is standing now, rubbing his eyes, trying to focus. "Hey, Gun. Guess you forgot how it goes. I been up since five o'clock, working on school stuff. Already taught my classes and made a faculty meeting. Be back out there on the field in a couple of hours. Gotta get my rest where I can."

"Ain't exactly educational tee-vee you're watching there." Billy Ray scrapes a metal folding chair across the bare concrete floor of the room, turns it around, sits on it backwards. "That set's so old, it probably gets Ed Sullivan live."

"We use it to watch game films, mostly. Doesn't roll like this when you use the VCR. Rest of the time, I just use it for company. Don't guess you'd know anything about fixing tee-vees, would you?"

"Everybody seems to think I'm a handyman these days. I don't do air conditioners or plumbing, neither." Billy Ray scratches the cat, which has reappeared and is sniffing his sneakers, looking for a friend. "Looks like you've got your rats under control, anyway."

"That's because Malcolm works for food. If it costs money, the Board of Education don't want to hear about it."

"Speaking of which, what you gonna do when the school closes?"

"Aw, hell, I don't know, Gun. There's a bunch of young coaches coming up that'll work cheap. The white schools like Lee, they don't want to mess with no old black coach with heart trouble. They got their own farm systems, booster clubs, their own bag."

"Looks like with the city government gone black, y'all'd get taken care of."

Herman stretches, yawns, and turns off the television. "Yeah, but the old white boys who write the checks don't have to run for office. Can't get rid of 'em. They know where the money's hid. They take care of the white schools."

"Reckon that explains it." Noticing a jumble of cardboard boxes and movie cannisters piled nearly to the ceiling in the far corner of the office, he wanders over for a look. "I guess *I'm* a Lee parent, since my daughter's in school there. God *damn!* It'll cost you a thousand bucks a year just for the privilege of belonging to the boosters club. About all that gets you is the right to buy good seats and get on the list for the Monday Night Quarterbacks meeting. They got a better stadium than we had at North Alabama. Five assistant coaches. A training room the Falcons would kill for. Hell, if they ain't got a tailback, they'll just go out and buy one."

"Tell me about it," says Herman. "Lost mine last year. Lee fixed up the boy's folks with a little store, moved the whole family to Crestwood, and the boy's liable to be all-state this year."

"Heard about that. One of my neighbors out there says the kid can run a four-four forty with a twenty-one-inch television set under his arm." Billy Ray cocks his head to read a scrawl on one of the boxes: Forrest '61. "What you got here?"

"That's what I wanted to show you." Herman slips into his shower clogs and shuffles along the concrete floor to the haphazard stack of cardboard boxes and pewter-gray cannisters. "Must be fifty years' worth of Forrest High stuff here. Game films, newspaper clippings, pictures, coaches' notes, everything. Probably got your jock size written down there somewhere."

"What's all this stuff doing here?"

"Didn't know what else to do with it. Found it in one of the classrooms upstairs, put out the word, but none of the old Forrest boys showed up to claim it. Principal said move it."

"That the one I met? The warden?"

"Miz Robbins. She ain't exactly a football fan."

"Don't seem to care much for white boys, neither."

Herman lets it pass, instead motioning for Billy Ray to follow him back to the corner of the room holding the Zenith and the cot and a school-issue gray metal desk, its top cluttered with loose sheets of paper with scribblings of offensive and defensive plays, X's and O's and arrows. "Check the big bottom drawer on the right."

From the drawer, Billy Ray hoists a foot-tall bust of himself, its original bronze now turned green, with a legend at its base reading BILLY RAY

HUNSINGER, Forrest High Panthers, HS All-America QB 1961. He doesn't quite know what to say except, "I'll be damned. Never even knew about this thing. Must've been in too big a hurry to get on with my life."

"Be nice for the Gun Room."

"What do you know about the Gun Room?"

"Oh"—Herman acts as though he has slipped up and leaked a secret—"I probably read about it somewhere, is all. Figured every old player's got a place for trophies. I've got one, myself. Ain't much in it, though, seeing as how there weren't many awards given out for grunts like me."

"Yeah, that never did seem very fair to me." Billy Ray holds the statue at arm's length to admire it. "*Parade* magazine. Back when I was a promising young man."

...

"Coach?" They turn to see the kid, Mavis, standing in the open doorway of the office. "Excuse me," he says when he sees Billy Ray, turning quickly as though to leave.

"It's all right, son," Herman tells him.

"I'll come back later."

"No, come on in. I want you to meet somebody."

In sneakers, blue jeans, and Panthers T-shirt, the boy takes a step into the room. Herman introduces them—*greatest quarterback this school ever had . . . this young man just might break your records one day*—but neither is listening. Rather, they are peering into each other's eyes, trying to see what's there, not sure whether to acknowledge their first meeting and its circumstances. Finally, they shake hands. Billy Ray makes a mental note that he has never felt a firmer handshake since his father's; a real bone-crusher, that one, developed from years of wielding a paint brush and crushing beer cans.

Herman coughs and says, "How's your mama, son?"

"They took her away," says Mavis.

"Same hospital? One in Macon?"

"Yes, sir."

"How long? They know?"

"When she's well. Three months, maybe."

"Anybody else at the house?"

"There's neighbors. Some uncles." The kid glances at Billy Ray, then at Herman, pleading with his eyes that his coach will let it stop right here. "I'm okay, Coach. I can handle it."

"You eating properly?"

"Enough. I cook a little."

"You need some help, you let me know, okay?"

"Yes, sir."

...

When the boy has left to take care of some chores in the gym, Billy Ray and Herman settle beside each other in a cracked brown leather sofa that has been there since the heyday of Coach Frank Hyder in the 'fifties and 'sixties. Except for the clattering of the fans throughout the locker room, an occasional grumble from plumbing in the showers, and the squeaking of sneakers on the floor of the gym across the way, there is a silence that stretches into minutes, not broken until Billy Ray says, "I already met the kid."

"I know," says Herman.

"He tell you?"

"No. Frank Lorino."

"What is this, a committee?"

"Sort of."

"Frank tell you the kid was stealing?"

"It wasn't like that at all, Gun. There's some things you don't know. This is a special kid."

"*Special*? Hey, the punk was boosting groceries right off the shelves in broad daylight. Helping himself. What the hell is going on here, Tank? You a football coach, or a social worker?"

"Both."

Over the next fifteen minutes, Herman tells Billy Ray the short version of Mavis Jackson's life up to this point. Father unknown, no siblings that anyone knows about, he has been raised in that rundown house in Fatback by a mother who cleaned houses in Inman Park for a while but in recent years has turned to prostitution in order to keep herself in booze and drugs. How the boy survived that, says Herman, is a story in itself. Taking the coach's view, he would like to think sports has a lot to do with it. He first met Mavis as an eight-year-old scamp in the Parks & Recreation Dapartment's inner-city athletic programs, a quiet kid who would do anything if they would let him stay one more hour shooting baskets or throwing footballs or hitting baseballs—mop the gym floors, mow the fields, tend the equipment, anything to keep from going home—and the result is not only a gifted athlete but a kid, a *good* kid, who has learned to fend for himself.

"Yeah," Billy Ray says, "but *stealing*."

"Not really. Lee High's got its boosters club, and so do we. Frankie Lorino was just doing his part."

"I notice the kid ain't exactly wearing rags. What's he got, a charge card at Rich's? And how about money? A kid's gotta have *some* cash."

"More 'boosters,' if you want to call 'em that. Our team chaplain's got a church that keeps the boy in used clothes. There's a banker that slips him some pocket money now and then. A foreman at Dixie Box Corporation, boy that played here a few years ago, he gave him a parttime job this summer down there on the loading docks when he got off the crutches. About all he had to do was keep track of stuff going in and out."

"Lord God, Tank, y'all are gonna get in some deep shit with the state athletic association if they find out about all of this."

"Never caught *you*, did they?"

"Say what?"

"Think about it." Herman leans back, hands behind his head, proud of himself. "I'll bet old man Lorino kept you in comic books, candy bars, even cigarettes and rubbers if you wanted 'em, for all four years you played here.

How about those 'fifty-dollar handshakes' every time y'all whipped Northside's ass? You ever pay for a meal around Little Five Points on a Saturday? I know about the shoes, the clothes, the summer jobs where all you had to do was punch the clock. I know about the old 'fifty-four Ford you got 'loaned' to you until North Alabama gave you that brand-new Mercury. Hell, I know about the painting jobs your daddy got, and the—"

"Okay, okay, but see, things were different then, Tank. Hell, we were drawing big crowds. We were great. People loved us."

"Gun, Gun, Gun. You think people don't love this boy? Yeah, it's different. They were helping you out because you made 'em happy every Friday night. They're helping Mavis out so they can save a boy's life."

"Aw, come on, Tank, that's a little bit too much, don't you think?"

"None at all. I don't know if you've read about this, but the odds are that about half of these boys could be dead or in prison five years from now. Look at me. I wouldn't be sitting here talking to you if it hadn't been for football. Probably the same with you, too, and you were a white boy with a mama and daddy to go home to."

...

In the gloaming late that afternoon, having passed the day trying but failing to take a nap in the searing heat, Billy Ray finds himself sitting high in the concrete grandstands at Grady Stadium, alone with the pigeons. Down on the field, Herman Graves is wheeling his electric golf cart from group to group of McGill Panthers, bellowing through his megaphone, exhorting the boys to extend themselves one more time. His one assistant coach, a pygmy of a man with a bald head and a voice like a bullfrog, literally kicks the butts of those who don't jump fast enough. They have been at it since mid-afternoon, following a full day of classes, and soon it'll be over.

To end the day, Tank has them working on the passing game. It is half-speed for the linemen—the middle of the offensive line dropping back to form a pocket for the quarterback, Mavis, the charging defenders jumping off the ball with an initial thrust but then backing off when contact is made—but for the receivers and the defensive backs it is all-out war. *Hut-hut.* Mavis is dropping back into the pocket, looking for a receiver, and airing it out. A bullet to the far sideline is dropped. A long bomb, arching sixty yards, is overthrown. An outlet pass to a fullback drifting out of the backfield hits him in the back before he can turn around. "Again," Tank Graves intones through the megaphone. More of the same.

Billy Ray has been giving body English to each throw, trying to will receptions, moaning with each dropped pass and errant throw. "Christ Almitey," he is saying under his breath when suddenly he feels somebody shove his Packers cap over his eyes.

"Thought I might find you here." Rima, in sandals and a one-piece sun dress, nestles in beside him and sticks an arm under the elbow at his side.

"You scared me," he says. "You're dressed funny."

"Thanks a lot."

"No, I mean a *dress*. Shoes, even."

"Well, you know, first day of school. Had to stay late in the art room. What're you up to?"

"Just checking out the meat, is all. Can't help myself."

Suddenly, Rima jumps to her feet, cups her hands around her mouth, and screams at full power: "Come on, Mavis, you can do it, kid! On the numbers, baby! Gimme six!" Just as suddenly, she is sitting down on the hard concrete grandstand, putting her arm under his, interlocking her fingers, a serene smile on her face, as though nothing has happened. Down on the field, the players turn their heads briefly to check out the commotion, then go back to their business.

"What the hell was that all about?"

"These boys need all the help they can get, don't you think?"

"They need more than a little yelling. Anyways, I got the idea you hate football."

"Oh, no. Even though I may speak as an academic, I recognize the importance of athletics in our society. A little ass-kicking never hurt anybody."

Tank is blowing his whistle again, ending the day, and as the boys line up for their windsprints Billy Ray and Rima stand up to leave. His knee having locked up on him from sitting there for nearly an hour, he needs help from her as he negotiates the steps down to the field and on to his wagon and her pickup. "Go, go, go, you little motherfucker," he hears the gnarly little assistant coach yelling at the players. *God,* he catches himself thinking, *I love this shit.* Mavis, in the meantime, is jogging around the track, all alone.

"I got an idea," Billy Ray says when they reach his wagon, parked on the street in front of the school. "How's about a steak tonight?"

She says, "Your place or mine, big fella?"

ELEVEN

He tried. Lord knows, he tried. For nearly three months he has been hanging around like a lap dog patiently waiting for a handout while she slinks around in her cutoffs and bare feet and torn T-shirts—no bra or panties, ever, that he can tell—with a wink here, a smile there, a touch, a giggle, here a navel, there a nipple, and all the while he's going nuts wondering if not now, when? After they put away the steaks the night before, he decided to make his move, throwing her across the bed on his side of the duplex, the two of them wrestling and tickling and laughing like kids in a sandbox, and then . . . nothing. Game called due to lack of interest. Scottie has told him there would be times like this, until the booze left his system and his body adjusted accordingly; but, hey, *What the hell is this?* Lying flat on his back, staring at the ceiling, fairly certain he has lost it, he felt her twirl the reddish hair on his chest, kiss him on the cheek, then slide off the bed. "Don't sweat it, stud," she said, hitting the floor with her bare feet. "Babe Ruth struck out one thousand, three hundred and thirty times. You can look it up."

Now, at daybreak, he has found a way to forget about it. With a steaming cup of coffee at his bare feet, a lit cigar in his mouth, swaying gently in the swing on the front porch, he has lost himself in work. Swirls of arrows and dotted lines, X's and O's, the language of field commanders and football coaches—Attack, Hold, LB, TE, QB, Curl, Fly, Fade, Pump, SE, FB, Trap, Screen—fly from the hank of charcoal in his hand onto the pages of the artist's sketchbook he has fished from the mess in her front room. He rips a page from the book and tosses it away, the curled paper drifting to the floor like a leaf falling to the ground in autumn, then starts on a fresh one. A madman at work, he doesn't bother to look up when a yellow school bus rumbles past on the street.

Holding a cup of coffee, wearing nothing but a long T-shirt this time, enough to cover her rump, Rima opens the screen door with a creak. He nearly jumps out of his skin when she explodes into song—*"Ooohhh, the hilllls are aliiiivve . . . !"*—but recovers when she tousles his hair with her free hand, leans over to peck him on the forehead, then squats on the doorstoop to pick up the Atlanta *Constitution* and the New York *Times* left on the steps.

He is doodling, mumbling to himself, oblivious to everything, when she says, "You think I'm pretty?"

"What?"

"I was Watermelon Princess one time."

"Jugs like that, you get my vote."

"What a terrible thing to say." Opening to the Style section of the *Times,* she sees a spread on Andy Warhol. "I could've been one of Andy's chicks, you know. Baby Jane Holzer. Girl of the Year." She gives up, joins him on the swing, peers at the sketches. "Whatcha doing"?

"Just scribbling stuff."

"Looks like you're planning the D-Day invasion."

"Come to think of it"—he holds the sketch pad at arm's length—"yeah, that's close. Push, pull, decoy, set traps, let 'em have it. Ike would be proud."

"Where's Mavis?"

"Huh?"

"You know, the quarterback. Which one's he?"

"The quarterback's the circle filled in with black, the one behind the center, the square with an X in it. Here's the blockers and the direction they block at, these little slashes in front of 'em. The X's are the defenders, where they're set up, and, hey, come on"—he tosses the sheet to the floor, starts with a fresh one—"you're puttin' me on. What I heard yesterday, all of that 'hit him in the numbers' and stuff, you know more football than, well, hell, more'n Tank's assistant coach, anyway."

"He needs help, you know."

"Rasslin' coach. Can you believe it?"

"No, I mean the boy. Mavis."

"Tell me about it. Damned kid couldn't hit a city bus if it was standing still, what I've seen so far. Worst part is, I don't think he much gives a rat's ass if he does or not."

"But you don't know for sure"—she's at it again, moving her thighs against his, dragging her nails through the wisps of hair at the nape of his neck, bringing chill bumps—"do you, now? Am I right? What do you say?"

...

Now it's his turn to be caught napping on the cot in front of the television set in Herman Graves's office, a soap opera rolling in free-fall, an organ punctuating breathless dialogue about bad hair and philandering husbands and other treacheries. He's been in the room since noon, long enough to fill the blackboard with plays transferred from his scrawls in Rima's sketchbook, so engrossed in it that he failed to make lunch at Manuel's. He bolts from his reverie when the television goes dead and he hears a voice: "I don't see 'Niggers Go Long' up there." In a pair of wrinkled navy blue cotton trousers and a short-sleeved white dress shirt with a clip-on tie, his teaching outfit, Graves is standing in front of the blackboard, hands on hips, studying the diagrams.

"Hey, Tank." Billy Ray sits up, rubs his eyes, sees that it's already past two o'clock. "Well, it's there, you just don't recognize it. That's the point, ain't it? If *you* don't see it coming, how's a bunch of teenaged defensive backs gonna pick it up?"

"Thing is"—Graves steps to the board to point at one play involving four deep receivers running elaborate routes en route to the end zone—"by the time it takes for these guys to get loose, the defensive line oughta have just about enough time to dig a hole and give my quarterback a proper burial."

"Way I look at it, that's your problem, Coach. You plan to teach blocking this year?"

"Ahn-hanh, I see. Know what you're gonna say next. 'Gimme ten good men,' right?"

"I would if I thought you had that many. Lord, God, Tank, this is about the sorriest lookin' bunch I've ever seen. This ain't a team, it's a gang."

Herman peels off his shirt and trousers, hanging them on hooks in the rusty locker canted in the corner behind his desk, then fishes for a pair of shorts and a T-shirt. Dressed for the second half of his day, he finds a clean pair of white socks in his desk drawer and plops into his chair to pull them on. The bell rings in the gym to announce the seventh-period classes.

"Saw you up in the stands last evenin', checkin' 'em out," Graves says. "You and Miz Byrd."

"Is that"—Billy Ray supresses a laugh—"is that what she calls herself around here?"

"She keeps trying to get the students to call her 'Rima,' but they're afraid of what the principal might say about first-naming a teacher, even if she's just parttime. She's a good one, though. Knows that art. The boys love her."

"I'll *bet* they do."

"You two got a *arrangement*, do you?"

"Me and her? So what? I can't see as how that's any of your damned business."

"Sorry, Gun, but I been listening to your show lately. Sounds to me like you're making your life *everybody's* business."

"Yeah, well, what can I tell you? Show business is my life."

Some of the players who don't have last-period classes have begun drifting in, high-fiving and playing grab-ass with each other, complaining about everything from the heat to sore muscles to women. Billy Ray finds himself comforted by it, the language of jocks probably dating back to the first Olympic games, and catches himself breathing deeply to take in the familiar smells of liniment and tape and old leather, the sweet perfumes of his youth. And he knows that somewhere in the room, barely perceptible to an outsider but there just the same, there lurks the smell of the fuel that drives it all, the musky odor of testosterone.

"Showtime," says Herman, sneakers laced, on his feet now, cap in hand. "Time to separate the men from the boys. Well, you 'bout ready?"

"Ready for what?"

"To help me out."

"Oh, no. *Hell,* no. What you see up on the blackboard, that's it, my friend."

Tank takes a deep breath and lets it out in a wheeze, rattling the loose papers on his desk when he exhales. "Come on, Gun, we been having some fun but let's quit messin' around. This thing's been building up ever since you just 'happened to be in the area' that day, joggin' around the track. You miss it so much you're about to die. You need me as much as I need you."

"God *damn,* Tank, I ain't no coach and you know it. For one thing, I've gotten to be an old fart all of a sudden. For another, I ain't got the patience."

Herman Graves pretends that he hasn't heard a thing Billy Ray is saying. "You just said the magic word," he says, coming around the desk and sitting on the edge, leaning forward to bring Billy Ray into his confidence. "'Patience.' This boy's got an arm that came from God. No doubt about that. He just doesn't know what to do with it. I'm a lineman, Gun, you're a quarterback. Besides, I got all these other boys to worry about. How 'bout it? I thought you might just sit down with him, check him out, see what makes him tick, maybe y'all even play a little catch."

"Hell, I can tell you right now what his problems are—"

"Tell the boy, Gun, not me."

"Don't do this to me, Tank."

"Aw, come on. What's an afternoon of your time? Tell you the truth, I thought you'd be honored to have a chance to share some of your *ex-per-teez*"—a bite in the word, a sardonic smile, a raised eyebrow, a slap on the knee—"with a kid who never thought he'd get to meet a real pro quarterback like yourself."

"Shit, Tank, he don't even know where Green Bay is."

"What's that got to do with it? *Tell* him. Tell him about Lombardi and the Packers, the Colts, the Cowboys, Canada, all that stuff."

"He ain't interested in what some old honkie's got to say."

"I was. Still am."

"You asshole." Billy Ray flexes his right arm, windmills it, curses when he hears the shoulder creak. "I reckon a little chat wouldn't hurt none."

"That's all I'm asking."

"Ought not to take too long."

"There you go. I'll get you home before dark."

...

Standing in the middle of the field in a pair of purple cotton shorts borrowed from Tank, a safety pin holding them up, shirtless and sweating beneath the broiling sun of late August, he feels as though he never left. Everywhere he looks, angry young men are committing mayhem, making him feel like a platoon sergeant in the heat of battle, bayonets drawn, a battle to the death. He hears the smack of leather on leather, helmets cracking, whistles blowing, Tank Graves bellowing into his megaphone, the cries of the wounded, the screaming of banshees. Such music! "Motherfucker! Yo' ass is mine! Dammit, hit him, don't kiss him! Dig-dig-dig! Git 'im, git 'im, git 'im!" In Billy Ray's memory, the donning of pads always brought the first drastic reduction in manpower: a trip home for the faint-hearted, to the loving arms of mama, to milkshakes at the Dairy Queen, to quiet hours in the library. But not here, not on this day. For whatever reasons a shrink might come up with—street kids, poor kids, *hungry* kids—this bunch loves violence, understands it, lusts for it.

Down behind the goalposts, in a sandy pit, it's every man for himself: hand-to-hand combat, under the eyes of the wrestling coach, Tank's only assistant, whose mandate now becomes clear to Billy Ray. The man is a sadist, right up there with Vince Lombardi and Bear Bryant and Marine drill instructors; the axe-man, the brute, the enforcer; the boys' first taste of what they'll find waiting for them in military boot camp if nothing else works; a frog with scarred knees and a glistening bald head and eyes that rage like the fires of hell. His charges are pit bulldogs, riled up, smelling blood, looking for the jugular. At the head of one line, bloody hands on his knees, a linebacker without a neck snorts like a bull and paws at the sand with his cleats, ready to spring at his prey, a kid at the head of the other line, an offensive lineman, helmet still askew from the last collision, eyes wild, legs splayed in a three-point crouch. "Goddamit, Rat, the only good thing about you ran down yo' mama's leg! Kill the sonofabitch! Go!" *Wham!* "I want blood, dammit, blood!" *Ka-blooey!* "Little pissants! If you're gonna quit, do it now, not when we're on the goal line against Decatur! What the hell you lookin' at, Pinky? Yo' mama ain't here! Kill him, Grunt!!"

Drifting away to join Tank beneath the canopy of his golf cart at midfield, where that sort of thing seldom happens, Billy Ray watches the "skill" players, a euphemism for the ones who actually touch the ball, as they mince through their paces. In direct contrast to the interior linemen, whose nicknames are like job descriptions (Grunt, Mole, Dog, Rat), these kids are of more delicate persuasions, the specialists with more civilized *noms-de-guerre* (Flea, Streak, Preach, Bambi), a more pensive group with an air of lordliness. Preening, stretching, back-pedaling, jogging in place, they are running some basic offensive plays at half-speed, with orders not to maim but to work on finesse.

"You ask me," Billy Ray is saying to Tank, "Coach Whatsisname ought to be committed."

"He was, once, but he's okay now."

"Where'd you get him, Parris Island?"

Tank interrupts to shout at a defensive back who has taken a head fake and been beaten by a receiver on a deep route—"Watch his hips, son, not his eyes!"—then mutters under his breath as Mavis overthrows by a good five yards. "Name's Pig Thomas. He was a warden up at Alto, the boys' prison. Lost his job as wrestling coach when he nearly choked a kid in practice."

Perfect. Billy Ray has noticed wholesale changes in personnel since he first glimpsed the team, that day a couple of weeks earlier when he was jogging and met up again with Herman Graves. Everybody seemed to be playing out of position then—fat boys running and catching the ball, tall skinny ones in the line, a little butterball pretending to be a punter—but all of that has changed now. He points this out to Tank and wonders aloud, "You have some more troops show up, or what?"

"It's just some more of those head games you gotta play with high school boys," Tank tells him. "First couple of weeks, before we go to pads, I always treat 'em it like it was recess. Throw out the balls and let 'em play. Don't want 'em gettin' bored and quittin' on the first day, you know. They all want to get their hands on the ball, get their names in the paper, show off for their girlfriends, so I let 'em choose their positions by seniority. Oldest ones get to play what they want to. Pretty soon, though, they figure it out for themselves that they're more cut out for the dirty work, blocking and tackling, than they are for catching passes in traffic or running away from eleven boys who want to tear their head off. They get the message. What I got now is pretty much the way you want it. Got the basketball and baseball players putting their hands on the ball, the grunts in the trenches. There's your ten good men for you, Gun."

All along, it's been more of the same from Mavis Jackson. With nobody rushing, he takes the snap, drops back four or five steps, locks in on a receiver, aims, and throws with the same results Billy Ray has seen before: the passes sail or hook like shanked tee shots, fall at a receiver's feet or zoom out of his reach, either hit his man in the back before he can turn to catch it or wind up in a defensive back's open arms. No throw suits the situation; outlet lobs are fired like bullets, bombs intended for the end zone die at the apex and drift down like parachutes. Now and then the kid is perfect—*yes!*—take the snap, drop back, pump-fake right, drill it in the numbers to a man streaking on a fly pattern down the left sideline, *bingo*, off to the races, touchdown. Then, on the next try, what's supposed to be a simple dump pass over the middle to a tight end, he hits his unsuspecting center in the back of the helmet with a shot that knocks the boy out cold. As everybody is gathering around the stricken player—"Get some ice!" "You all right, T-Bone?" "Air, give him some air!"—Herman Graves blows his whistle and calls for a water break.

...

Sitting in the shade of the east stands, traffic rumbling past Grady Stadium's main entrance on Monroe Drive during the late-afternoon rush hour, Billy Ray has finally managed to light his mangled cigar when he looks up to see Mavis sidling toward him from the other side of the field, where the others are playfully spraying hoses on each other in the shade cast by the grandstand across the way. Like the others, the kid looks as though he's been run through a wringer. His hair is a wet Brillo pad, his dingy gray practice uniform nearly turned to mud from the dirt and sweat, his face streaked with rivulets that drip from his chin. When he reaches the shade, holding his helmet in one hand and a football in the other, he stops a few feet in front of Billy Ray and says, "Coach said come see you."

"Right, right. Pull up a chair, son."

"You ain't my daddy. Let's get that straight right now."

"Aw, hell, kid. Back off. It's just a figure of speech. Come on, take a load off." Billy Ray pats the gravel, puffs on the cigar, all the while trying to read the boy's eyes. "Heat's gonna kill us all. Man and beast alike."

Waving the cigar smoke away from his eyes, Mavis drops the helmet and football, then plops onto a patch of grass. He draws his ankles together and sits cross-legged, Indian-style, the same as Billy Ray. "*Man.* Thought I was gon' throw up there for a while. It's a hot motherfucker." He engrosses himself in plucking at strands of grass, now and then stealing a glance at this white man, trying to guess what's up.

Billy Ray says, "What'd you have for breakfast?"

"Say what?"

"You eat breakfast, do you?"

135

"Hey, man, everybody eats breakfast."

"So?"

"Hanh?"

"So what'd you have?"

"Shit, man, you still on breakfast? Coach said we was gon' talk some football."

"Look, sport, it's a simple question. What was it, a beer and some crackers, or did you drop by the Majestic for eggs and hashbrowns and a short stack? Bacon on the side. Good tip for Moselle, the one with the big tits? I don't want to tax your memory, ace, but I *would* appreciate an answer."

"I don't drink no beer."

"That's a start. Well?"

"Breakfast. *Shit.*" The kid shrugs, tosses a grass stem to see if a breeze might catch it, looks Billy Ray in the eye. "I was in a hurry. Had me a banana and a Coke. Okay?"

"Great. Breakfast of Champions. That brings us to the noon meal. How 'bout lunch? You able to work that into your schedule?"

"Get off my back, man. You ain't so old you can't remember that shit they give you at the school cafeteria. It was hot dog day at the Gag. Had me three dogs and some chips. Two bags of 'em."

"And how'd you sleep last night?"

"Aw, *maannn* . . . What the hell are you, the new principal? Slept like a baby, okay? They was some fightin' outside. Broke up 'bout three or four o'clock, I don't know. I slept all right."

"And studying. You manage to get any studying done with all that excitement going on?"

"Studyin'. Shit. We ain't got to that yet. Classes ain't really got started. Signed up for classes, answered roll call, checked out some books at the library, that's all we had to do. Hey"—the kid seems poised to bolt—"when we gon' get around to talkin' football, passin' the ball, all that good stuff?"

"I'm a-comin' to that."

"Eatin', sleepin', studyin'. Shit."

"It's *all* about football, kid."

"Don't sound like it to me." Mavis begins wildly waving his hands to bat away the smoke spiraling from Billy Ray's cigar. "Those things are *bad* for you, man. Why'n'cha put that damned thing out? Askin' me 'bout eatin' breakfast and sleepin' and shit, look at you. Gon' go up in smoke some day. Shit. *Maaann.*"

"Fair enough." Billy Ray snuffs out what's left of the cigar and flips the butt away. Out on the street, now snarled with traffic, a fender-bender has brought some old white guy out of his delivery truck, yelling and brandishing a tire iron at a load of black teenaged boys in a smoking Ford Galaxie who have spun out of the stadium parking lot and creased his driver's-side door. The white guy is shouting at them in Italian, the black kids answering in street slang ("Spic motherfucker!"), the battle enjoined. Billy Ray has been engrossed in the sideshow, wondering what the old guy's chances might be, when he turns back to see that the kid has been studying him all along.

"Coach says you was a cool dude."

"I had my moments."

"Says you was a pro."

"I know some things."

"Like what?"

"Like you ain't nearly as good as you—. Naw, I ain't gonna do it like that." Billy Ray nods his head toward a large plastic trash barrel in the shadow of the grandstand, about three feet across at the mouth, maybe fifteen feet away from where they sit. "Tell you what. Lemme see you throw one in that barrel."

"That thing over there? Little ol' barrel? Shit. You wanna put some money on it?"

"I would if you had any."

"I ain't broke. I'll come up with something."

"Tell you what. You drop one in on the first throw, I'll buy you lunch Saturday at Manuel's."

"Manuel's. That honkie joint on Highland?"

"Yeah. Make it, you get lunch on the house. Miss it, you wash my car."

"That ol' heap of yours still runnin'? Thought maybe you'd junked it by now."

"You remember that, huh?"

"Already told you I 'preciated the ride."

"I keep leaving it unlocked, hoping somebody'll steal it, but I can't find any takers. How 'bout it, kid? We got a deal?"

"Deal." Mavis jumps to his feet, grabs the football, sights on the trash barrel, curls his tongue over his lips, pumps his arm a couple of times, then unloads. *Whap!* Not surprising to Billy Ray, the kid has thrown the ball with such force that he knocks the barrel over on its side, spilling its contents of stagnant water, crushed beer cans, candy wrappers, and used condoms. *"Motherfucker!"*

"Saturday morning, ten o'clock sharp."

"Fuckin' barrel. Just standin' there!"

"Three things." Billy Ray has fetched the football and set the barrel upright. Now he is windmilling his arm, football in hand, focusing his sights. "Number one, you're throwing across your body. Like this." He points his left toe to the right, then feigns a throw to the left. "Two, when you let go you watched the ball, not the barrel. What you oughta do is lock on to your target and let the ball find it. The crowd, they'll let you know if you've hit your man. Okay? Last thing, the worst thing, this ain't no contest to knock the fat man into the water barrel at the county fair to win a Teddy bear for your girlfriend. You *drop* it in there*, lay* it in there, real easy, like puttin' a baby to bed. Like this." He's pretty sure he's going to blow the whole thing, it's been so long, but he's hoping that there are some things a man never forgets. *Fourth and long, ten seconds on the clock, Stick Sims running the Z-Fade, got his man beat in the corner of the end zone.* Billy Ray takes a deep breath, locks in on the target like a heat-seeking missile, steps with his toe pointed straight ahead, lobs the ball in a perfect soft spiral, following through with the index finger of his throwing hand pointed to the mouth of the barrel, and when the ball disappears it rattles around in the bottom of the barrel, sounding like a drum roll.

...

Late in the afternoon, close to quitting time, Billy Ray borrows three of the more promising receivers he's noticed so he and Mavis can work on some things. Down on the ten-yard-line, with Mavis under center (T-Bone's better now, thanks), he has the kid working on three simple passes: a lob over the middle to a slotback who is supposed to have sneaked behind the linebackers, a soft fade to the fastest receiver in the corner of the end zone, and a bullet into the gut of the big tight end on a simple button-hook pattern at the goal line. It's been like taming a wild horse, running the three plays over and over again, but Mavis is coming around and gaining some confidence.

"Okay, here's the deal," Billy Ray tells them. "Coach Graves wants to wind it up today with some work in the Red Zone. Eleven-on-eleven from the ten. Full-tilt. Bust-head."

"Already got me one busted head," says T-Bone. "Don't need no more."

"Shit, man, we ain't ready yet," says Mavis.

"They gon' clean us some new assholes," says Runt, the little scatback.

"Ain't got no plays," says Tree, the tight end.

"You a crazy motherfucker," says Streak, the flanker.

"Wrong," says Billy Ray. "These boys are so pissed off about what they've been through today, they're ready to kill somebody. We're smarter'n they are. We're gon' run four plays and score three touchdowns. Trust me, they're—"

A blood-curdling roar goes up at midfield, causing Mavis and the other four to go wide-eyed with terror. Like an army of desert bandits, issued sabres and told to take no prisoners, the grunts who have been grinding away under the tutelage of Pig Thomas for most of the day are thundering toward them now with murderous intent; screaming, whooping, running into each other, raising great clouds of dust, making the earth move. A football is placed on the ten, between the hashmarks, and fistfights break out immediately over who gets the first shot at the quarterback. Tank Graves is trying to bring order. Pig Thomas is drooling. "Stay cool," Billy Ray says to Mavis, slapping him on the butt and sending him into the huddle with the series of four plays.

Hut-hut! Too bad about Mojo, the sacrificial lamb in Billy Ray's scheme of things, for it is he, the fullback, who takes the handoff from Mavis and is forthwith swarmed, flattened, steamrolled, pulverized, swallowed alive by a tidal wave of brawling defenders. All eleven of them are peeled off the pile, even the backs who should have been sitting back and thinking pass, and poor Mojo has to be dragged away while his muggers are leaping with unalloyed joy, high-fiving each other, chanting, "*Dee*-fense, *Dee*-fense, *Dee*-fense."

Hut-hut! Same play, different fullback, except this time, just as the two deep backs are landing on top of the pile with shouts of glee, they discover that Mavis has kept the ball and flipped it to Runt, who has slipped unmolested to the back of the end zone and caught a touchdown pass. The defenders are stunned—*Hey, wait, what the hell?*—to see Runt spiking the ball, Mavis pointing at them and laughing, Pig Thomas, their master, trembling with rage.

Hut-hut! Same play, another fullback, same result. This time the tight end, Tree, mighty as an oak, has executed a buttonhook at the goal line and is wrapping his arms around a cannon shot at the numbers from Mavis.

Hut-hut! Same thing, Mojo back in at fullback, defensive backs staying home this time, but no matter. Mavis hasn't forgotten the trash barrel. Untouched at the line of scrimmage, Streak is all alone in the left corner of the end zone. Before the linebackers and deep backs can get to him, he is leaping for Mavis's soft fade and hauling it in, making certain that his feet land in the end zone, then taking several long strides before slam-dunking the ball over the goalposts.

Mavis is beside himself, pointing and laughing and taunting the defenders. "Y'all had enough, or you want some more?"

"You bunch of goddam *morons!*" Pig Thomas is screaming, hitting the first kid he sees.

"Hey," one of the linebackers is yelping, "they can't do that, coach. We got suckered. They playin' volleyball, not football."

Tank Graves is all smiles as he blows his whistle. "See y'all tomorrow," he says. "Eat good, study, get some sleep. We might make something out of y'all before this is over."

TWELVE

T he old man's still got the juice, no doubt about it, and what amazes him is how easily it's all coming back; as though he's just been away for a couple of weeks to let the muscles regenerate. Oh, sure, the old spring in the legs and the zip on the ball aren't there yet, not after all of that dissolution he's put himself through, but with every hour he spends on the field in the company of these teenagers, kids whose capacity to endure pain seems endless, the more the years seem to fall away. And to make the whole thing sweeter—*Yo, Gin, got another irony for you*—it's all taking place right there where he first found something he was good at, under the craning necks of the light standards at Grady Stadium, home of champions.

It's not a bad deal, the way he looks at it, not bad at all. There's no making reveille in order to teach classes, meaning he can sleep late and plan the day's lesson for the kid. No baby-sitting or butt-kicking or attending strategy sessions with Tank Graves and Pig Thomas, that being the domain of the bosses, leaving him free to do what he does best, and nothing else. Except for the fact that he has no official position and isn't being paid for his services, he feels like a visiting lecturer or a high-powered consultant who's been lured out of retirement to fix things as only he, the great Billy Ray Hunsinger, the Gunslinger, can do. A tutor to the stars. Nice gig.

So far, everybody seems to be happy with the arrangement. About all it takes to please Pig is to show him a little blood now and then, even if it's his own when he gets pissed at a lineman and goes down into the sand pit with him, *mano a mano*, just to teach him a lesson that sometimes backfires. Tank might have been a great offensive lineman at Grambling but he was a mere center lost in the maelstrom, charged with flattening anybody who got in his way, the first to admit that the intricacies of modern offensive football are as mysterious to him as aerial combat or hieroglyphics. That leaves Mavis and his teammates, a situation that ameliorated when Billy Ray showed them what a little chicanery can do. He knows that what he did was shameless, stacking the deck in favor of Mavis and his receivers, taking advantage of the over-eagerness of a bunch of wild-eyed kids like that, but it worked and that's what counts.

One positive residual from all of this is that he has settled into a healthy routine for the first time in five years. If he's going to instruct the kid to get plenty of sleep and eat three squares a day, he might as well do the same. Amazing, what a little structure can do: in bed before midnight, up by seven, whipping up some breakfast and taking a stroll through the neighborhood; all morning at the drawing board, as it were, scribbling notes and drawing up plays, like a schoolteacher planning the day's lessons; a decent lunch, most days, at Manuel's; three hours on the field with Mavis and the Panthers' offensive unit; some meat and potatoes for dinner, a little television, in bed after the eleven o'clock news. Giving up the whiskey hasn't been the easiest thing he ever did, and a day seldom passes when he doesn't think fondly of the Jim Beam he hid from himself in the pantry—still waiting patiently like an old girlfriend—but hey, he can do this.

...

In the glare of a bright Saturday morning, Fatback looks even worse than Billy Ray remembers. Old cars litter the neighborhood at the precise spots where they died, parked haphazardly at curbside on the cracked streets, blocking sidewalks, or in bare dirt yards where they are being cannibalized piece by piece as the need arises. Most of the single-story frame houses are beyond salvation, their foundations perched tenuously on bricks and cinderblocks, screen doors sprung from their hinges, windows busted, paint flaking and curling to reveal bare wood now rotting. Front porches sag beneath loads of old sofas, splintered chairs, castoff refrigerators and washing machines, and rusty automobile parts. Neither taxi drivers nor cops in patrol cars are eager to respond to calls from Fatback, he has heard, and he can see why. Clutches of listless black teenaged boys crouch on curbs or sit on the hoods of the junk cars, smoking cigarettes and passing half-pint bottles and shouting at young girls in ragged dresses. Mongrel dogs and feral cats chase everything that moves. Like the strip along the Bankhead Highway, near the radio station in Austell, it is a civilization marked for death.

Billy Ray parks his old Chevy wagon on the street in front of 745 Dixiana and makes sure that everybody sees him locking the doors—she may have seen her better days, but *Rosinante* looks like a luxury car in these parts—then walks across the gullied dirt yard toward the front porch, where two men of indeterminate age sit in molded white plastic chairs at a rickety Formica dinette table, playing cards, sharing a half-gallon jug of wine. The shrieks and implorations of a fundamentalist preacher come from a radio somewhere inside the house.

"Brother must be lost," one of the men says as he glances up at the intruder, drawing cackles from the other.

"I'm looking for Mavis," says Billy Ray.

"Don't look like no *po*-leece to me. Look like it to you, brother?"

"Might be come to repossess the furniture, ast me. Gon' take the last stick."

"Is the boy here?"

"He be in there somewhere."

The house is even less promising inside. Old blankets and tattered sleeping bags cover the floor of the living room like wall-to-wall carpeting. The place reeks of wet rugs and beer and cigarette smoke and stale grease. Straight ahead is a cramped kitchen, the sink overflowing with unwashed dishes and pots and pans, the walls spattered with cooking oil and ketchup and jelly, the cracked and curled linoleum floor slick with rusty water from a plumbing leak, strewn with what a plastic garbage can can't hold: coffee grounds, crushed beer cans, leftover pork-and-beans, curdled milk, molded hanks of bread, chicken bones. Roaches and flies and ants are everywhere, feasting.

In the dank back bedroom, across the narrow hallway from a bathroom reeking of urine, he finds Mavis sprawled across an old rollaway cot, dead asleep. Billy Ray stands in the doorway for a moment to take it in: a plastic basket full of dirty clothes in one corner; a bureau with clean clothes neatly folded and stacked in its open drawers; walls holding framed photographs of Mavis in his football uniform, last year's team photo of the McGill Panthers, Martin Luther King Jr., Auburn's black running back Bo Jackson, a pretty girl in a McGill cheerleader's outfit, and a woman he guesses to be the boy's ailing mother; a doorless closet revealing a dozen hangers, neatly spaced, holding a sports coat, some khaki trousers, a white dress shirt and a blue one, the bulky suede great coat of that day at Lorino's Grocery; a bed-side table laden with schoolbooks, shoelaces, crinkled cellophane wrappers that once held Honey Buns and Twinkies and Snickers, a tea glass holding pencils and ball-point pens and lollipops, an empty Coke bottle. It's not much, Billy Ray is thinking, but there are signs that there is some pride here: the neatly spaced hangers, the four pairs of sneakers and shoes arranged on the floor of the closet, the folded stacks of clean jeans and T-shirts in the bureau, the perfectly aligned framed photos on the wall, even the frilly window curtains covering the two windows. There are no cobwebs, no roaches, no balls of lint here, not in this room.

When Billy Ray raps on the door frame, the kid bolts upright as though to defend himself. "What? Hunh?" Seeing who it is, he relaxes and begins kneading his eyes with his knuckles. "Oh, it's *you*."

"I told you. 'Billy Ray' or 'Gun' would do nicely."

"Far as I'm goin' is 'coach.'"

"Whatever you say, kid." Billy Ray feels odd, breaking in on some-body's bedroom like this, but doesn't know what else he could do. "Surprised I got past your bodyguards."

"They still out there? Must've been at it all night." With the mention of the two men on the porch, Mavis sits up, lifts his pillow, finds his billfold, and counts the bills. "Motherfuckers think I'm their banker."

"Ready to wash a car?"

"Aw, man. I thought you'd forgot."

"A deal's a deal. Tell you what, though. Make 'er shine, I'll spring for lunch at Manuel's. Come on, shake a leg."

While Mavis is sliding into a pair of jeans and a T-shirt, Billy Ray walks around the bed to take a closer look at the photographs on the wall. *Love Forever, Shanikah* is scribbled on the one of the young cheerleader. There is nothing written on the other.

"Who's the chick?"

"*Was* my girlfriend," says Mavis, now sitting on the cot, pulling on some socks.

"Must still be, if you're keeping her picture."

"She still around. Ain't around me no more, is all."

"What happened?"

"Hey, man—"

"Aw, hey, no, my fault. Sorry I asked."

"What the hell." He's in his sneakers now, tying the laces. "Ain't nobody exactly rich from McGill, understand what I'm saying, but this one's got it pretty good. Daddy owns a grocery store, got big plans for her. College and all that stuff. Plans don't include marryin' no football player that lives in Fatback."

"The other one's your mama, right?"

"Yeah. When things was better." Mavis looks up at the framed photo, his eyes lingering on it as though to say more, but drops it. Instead, he slaps a baseball cap on his head and darts for the door. "Let's blow. *Coach.* Gotta wash that thing 'fore somebody hauls it off to the dump."

...

On any other Saturday this time of the year, hoping to "get some rays," as she puts it, Rima would be sprawled out on a blanket in the grass wearing practically nothing, attracting randy teenaged boys cruising past in their pickups and jalopies to get a peek. Not so today. Everything is relative, of course, but this morning she is dressed downright demurely in jeans and sandals and a long-sleeved denim shirt, not wanting to give the boy the wrong idea, while she hoses down her kiln under the shade of the sweetgum tree in the side yard. With the football season coming on, she has dyed her hair purple in support of the McGill Purple Panthers.

When Billy Ray jumps the curb and wheels *Rosinante* onto the grass, causing Rima to rise halfway from her chores, smile, and wave, Mavis's eyes pop out. "That Miz Byrd, ain't it?"

"In some circles."

"What's *she* doin' here?"

"Tidying up the place, looks like."

"She your old lady?"

"I ain't that crazy, kid."

"Sure looks like it. Scrubbin' and stuff."

"Naw, naw. Just another tenant, behind in her rent." When *Rosinante* shudders to a halt in the yard, belching one more time, they dismount. Mavis lingers behind, nervously, while Billy Ray walks through the weeds to where Rima now stands, fully erect, wiping her brow with the back of her leather work gloves. "Wondered when you'd get around to cleaning that crap."

"Good morning to you, too, dear. I trust you slept well."

"You might give some thought to bulldozing the front room while you're up."

"Yes, sir. Aye-aye, sir. Anything for art, sir." Rima looks past Billy Ray to the kid, still hanging back, not sure how's he supposed to act upon seeing his art teacher away from the classroom. "Hi, Mavis. Where y'at?"

"Miz Byrd."

"I'm gonna try this one more time, Mavis. My name's Rima. Can we say 'Rima,' boys and girls?"

"Yes, ma'am."

"We'll have to keep working on that." She tosses the hose aside and pulls off her gloves, stuffing them into the hip pockets of her jeans. "Come on in, boys, while I rustle up some tea. Mavis, I want to show you something."

While Billy Ray goes to his side of the duplex, Rima opens the screen door to hers for Mavis, and the first thing he sees is one of her fanciful creations serving as a doorstop: a three-foot-tall ceramic penis with blue veins and a purple head with a smiley face, sprouting wings. It stops him in his tracks, has him looking wildly about for a graceful way to get the hell out of there, but she pulls him into the front room before he can bolt. She says nothing about the statue, instead drawing him by the elbow to the Ping-Pong table, standing upright on its side to serve as a giant easel, with four sheets of drawing paper taped side-by-side. They hold preliminary charcoal sketches of a football player in various poses: arm cocked to throw, stiff-arming a would-be tackler, kneeling on the sidelines, helmet off while he drinks from a ladle.

"Ta-*daaa*!" she says. "What do you think?"

"What's this?"

"You don't recognize this fella?"

"Well, it looks a little bit like, I don't know, man. This ain't supposed to be *me*, is it?"

"Thanks a heap, sport. Here you are, being eulogized before your time, and all I get's an 'I don't know, man.' I'm calling it 'Portrait of the Jock as a Young Man' right now. Maybe 'Young Stud,' 'African Prince,' something like that. That is, if you don't mind. I mean, I don't want to invade your privacy and all of that, you know. Say the word, I'll tear 'em up and forget about it."

"Aw, naw, I don't mean it like that. It just looks like, aw, you know, sort of rough-like."

"Don't you remember last year when I had y'all doing portraiture, starting out with sketches and then building from there? You were doing your girlfriend, what's-her-name. Pretty good stuff. Rough at first, just like this, but it was going somewhere."

"Yeah. Shanikah. We broke up, so I quit. Started doin' a cat instead. Ol' Malcolm, the one that hangs out in the gym."

Rima skitters a dinette chair across the floor and places it before the makeshift easel, front and center. From Billy Ray's side of the duplex, they hear the rumble and shudder of old galvanized plumbing, a toilet flushing. "Tell you what," she says, practically pushing Mavis down into the chair like an usher arranging the seating at a private art show. "Check 'em out while I fetch some iced tea, will you? I need your technical advice on some things." She heads toward the kitchen, then turns. "Oh, one thing, what's your number? Gotta put that on there."

"Ma'am?"

"Please. 'Rima.' What number do you wear? On your uniform."

"It was forty-five last year."

"Forty-five it is, then."

"Make that thirteen." They turn their heads to see Billy Ray clattering through the screened door, securing the fly of his jeans.

Rima says, "Unlucky thirteen? What's it gonna be, boys, forty-five or thirteen? I can't imagine anybody wanting to wear the number thirteen."

"Me and Tank just drew up the new numbers for this year. Forty-five's a fullback number. Anyway, we need to change the boy's luck. A new number might help."

"Whatever you say, ace."

With Rima rummaging through the refrigerator for the tea and some ice cubes, Billy Ray pulls up a stool and joins Mavis in front of the sketches. The boy seems embarrassed and flattered at the same time, cocking his head this way and that, not quite knowing what to say. "Fingers ain't quite right on the laces," he says. "Stiff-arm's all right. I like that pourin' water on my head. Don't know 'bout that kneelin' on the sidelines durin' a game.

Coach Thomas don't allow it." He leans back in the chair, scrunches up his face like a prune, takes a longer view. "She's pretty good, though."

"Whatever." Billy Ray is nonplused about Rima's sketches, doesn't understand the point, figures she must have gotten bored during the night and was looking for something to do. "She's okay, I guess."

Shooting a glance toward the kitchen, not seeing Rima, hearing the toilet flush instead, Mavis drops his voice to a whisper. "If she ain't your old lady, then, what's up?"

"I told you. She's just a tenant."

"But y'all next door to each other and all."

"Nothing's happening, believe me."

"Seen your wedding ring. You got a old lady *somewhere*."

"It's a long story, kid. I'll tell you all about it sometime. Right now, you owe me a car wash." Rima is back now, bearing tall gimme plastic cups, courtesy of the Clermont Lounge, full of iced tea. "Soon's we get this car washed," Billy Ray tells her, "I'm buying lunch at Manuel's. Ladies included. Maggie's coming in to join us."

"Maggie?" says Rima.

"You know, my daughter."

"Oh, I don't think so, ace."

"Aw, come on. You'll like her."

"I'm sure." It's the same look he has seen on Ginny's face, with the tight lips and all, a woman thoroughly put out with him. "I look like crap, and I've got things to do."

"We're talking a free lunch here."

"Thanks a bunch. Some other time."

...

Ever since Manuel Maloof was elected Chief Executive Officer of DeKalb County, a turn of events that continues to astound all of the professional politicians in Atlanta (a gruff second-generation Lebanese Melkite Catholic, and a Democrat to boot, who owns a saloon in a county full of

Baptist churches and blue-haired Republican ladies?), about the only time he can be found at his own establishment is on weekends. His brother and his sons are running the place these days, but on Saturdays the man himself is likely to be there, ensconced like a potentate at a big round oak table in the back room, arguing politics and sports with cops and Emory professors and plumbers and black and white activists from the Civil Rights days, now and then shuffling behind the bar to pull a few draft beers just to stay in practice. This is one of those days.

Billy Ray hears himself being hailed as he and Mavis come through the front door. "If you think you're gonna get a beer in here, you better think twice." It is Manuel, behind the bar, wiping his meaty hands with a towel.

"This a bar or an AA meeting?"

"Heard about your adventures."

"So'd I. They tell me I missed a hell of a show."

"Never thought I'd see the day the Gunslinger'd give up drinking." Manuel gives Mavis the once-over and nods toward the back room. "Got a pretty little thing waiting for you back there. Says she's a big fan of yours. I'll be with you in a minute."

With Mavis following him like a shadow, Billy Ray walks past the dark wood booths lining the wall opposite the long bar and turns left into a large smoky room crowded with tables where Georgia Tech students sit, sharing pitchers of beer and following a college football game on giant television sets suspended from the ceilings in every corner. "Daddy!" Maggie, auburn pigtails flying, hurls herself at him. They hug, he introduces her to Mavis, who seems to have been struck dumb all of a sudden, and the three of them take the big round table usually reserved for the cops from the nearby precinct.

Except for the call he made that morning to invite her to lunch, he has barely spoken to his daughter in a month. She's as perky as usual, seems happy enough to see him, but he has no idea what's been happening around the house in his absence. Does she miss him? Is Ginny still pissed? Do they talk about him at all? Is the Gun Room still there? He's got hundreds of questions, but they won't come. The lyrics to an old song hit him—*Please don't talk about me when I'm gone*—and all he can think to say is, with a cough, "Your car's still running okay, I guess. I mean, you made it here, didn't you?"

"It's fine, Daddy. Fine."

"Remember to get the oil changed regular."

"Oh, *Daddy.*"

"So"—*damn this*—"how's Mom? She okay?"

"Oh, she's great. Busy as usual, especially since school started."

"Oh, yeah, I almost forgot what I wanted to ask you." *What the hell is this, a first date?* "How'd that business about the band playing 'Dixie' turn out? I ain't seen anything else in the papers."

"We lost. Can you believe it? Bunch of Neanderthals. I swear, you'd think the Civil War is still going on."

Mavis has been following the exchange closely, as though he were watching a tennis match. This is a Coach Hunsinger he doesn't know about. Wife. Daughter. Car. School. Oil changes. Where's the Gunslinger, kneeling in the huddle, drawing plays in the dirt, saying motherfuckers-this and sonsabitches-that, raising hell when a play doesn't work, grabbing the ball and doing it himself? Now they're talking about some band playing "Dixie"? What the hell is this? He, Mavis Jackson, is thinking about the many places he would rather be at this moment when a waiter arrives and Billy Ray places the orders: chicken wings and a side of onion rings for Maggie, the Manuel's Burger for himself, the meat loaf blue-plate special for the kid. "Gotta fatten you up," Billy Ray is saying, just when Manuel arrives.

"So who we got here, Gun?"

"This here's my protege. Manuel, meet Mavis Jackson. Quarterback for the McGill Panthers."

"Protege? You're coaching now?"

"Well, sort of." This being all news to Maggie, she looks first at Mavis and then at her father, puts her elbows on the table and leans in as Billy Ray continues. "I still don't know how it happened, myself, but, yeah, I'm kinda helping out a little bit. Mavis here, he's got an arm you wouldn't believe, Manuel."

"That a fact?" Mavis wriggles under the gaze of Manuel, whose eyes are checking him out from head to feet. "He as good as you were?"

"Well, I don't know about that."

"Son"—Mavis jumps when Manuel taps him on the shoulder—"if you can throw a football *half* as good as the Gunslinger could when he was your age, I ought to invest some money in your career right now. *No*body, *no*where, *never,* could put on a show like the Gun. Lord have mercy, I used to go down to Grady Stadium on Friday nights just to watch him play. Billy Ray, you remember that story old Charlie Roberts did that night y'all killed Murphy? Something like, 'Even the light poles bowed their heads . . .'?" Billy Ray is about to finish it when a commotion breaks out and they all turn to see Bernice, the cook who has been there forever, descending on them with a pile of meat loaf and potatoes and collard greens big enough to serve three.

"Lord, Lord, it's one o' my babies," she says, plopping the plate in front of Mavis and then embracing him in a bear hug that nearly lifts him out of his chair.

"What are you *doing,* Bernice?" says Manuel. "We got waiters to deliver the food."

"Don't matter, Manuel. This is Mavis."

"And look at all that food. That's enough to choke a horse."

"We gon' put some meat on this boy's bones."

"Yeah, but hell, Bernice, I'm in business."

"You'll just have to take it out of my pay, then."

"You say you know this kid?"

"*Know* him? Lord, Manuel, where you been? You ain't heard 'bout the Touchdown Mamas from McGill High? We're goin' to heaven, and this is the boy that's gon' take us there. 'Mavis Jackson, he's a dream, he's the captain of our team.' *Yes*!!" Bernice hugs Mavis again, kissing him on the top of his head for good measure, then hustles back toward the kitchen. "Panther Power!" she yells as she walks away, pumping her fist, causing heads to turn throughout the place.

...

When they are finishing lunch, Maggie advises her father that the Robert E. Lee Rebels will be opening their season at home next Friday. "We've got a super halftime show planned. You're gonna love it."

"Aw, babe. I'm afraid I can't make it."

"Can't make it? What do you mean? You've never missed a home game yet."

"Like I said, I'm coaching for McGill now."

"I thought you were just helping Mavis. I didn't know you'd actually coach the games."

"Afraid so, babe."

"Daddy!"

"Sorry."

"Well, shoot." This is taking her some adjustment. "Tell you what. If he's as good as y'all say he is"—she shoots a dart at Mavis—"how about he just comes and plays for us. Our quarterback can't squat. Well, he can squat but when he does he can't get back up. Brian Jamison. *Boooo!* He's awful. Anyhow. See, it's simple. Just come on out to Crestwood right now, you and Mavis, and everything'll be perfect. We've got a quarterback and I've got my daddy back, and so there you go!"

"Honey, it doesn't work like that."

"I don't see why not. We've got a lot better school than McGill. That old place is about to fall down. Everybody knows that."

Billy Ray has to explain to his daughter what she already knows but doesn't want to admit. You have to go to school within your district, and the same applies for where athletes play. Besides, on the eve of the season, it's too late for a transfer. On top of all that, he tells her, Mavis is McGill and McGill is Mavis. "You have to dance with the one that brung you."

"Well, why don't you just come on home, then, Daddy? I miss you. Mom misses you, too, even if she won't admit it."

"Sorry, Mags, but it's too late for me, too."

Maggie decides to roll the dice. "It's that girlfriend, isn't it?" She settles back in her chair, crosses her arms, and awaits an answer.

At this, Mavis rises and asks Billy Ray for directions to the restroom. From the stricken look on the boy's face, there's no guarantee he'll be back. Billy Ray would like to go with him and keep on going. But duty calls.

"There's nothing there, Mags, believe me."

"Hah!"

"No, listen."

"I'll just bet!"

"Listen, sweetheart." It seems hot in here. He flaps his T-shirt to create a breeze. "No girlfriend, no lover, no nothing like that. Your mom kicked me out, I had to live somewhere, and since I own the dump that's where I went. No hanky-panky. No foolishness. Really."

"Nice try, Daddy."

"You'd like her, Mags, you really would."

"That does it," she says, slamming her napkin to the table, shoving her chair away. "I'm outta here."

And then she's gone, just like that, leaving Billy Ray with a tab to pay and another mess to clean up. He looks everywhere for Mavis, finally finding him in the kitchen sitting on a stool and devouring a bowl of banana custard under the matronly watch of Bernice, grandmother of Melvin ("T-Bone") Williams, stalwart offensive center for the McGill Panthers.

THIRTEEN

Well, folks, a lot's been going on since I talked to y'all last week. Remember how I was talking about how there wadn't no way the Gunslinger would ever stoop to coaching, especially baby-sitting a bunch of little old high school boys that don't hardly know an X from an O? Turns out the joke's on me. You're now listening to the unofficial, unpaid, unrecognized, unappreciated, un-whatever part-time offensive coordinator for the McGill High School Panthers football team. I don't exactly understand how the hell it happened, pardon my French, but here I am. By the way, the name of that quarterback I was talking about, the one that's walking around with a six-shooter on the end of his arm, it's Mavis, Mavis Jackson, and the deal is I'm supposed to show the boy everything I know about throwing a football. All I can say is, Aw, naw, man, don't throw me in that brierpatch. Turns out, I kinda miss it, you know. Boys sweating and yelling and banging away at each other, having a good old time. Can't say I miss the pain, whether it's getting plowed under by a whole defensive line or just losing. But anyway, I'm back at it for a while, trying to pass on to this kid whatever I can remember, so that's the latest from these parts. Lookie here now, would you, looks like I woke up the troops. Line one, talk to me.

...

Hallelujah, brother.

Sounds like the Rev to me.

Reverend T. Vivian Beaumont here, First Calvary AME Revival Assembly.

How come hallelujah, Rev?

We been prayin' for you, Brother Hunsinger. Waiting for you to answer the call, if you understand what I'm saying.

Well, I don't. Who's we, anyway?

Don't suppose Coach Graves told you, but I'm the chaplain for the McGill Panthers.

Didn't know that, Rev, although I can't say I'm surprised they've got their own personal preacher.

In these coming times of trial and tribulation, these young men are gon' need the Lord on their side.

What I've seen so far, this bunch is gonna need more'n that.

There's a lot of us out here that maybe you don't know about, doing the best we can to help these boys find their mission in life.

Ask me, be a big help if God can block.

He probably can, in His mysterious ways, Mister Hunsinger. There's people like the Touchdown Mamas, His servants on earth, trying to make all things possible.

Oh, yeah. The Touchdown Mamas.

You heard about the Mamas?

How 'bout hanging up, Rev. I oughta tell the folks out there what we're talking about.

You have a nice evening now, you hear?

I'll do that, Rev. Now, see, folks, I took the boy to lunch at Manuel's Tavern yesterday, and out of nowhere here comes this cook, Bernice something or other, and she starts making over Mavis like she's the mama this boy ain't got, says she's a Touchdown Mama. Got a grandson playing for us named Melvin, Melvin Williams, but we all call him T-Bone since he looks like he just had about four of 'em for breakfast. Soon's I got home I called Tank Graves to find out what that's all about. Found out they're a bunch of mamas and grandmamas that's got kids playing for McGill High and they help 'em out. Cook the pre-game meals, wash the uniforms, root for 'em at the games, all of that good stuff. In my time, which is longer ago that I'd like to talk about, that's what your regular mamas and papas would do, but there you go. Things change. I mean this boy, Mavis, hell, you wouldn't believe it. Ain't got no daddy. Mama's in the hospital. Lives over in Fatback, if you know where that's at, pretty bad place, more or less takes care of himself. The way it works out, there's this kind of community thing going where everybody's behind the McGill Panthers, the Forrest Panthers when I was there, like it was their team or something. All I can say is, Go, Panthers, beat Cross Keys, which is who we play Friday night. What time is that, anyway? Yeah, here it is, seven-thirty, Grady Stadium. Hope God shows up to help out. Line two, where y'at?

...

Hey there, Gun?

Speaking.

I keep up a little with high school football around here, and I got to wish you lots of luck. That McGill team's B-double-B bad.

Now you're gonna get my back up, bubba. It's okay if I say it, understand, but these are my boys you're talking about. Them's fighting words.

Check it out, Gun. They was four and six last year, couldn't beat nobody that counted. The way I hear it, they graduated the only good ones they had except that kid quarterback you keep talking about. Then they lost that tailback to Lee High. Don't think I'd be putting my money on 'em just yet.

Lemme know if you change your mind, pardner, 'cause I know some things you don't. For one thing, we got some new players this year that don't nobody know about. Wadn't nobody around to catch Mavis last year, but I guaran-dam-tee you these boys can. I don't know how he did it, but Tank

159

Graves talked half the basketball team into playing this year. Another thing is, it could be these boys have been down so long they're tired of looking up. We had a practice the other day that, Lord God, you should've seen it. Even scared me, and I've seen some hurt *in my time. This ain't no bunch of little old pussy-cat white boys we've got here. These boys have had it rough. Know what I mean? This other coach they got, name of Pig Thomas, he knows where they're coming from. Runs practice like it was the first day at Parris Island, gets 'em so riled up they're ready to go to war. Matter of fact, with this first game coming up next weekend, we're gonna have to go back to messing around in shorts all week before they kill each other.*

I'll keep that in mind, Gun. In spite of what I said, though, I got to admit I love to watch these kids play. The ones from what they call the inner city, you know? These boys put on a show. Them marchin' bands, all that celebratin' they do when they score, the whole package.

Yeah, but I'm trying to get 'em to tone it down a little, you know. Stay cool. Quit acting like that's the first time they ever saw the end zone.

But that's the fun of it, don't you see? Hell, this ain't the pros. It's high school. I gotta go, Gun. Keep up the good work.

...

Line three, you been waiting for awhile.

You've certainly changed your tune in a hurry, ain't you? The NAACP must've got to you.

Who's this?

Never mind. Just call me a concerned citizen.

You sound like one, all right. What's bugging you, bubba?

Why don't we just call a spade a spade? You keep talking about these poor colored boys from the so-called inner city. Hell, everybody knows it ain't nothing but nigger football. Them colored kids ain't never had no discipline and they never will . . .

Whooaa, there, bubba. Back off. If you've got anything done today it was to get my telephone lit up like the Fourth of July.

160

Seems like yesterday you was talkin' 'bout the Fal-coons, tellin' it like it is, and now look at you.

What can I say, my man? I've already gone through this before. Things look different when you get up close for a look. You might ought to try it.

Hell, I know the facts already. Half of these spooks are gon' be dead or in prison in two years.

Let me issue you a personal invitation, my friend. Friday night at Grady Stadium, McGill versus Cross Keys. I'll leave you a ticket, okay? Gimme your name.

I ain't nuts. If I did go to watch a game at Grady, I can guaran-dam-tee you I'd leave my hubcaps at home. What're you, a Communist or some-thing? I ain't talkin' to you no more, you damned turncoat.

Ouch. Look here, folks, from the look of all these callers lined up, I know all of y'all would like put in your two cents' worth, but I don't think we ought to be wasting our time on that old boy. Spider says there's a lady that's got something else on her mind. Line three, is it?

...

Am I on?

Yes'm, go ahead.

Mister Hunsinger, there's been all of this talk tonight of violence, and it concerns me.

That's probably what they're saying at Cross Keys High along about now, ma'am. They got a week to think about it.

No, I'm being serious. Are these the proper lessons to be imparting to our young men, with all of the violence going on in the world as it is? Don't we have enough?

Ma'am. I reckon I understand where you're coming from and I respect it. It'd be nice if everybody'd be nice to each other, but it don't always work out like that. Coming from where these boys do, if you turn the other cheek you're gonna get your head busted. Ma'am? Must've lost her. Line what? Line four it is.

My goodness. That nasty man. Whatever became of the City Too Busy to Hate? I thought we had made some progress in race relations in Atlanta since Doctor King laid down his life. Anyway, with all of that aside, Mister Hunsinger, didn't you mention last week that you recently underwent some personal pain in your life, lost a loved one, perhaps, and what carried you through were the lessons you learned from your old coach?

Yes, ma'am, I did.

Would you care to elucidate on that?

You're one of the Ansley Park ladies, ain't you?

I live on The Prado, yes. How would you know?

We don't get to elucidate *much around here.*

But you know what it means. I get the idea that you're a lot smarter than you let on to be. I loved your story about Dizzy Dean and the school-teachers, by the way. I grew up in St. Louis and I remember when that happened. At any rate, would you tell us more about your coach's advice? Did someone die? What happened?

I really don't want to talk about it, ma'am.

Maybe some other time, then.

Yeah. Yes, ma'am.

Oh. One more thing. You also mentioned that these poor kids at McGill don't have much training equipment now that the school's closing down.

You wouldn't happen to have any blocking sleds around the house, would you?

Well, no, of course not.

I'm just kidding, ma'am.

But I do have a rowing machine.

No kidding? Those things are great for conditioning. Make you hurt all over as much as anywhere else. You into rowing, are you?

My husband was, but he left it when he died. It's just sitting here now. If you can get someone to come by and pick it up, it's yours.

That's great. I know somebody that's got a good pickup truck. Tell you what, don't hang up. Give your address to Spider, my trusty engineer here, and we'll take you up on it, okay? We got time for one more call, folks. Line whatever it is.

...

I've got some boxing gloves, if they'll help.

How'd a nice lady like you wind up with boxing gloves?

Beats me.

Beats me. That's good, lady. Real good.

Well, thank you. Maybe if the boys want to duke it out sometimes. Is that right? Duke it out?

Stop it, lady, you're killing me.

I thought, if Eleanor can donate a rowing machine, I should be able to do something for the boys, myself.

You two are neighbors?

Next door to each other.

In Ansley Park, you say?

You've got yourself a regular fan club down here, if you didn't know it, Billy Ray. Is it okay if I call you that?

Be my guest. I've been called worse.

No, really. Ever since we discovered your show, we've been gathering at somebody's house every Sunday night just to listen.

Well, if that don't beat all.

There's just nothing else worth listening to at night.

Lemme guess. Your husbands are out of town, and you don't do the disco clubs no more. Frankly, I'm shocked. You hussies, you.

Oh, you kidder.

You like it when I talk dirty, right?

You're the man, Billy Ray. You're the man. Now don't forget to take my address, you hear?

Just give it to Spider and we'll be there. Thanks for calling in, ma'am.

Wait, wait. Margaret wants to talk to you. She's got a—what?—she's got one of those Nautilus machines for you that builds up the legs. Here, let me put her on. It's Margaret. I'll let her tell you about it herself. . . .

FOURTEEN

voiding the office of the principal, Clarice Robbins, is easy
enough. All you have to do is drive around back and park next to
the Music Building, which is what he does on this Monday afternoon, slipping right into the gym without having to wear a visitor's badge
like a suspected pervert or drug pusher. When he pushes through the doors
marked Football he hears a whirring sound and sees Pig Thomas pumping
away on an exercise bike in the corner of the room; bald head glistening
with sweat, teeth gleaming, sheer ecstasy in his eyes. It reminds Billy Ray
of the Christmas when he got his first bike.

"You tough enough, coach?" Pig says.

"Depends on what for."

"Got a long season ahead of us."

"Yeah, but I ain't gonna be playing. Where'd the bike come from?"

"Georgia Tech. Truck rolled up this morning with all kinds of stuff.
Couple of these bikes, real barbells, towels, must be ten miles worth of tape,
even some crutches. This ain't nothing, though. You oughta see what's on
the field. We got some real blocking sleds now."

"Tech? What's this all about?"

"I figured you were behind it."

Billy Ray has to think about this. "I might've said something on the radio about the piss-poor facilities here, if you can call 'em that. Hell, I don't know. When I get to going I talk about a lot of things. Far as I know, there ain't nobody listening."

"Looks like somebody at Tech did, anyway. The boys that brought it said they found the stuff sitting in a warehouse over there." Pig dismounts and wipes his face on a gold towel embroidered with the GT logo.

Billy Ray says, "It's too damned late for their apologies."

"I don't follow you, Gun."

"Sonsabitches wouldn't even give me a look when I was being recruited. Homeboy, too. Can you believe it?"

"Well, that was before my time."

"Where's Tank at, anyway? He napping again?"

"Oh, yeah, I was supposed to tell you," says Pig, now casting his eyes on the jumble of newly arrived barbells. "He wants to see you up at the principal's office."

...

This doesn't look good. Even before he reaches the office, Billy Ray can see through the glass double doors that Mavis is sitting on the sofa, being consoled by the matronly secretary. She has taken him to her ample bosom and is stroking him, cooing to him, letting him talk.

"It hurt my heart," Billy Ray hears the boy saying when he enters the anteroom.

"There, there, child," says the secretary.

"I been doin' the best I could."

"I know, I know."

"They got to give me another chance."

"You poor baby."

Billy Ray lets the doors close behind him. "I don't know about the 'baby' part." When they look up to see him, the secretary starts bawling and

Mavis tries to conceal that he's been crying. "What the hell, kid. We give you a day off and you get in trouble?"

"Wadn't my fault," says Mavis.

"No, it certainly wasn't," says the secretary. "There, there, now."

"Will somebody please tell me what's going on around here?"

"They in there, waitin' for you," she says, nodding toward the closed door leading to the principal's office.

...

He is taken aback to see what appears to be a full-scale board meeting in progress. Seated around a long oval table, one he remembers well from his days of being hauled onto the carpet for skipping class or otherwise disrupting the orderly flow of academic life, is a grim collection of eight people from his immediate past. At the head of the table near the door there is Clarice Robbins; at the other end, Tank Graves. Down the left side are Frankie Lorino, Rima Byrd, and, of all people, B. D. Spotswood. Seated across from them are Scottie Burns, with a shit-eating grin on his face; Bernice, the cook from Manuel's; and a large affable man in a shiny black suit and a silver tie whom Billy Ray has never seen before. They seem to have been caught in mid-sentence when he opened the door, and now they all sit staring at him as though he has interrupted a prayer meeting or maybe a poker game.

"Deuces are wild," he says, trying for some humor, but nobody laughs or even smiles at him. Out of the corner of his eyes, he sees Tank Graves running a finger across his lips as though to say, *Zip it.*

"Please be seated, Mister Gunn," Clarice Robbins says, officiously, indicating the empty chair beside her.

"Hell, I could've baked a cake. Anybody remember to bring the cole slaw?" Still no response. This time Tank is slowly moving his head from side to side, putting his finger to his lips. *Sit down and shut up.* As Billy Ray is plopping into the chair with a thud, the principal is busying herself with a bulky old tape recorder in front of her on the table. *Click*. She has engaged the Record button.

"Testing, testing, testing," she says. She hacks to clear a glob of phlegm from her throat. "These are the official proceedings of the case against—"

"What is this, a kangaroo court?"

"There are regulations we must follow, Mister Gunn."

"Get the honkie, right?"

Paying him no mind, Clarice Robbins plunges ahead. "Mister Gunn," she says, leaning forward and speaking directly into a microphone mounted on a flimsy tripod, "it's come to my attention that you are not exactly a credit to your race"—here she pauses for effect, proud of herself, drawing a chuckle from the imposing black man in the shiny suit—"nor are you, more to the point of our investigation, the sort of man that our *chill-ren* can look up to as a role model."

"What the hell business is this of yours—"

"Later, Mister Gunn," she says. "You'll have your opportunity to speak in due time. Now. Here are the charges. Number one, that you are an alcoholic who spends his days with other drunks at Manuel's Tavern, that, that *saloon* on Highland Avenue. Two, that you use the Lord's name in vain. Number three, that you are subsisting without any visible means of financial support. Four, that you have left your wife and child to fend for themselves in order to live in sin with another woman. Fifthly and finally, that you now reside, with your meager belongings, in slum housing of your own making. You have the right to respond to these charges, although, frankly, the initial evidence we have gathered seems overwhelmingly against you. How pleadeth ye?"

"It don't seem to matter much. Hell, this is an inquisition. Guilty until proven innocent, right?"

"It's just a hearing of the facts, Mister Gunn."

"Well, I ain't hearing no facts here. You've got everything all mixed up." Billy Ray frantically looks at Ben Burns. "Hey, Scottie, is this one of those AA interventions? Come on, buddy, tell her. I'm clean." Burns merely smiles back at him, indicating nothing.

"Is that your plea, then, Mister Gunn? 'Not guilty'?"

"Hey, wait a minute. Now I get it. You don't want me hanging around the football team, right? Afraid I might teach 'em bad habits."

"These are among the issues under discussion, yes."

"Well, I got news for you, lady. You can't fire me if you never hired me. Right, Tank? Help me out here, buddy."

"Listen up, Gun." It is Tank Graves, finally breaking his silence. "Listen up."

Clarice Robbins shuffles through a pile of papers in front of her, then looks around the room. "On the other hand, while I was in the process of gathering evidence, I was able to contact these witnesses you see before you. To a man, and to a *woman*"—she glares in disgust at Rima, who perks up and grins like a cat with bird feathers in her mouth—"all of these people have refuted the charges. In fact, they say that none of what I heard is true. We'll go around the table now. Mister *Lorenzo*?"

Billy Ray feels like the celebrity guest in the old television show, *This Is Your Life*, where everybody he has ever known, from old girlfriends to grandchildren, pops from behind a curtain to say wonderful things about him. The catch here is that, except for old Frankie Lorino and Tank Graves from the old days, he has vaguely known most of these people for just a few months. Although the question of why he is being treated like this is quite another matter, he knows that they can go either way, for him or against him. *This is gonna be good.* He leans forward, both elbows on the table.

Frankie Lorino, slumped like a gnome in his chair to the left of Clarice Robbins, obviously would rather be at the store. "Well, I've known Billy since—"

"Speak up, please! State your name, who you are, and address the microphone."

"All right. I'm Frank Lorino. I own the store up the street. Like I said, I've known Billy since he was a student and a football player for the school when it was called Forrest High. My wife and I always loved Billy like he was our own son. I lost track of him over the years, but he's a good boy. One day it was raining hard and he volunteered to take the boy home because he felt sorry for him. That's Mavis. The boy."

"Thank you, Mister Lorenzo. Next?"

They proceed around the table, and soon Billy Ray is sitting back, enjoying the show. *This Is Your Life*, indeed. Scottie Burns testifies that he has never seen a man turn his life around so effortlessly, describing Billy Ray as "a man of great fortitude, the utmost honesty, yeah, verily, a man for all seasons." B. D. Spotswood, testifying that Billy Ray is, indeed, a paid employee of his station, has to be cut off when he spirals off into a commercial about the soaring prospects at WWJD ever since Billy Ray came aboard. Bernice verifies that Mister Gunn paid for Mavis's meal Saturday at Manuel's, like he was the boy's father, and assures everyone that he was, indeed, drinking only iced tea, no beer. The man in the suit—"Reverend T. Vivian Beaumont, First Calvary AME Revival Assembly, also chaplain to the McGill High football team"—has to be stopped in the middle of an impassioned sermon about the joys of watching a brother finally seeing the light. Tank says that the mere presence of the Gunslinger on the Purple Panthers' playing field has given these boys, particularly young Mavis Jackson, renewed hope that there is a future in their lives. Finally, Rima brings some levity to the proceedings by saying it's foolish to think that there might be some hanky-panky going on between them when "some old guy Billy Ray's age can't be expected to, like, you know, *perform,*" drawing laughs and downright guffaws from everyone around the table except Clarice Robbins and Billy Ray.

...

When the merriment has subsided, Clarice turns off the tape recorder and says, without a trace of emotion, "So you seem to have been absolved, Mister Gunn. Congratulations."

"Well, that's a load off," says Billy Ray, hiking up his jeans with a thumb in the belt loop. "That means I get to keep a job I never had."

"Not so fast, Mister Gunn. There's more."

"You're gonna start paying me, right?"

"In fact, yes. It's only a pittance, you understand, but that doesn't seem to be an issue with you. We need to make your employment official, you see, get it onto the records. We're prepared to pay a dollar a year for your services."

"I take all this crap for a buck a year? Excuse *me,* lady."

"It's only paperwork. Surely, you'll take it."

Whatever this is all about, he would like to drag it out, make *them* sweat for a change, but then they might change their minds. "What the hell," he says, reaching down to scratch his crotch. "If the lovely Miz *Byrd* here keeps paying her rent on time, I'm okay."

"Good. That's settled, then. Now for the *real* business, Mister Gunn. We have a situation that came up over the weekend, and we need your help." Then she lays it out. There was another ruckus in Fatback on Sunday morning, she says, so bad that the police finally showed up. They went inside the house at 745 Dixiana to check things out. What they found was this teenaged boy, asleep at the time, apparently an orphan raising himself without any proper adult supervision whatsoever. The police reported it to the Department of Family and Children Services, whose workers showed up and were appalled by what they saw, resulting in a phone call this very Monday morning to her, Clarice Robbins, the principal of McGill High. "We've got to find this boy, Mavis Jackson, a home," she says. "Not tomorrow, not next month. Right now. This minute."

Billy Ray bolts up from his chair like a rocket leaving a launching pad. "Oh, no. *Hell,* no."

"Just for a little while, Mister Gunn" she says.

"Football season, Gun, that's all," says Tank Graves. "We'll get you plenty of help."

"But he's gotta have some kinfolks *somewhere.*"

"Ain't nobody, Gun, unless you want to count those 'uncles' hangin' around the house."

"God *damn.* Well, how 'bout the Touchdown Mamas? Bernice? He's one of y'all's. You were making all over him the other day."

"Not me, mister. I got so many grandbabies I can't count 'em. Don't even know half of 'em's names."

"How about the others, then?"

"Same thing. That's why we're called the Mamas."

"How 'bout you, Rev? Ain't this what churches are for?"

"Souls, Brother Hunsinger. Not stomachs."

"Frankie?"

"Stomachs, Billy, not souls."

"Hey, lookie here now"—around the table, he sees nothing but smiling faces—"I've been railroaded. This whole deal's been a setup, right? Sucker me in, then try to make a baby-sitter out of me."

"You're our only hope, Mister Gunn."

"If that's the way it is," says Billy Ray, "then this place is in worse shape than I thought."

...

At dusk that day, the clothes he has brought with him from the house still slung over his shoulder on hangers, Mavis sniffs and pokes around Billy Ray's side of the duplex like a cat in strange new surroundings. Walking through the dusty living room with its ratty used sofa and matching side chairs and the big television set and not much else, past a kitchen spilling over with unwashed pots and pans and dishes, down a hallway strewn with dirty clothes tossed where they were shed, past the front bedroom dominated by the garish unmade French Provincial bed left behind by Walter and Robbie, the kid is stopped short when Billy Ray opens the door to the back bedroom, formerly known as the Bunkroom. It is knee-deep in a sea of smelly sleeping bags, futons, wire hangers, cushions, stained pillows, blankets, sheets, newspapers, magazines, empty boxes, and all of the other detritus remaining from The Ranch's heyday as a house of orgiastic joys and revelries.

"Place looks like crap, man," says Mavis.

"I kinda got behind on my housecleaning," Billy Ray tells him. "Busy weekend, you know."

"You expect me to live like this?"

"Last I heard, you ain't got much choice, sport."

"I thought white folks was better'n this. *Shit.* You live like a pig."

"I'll ignore that." Billy Ray kicks the door fully open and deposits the cardboard box full of Mavis's other belongings on the floor. "There's one of those hippie whatchamacallits, a futon, somewhere under all that stuff. We might want to go back and get that rollaway you were sleeping on, for a bed."

"That's all right. I ain't gon' be here long, anyway. Soon's my mama gets home, I'll be outta here."

"Suit yourself." They hear Rima calling from the front door, back from a run through the take-out window of a barbecue joint on Moreland Avenue. "Why, there's Mom right now, just in time with dinner," Billy Ray says. "Welcome home, son."

...

It's been a day fraught with parrying, raised eyebrows, unfinished questions, silences. The man and the boy have hardly spoken to each other since being called together and given their orders, as it were, with instructions to do the best they can with an imperfect solution to an unfortunate situation. During the light practice of the afternoon—no more pads this week in order to avoid injuries—Mavis went through the motions and Billy Ray merely watched and made suggestions from time to time. Then, wordlessly, Billy Ray drove the wagon to the house on Dixiana and helped Mavis strip his room of the clothes he wanted and the photos on the wall and any other treasures the old drunks on the block might steal in his absence.

Now, having feasted on the barbecue, Billy Ray and Rima are rocking gently in the front-porch swing, listening to the traffic and watching the fireflies play, while Mavis tries to make something of the bedroom he has inherited.

"Well, Mom, here we are."

"Hi, Dad."

"Kinda weird, ain't it?"

"You know," says Rima. "I can't help wondering what your wife would think about all of this. You ever think about that?"

"Sure."

"Miss her?"

"I guess." Billy Ray hears hammering from the back room. *Hanging pictures. That's a start.* "Sure, I miss her. I mean, hell, seems like we've been married forever. What's the line from that song, 'I've grown accustomed to her face'? Aw, Christ, it's more'n that. I love her. I just screwed up, that's all. Can't blame her a bit, now that I've had time to look back at everything. I was a sorry-ass no-good motherfucking wall-to-wall sonofabitch."

"That certainly seems to cover all of the bases," she says. "But you're a lot better now, don't you think?"

"Ninety percent, at least."

"Why not a hundred?"

"Nobody's a hundred percent happy, girl. You know that. There's always some spooks to keep you awake at night. Things you've done, things that just happened, stuff that won't never go away. The way I look at it, ninety percent ain't bad at all."

"Well, hoss, I've been thinking"—she has finished a beer and is cracking another—"thinking *again*. It's always dangerous when Rima the Bird-Girl starts playing philosopher. Anyway, what I've been thinking is how we might be killing two birds with one stone here. You know? The preacher and that ghastly principal keep talking about saving this boy's life and his soul, giving him a future, but I don't see anybody talking about you. The big bad Gunslinger. Ol' Billy Ray. *The Man.* We might be saving two lives here, you know, not just one. Is this neat, or what?"

"*Neat?* We're the Odd Couple. Apples and oranges. Bluebirds and redbirds. An Eskimo and a hula-dancer."

"Come on, sport. You're both jocks."

"Yeah, one coming, one going."

"But you can *learn* from each other. Don't you see?"

"What the hell can I learn from this truant besides boosting hubcaps and dodging bullets? Hunh? He's a kid. He don't know anything. I've barely got my own act together, and now I'm supposed to be his daddy? What the hell kind of thinking is that?" He's too tired to talk about it anymore. Maybe tomorrow. "Anyway," he says, getting to his feet, "I've been doing some thinking, myself."

"Now *that's* dangerous. What?"

"Your rent's late again, that's what."

"Oh, didn't I tell you?" she says. "It's in the mail."

"Right. That's what Walter and Robbie kept saying."

He pats her on the head, like a father would his daughter, stretches and yawns, mumbles a goodnight, then goes inside. Hearing no more sounds from the back bedroom, he shuffles down the hall in his bare feet to check on the boy, curious to see what he's made of the mess. In one corner, piled nearly to the ceiling, he finds that Mavis has neatly stacked all of those extra blankets and sleeping bags and cushions. In another corner are two cardboard boxes, one full of wire hangers and magazines and newspapers, the other with usable sheets and pillowcases that need to be washed. On a laundry table borrowed from Rima, neatly folded, are the few clean clothes he brought with him. In the closet, his scant dress-up clothes, the jacket and the shirts and the trousers, hang evenly spaced on a bar. The boy himself sleeps atop the one salvageable futon in his jeans and T-shirt, below the framed photographs he has nailed to the wall. Mother, team, Martin Luther King Jr., Bo Jackson, girlfriend. Like it or not, it's the only family he's got.

FIFTEEN

The new regimen at The Ranch begins the very next morning when Billy Ray assembles a breakfast of scrambled eggs, grits, sausage links, toast, orange juice, and milk to get the kid's day off right. Jostled awake at daybreak, complaining at first, Mavis goes through twenty minutes' worth of calisthenics—pushups, situps, then leg-lifts to strengthen his quadriceps—before eating and showering and dressing for school. Next door, Rima has been putting together a sack lunch for the boy, sure to be an improvement over whatever the school cafeteria would have to offer that day. At a few minutes after eight, Rima and Mavis are wheeling away to school in her pickup truck. Billy Ray stands on the doorstoop, waving goodbye to them, feeling like a househusband.

He's tired already. Wake up the boy, make sure he does the exercises, lay out some clean towels in the bathroom, cook breakfast while the shower runs, drag him to the table, make small talk about the day ahead, promise a steak dinner at night after practice, be sure he's got his school books, advise him to keep his nose clean. Thousands of mothers and children throughout the city must have been going through the same routine this very morning, including Ginny and Maggie, but they're used to it. He doesn't even own an apron.

Only now, alone with the whole day ahead of him, can he fully ponder what the circumstances have wrought. He hears Rima's observation from the night before—*Is this neat, or what?*—and that's what kept him up late and got him up early. It's been *too* neat. He still can't figure how it came about that all of those disparate people happened to converge on that room at the same time, without his knowing anything about it. The presence of the principal and the coach and the team chaplain made some sense, each of them having a more or less official vested interest in Mavis's welfare, but he can't say the same of the others. Well, okay, maybe they were character witnesses: Scottie to swear the Gun is sober now, B. D. to attest that he gets a paycheck every week, Rima to say that the two of them aren't exactly living in sin, Frankie Lorino with a story about how Billy Ray had driven the kid home in the rain, even a Touchdown Mama to testify that she saw him buy the kid a lunch. It reeks of a setup.

Just like that, any way you cut it, he has become a foster parent without any portfolio whatsoever. The only things to recommend him as a temporary guardian for Mavis are that the two of them seem to get along and he, Billy Ray, is old enough to be the boy's father. That's it. There is nothing else he can think of that would merit the unadulterated praise he heard flying around that table from people who know him only in the most tenuous sense: a recovering alcoholic, an adoring fan who happens to be his employer, some kind old Italian grocer from his high school years, a black short-order cook, a hippie "artist" who could be arrested any day now for creating and selling pornography.

He's a coach, not a parent, but he has to admit that having his pupil living under the same roof enhances the teaching process. This way, like an eager son and a doting father, they can wake up and go to bed talking football. Which reminds him: he should run out to the house in Crestwood and fetch the projector and the film of the Alabama game, and that piece of Nautilus equipment the Ansley Park lady offered can do wonders for the boy's leg. He allows himself to fancy what things can be like. Rima is book-smart, what with her Agnes Scott education and always reading the New York *Times*, so maybe she can help the boy with his classwork. He'll stuff him with meat and potatoes as long as he can stand the kitchen. They'll dissect the college and pro football games on television as students of the game, not fans, a coach tutoring his prized student on the finer points of the game. That's the stuff, that's his mandate. Fatten him up, strengthen his body, keep the grades up, tame all of that raw talent, make the boy the best he can be. Then, who knows who might come knocking at the door.

...

At Manuel's, hamburgers on the way, Billy Ray and Scottie Burns guzzle iced tea and reconstruct the events of the day before at the school principal's office.

"Ol' B. D. did seem a little nervous, come to think of it," Billy Ray is saying. "That principal's enough to scare anybody."

"No, it was all those black folks in one room, plain and simple," says Scottie.

"Aw, hell, he ain't that bad."

"You didn't see his Cadillac out front?"

"Naw, I went through the back door."

"His hubcaps were gone. He told me he took 'em off and put 'em in the trunk before he came to town."

"Ain't that something. B. D.'s all right, he just don't get out much." Billy Ray sees Bernice grinning and waving at him from the kitchen, and waves back. "I'm curious, though. Where do you know him from?"

"I get around. I know lots of people. This Rima, hell, everybody knows about the Bird-Girl. I've been stopping by Frankie Lorino's place for years, for Cokes and stuff, cigarettes when I smoked. Bernice"—he, too, is waving at her—"anybody who ever ate at Manuel's knows Bernice."

"That don't explain the Rev. Y'all acted like old pals."

"The civil rights days, Gun. I didn't just stand back when it hit the fan, you know. I was there at the Pettus Bridge in Selma in 'sixty-five. Got me a pretty good bump on my head for my troubles. Why are you asking?"

"Well, the whole deal just seemed odd to me, is all. It seemed like a setup, an ambush, the way that thing got rubber-stamped. I mean, who put all of that together?"

"You're paranoid," says Scottie. "I don't see how it matters, anyway. You just said the boy's taking it well. You seem to be okay with it."

"I just like to be in charge of things, is all. Calling the signals. Old quarterback, all of that. It was the Rev, wasn't it? Come on, Scottie."

"Team chaplain. What can I say?"

"Frankie Lorino."

"As McGill High goes, so goes his business."

"Okay, it was Rima."

"The girl had to defend her honor, for God's sake."

"Spotswood, then. How the hell do you explain him coming in all the way from Austell?"

"Between you and me"—Scottie looks around and drops his voice—"B. D.'s money trail's been pretty messy ever since he started getting contracts while they were building I-20."

"So it was blackmail, then."

Scottie says, "Could be. I just don't know. You've gotta remember, the guy's loved your ass ever since that Bama game."

"That seems like a hell of a lot of trouble to go to, just to rope me into being this boy's daddy."

"Look, Billy Ray. It worked. Everybody's happy. This kid can be something, and you're gonna help him. The Gunslinger lives." Scottie reaches across the booth and cuffs Billy Ray on the shoulder. "So. How's it going with Ginny? You seen her lately?"

...

It's Picture Day for the McGill Panthers, pretty exciting stuff for kids who've been pummeling each other for the better part of a month, and when they gather on the field in their clean new uniforms it's as though they have to introduce themselves to each other. They have four color combinations they will wear during the ten-game season—all-purple with white numbers, all-white with purple numbers, purple pants and white jerseys, white pants and purple jerseys—and the latter set has been chosen for the team and individual photos to be taken on this day. The Atlanta *Journal-Constitution* and the weekly DeKalb County *Neighbor* have sent photographers, and they are joined by two dozen girlfriends and siblings and parents who have brought cameras of their own.

While Pig Thomas tries to calm them down and get them seated for the team photo, Herman Graves and Billy Ray sit in the shade of the canopied golf cart watching the proceedings.

"Everything okay with the boy?" says Herman.

"Could be better, could be worse, Tank. Ain't no telling how long it's been since he slept in a real bed and had a real breakfast."

"He slept and ate all right, then?"

"Like an honored guest. Can't say the same for myself. I didn't get any sleep 'til he left for school."

"Ah, well"—Tank lifts one cheek off the padded seat to fart, a thunderclap, enough to turn heads—"I figure y'all can work it out. Didn't expect everything to be perfect the first day. Y'all are too much alike. Sorry about how we did all this, by the way."

"Thanks, Tank, thanks a whole heap. Hell, all I wanted to do was help a kid throw a football. Now look what you've got me into. It was a lot more fun just being an ordinary drunk, hanging around the house, watching old films, taking out the garbage."

"See there? Made you a better man already." Having apologized the best he can, Herman gets back to Mavis. "He do his work this morning?"

"Aw, hell, he's a regular leg-lifting fool. Kid *loves* it."

"He's gon' be all right, Gun. Boy's been taking care of himself for a long time."

"Things have been happening so fast, I haven't even asked about last year," says Billy Ray. "How'd he do? What were his stats?"

"Pretty bad, if you just look at the numbers. Didn't complete but forty-eight percent of his passes. Might've been sixty or thereabouts if we'd had anybody who could catch the ball. Seventy if he'd had more protection and knew where he was throwing it."

"Touchdowns and interceptions?"

"Awful. Something like twenty touchdowns and thirty interceptions."

"Sacks?"

"Ten games, forty-three sacks."

"Good God almighty. Must've spent half his time on the run, and he can't even hardly run."

"It'll help some if that hamstring keeps coming around," says Tank. They pause to watch Mavis insinuate himself, claiming the center of the front row as his position in the team picture. "That's good. See how they're letting him have his way? We ain't got a prayer if he doesn't come around. He knows it, the boys know it, and we know it."

"You gonna give him those ten good men?"

"Ten *pretty* good ones, anyway. Look here"—Tank points to the clipboard on his lap, showing the depth charts for the offensive and defensive units—"you've got all of the best boys on offense. Pig's plenty pissed, but he'll get over it. Tell you the truth, with what we've got left on defense, we're gon' probably give up forty points a game."

"Well, coach," says Billy Ray, "I reckon we'll just have to score forty-one, then."

...

Tank doesn't want to risk any more injuries for the rest of the week leading to Friday night's opening game. Once the picture-taking is done and the uniforms have been hung in the stalls, like rented tuxedos, the players return to the field in their shorts and practice jerseys and helmets for an afternoon of working on techniques and assignments. Pig Thomas is haranguing the defense at one end of the field, while Tank and Billy Ray patiently walk the offensive unit through its basic set of plays at the other. The Labor Day weekend is coming up, the weather has brought some relief from the heat, and it is an altogether perfect day.

"Okay, boys, gather 'round and listen up," says Tank, motioning for the fifteen offensive players to form a semi-circle around the portable blackboard he has brought over from the gym. "If you don't know by now, this is Billy Ray Hunsinger, the greatest quarterback this school ever had. They didn't call him the 'Gunslinger' for nothing. Made high school All-America, College Hall of Fame, spent ten years in the pros. The Gun's gon' be with us all year, if you don't make him so mad he quits, so I want you to listen to him and do what he says, okay? Gun, you want to say something?"

He has been watching them closely while Herman Graves speaks, trying to bore a hole through their eyes in hopes of discovering what's there, and what he sees is a bunch of teenaged boys no different from what he was at this age: scared but won't admit it, dreaming of flying when they've barely learned to walk, baby sparrows about to leave the nest. He can see it in the way they chew their gum, roll their eyes, cock their hips, swagger when they walk, scratch their crotches, talk too loud, laugh too hard; boys wanting desperately to be men.

"Thanks, coach," says Billy Ray. He looks downright coach-ly himself, now that they've found his size in a pair of purple shorts and a gold T-shirt with the Panthers' logo over the heart. "Sorry if about all I know right now are your street names. I'm having some trouble with these 'Octaviuses' and 'Markeses,' understand. . . ."

Hoots and hollers erupt: "Billy Ray *what?*" "Billy Ray Bubba!" "Gun *who?*" "Gun *shot?*" Somebody spits the word "honkie," not kindly. Another mumbles something about whether he's going to be passing out food stamps. It takes a fixed stare from Tank to calm them down.

"Fair enough," says Billy Ray, lowering his head to indicate contrition.

"Let's get down to business, boys," says Tank. "Coach Hunsinger's gon' set up our offense. Go ahead, Gun."

"All right," says Billy Ray. "We're gonna have us some fun, boys." Although it can look complicated when it works, with receivers waving their hands all over the field, it's always been a simple offense; touch football, right off the street, but played under control. The trick here, with these kids, is to convince them that it isn't all that complicated, that it works. He goes to the blackboard, takes a piece of chalk, and draws the basic offensive set: a five-man line, two split ends, a slot back set between the tackle and the end on each side, a quarterback under center and a fullback behind him. Hands fly up immediately.

"We ain't got but five blockers, coach," says the kid Billy Ray recognizes as the center who got whacked silly by an errant Mavis pass one day.

"'T-Bone,' right?"

"Uh-hunh. Melvin Williams. What if they rush seven against five?"

Billy Ray licks his lips, flashes his teeth, and diagrams a quick toss to either of the receivers set up at slotback to the spot where the linebackers should have stayed. "They'll try it once," he says. "That's all."

The fullback, Mojo, Demetrius Anthony, lets out a squawk. "They don't block, I'm a dead man." He still remembers the day when they were scrimmaging at the goal line and the fullback, as a decoy, got creamed on four straight plays.

"That mean you don't want the ball?" says Billy Ray.

"Sure, I want the ball, man. Don't look like he's ever gon' give it to me, that's all. I don't want to be no damn play-actin' tacklin' dummy."

Billy Ray goes to the blackboard again. "Almost every play we've got starts like this right here"—Mavis takes the snap from T-Bone, pivots, either fakes a handoff to Mojo or actually gives him the ball, then steps back into the pocket whether he has the ball or not—"so that means everything keys on you, my man. Before they can even think about what Mavis is gonna do, they gotta deal with Mojo. Has he got the ball, or not? 'Mojo gonna blow right past me and score, or is he gonna knock me on my butt?' Either way, you're worth three blockers. Do your job, we'll give you an Oscar for Best Actor. Understand what I'm saying?"

"Yo, 'Make my day,'" somebody shouts.

"Naw, man, *Shaft*."

Mojo is loving it. "Anh-hanh. That's good. Gotta deal with Mojo first." He strikes a Charles Atlas pose, half-squatting and flexing his biceps, drawing jeers from the others.

Tank steps in. "It's a lot like building a house, boys. If you don't lay the first brick right, the whole thing'll fall apart. T-Bone, you and the guards and tackles, y'all are the foundation. Ain't nothin' gon' happen if y'all don't hold it steady." He is addressing the front five. "I'll put it another way. Play like you're a bunch of cops in charge of keeping the crowd off of God. If they get to him, they're gon' kill him, so you got to be ready to give up your life for him. Mavis here, he's God, got the Baby Jesus in his hands, lookin' for a friend to pass him off to. Understand what I'm sayin'? Got to give God a chance to find somebody he can trust to toss the Baby Jesus to. Let the crowd get to him, it's all your fault. You killed God and the Baby Jesus with him."

...

"Christ, Tank, I hope they ain't *that* dumb."

"Gives 'em something to think about, anyway."

Billy Ray and Herman are standing beside each other, behind the offensive players as they line up in the basic set, T-Bone over the ball, Mavis crouched under him to take the snap. There are no defenders, those fifteen going through drills of their own with Pig Thomas at the other end of the field, straining against the used blocking sleds sent by the good souls at Georgia Tech. The plan now is to walk through the motions against phantom defenders, step by step, one play at a time, until they've put together the basic repertoire that will carry them through the season.

Instead of huddling, they gather around the blackboard as Billy Ray and Tank draw up X's and O's to show blocking assignments, feints, traps, passing routes, play designations. Mojo Slant Left, Mojo Slant Right, Mojo Plunge. They go over the ball, line up, try it out. *Hut-hut.* "Do it again." Sprint Right, Sprint Left. *Hut-hut.* "No, no, no, like this." Tank goes over the ball, Gun takes the snap himself, and the two old guys demonstrate. "Okay, y'all try it. Better." Flood Right, Flood Left, Z Fade on two. Sneak, Hail Mary, Fly Right, Screen. "No, no, no, dammit."

"*Christamitey!* Tree? That your name?"

"Anh-hanh. Markese Fleetwood."

"Basketball, right?

"Center."

"Ain't nobody in Georgia taller'n you, son. All you gotta do is haul ass into the corner of the end zone and camp out like you're under the basket. Mavis is gonna play keep-away. He puts it up, you catch it. Game over. You dig?"

"Yo, coach?"

"Runt?"

"Yeah. Jerome Armstrong. What if my man stays on me, won't let me go?"

"That's the idea. You're the decoy. Mavis pump fakes to you, then hits Streak on the fly down the sideline. Streak?"

"Rashad Lattimore, coach."

"It's your time to shine, son. We're gonna make a star out of you. Smoke him, don't look back, leave him on his butt. 'Adios, motherfucker.' Got it?"

"I can live with that."

They end the day running windsprints, Mavis included, as the rush-hour traffic picks up on Monroe Drive. The kid is holding up well. All of those leg-lifts and what little work he has been able to get in on the stationary bike newly arrived from Georgia Tech have fine-tuned the hamstring. Their leader is just about ready. Two more days of this, and it'll be showtime.

...

"I thought that went pretty good, Tank, didn't you?" Billy Ray and Herman Graves are in the coaches' office afterwards, in various stages of undress, discussing the day's work. From across the way they hear the boys singing and whooping in the showers.

"That remark about whether you're gon' be passing out food stamps bothered me," says Herman, "but I guess that'll pass when they get to know you better."

"Guess so."

"One thing you gotta remember, these boys ain't had much more practice at integration than *you* have. They weren't even born when you and me integrated the Blue-Gray, and as quick as the public schools got integrated they got re-segregated." Herman looks up to see Billy Ray stripping naked, slipping into a pair of shower clogs, wrapping a towel around his waist. "Where you headed?"

"The showers."

"Now?" Herman's eyes are as wide as saucers.

"Christ, Tank, I smell like a whore."

"But we don't shower with the boys, Gun."

"Sweat's sweat, way I look at it."

"Usually, I just wait 'til I get home. The boys, they—"

Too late. The last Herman sees of Billy Ray is his rear end as he shuffles out the door. The Gunslinger isn't sure he has had a better day in, oh, hell, five years. A good hot shower to top it off, that's the trick, he's thinking, as he heads toward the sounds of merriment emanating from the swirling clouds of steam. *One of the guys, just like the old days.* He hears one of them in the middle of a story about maneuvering a cheerleader into the back seat of a car, as eager as anyone to hear how it came out, when he kicks off his clogs and tosses his towel atop them onto a chair and noisily opens the haphazard glass door to the shower stall. "She's saying, 'Hurry, dammit,' and I'm like—"

He is greeted with utter silence. Eyes widen. Mouths open. Bars of soap are suspended in midair. Frothy suds begin to slide down glistening black bodies, past squinting eyes, onto shoulders, down muscular chests, slithering toward the bushy nether regions. There are six of them, sharing the spray from the three nozzles that still work, and when Billy Ray enters they move aside without a word being spoken. It's as though a spy has entered their midst.

187

"Where's Mavis at?" It takes a moment for Billy Ray to adjust to the steam roiling in the stall. All he can make out are six shadowy black figures, unmoving, silent, frozen. "Mavis?"

"He gone."

"Yeah." There's an edge in the voice. "Time for his massage."

"Gon' get his hair conked, too."

"Bet Miz Byrd, she take care of him."

Stunned, asking himself what the hell he expected, Billy Ray gropes for a bar of soap and begins lathering himself. He senses they are checking him out, from the size of his pecker to the surgical scars on his knees, trying to see how far they can push. He can't see a thing through the steam and the soap on his face, figures that's a good thing. "Yeah," one of them says, "I remember when Mavis was a nigger." That does it. They aren't laughing over this one. He begins madly rinsing the soap from his eyes, turning to confront them, but when his eyes are clear he finds that he's all alone.

...

"Mavis," Rima says, "I'm going to have to insist that you eat the green stuff."

"What the fuck is it?"

"Watch your mouth, buster. It's spinach. The same stuff Popeye eats all the time."

"Well, he ain't no quarterback. That stuff looks like something a cow shit."

"You, too, ace," she says to Billy Ray. "Here I am, trying to put a nutritious meal on the table, and you look like you're going to throw up. Come on, set an example for the boy."

"She's right, kid," says Billy Ray. "It'll put hair on your balls."

"That does it." Rima slams her napkin onto the dinette table in a corner of what passes for Billy Ray's kitchen, grabbing her plate and emptying the steak bone and potato skins into the trash. She says to Mavis, "Soon as you finish, come to my bedroom and we'll go over the history lesson."

"Aw, *maaann*. Eat, eat. Study, study. I want to watch some tee-vee. Gimme a break, man."

"Hey," says Billy Ray, "no grades, no college."

"Thought you wanted to go over the playbook with me. Where you at, man? Help me out here."

"I told you, kid, it's a package deal. Eat to put on weight, exercise to strengthen the leg, study to stay in school. Gotta do 'em all, not just part of 'em, or you'll wind up on the street. We'll get to the playbook later. Then we'll catch the news, okay?" They stare at the globs of canned spinach left on their plates, look at each other, and try to keep from laughing so loudly that she might hear. Billy Ray twirls the stringy mess on his fork and makes a face. "What the hell. Do the best you can."

...

When the news comes on at eleven, Billy Ray is sprawled out shirtless on the sofa and Mavis is wearing only jockey shorts and a T-shirt, straining at the exercise bike that Rima collected from the mansion of the matron in Ansley Park after school. This way, the boy can get his work in and watch television at the same time. He'll have to take the McGill playbook to bed, hoping to memorize a few more of the plays before he falls asleep.

As usual, the first ten minutes of the evening news sounds like a police drama. Drug busts, traffic fatalities, house fires, robberies, and general rowdiness roll forth, along with the promised "film at eleven," plenty of evidence that Atlanta is no longer the mannerly overgrown Southern town of Billy Ray's childhood. Over the squeaks and clanks of Mavis at his labors, listlessly biding time until the sports report is due at eleven-twenty, they hear about a robbery gone bad. A black teenager wearing a ski mask has killed the Korean owner of a liquor store when the man pulled a gun on him and they shot it out. When the boy's face shows up on the screen, being hauled off in manacles, the noise of the exercise bike stops.

"Hunh," Mavis says. "Sarge."

"Say what?"

"That's Lucius."

"You know that guy?"

"Hell, yeah." Mavis can't believe this. "Lives across the street from me. Lucius Franklin. Call him 'Sarge.' Played a little ball."

"For McGill?"

"Did until he hit Coach Thomas last year. Said he wasn't gon' put up with that shit no more. Knocked Coach flat. Walked away. Quit school."

Billy Ray hacks to clear his throat. "Need I remind you of the lesson to be learned here?"

"Naw, you don't. *Lucius*. Humph. Ain't that something."

They endure the commercials and the medical report about asthma sufferers and the first of many weather updates, then lean forward for the sports segment. The Braves are hopelessly out of the National League race again, just playing out the schedule; the Falcons are crippled up as they await the Rams; Tech is at home this Saturday, Georgia on the road; here are some of the top games on tap for the opening of the high school football season, Cross Keys versus McGill at Grady Stadium among them.

Suddenly, as big as life, Ginny's face fills the screen. "It looks like they'll still be whistling 'Dixie' at Robert E. Lee High School games after all, or at least playing it," the announcer is saying. "At an impromptu press conference today, a Lee High teacher who had organized students to protest the band's playing of the controversial tune during football games, said she was appealing the decision . . ." Beneath the picture there is the name, Virginia Hunsinger.

"So *that's* your old lady."

"Could be."

"Can't be that many Hunsingers."

"Okay, okay," Billy Ray says. "That's my wife."

"Robert E. Lee? Those honkies out there? Hey, man, what's happening?"

Clearly, Billy Ray would rather talk about something else. "Things happen. That's what's happening."

Mavis is loving this. He cuts a look to be sure Rima is still gone, hasn't somehow slipped back into this side of the duplex to tuck him or, for all he knows, bed down with Billy Ray. "What the hell you doing with *her*?" He nods toward Rima's apartment, then back at the television screen. "Man, that's a fine-lookin' lady there. You out of yo' mind, or what?"

SIXTEEN

A ll through the night, in spite of a light rain sometime before dawn, two dozen of the fathers and grandfathers and uncles and assorted cohorts have been roasting a pig over a fire in the gravel parking lot behind the gym. By two o'clock in the afternoon, when Billy Ray drives up to begin the countdown to kickoff, he can't believe what he's seeing. The pig has been cooked, all right, but at a terrible price. Those men who aren't passed out in the weeds, or napping against the trunk of the giant oak that hovers over the Music Building, are being scolded and whacked with umbrellas by their women, Touchdown Mamas all, outraged by their demeanor on such a solemn occasion as the Panthers' first game of the season. Chastened, the men cower away to the safety of the gym while the Mamas begin carving the pig into manageable portions and lugging the chunks into the school building.

Bernice is in charge at the cafeteria, where the pre-game meal will be served promptly at four o'clock. The cheerleaders have made the place as festive as possible: draping purple-and-gold bunting from the ceilings, placing folded place cards and little panther cut-outs on long laundry tables covered with white butcher's paper, hanging the walls with slogans (*Purple Power!* and *Scalp Indians!*), pasting purple paw tracks to the linoleum floor along the cafeteria line, putting rap music CDs into a boombox and turning the volume on full power. The Mamas, meanwhile, are pulling pork, stirring baked beans, chopping cole slaw, cutting mayonnaise and mustard into potato salad, heating buns, brewing tea and ripping open plastic bags of ice. Oblivious to the rap music, they are chattering away among themselves like mother hens.

His paper plate loaded with goodies, Billy Ray joins Herman Graves and Pig Thomas at a small table in the corner where they will be apart from the players when they come in. The two are on their second plates and thinking about thirds when Gun takes a seat in a metal folding chair. There is a place card before him: Coach Gunslinger.

"Looks more like a party than a pre-game meal to me, Coach," says Billy Ray.

"I learned a long time ago not to mess with the Mamas," Tank tells him.

"That crap is music to kill by."

"Damned right it is," says Pig, barbecue sauce dribbling out the sides of his mouth. He holds his paper cup in the air, rattling the ice cubes, and a cheerleader swoops in to refill it with tea. "Had my way, we'd play the Marine Hymn."

"Could play some Mozart, I guess." Tank isn't wasting any time shoveling in the food, himself. "Maybe you'll want to bring your Hank Williams next time."

"They'd kill me and you know it, Tank." Billy Ray has already had his usual lunch at Manuel's, and is dabbling with his food. "Is this what they did for pre-games at Grambling? Rap music and barbecue? Steaks and quiet, that's what we used to do. Gave us time to think."

"Last thing we want, Gun. They're scared to death already. The idea is to stuff 'em and let 'em work off the willies so they'll take a nap. Don't worry, they'll be riled up again come kickoff. Pig here, he'll take care of that."

"Steaks would be better'n barbecue, anyway, what I'm saying. They're gonna be throwing up before halftime."

"Find somebody to buy 'em, we'll serve 'em. Maybe you could say something on your radio show. The way it's going, ask and ye shall receive."

...

With so many new players of their own to break in, it's a good thing the Panthers have drawn the Cross Keys Indians for their first game. Both schools can remember days of glory but now find themselves in transition: McGill in its last year of existence, Cross Keys with a smorgasbord of immigrant students from countries in Latin America and Southeast Asia where American football is a mystery. The only consistent strength of the Cross Keys Indians in recent years is in the kicking game, where there always seems to be a soccer-style kicker from South America. Consequently, with only a handful of native-born Americans, a mixture of black and white, the school hasn't had a winning team in years.

Later in the afternoon, with the sun slanting through the windows and the thirty players finally dozing fitfully on wrestling mats strewn across the floor, Herman and Billy Ray are alone in the coaches' office, biding their time. Pig Thomas, the enforcer, has already put in a full day's work, breaking up the basketball games and general horseplay that followed the pre-game meal, taping the ankles of the boys who need it, seeing that they got half-dressed in their white jerseys and uniform pants *sans* pads; now he is outside, checking out the conditions of the playing field in an attempt to calm himself down.

"It's too late now, but this passing game scares the hell out of me," Tank is saying. "Like Coach Bryant used to say, three things can happen when you pass and two of 'em are bad."

"Make it four things, and *three* are bad," says Billy Ray. "You can expect the incompletions and an interception now and then, but it's the sacks that'll kill you before you can even get airborne."

"We lost almost four hundred yards on sacks last year. Can you believe it?"

"What I hear, the defenses didn't have to worry about covering any-body. All they had to do was keep Mojo in check, and then go after Mavis."

No doubt about it, talking the stars of the McGill basketball team into coming out for football can be the difference this year: Markese ("Tree") Fleetwood, the towering basketball center, is the new tight end; Rashad ("Streak") Lattimore, the athletic scoring forward, is the wide receiver who will be Mavis's primary target; Jerome ("Runt") Armstrong, the point guard and playmaker, is the scatback who can either run the ball or slip through to catch passes. With Demetrius ("Mojo") Anthony up to a rotund 220 pounds now, a year older and wiser, they have a cement truck to stand between Mavis and oncoming linemen. And, of course, none of it will work if Melvin ("T-Bone") Williams and the other offensive linemen can't give Mavis enough time to throw; to protect God and the Baby Jesus.

"I been coaching for about twenty years now, and this is the part I hate the most," says Tank. "First game is like trick or treat. You never know what's gon' be in the bag. If I had any sense I'd go to selling burial plots."

"Don't see as how there's a whole lot of pressure on you, Coach, not with the school closing."

"You got that part right. Win or lose, I got to figure out something to do with the rest of my life. But it ain't me I worry about as much as the boys."

"They're young. They'll be all right."

"You think Mavis is ready?"

"He ain't gonna panic. I can say that much. A bunch of linebackers try-ing to tear his head off ain't nothing compared to what he's been through. I been there, remember?"

"Look, Gun, I want to thank you for helping me out here. Me *and* the boy. No matter what happens, we can at least say it's been interesting."

"I'll buy that, all right." Gun leans back and looks through the doorless entrance and sees that Pig is walking around like a barracks sergeant, stir-ring the players from their naps. Looking around for Mavis, Billy Ray sees the kid sitting at his stall, moving his lips as he flips the stapled pages of the Panthers' playbook. To Tank he says, "It's almost showtime, Coach."

...

After a brief warmup on the field, at a few minutes before the seven-thirty kickoff the players are gathered in the middle of the football locker room. Tank, Pig, and Billy Ray stand together amid a circle of players, arms crossed and looking cool, hoping the boys will take their cue. Both Pig and Billy Ray wear khaki trousers, purple T-shirts and black rippled-soled sneakers, standard coaches' garb, but Tank is a sight to behold in a wrinkled iridescent purple suit that he would have trashed years ago if it hadn't become his trademark. Scanning the eyes of the boys, wearing their all-white uniforms for this game as a ploy to make them appear to be bigger and faster than they really are, the coaches see not the cocky band of row-dies from the brutal days of practice but rather a bunch of kids scared to death. Rev. T. Vivian Beaumont, the chaplain, isn't helping much by equating the next two hours of combat with some kind of Armageddon between the forces of good and evil. "And ye shall be *judged!!*" he shouts, rattling the windows around the room. When the preacher dismounts the bench whence he has been gesticulating, Pig steps forward. "Thanks, Rev," he says, nearly bowling him over, then smacking the nearest kid on the helmet and exploding: "Now get out there and *kill the bastards!!*"

There are about a thousand fans wiggling into their seats in anticipation of the kickoff this night at Grady Stadium, quite a comedown from the heyday of Billy Ray's years when there would be nearly ten thousand for a big showdown between arch rivals. If the fans get boisterous they'll have to deal with the players and others who are there in an official capacity. Each school has brought a marching band of nearly a hundred members, two dozen majorettes, thirty cheerleaders, and a dozen eager students to fetch things on the sidelines. Throw in the players, coaches, trainers and doctors, referees, cops, concessionaires, college recruiters, scouts from other high schools, sportswriters and photographers and statisticians, groundskeepers and electricians and plumbers and others necessary to tend the stadium, that total comes to nearly five hundred.

As far as the Panthers are concerned, there might as well be fifty thousand people in the stands. They are gathered in the end zone, concealed behind a paper curtain stretched across the goal line by the cheerleaders, the Pantherettes, jogging in place and slapping each other's shoulder pads and bumping helmets, nervously awaiting their grand entrance. Billy Ray sees that one of the freshmen playing his first game has peed in his pants, a yellow stain spreading across the crotch of his white uniform britches. From the Mighty Marching Panthers Band in the stands a drum roll begins to build, rising from a funereal pace to a crescendo, and the place explodes when an ominous voice over the public-address system booms, "And now, the McGill High School Panthers!!" Mavis and his co-captain, a linebacker named Travis ("Pac-Man") Dukes, lead the way as the players burst through the curtain and charge onto the field through a corridor formed by Pantherettes jumping and shaking pom-pons and screaming encouragement. The poor Cross Keys Indians, meanwhile, have simply strolled away from the yellow school buses parked on the track beyond the far goal posts and trudged to their places on the visitors' sideline, where now they are forced to suffer the Panthers' noisy entrance.

"If we win, son, we want the ball," Tank reminds Mavis as he and Pac-Man head for the center of the field for the coin toss. It's heads, McGill wins, and that's about the only thing that will go right for the Panthers in the first quarter. Runt Armstrong loses the opening kickoff in the lights, has the ball hit him in the shoulder pads, and is lucky to recover at the seven-yard-line. Billy Ray's game plan is to try a deep bomb over the middle to Streak Lattimore on the first offensive play, hoping to spread the defense from the very beginning, but Mavis's throw sails ten feet over his hands at midfield. A bullet to Tree behind the linebackers gets a first down at the twenty, but then the Cross Keys defenders rise up to swarm Mojo on a draw play and then Mavis on two straight sacks. Ali Allen gets off a majestic punt high into the lights, but the Indians' returner pulls it in at midfield and takes off on a cross-country gallop against Pig Thomas's over-eager troops that zigs and zags for what seems like half a mile and doesn't end until he winds up in the end zone. A chunky Korean placekicker by the name of Ho Win slams home the extra point, and the score is 7-0 before anybody besides the Indians' punt returner has worked up a good sweat. The scant crowd of Cross Keys followers, maybe two hundred of them, can hardly believe what they are seeing. It's the first time in two seasons that their boys have had a lead on anybody, anytime, anywhere.

Runt doesn't lose the ensuing kickoff, instead taking in a short line-drive kick at the twenty-five and blowing straight up the middle of the field like a cat on fire for a touchdown that, with Ali's extra point, ties the game. It gets better after that electric opening, but not by a lot. In its earnestness, Pig's defensive unit is buying every feint presented them by the smaller Cross Keys offense: the pump-fakes by a little quarterback named Joaquin Toyo, the trap-blocking scheme, the belly series they are running, even a reverse off of a fake punt that sets up a field goal. The Panthers' offense, in turn, is the same mess Billy Ray has seen since he first laid eyes on them: no running game to speak of, passes either dropped or overthrown, little protection for Mavis, offensive linemen jumping the gun for drive-killing offsides penalties.

Each of the kicking teams has scored once, the difference in the score being three field goals by Ho Win, and McGill is trailing late in the first half when Mavis finally engineers the first sustained drive of the game. Taking over at his own twenty after Win's third field goal, he begins to move the Panthers up the field with a mixture of short passes and keep-'em-honest blasts at the line by Mojo. They finally score again on fourth-and-goal at the five when the defense swarms Mojo at the line, only to find Tree hauling in a soft fade from Mavis in the back of the end zone just like they had practiced on that day of vigorous red-zone scrimmaging. It's 16-14, Cross Keys, at the half.

...

In the locker room, with the faint strains of the Mighty Marching Panthers Band's rendition of "Sweet Georgia Brown" drifting in from the field, the Panthers have the shell-shocked look of a platoon that has been ambushed during a night patrol in the jungles of Vietnam. Pig is ranting at his defensive players in one corner of the room—even as student trainers and a volunteer doctor administer to the wounded—saying the vilest things about their manhood and their families, jabbing and poking at every soft spot he can find: "I don't want to see no more field goals from that slant-eyed motherfucker! I just found out his daddy killed my daddy in Korea and made me an orphan!" Tank and Billy Ray, meanwhile, are still doing their best to remain calm in the face of what they regard as a disaster. While Tank sits on a mat in one corner, squatting with T-Bone and his other four offensive linemen like an Indian chief at pow-wow, once again reminding them to form a pocket that will allow Mavis to do his work, Billy Ray has Mavis and his running backs and receivers sitting on a bench in front of the big blackboard. Chalk in hand, he is going over every formation in the playbook.

"Streak, son, the play calls for you to take eight strides before you stop and turn. Not seven, not nine. Eight. . . . Runt, don't keep bitching about how three guys are covering you everywhere you go. Hell, that's what we want. Means you just took three guys out of coverage. You dig? . . . All of y'all, I wadn't just sitting around doodling when I drew up these plays. Hell, they work, they been working since before y'all were born. . . . Another thing. Tree, for God's sake, use your height. Pretend Mavis is feeding you a lob so you can dunk the basket that wins the game. . . . Y'all go over there and swallow some more water now, cool down, try to picture yourselves making these plays just the way they got drawn up. . . . Mavis, we gotta talk."

His stats for the first half could be worse—ten for twenty-one with the one touchdown and one interception—and they would have been better with more protection from T-Bone and the others whose job is to be Mavis's bodyguards. There were three sacks in all, two of them on that first possession, a situation that might have been helped if he could run to safety on his gimpy leg. At least six of his incompletions were flat-out dropped by receivers who were, more often than not, in the wrong place at the wrong time. He seems to be throwing all right, nice and easy, none of that throwing across the body except when he's running for his life. Unlike the five of his teammates who vomited on the sidelines early in the game, the overweight Mojo and T-Bone among them, he seems to have survived the Touchdown Mamas' unpropitious pre-game meal.

"It might be time to kick some butt," Billy Ray is saying. The two of them have gone into Tank's office to be alone. Mavis sits on the folding cot and Billy Ray is at Tank's desk, shoes off, stockinged feet dangling.

"We'll do that, all right," says Mavis. "Those guys ain't shit. 'Indians,' my ass."

"Naw, I mean our guys."

"Hey, man, that's your job. I ain't the coach."

"You're *more* than that, kid. You're the pilot, the engineer, the driver, the captain of the ship. I can't run this team. Tank can't run this team. Pig sure as hell can't run this team. You're the man."

"Aw, man, I can't do that. These are my friends."

"What kind of friend lets your ass get mugged?"

"They just got to do better, that's all."

"Tell 'em about it, then. Next time Squat jumps offsides and costs us five yards, I want you to kick him in the butt."

"In front of all them people?"

"God and everybody."

"Hell, Gun"—they both pause, realizing that this is the first time he's ever used the nickname—"they'll up and whup the shit out of me, right in the middle of the game."

"Better him than some linebacker. Understand what I'm saying?" They hear Pig cut loose with a blast on his whistle to indicate it's time to go. Billy Ray drops his feet to the floor and reaches over to rub Mavis's head. "First rule of quarterbacking: 'don't take no shit off nobody.' You're the king. Now go get 'em."

...

Billy Ray has seen some turnarounds in his time, but nothing to compare with this. All of that bile directed at the defensive players by Pig Thomas at halftime has turned them into maniacs. On the opening kickoff, a rainbow to the twenty, the hapless Cross Keys returner momentarily takes his eyes off the ball when he hears eleven Panthers thundering toward him screaming like Apaches, fumbles, is steamrolled, and looks back from his position on the ground to see a raucous celebration taking place in the end zone, where the kid who had peed in his pants before the game, Anterrius ("Mouse") Leonard, has recovered the ball and run it in for a touchdown. Clearly shaken by this turn of events, the Cross Keys Indians will never be the same.

Although in their zeal Pig's defensive players will continue to make errors of commission, allowing the spunky little Mexican quarterback to fake them out of their shoes on the option play and piling up a season's worth of penalties for leveling receivers when the ball is still in the air, they hold their own in the red zone. The next time Ho Win tries a field goal, he is swamped by a tidal wave of Panthers and is hauled off the field on a stretcher, effectively removing half of the Indians' offense. Before the third quarter ends, Joaquin Toyo himself simply collapses from exhaustion and is hoisted into an awaiting ambulance on the track. When that happens, Pig sidles up to Billy Ray on the sideline, smirks and bows and says, "Your ball, coach."

Now, with the lead and little chance that Cross Keys will score again unless McGill gives it to them, Billy Ray and Herman can turn their full attention to Mavis and the offense. There has been precious little practice time for them to work on the important matters of timing and protecting Mavis so his receivers have time to run their routes, and here's the chance to learn things on the job.

"Okay, kid, here's where we change the game plan," Billy Ray is telling Mavis while the ambulance attendants are trying to revive the stricken Cross Keys quarterback. The Gun has his arms draped over the kid's shoulder pads as they stand beside the bucket of Gatorade in front of the Panthers' bench. "First thing we're gonna do is wear 'em out."

"'Niggers Go Long,' right?" says Mavis.

"Where the hell did you hear that?"

"I keep up."

"Look, I never really—"

"It don't matter. Let's cut out the crap and get on with it. What's up?"

If it worked on that glorious day against Alabama at Tuscaloosa, it sure as hell ought to work tonight against a poor high school team already back on its heels and thinking fondly of being home in bed. The essence of it is to wear down the defensive backs by flooding the secondary with waves of potential receivers on every play, whether throwing to them or not, at the same time managing to keep the drive alive with little short outlet passes to Mojo or to Runt. "You find Tree or Streak open, hit 'em," says Billy Ray. "Just make sure you've got a third man loose to dump it to. Main thing is, keep the backs on the run in coverage 'til they're about to drop. Then you can do any damned thing you want to with 'em. Got it?"

Mavis has it, all right. When he trots back out onto the field to the encouragement from the Pantherettes—

Say what?
>*Panthers!*
Say who?
>*Mavis!*
Say how?
>*Touchdown!*
Say when?
>*Now!!!*
Panthers, Panthers, Panthers!!!

—he crouches under T-Bone at center, first and ten at his own thirty-five after a punt, checking to see that four of his receivers are spread out from sideline to sideline, and begins the count. *Hut-hut!* When his left guard, Antwan ("Squat") Jenkins jumps offsides and draws a five-yard penalty, Mavis takes a step toward him and knocks him to the ground with a violent shove to the shoulder pads. "What the fuck, man?" says Squat, scrambling to his feet, being held back by T-Bone. "I'm gon' stick this ball up your ass next time you do that," says Mavis. "You with us, or against us?" From the visitors' stands across the way come laughs and cheers, from the McGill stands a stunned silence, from a press box filled with sportswriters and college scouts and rival high school coaches nervous chuckles. Billy Ray can only smile when Mavis goes under center again, checks his receivers and the secondary, and begins the barrage.

After twelve completions in his next fourteen attempts, two of them for long bullets to Streak and then to Tree on crossing post patterns in the end zone, McGill is up, 28-16, and the Cross Keys defensive backs are bent over, wheezing, hands on their knees, begging for the last of their remaining timeouts. It seems that they have spent the entire third quarter running backwards, smacking into each other in man-to-man coverage, pointing fingers when they go to zone coverage and the Panther receivers find the seams. In due time, needing all of the help they can get in the secondary, they are rushing only three men, giving Mavis all day to find a receiver and allowing Mojo to have the time of his young life by blowing up the middle for runs of five, ten, and twenty yards before he can be hauled down. In their elation following another touchdown and another kickoff, the McGill defensive players let a Cross Keys scatback named Tico Sanchez get loose for a ninety-yard return for a touchdown, but when the game winds down Pig Thomas is kicking back on the bench, enjoying his Gatorade, while the boys are carrying Mavis off the field on their shoulders. McGill has won, 41-22. It's a start.

SEVENTEEN

Noon Saturday finds Billy Ray wheeling through the shady streets of Crestwood with Mavis slumped beside him in the shotgun seat. The kid is swollen and bruised from the beating he took the night before, but a breakfast of steak and pancakes has perked him up a bit. It is the first fall-ish day of the year, and the men of the neighborhood are out in force with their mowers and blowers and trimmers, an army of suburban pioneers intent upon leaving their mark on the land. For Billy Ray, who hasn't been back to the neighborhood since his exile, there are no surprises; he could drive the route blindfolded after all of these years. But for Mavis, this is new territory. He is silent, all eyes, as this bright new world unfolds: picket fences and stone walls, neat split-level and two-story houses, teenaged white boys shooting basketballs at hoops nailed to garages, younger kids riding bicycles, shiny new station wagons parked in carports, trees and privet hedges and real sidewalks.

"Man," Mavis says. "Place looks like Disney World."

"All this can be yours if you're dumb enough to want it, kid."

"Leaving this? Now I *know* you're crazy."

"Flip side is, you gotta pay for this stuff."

"Money ain't yo' problem."

"Well, pardner"—Billy Ray rolls the cigar in his mouth—"the truth is, I wore out my welcome."

"Your old lady know we're coming?"

"Thought we'd surprise her."

...

Ginny's red Blazer is in the carport as he pulls into the circular drive-way. When the last juddering of *Rosinante*'s engine ends with a pop and a belch of blue smoke, they can hear the unadulterated sounds of Crestwood on a crisp weekend: gas-powered lawn machinery blatting and whining, bluejays squawking in the trees, dogs and little kids yelping, a boombox turned up full-volume somewhere, the distant purring of a car engine being fine-tuned.

Seeing his next-door neighbor out in his tennis shoes and Bermuda shorts and wide-brimmed straw hat, trimming the grass from his stretch of sidewalk, Billy Ray can't resist. "Yo, Ham," he shouts, wildly waving both arms to get his attention, then slicing a hand across his throat as a signal for quiet.

With a look of disgust, Hamilton Sutton releases the switch to turn off the weed trimmer. "Why, hello, Bill," he says, fishing a bright red bandan-na from his hip pocket to wipe his flushed face, all the while peering at this black boy standing before him. "Long time no see."

"Been out exploring the provinces."

"I see."

"They be monsters out there."

"Wouldn't surprise me."

"Hey. Understand you and the bride been collecting art."

Sutton stiffens, unsure where Billy Ray is going with this, then points to a new centerpiece in his carpet of plush zoysia. "Wouldn't call a concrete birdbath 'art,' exactly."

"Come on, Ham, we can talk." Billy Ray feigns a look over both shoul-ders, then lowers his voice, conspiratorially. "Where do y'all keep it at?

Bedroom? Bathroom? Frankly, I think 'Eden Redux' seems a little, what, theatrical, wouldn't you say? But, then, I ain't much on the Bible."

J. Hamilton Sutton IV—downtown lawyer, church deacon, Boy Scouts leader—is staring back, trying to compose a response, reduced to sputtering, when Billy Ray winks, throws an arm around Mavis, and crunches through the pea gravel toward the front doorstoop. He presses the doorbell of his own house, feeling like a Jehovah's Witness out making the rounds on a Saturday.

...

"Oh." Ginny opens the door from the inside while Billy Ray is still trying to find the right key on his keyring. She stands in the doorway, her mouth agape, wearing ragged cutoffs and one of his old long-sleeved dress shirts and sneakers without socks, a bandanna tied around her forehead to keep the wisps of blonde hair from falling over her eyes. Seeing these two on the doorstoop, unannounced, has caught her by surprise. Her knees are caked with dirt, her cheeks streaked with sweat, and when she tries to wipe her forehead with the back of her hand she forgets she is wearing muddy gardening gloves. "Oh," she repeats. "Hi."

"Ain't nothing sexier than a woman in a man's shirt, I always say."

He wants to believe she's blushing. "Well, you know. Keeps the bugs off."

"Hi, babe."

"You should have called."

"Probably right."

"I was just"—flustered—"well, obviously, I was doing some planting. Chrysanthemums."

"Sorry to pop in like this." Billy Ray bows slightly and sweeps a hand between the two of them. "Mavis, this here's the former Virginia Sue Bradford, my wife. Ginny, meet Mavis Jackson."

She quickly recovers her Southern manners; shucking her gloves to shake hands with Mavis, asking them inside, shutting the door, inviting them to sit in the living room, then hustling off to the kitchen. Soon the three of them are seated around the glass-topped coffee table, Billy Ray and Mavis beside each other on one loveseat, Ginny alone on the other, sipping iced tea and nibbling at oatmeal cookies and trying to start a conversation.

"Mags home?" says Billy Ray.

"The cheerleaders are having a car wash. They're at the church parking lot, if you have time to go see her."

"We just might do that. Ol' wagon can always use a wash, that's for sure."

"Is it running all right?"

"For an old broad, yeah."

"Good. Good." Ginny turns to the kid. "So. It's good to finally meet you, Mavis. I've heard so much about you." Mavis and Billy Ray cut looks at each other, puzzled. "You know. From the radio show."

"Yes, ma'am."

"Oh. And I saw where you boys won last night."

"Yes, ma'am."

"Lee High won, too. Thirty-to-something, I think it was."

"I saw that in the paper. Yes, ma'am."

"It was a good game."

"They're tough."

"Too bad you two don't play each other."

"Yes, ma'am."

"That'd be something, wouldn't it?"

"Well, they're tough, all right."

The lines go dead. Mavis looks like he's been flushed out of the pocket again, no open receivers in sight, desperately looking for somewhere to run. Billy Ray thinks he would like a Scotch-and-rocks, or maybe at least to light his cigar, but the moment passes. What he would really like to do, along about now, seeing when Ginny leans over to aimlessly rearrange the cut gladiolas resting in a glass vase on the table that she is braless, is to throw her to the shag carpet and resume life as he knew it. That passes, too.

"So," Ginny says, perking up. "Would you boys like some lunch?"

"Thanks, hon, but we ate a horse for breakfast." *'Hon.' Is that all right?* "We just came to get some things."

"I could make sandwiches."

"Naw, really. If it's okay, I'd like to fetch that film of the Alabama game and maybe some of the exercise equipment."

"You're working out now?"

"Hey, I'm even jogging these days. A regular runnin' fool. It's about to kill me. Naw, really, it's for Mavis here. Trying to build the boy up. Okay?"

"Well, sure. It's your stuff, isn't it? Careful in the Gun Room. It's been closed off ever since you—. Since June."

"Fourteen weeks." He glances at the grandfather clock canted in the corner of the room, the one his parents left for them. "And two hours."

"Whatever."

...

In the Gun Room, while Billy Ray assembles the film cannister and projector and portable screen on the pool table, Mavis gawks at the trophy cabinets and the framed photographs and other memorabilia of a long career in football. Up until now he has been thinking that it's been the bluster of some old honkie, all that stuff about the great Gunslinger, but the evidence on the walls says otherwise. Here is Hunsinger standing beside Vince Lombardi on the Green Bay sideline. There he is being carried off the field on his teammates' shoulders. Here's the cover of the North Alabama State media guide for the 'sixty-five season, Billy Ray wearing a coonskin cap and buckskin jacket and brandishing two six-shooters: "The Gunslinger Loaded for Bear." The plaque commemorating his election to the College Football Hall of Fame.

"So it really happened, huh?"

"What, you think I made it all up?"

"Well, you know." The kid trails off. "*Man!* That you with Bear Bryant? He don't look so happy."

"Might've been the longest day of his life."

"You're always saying you *almost* beat him. What happened?"

"It's all right here, my man," says Billy Ray, thunking the cannister of film with his finger. "We got plenty of time for that. Okay. Checklist. Film, projector, screen, exercise bike over there, and—*damn!* The barbells are upstairs. Let's load all this in the wagon first, okay? Might have to roll the damned things down the steps."

...

At the top of the stairs, laid out in a fashion typical of split-level houses built in the 'sixties, there are three bedrooms: the master bedroom and bath running the length of the upstairs facing the street and, across a carpeted hall between a large closet, two other, smaller, bedrooms connected by a shared bath. The door of the first, hastily left wide open to reveal a canopied four-poster bed and the typical mess of a busy teenaged girl, bears the legend MAGGIE in block bronze letters. The second door, at the end of the hall, is closed tight and the letters on this one read RICKY.

That door being stuck, Billy Ray has to lean into it with his shoulder to pop it open. He is overcome by the musty air, and when he flips the switch for the ceiling fan cobwebs fly. Nothing has been moved in years. It is no less a museum than the Gun Room downstairs, the decor being football: bedspread, curtains, wallpaper, even a throw rug crocheted with the Robert E. Lee High Rebels' logo of the familiar old *"Forget, Hell!"* Confederate general brandishing a sword. The base of a bedside lamp is a miniature gold-and-white football helmet with Georgia Tech's GT logo. A pair of black low-cut cleats, tied together with their laces, hangs from a nail. Tossed into one corner is a set of shoulder pads, the leather turned a moldy green, and a couple of scuffed footballs.

"Man, I could use a place like this." Mavis would like a better look, but Billy Ray is standing in the doorway.

"What?"

"I said it's a hell of a room."

"Watch your mouth, okay?"

"Well, shit—"

"Hey"—Mavis has never seen Billy Ray so agitated—"I said knock it off."

"Okay, okay."

Billy Ray walks briskly toward a wall-length closet with louvered doors, allowing Mavis to step inside the room, and the first thing the kid sees is an oil portrait hung above the headboard of the bed. It is a full-length painting of a red-haired teenaged boy in the classic pose of a quarterback, both hands holding a football cocked behind his right ear, bright green eyes wide in anticipation. Centered beneath, on a strip of tarnished copper nameplate, he reads RICKY HUNSINGER, LEE J.V., 1980.

"That your boy?"

"What?"

Billy Ray is bent over, rummaging through the closet. Mavis speaks up. "Said I didn't know you had a son."

"I don't."

"Who's Ricky, then?"

There's a pause. "It's just a painting."

"He looks a lot like you. Tall, red hair—"

"Look, goddamit"—Billy Ray is flushed in the face, already sweating in the clammy room—"you gonna help me, or what?"

"I was just asking."

"Here." A set of barbells comes rolling out of the closet, a thick shiny bar with a twenty-pound cast-iron disk locked to each end, and slams against the foot of the bed. Mavis hops to avoid being hit in the ankles. "How 'bout hauling that down the steps. I'll bring the rest of it."

Puzzled, Mavis bends to lift the barbell, gets a firm grip, gingerly backs down the steps, and deposits the load with a loud thump that brings Ginny to the landing. He figures she's going to raise hell, but instead she is looking at the barbell and smiling. He smiles back at her, even though he is busy assessing how much pain this damned thing is going to cost him, and trudges back up the stairs to help with the rest of the weights. He picks up a pair of ten-pounders while Billy Ray gathers up four little five-pound weights in his hands. "That's about it," Billy Ray says, nodding for Mavis to precede him out of the room. Billy Ray simply walks away from it, not looking back, and this time he leaves the door wide open. The ceiling fan is still purring, gently stirring the air.

...

"Billy, I—"

"The kid's—"

"I'm sorry."

"No, go ahead."

Mavis has been dispatched to the station wagon with a plastic cup of iced tea to-go, told to secure the load and wait up. Ginny is getting some more cubes from the refrigerator while Billy Ray stands in the doorway of the kitchen. They act like teenagers who have just met, tentative and shy, circling each other, each waiting for the other to commit.

"You're looking better," she says, running tap water over the tray of ice.

"Clean living, pure and simple."

"Mavis seems like a nice boy."

"For the kind of life he's lived, yeah. The street toughens 'em up. Makes you think twice about Crestwood."

Ginny twists the plastic tray until the ice cracks, then plops a handful of cubes into his tea. "What's your, you know, what's the arrangement?"

"Thanks," he says, swirling the cup to cool the tea. "Me and the kid? He's living with me now. Damned near had to kidnap him, but he's got a room of his own. I'm trying to fatten him up, teach him some football, get his grades up."

"Won't you get into trouble for that? The DFACS people are pretty strict."

"What, kidnapping? Aw, hell, he was practically living on the streets when I came along. I tell you, this kid—"

"Is *she* still there?"

"Who?"

"The artist. Whatshername."

"Oh." *Well, now.* "You mean Rima. Rima the Bird-Girl."

"Well?"

"What?"

"Did you kick her out like you said you were going to do? Come on, Billy, don't play games with me."

"She's good."

"I'll bet."

"I can't believe this."

"Sounds like a big happy family to me. You and the boy and this, this *honey.* I thought you'd gotten over all of that. In the meantime, I'm out here being a single parent to your daughter, whom you've found time to see exactly once since you left her."

"Whooaa. I *left?* You kicked me out, remember?" Billy Ray twirls his unlit cigar. "You wouldn't be jealous, would you?"

"Don't flatter yourself. If I were, I'd tell you. I was just curious."

"What she's good at is English, geography, math, art, and a lot of other stuff the kid's gotta know to get into college. You want to believe otherwise, that's your problem."

"It just seems, you know, *odd.*" They hear a beep of the horn from outside: Mavis, ready to roll. "I mean, things haven't exactly turned out the way I'd thought they, well, the way I'd planned."

"This whole damned thing's odd, if you ask me." There's something in her look, her voice, that brings him up short. "Wait a minute. The way you *planned?*"

"Don't get mad, Billy. We can talk about that, if you want to. Just don't get mad."

"So it was *you,* all the time."

"Somebody had to do something. You sure weren't going to do it by yourself."

"Son of a *bitch.*" When he hears a sustained wail on the horn he bolts to the doorstoop and yells at Mavis to knock it off, cool it, he'll be there when he gets there. "I'm not sure I want to hear this, but let's have it."

213

"Sit," she says. They take seats opposite each other, across the coffee table. "Except for the girl, I know all about everything that's happened. The radio show, the Ranch, the seizure, the wreck, Mavis, the coaching job, everything."

"Of course you do. Hell, I've told everybody that can pick up WWJD. I'm sure Maggie filed a report last weekend."

"She's not the only one."

"You've been spying on me. So what?"

"It's more than that, Billy." She smiles, jiggles the ice in her cup, then winces. "Oh, God, you're not going to like this a bit."

"Let's have it. Try me."

It takes Ginny a full ten minutes to explain the tenuous connections and fortuitous happenstances that have brought them to this point. Long before she kicked him out of the house, the first thing she did was call B. D. Spotswood, who had been sending those "birthday" cakes for all of those years, telling him that now was the chance to really help his hero, the Gunslinger, who would be perfect for a talk show on WWJD. She knew Scottie Burns from that homecoming weekend in 1965, when they met during a pre-game brunch for the bands and cheerleaders of Alabama and North Alabama State, and enlisted him to work on the Gun's drinking. She called Tank Graves, whom they had both met during the parties leading up to the Blue-Gray Game that Christmas Day in Montgomery, to alert him that Billy Ray just might be available to help out with some coaching if he could use him. She knew Rev. T. Vivian Beaumont from her days of volunteering on the Selma-to-Montgomery march in 'sixty-five. *No*, she is telling Billy Ray now, she wasn't going to let him throw away his life. "They wanted me to be there at the principal's office last Monday, but I thought that would've been a bit too much."

"If that don't beat all," Billy Ray says when she is done. "So it *was* a setup, all along."

"Pretty good work, don't you think?"

"I've got egg all over my face, that's what I think."

"So? You're sober. You've got a job. You're back in football. You're helping a boy who needs it. What else matters?"

"Here I am, thinking what a good boy I've been, turned myself around, and now this."

"Billy," she says, rising from the loveseat and walking around behind him, then beginning to rub the back of his neck. "Why don't you stay?"

"Afraid we gotta scoot. From the sound of it, the kid's had about all of Crestwood he can stand in one day."

"I mean *you*, hon. Come home."

"Don't say it if you don't mean it."

"I'm not sure what I think, Billy. I think you're ready now. Don't you?"

"Well, we've got a problem there, babe. I mean, I've sort of made myself this boy's daddy, you know. This thing's gotten complicated."

"You could bring him with you for a while, couldn't you? There's Ricky's room, you know."

"The problem is, we're into the season now and he can't play for anybody if he moves out of the school district. You know the rules."

"Oh, Christ, Billy, those rules don't mean anything and you know it. This one black player we've got spends half his time downtown with his grandmother, where all of his friends are." Mavis is on the horn again. "This is all about the girl, isn't it?"

"Not anymore, it isn't."

"So it *was*, then. In the beginning. You just admitted it."

"Believe what you want, babe."

"Dammit, Billy." Ginny is seething now. If he didn't know better, he thinks she might cry. "You asshole. I'm not going to let you do this to me again. Go. Get the hell out of here."

He snaps his fingers. "Forgot something. Be right back." Billy Ray bounds up the carpeted stairs and is back downstairs in less than a minute, holding the two scarred footballs against his chest with one hand, the jumbo plastic cup of tea with the other, heading out the front door. He stops and turns to face his wife, the mother of his children, trying to make a pronouncement that at least he can claim to be his own idea. "You might want to give some thought to turning that room into an office or something," he says. "Seems a waste, sitting empty like that."

...

He has forgotten that Georgia Tech is playing at Grant Field that afternoon, and they get stuck in traffic near the North Avenue exit on I-85. The kickoff is still an hour away, but they are surrounded by a swirl of Tech and North Carolina fans in cars and pickup trucks decorated in their teams' colors, gold-and-white and heavenly Carolina blue, blowing horns to assert themselves, eager to get off the interstate and into the parking lots.

"Sorry to jump on you like I did back there," says Billy Ray, trying to find the pre-game tailgate show on the car radio. "I've had a lot on my mind lately. Didn't mean to take it out on you."

"Your old lady don't seem all that mad at you," Mavis tells him.

"Finally meeting you gave her some funny ideas."

"Yeah, I know."

"Know *what*? Christ, you were outside."

"Hey, man, you don't think I can see what's happening? White lady gon' get herself a replacement son. *Nigger* boy on top of that. Impress her honkie liberal friends. 'Lookie here. Me? I ain't prejudiced. I *love* black folks.'"

"Come on, pal, give her a break."

"Unh-hunh, I can see it now. Mom and Dad and their colored boy."

"What're you talking about? It ain't like that at all."

"You know what I'm talking about. I ain't no toy. Ain't no orphan y'all can play with just to make you feel good. I got my own mama. Got my own life. I ain't yo' boy, never will be. You can just get that out of yo' mind right now."

Billy Ray's throat is dry. He longs for simpler times, when black was black and white was white—no, that's not it, he can see that doesn't work anymore—it's just that, well, how come everything has gotten so damned complicated? There's an empty room in the house with somebody to use it,

216

and an empty side of the bed next to Ginny that she's ready for him to fill again, so why can't we just do this thing without having to make a big deal out of it? She's right about how they could work around the rules about where the boy actually sleeps at night. Now that he's gotten his back up about it, though, Mavis is the problem, not the school board.

His mind somewhere else, wondering if the traffic will ever break, thinking this simple chore might take all day, Billy Ray is startled to hear Mavis speak in an almost fatherly tone: "He'd be about my age now, wouldn't he?"

"Who?"

"Ricky. Your son."

"What're you, eighteen?"

"Un-hunh."

"He'd be the same. November the fifth."

"Was he good?"

"Would've been. Could've been." Billy Ray can't go on. He turns his head away from Mavis, pretending to see something of interest up on the hill at the Varsity Drive-In, swamped with fans showing the colors, not wanting the boy to see his stricken face. He's trying to take a quick swipe at his eyes when he feels a hand pat his knee, as though the kid understands some things now, and when he looks up at Mavis he sees a smile as big as sunrise.

EIGHTEEN

L ooking back, he's pretty sure he knew what he'd be doing on the show the instant he lost it in front of Mavis. There was the kid, consoling him, of all things, which isn't the way it's supposed to work at all. Who's in charge here, anyway? He had no idea he would be so affected by the trip back to the house—the sight of Ricky's room again, the conversation he had with Ginny, that moment with Mavis in the car as they were coming back to town—and he knows now that it's time to bite the bullet, put it away, move on.

He could hardly sleep Saturday night for thinking how he'll handle it, and it's been the same all through a long Sunday awash in a downpour that knocked him and the boys out of their weekly frolic at Grady Stadium. Ginny and Maggie might not like what he's about to do, which is to air out the family laundry for all of the city to hear—like they say, let it all hang out—but he'll go nuts if he doesn't do it, and do it now.

Having brushed past B. D. and gone straight into the booth without a hello, settled into the chair and slapped the headset on, looked for the countdown from Spider, gotten the go-ahead, he finds himself launched into it before there was a chance to change his mind.

...

We didn't know whether it was gonna be a boy or a girl, see, wanted it to be a surprise, but I don't mind telling you I acted like a fool when the doctor says to Ginny, says, Come on, now, gimme one more good push, he's coming. I'm thinking, Hot dang, I got me a boy. Well, it turns out Ginny probably wanted a girl about as much as I wanted a boy, 'cept she never let on. She's all doped up and everything, but when she hears that, she raises up and says, He? Doctor says, Hey, it's just a figure of speech, come on and push for me now. I tell you, I never saw such a mess with all of that blood and her yelling and nurses running around and all.

You can say that again, Gun.

At any rate, here he came, sticky little monkey with my red hair and all, and I about lost it. I'm jumping up and down in that stupid-looking cap and gown like it was Christmas morning. Ma in her stirrups and Pa his cap, if you know what I mean. I'm saying, That's about the damnedest thing I ever saw in my whole life, excuse my French, and the doctor's saying, All right, let's calm down, now, just calm down, happens all the time. Thing is, it never happened to me before. Nurse sticks this little bundle at me and says, Wanna hold him? and I says, Ma'am, I set records that's still standing for not fumbling the ball, but I'd just as well you hand this one off to somebody else. Gun, he don't want the ball.

Nervous, were you?

Scared to death, is more like it.

Sometimes I think it was better in the old days, when you went to the fathers' waiting room and sat there with your cigars 'til they called you so you didn't have to see all that stuff.

Maybe. I don't know. Lot to be said for being there the minute they pop out. This was about ten years before they started letting daddies in the delivery room. I had to pull rank, remind 'em I was a Packer, I was man enough to take it, just to make 'em let me in. That's how much I wanted to be there.

So, anyways, you had yourself a son.

Right. That was a Saturday night. I was with Green Bay then, mostly sending in plays from the sideline just to keep busy and earn my pay, but the next afternoon we got into a blowout at home against the Giants and

Lombardi finally sent me in and I'll be danged if I didn't throw for a touch-down. It was on the Z-Fade, to my tight end, where he wiggles loose and I lob it to him over everybody in the corner of the end zone. If you've got some old boy that's tall enough, there can't nobody hardly stop it. Anyway, Ginny and the baby were still at the hospital, understand, so I grab this radio guy's microphone in the locker room after the game and say, This one's for you, Ricky, hoping maybe Ginny and the boy might be listening. Chicago Tribune *had it the next day about me and my Touchdown Baby. So you might say it was me and the boy and football from the git-go.*

Lookie here, Gun, how 'bout I hang up and just listen. While I got you, though, you wouldn't happen to know how Rabun County came out Friday night, would you?

What do you think this is, a sports show?

That's a good one, Gun. Catch you later.

Okay, where was I at? Green Bay. 'Sixty-seven. Anyhow, by the time that boy was walking, he was a regular mascot in the Packers' locker room. Fixed him up with a Green Bay jersey with my number on it, ol' lucky thirteen. Same thing up at Calgary when Lombardi and them screwed up and let me go and I caught on with the Stampeders up there in the Canadian Football League. Our little girl came along a year after Ricky, that's Maggie, so it was like a boy for me, a girl for Ginny. I don't really know how it is with mothers and daughters, but there can't be nothing quite like the deal between fathers and sons. I love Mags, understand, but it's different with a boy, you know. It's like, aw, hell, it's like looking in a mirror. Like he's this little baby brother some-body gave you to play with, and if you're lucky he looks up at you like you're God or something and he's counting on you to teach him what he's gotta know. Being an only child whose daddy stayed drunk most of the time and didn't know pig-squat about football, I never got any of that. So I wanted it real bad. Me and the boy. Father and son. Dammit, Spider, I see it. Line One, what's buggin' you?

Yeah, y'all got the Valdosta score? It wadn't in the paper this weekend.

We ain't got no Valdosta score. Call WSB.

What th—

Can't you see I'm talking here?

Yeah, but—

Hold them calls for a while, Spider, okay? A man can't hardly ruminate with all of these interruptions. At any rate, like I was saying, I loved this little boy more'n I'd ever loved football or much of anything else, watermelon and angel-food cake included, so it wasn't all that hard to take when my knees got so bad that I had to give it up. I figured now I could spend all my time with my son, teaching him everything I knew about football and life and all that good stuff. That was in 'seventy-five. The season up there runs from about the Fourth of July to early November. Both the kids were in school by then and it wadn't doing them no favors to have 'em spend the fall semester in Canada and the spring down here, so that's when we moved back home to stay. I'd had my fun, don't you see, and now it was the boy's turn. This is when it really got good, folks. Ginny and Mags had their thing, dance classes and piano lessons and all that, girl stuff, you know, and me and Ricky had ours. School had him for seven hours every day, but I got all the rest. Like I said, it was me and the boy and football nearly twenty-four hours a day, if you want to count the time dreaming and I reckon you can. He'd be up at daybreak, lifting weights and building up his legs on an exercise bike in his room, which was practically wallpapered with pictures of his favorites he'd clipped out of magazines—eat a big breakfast, then walk to school since it wasn't but a mile and it was good for his legs. I'd go off and work somewhere while he was in school, selling cars or whatever, just to keep myself from going crazy more'n anything, and I'd be waiting for him when he got home. Then it was time for us to go to work, and the boy couldn't get enough of it. Sometimes we'd work out in the back-yard, where I'd strung up this old tire from a tree limb so he could throw at a moving target, other times we'd play 'til dark at the Lee High stadium near the house. Passing to me, the tight end. Running the option against me, the defensive end. Taking snaps from me, the center. Working on handoffs, the head fake, the double pump, the bootleg, checking off defenses, all of it. At night, we'd watch some of these old films I had of me playing, and on week-ends during the football season we'd watch every game they had on television, college and the pros. We weren't just watching, understand, we were studying. He'd say, How'd that play work, Daddy? and I'd walk him through it. He wasn't even ten yet, but the boy couldn't get enough of it. Me, neither. What? Folks, we got to take a break here so B. D. can pay some bills. I'll be right back.

...

... During the commercials I got to thinking how it might sound like the only thing me and the boy had was football. It wasn't like that at all, although I got to admit I don't know how it might've been if he'd turned out to be a clarinet player. I guess maybe I'd've done whatever it took to make sure he got to be the best damned clarinet player in the world, right up there with Woody Herman and those boys, because the bottom line was that he was my own flesh and blood. I'd run my hands through that frizzy red hair and it might as well have been my own. Look into those big green eyes and it was, well, like I said, it was like looking into a mirror. Same old long skinny legs like I had when I was that age. Even the freckles were in the same places. Sometimes when I'd stick my head in the door to his room late at night to make sure he was okay I couldn't help myself. I'd go over and sit on the bed, him all sprawled out like a little colt in a pile of hay, his whole life ahead of him, and I don't mind telling you I'd get all choked up. What's he dreaming, you know? Is it gonna be better for him? That last part, that's what it's all about, I reckon. From the father down to the son and on to whatever grandsons that might come along, about all you can ask is that each one of 'em turns out to be just a little bit better than the one before. He wasn't even old enough to know anything about girls yet and here I was already thinking about stuff like that for him. So you see it wasn't all about football, it was about whether he was gonna handle his life any better than I did. Lord, I'm about to talk my head off. Line Two, what you got?

Hey, Gun, for me and my boys, it's huntin'. Y'all ever go out deer-huntin' together? Now that's some real father-and-son stuff, you ask me.

Naw, in spite of me being called the Gunslinger, I never developed much stomach for shooting animals because an uncle of mine got killed in a hunting accident when I was just a kid. We loved the camping out part, though, just being together out in the woods. What we'd do when we came across some deer was shoot pictures instead of bullets. Line Three?

If you don't mind my saying, Gun, sounds like you was raising a bionic quarterback, with all that exercise and diet and training. How'd the boy turn out, anyways? I don't remember reading about no Gunslinger Junior. . . . Hello? Gun? You still there?

Here I am.

Well, how 'bout it? What happened to the boy?

Just a second while I drink some water.

I'm outta here, Gun. I'll hang up and just listen. Tell it like it is, buddy.

Well. To answer the first part, they'd never seen anything like Ricky Hunsinger in the pee-wee leagues. Some folks got to calling him Gunslinger Two, The Pistol, Son of a Gun, things like that. He was so good that when he was ten they made him play with the twelve-year-olds, and when he was thirteen he was quarterbacking what might as well have been the Lee High junior varsity. They used the pee-wees like a farm system in baseball, see, right down to the same uniforms and the same defensive and offensive sets. Still do, as a matter of fact. Hell, it looked like he was gonna step right in and be The Man for Lee High when he got to be a freshman, just an eighth-grader. To answer the second part ain't that easy. The worst thing about it for me was that there wasn't anybody I could blame. It was just one of those stupid accidents you hear about all the time, where a kid happens to be in the wrong place at the wrong time. Excuse me a minute. I need some more water here, to clear my throat. Okay. It was a Saturday in November. November the twenty-second, to be exact, nineteen-eighty, moving up on Thanksgiving. He'd just completed fifteen out of twenty-one passes for five touchdowns, the other ones being flat-out dropped. So he'd won his last pee-wee game, big-time, before he'd go on to high school and college and maybe the pros. Who knows? Who'll ever know? Anyway, what happened was, an older buddy who had his driver's license came by the house and picked him up so they could run over to the Steak 'n' Shake to get milk shakes and cheeseburgers. Said he'd be back in time for us to watch the FSU game that night on television. FSU was using the pro sets, you know, a real air show, and we were gonna chart the passing routes, figure out how they were doing things. He just, well, he just never came back. Look here, this ain't easy. If anybody wants to butt in, be my guest.

...

Hello? Goodness, it's after eleven. Am I on the air?

Yes, ma'am.

Is all of this true? I was seeing what's on the radio this time of night and I came across this show.

Yes'm. It's true, all right.

There used to be a radio show called You Are There, *with Edward R. Murrow, where they dramatized historical events such as the burning at the stake of Jean d'Arc. This isn't one of those, is it?*

No, ma'am, this is for real, the best I can remember it. Let me finish, okay?

I'm sorry. Lord, I feel like a voyeur.

Whatever. Anyway, to pick up the story, there's this road that takes you over to the Steak 'n' Shake on Roswell Road in Sandy Springs. Lots of curves and trees and parked cars. It was dusk when they left, getting hard to see, you know. What the cops guessed happened was, a dog jumped out from between some parked car, probably chasing a cat or something, and the boy that was driving swerved to keep from hitting it. The skid marks showed 'em going into a slide and then they went into a roll, banged off a car, went airborne, and hit a tree. They weren't wearing seatbelts, and both of 'em were killed instantly. They were still cleaning up the mess when me and Ginny got there. There was my son. Covered up with a sheet on the sidewalk. What was left of him, anyway.

I'm—I never . . . You poor man.

Yes'm, that's about the way I looked at it. Got on my pity-potty, all right.

But when you lose a child, you're entitled to all the grief you want.

Yeah, but I sort of overdid it.

We can't survive disasters alone. My husband and I suffered a similar experience with a child of ours, and we spent thousands of dollars on psychiatrists just to get over it.

The way it turned out, a shrink would've been cheaper for me.

So you did seek therapy, then?

Yes'm. Jim Beam whiskey. Enough to fill the Atlantic Ocean.

Goodness.

That, and women.

Oh, my.

I didn't know what else to do with myself, see? Soon as we buried the boy, I locked up his room just the way he left it, made a museum out of it, and then I fixed up this little memorial for him out in the backyard. Dug a hole for a pond, lined it with flatrocks, put in a fountain, bought some goldfish, drug a bench out there, put up a headstone, all of that. A whatchamacallit.

A grotto.

Yeah, that's it.

That's sweet.

We had ourselves a little ceremony out back when I finished it, me and Ginny and Mags. Ginny remembered this poem about an athlete that died before his time.

How touching. Let me guess. "To an Athlete Dying Young." A. E. Housman.

Sounds about right. At first, I thought she said Heisman, like in Heisman Trophy.

Perfect choice.

Well, you know what the poem means, then, how it's supposed to be better to go while you're on top, before you grow up and find out that life can be a bitch. We all had a good cry, like we were saying a proper goodbye to Ricky, and Ginny, tough as she is, she just got up and walked away and never looked back. It took Maggie a little longer, but she got over losing her brother soon enough. Me, I didn't do so hot. I wound up spending half my nights out there around the fountain, what you call the grotto, drinking and thinking, playing with the goldfish, watching the moon come up, missing Ricky something fierce. I don't mind saying I cried a lot. Pretty soon I wadn't no good for nobody, especially Ginny and Mags. I didn't even care about watching football anymore if I couldn't watch it with my son. Ginny kept telling me, It's over, he's gone, nothing we can do about it, but that didn't do me any good. An athlete dying young, my ass. It just got worse and worse. I kept picking fights, losing jobs, getting drunk, chasing women, making a general ass out of myself. Wadn't helping nobody, especially myself. With all due respect, ma'am, I don't think there's a shrink in the world that could pull me out of something like that, do you? Hello? Ma'am? Guess I lost her.

...

Gun. If I've got my dates right, wouldn't the boy be quarterbacking Lee High this fall?

You can count on it.

They're pretty loaded this year, way I hear it.

Always are. It's a regular football factory out there.

How do y'all stack up with 'em this year?

We don't play 'em, thank God. Tell you the truth, a little ol' school from in town like McGill can't compete with the Robert E. Lees. They've got facilities you wouldn't believe. Looks like a small college.

From what I read in the paper, what they ain't got they just go out and raid.

Yeah, well, McGill lost a tailback to 'em. It's a lot like what's happened to Grambling. Used to be, Eddie Robinson could get any black kid in America. Grambling was called the black Notre Dame, remember, back before integration. Nowadays, if a black kid's got any smarts, he'll go to the big white schools. Ones that used to be white, anyway.

If that quarterback you've got is that good, then how come he's still at McGill? Looks like his chances would be better at one of the big mostly white schools.

About all I can say is, things happen. Too late for him to change, now that the season's started.

That was a pretty good game he had the other night. What was he, twenty-two for thirty-five passing? Three touchdowns?

Something like that. Three sacks hurt. We got it going pretty good in the second half.

Thanks, Gun. Lots of luck, okay?

Lord willing, and the creek don't rise.

NINETEEN

So that's all it took. By the middle of the week, when he meets Reverend T. Vivian Beaumont for lunch at Deacon Burton's Soul Food Cafe, Billy Ray feels as though the weight of the world has been lifted from his shoulders. To come out with it about the loss of his son has served as an exorcism, a confessional, a house-cleaning, a settling of debts. He doesn't know why it took him so long to make a separate peace, why he had to put himself and Ginny and Maggie through all of that pain, but he isn't asking any questions. Neither is Ginny, apparently, because there was not a word out of her, not even another cryptic message about how "the goldfish died," following his very public exorcism. All she had asked of him when she kicked him out in June was to "get yourself fixed," and now he feels it's been done. Ricky is gone and, much to Billy Ray's surprise, the world proceeds without him. So be it.

Their plastic trays loaded with plates of fried chicken, mashed potatoes, collard greens, fluffy biscuits, and pecan pie, balancing tall plastic tumblers of sweet iced tea to wash it down with, he and the preacher claim a Formica-top table in the corner beneath a roaring floor fan. Deacon Burton's emporium, occupying a squat redbrick building across the street from the Inman Park MARTA station on DeKalb Avenue, has become hugely popular with young white lawyers and plumbers and secretaries these days, all of them more than happy to inch along a cafeteria line while the deacon himself, in an apron and a tall white chef's hat, stands behind the steam table, imploring them to keep it moving and have their cash ready.

"Well done, Brother Gun, well done," the Rev is saying as they settle in. "That was a fine tribute to a fine son, I'm sure. Got those devils under control now, do you?"

"Reckon it took me long enough," says Billy Ray.

"A certain amount of mourning is necessary in the healing process."

"Guess you'd know more about that I would, you being in the Jesus business and all."

"I do, indeed." Greasy fingers or no, the preacher can hardly eat for being hailed by fans, both black and white, who keep on coming by the table to shake his hand.

"But I can see you've got something else on your mind," says Billy Ray, mildly perturbed that no one recognizes *him*.

"For starters, I just wanted to thank you for what you've been doing for these boys, Brother Gun."

"Think nothing of it, Rev. I gotta admit I'm pretty surprised how things are going, myself."

"The Lord works in mysterious ways."

"Downright weird, if you ask me."

The preacher says, "Did Coach Graves tell you about the frozen steaks that showed up at the school this morning?"

"Well, I haven't checked in with him today. Steaks, you say."

"Got a box of 'em. 'Anonymous' sent 'em. A note said there's gon' be forty more every Thursday so the Mamas'll have to time to thaw 'em out for the pre-game meal every week. Got you to thank for that, too, I'm sure."

"'Anonymous'? Reckon they're safe to eat?"

"Had 'em checked out. Grade-A prime, hard as bricks. These boys never dreamed they'd be eating like this."

"Ain't that something." Billy Ray suspects that the Ansley Park ladies are at work again, that he ought to thank them on the radio show. "Looks like the ol' McGill Panthers have got fans they didn't know about. Some of these folks helping out wouldn't go to Grady Stadium without bodyguards."

"That's what I wanted to talk to you about, Brother Gun." Reverend Beaumont leans forward across the table conspiratorially, drops his voice, lays a hand on Billy Ray's arm. "We appreciate everything you're doing. Want you to know that. But I've got a word of caution for you, and I hope you'll understand where I'm coming from. What we got to watch out for is making it look like here's some more of that same old business about white folks feeling sorry for black folks. You know. 'Here's some more sorry old clothes we don't need anymore, hope y'all will be beside yourselves with joy if we pass 'em on to you.' Understand what I'm saying?"

"But we ain't talking about used clothes here, Rev. We're talking about forty steaks every Friday afternoon. Blocking sleds, barbells, fancy new exercise equipment. And I ain't even got to what I'm laying out just to keep this kid fed."

"No, no, that's beside the point, Brother Gun. The point is, this can't be a black-and-white thing. We can't be telling the Mamas that if it wasn't for white folks these boys would still be riding a busted bike and getting sick on barbecue. They don't want to hear that anymore than they want to be reminded they're mostly on welfare."

"But I don't see how we're gonna get around that, Rev."

"It's easy, Brother. Just don't say anything. Those steaks are *there,* that's all. Just showed up. See where I'm coming from?"

"I guess so."

"Your thanks comes from the smiles on the Mamas' faces. The full stomachs on the boys."

"Yeah, well, I reckon that ought to be enough."

"And by the way"—the preacher is neatly stacking the chicken bones on his platter now—"you won't be seeing the need to go celebrating your victories now, will you?"

"I don't follow you, Rev."

"Shaking hands with your old friend Jim Beam?"

"Aw, naw. I kicked him out of the house."

"You're sure about that, now?"

"Oh, there might be some in a closet somewhere."

"Don't be playing with it, would be my advice, Brother Gun. That'd be like messing with a rattlesnake. Jump up and bite you before you know it."

"Truth is, Rev, I forget where I put it. Hadn't thought about it 'til you brought it up."

"Well, hallelujah, then, Brother Gun. Looks to me like we beat more'n Cross Keys High School the other night. Got the devil on the run, too." The preacher lifts his tumbler of melted ice and presents it for a toast. "Hallelujah and a big amen, Brother."

...

Except for the Friday-night games themselves, the signal event of each week for the football program at McGill High is Film Night each Wednesday during the season in the basement of Rev. Beaumont's church, First Calvary AME Revival Assembly, just south of Little Five Points on Moreland Avenue. What started out as a private screening of the previous week's game film for those parents who might be interested has evolved into an all-out celebration, replete with gospel music, a church supper, and introductions of each and every one of the Panthers and, finally, a florid narration of the game film by Coach Herman Graves himself. Tank insists that his players wear coats and ties. The Mamas can be counted on to show up in their Sunday dresses. The cheerleaders are there, too, wearing their scanty outfits.

Billy Ray is reminding Mavis of this, trying to convince him that passing up Film Night is not an option, but he is getting nowhere. It is past six o'clock already, less than an hour before the start of the program, but the kid has locked himself in his room.

"Come on, ace, you can help make the Mamas' week." Billy Ray is outside, in the hallway of the duplex, talking to the door.

"I told you, man, I ain't got no tie to wear."

"Ties, I got. Take your pick."

"Probably won't match my coat."

"Christ, anything goes with a blue blazer."

"It's wrinkled from all this movin' around. Rats probably got to it."

"Coats, ties, what's the difference? Hell, you can wear one of mine. We're about the same size. This ain't no fashion show."

"I've seen the film already, okay? Half a dozen times. Upside down and backwards. Hell, I got it memorized."

"Well, the Mamas ain't. Come on, Mavis, knock this crap off. You're gonna make this thing if I have to knock the door down and drag your ass out of there." Billy Ray is about to run out of ideas. "Hey, you know what? The cheerleaders are gonna be there. Shanikah. Hanh? What do you think?"

"Now I *know* I ain't going. She'll laugh at me. Hell, no. Ain't no way."

"*Damn!* Hey, sport, this is the new Mavis we're talking about here. You don't live in Fatback anymore. Hell, you're a star now. Her old man's probably begging her to wise up before you sign with the pros and get rich. What do you think? Hello?"

Rima has come up behind Billy Ray while he is arguing through the door with Mavis. She pushes him aside and takes over. "Mavis, honey," she says, "I think I know what this is all about."

"Don't call me that. You ain't nothing but my teacher."

"Whatever. Look, Mavis, this is about your mama, isn't it?"

There is a pause this time. "Maybe."

"She happens to be unavailable at the moment, see? We're filling in for her, that's all. You don't want to be the only player there without family, do you?"

"Y'all ain't my family."

"We're as close as you can get right now, hon."

"Tell you what," he says. "She'll be out in a couple of weeks. I'll go then, okay?"

"Won't work, Mavis. You're the captain, the star of the team. You're going to go to this damned thing whether you want to or not. Now get your ass out here. Let's go."

The door opens. Mavis is still wearing his jeans and a T-shirt, bare-footed. "Y'all be the only white folks there."

"That's their problem, sport, not ours," says Rima. "You've got fifteen minutes. Coat and tie, a shoeshine and a smile. Move it."

...

The First Calvary AME Revival Assembly is housed in a low granite building on a knoll at the corner of Moreland Avenue and Jones Street. Built when times were good, in the 1920's, the church has survived the Depression and the Second World War and even the migration of wealthier families who found greener pastures when it became possible for black people to live wherever they chose. Church enrollment is down from a high of nearly five hundred in 1960 to fewer than one hundred. Now the surrounding neighborhood is poor and black and old, a blight of creaky cars and wheelchair ramps and Craftsman homes in need of repair, and the mission of the church has changed. "From the Cradle to the Grave," reads the hand-lettered message on a billboard out front, nailed to four-by-four posts sunk into the weedy lawn, but there are more funeral services than baptisms inside the church these days. Reverend Beaumont is especially proud of the services his church provides for the needy: used clothing, free lunches for the aged and out-of-work, cots for the homeless at night, AA meetings, Bingo games, a jerry-built shelter on the corner where laborers can queue up and hope for day jobs every morning.

They are the last to arrive, in Rima's pickup, and when they descend to the commodious basement of the church they come upon a scene that has the feel of a revival meeting. The cots for the homeless have been folded up and pushed aside, making room for a sea of laundry tables and metal folding chairs prepared to seat nearly a hundred parents and grandparents and siblings. Up on the stage, where a four-piece band (two lead guitars, a bass, and a drummer) swings away on "When the Saints Go Marchin' In," there are three long tables where the thirty McGill players will eat, facing the crowd for all to behold, and a projection screen with a lectern beside it. The cheerleaders who aren't dishing out spaghetti, salad, and slices of white bread on paper plates along one wall of the room are stapling a long roll of paper to the curtains behind the stage that reads, Panther Power!!

Mavis's reluctance to attend is forgotten the minute he enters the room in a faded blue blazer, still fussing with a garish green-and-gold Green Bay Packers necktie loaned to him by Billy Ray. From the whoops and shouts that greet him—*Air Mavis!* from Pig Thomas, and, from the cheerleaders, *Mavis, Mavis, he's a dream!*—he is obviously regarded as something more than just one of the boys. His primary receivers, Streak and Runt and Tree, crowd around, giving him high-fives. Antwan ("Squat") Jenkins, the guard he chewed out in front of the crowd for jumping offsides during the game Friday night, fakes a playful punch before embracing him in a bear hug. A Touchdown Mama rushes him like an incoming linebacker, causing him to flinch in self-defense, then thrusts a paper plate loaded with spaghetti and salad and bread into his hands. A good-looking cheerleader, recognized by Rima as Shanikah Jackson, the erstwhile girlfriend, sidles up to him and whispers into his ear. Soon, he is joining the other players at the special tables set for them on stage, leaving Billy Ray and Rima to feel like empty-nesters.

...

Having been the last to go through the serving line, they have no choice but to sit at the same table with Clarice Robbins and Herman Graves. It's bad enough that they are the only white people in the room. Now this. Billy Ray is idly conversing with Tank—practice schedule, the upcoming game with the Tucker Tigers, a wrinkle on a new play he has devised, anything—when the principal starts in on Rima.

"That's an interesting color, dear," she says, nodding at Rima's purple hair. "Did you spill some paint?"

"Nope," says Rima. "It's straight out of a bottle."

"How inventive. For Halloween, I suppose."

"For McGill High. I call it Panther Purple."

"Oh, it's *purple*. I wasn't sure."

"What I wanted was blue, just like yours," says Rima, peering at Clarice Robbins's salt-and-pepper Afro with its hint of blue. "How do y'all get that color, anyway?"

"I beg your pardon. '*Y'all*'?"

"Older women. I never could figure—"

"This is my natural color."

"Oh, I'm sure. But let's say if you wanted to look younger, my age, for instance, I could mix up a batch for you. We could have a hen party, just the two of us, you know."

Clarice drops it and turns on Billy Ray. "Too bad your wife couldn't come, Mister Gunn. Is she at home, caring for the *chill-ren*, while you're, while you're *out?*"

"Well, ma'am, she's pretty busy."

"Ah, Miz Robbins"—Tank jumps right in before it gets nasty—"me and Coach Hunsinger were talking about how nice the boys look tonight in their coats and ties. Wouldn't you agree?"

They do look nice. There might be a future in football for Mavis and perhaps a couple of the receivers, at what the college scouts and sportswriters call "the next level," meaning college football games on Saturday afternoons with huge crowds cheering them on from the stands, but for most of the boys this probably marks the peak of their young lives. It may not get any better than this. They are young, healthy, cocky, certain of their indestructibility, full of themselves. There has been a remarkable transformation from the thirty boys in dirty practice uniforms who withstood the drudgery and berations of that afternoon's practice to the collection of sleek ramrod-straight young men now occupying the stage as guests of honor on this splendid autumn evening. With their glistening ebony faces, trimmed hair, high cheekbones, and sparkling teeth, growing chests about to burst through clean white dress shirts, they look something like handsome black princes who have come in from the provinces to collect their homage from a grateful nation.

...

The official photographer for the Panthers is Herman Graves's son, Sidney, a junior at McGill, skinny as a pencil, who affects bowties and suspenders and has been committed to a career in filmmaking ever since a chance meeting with Spike Lee, who graduated from Morehouse College right here in Atlanta. Even before he entered high school, Sidney was hauling a camera on a tripod to every McGill Panthers game, at Grady Stadium or away, to set up in the press box or high in the grandstand in order to record every play of every game. For "color," his younger brother Arthur roams the sideline and the stands and even the locker room with a hand-held camera. Sidney's charge is to have the film ready as soon as possible on Sunday afternoon so his father and Coach Thomas can begin the long process of critiquing every move made by every Panther on every play, first for themselves and later in team meetings. Multiple copies are then made and shipped out, as a professional courtesy, to every team remaining on McGill's schedule. The only public showing comes on Film Night, in the basement of Rev. Beaumont's church.

"You about ready, son?" Now, with the tables cleared and everyone seated—the players on the stage, the families in their chairs on the floor of the hall—Tank, in his familiar purple suit, stands at the lectern beside the big screen and speaks over the microphone to Sidney, who stands beside a movie projector at the other end of the long room.

"All set, Pop."

"Somebody cut the lights, will you?"

Let the celebration begin. Sidney has instructed his sister, Shirelle, a freshman cheerleader, to aim a pinpoint spotlight on the individual players as their names come up during Herman's ad-libbed narration of the game film. When the house lights are dimmed and the film begins to roll, the only sounds are of the whirring projector and of Herman Graves's voice. It's a lot like watching a silent home movie, with special remarks and asides by the host, except in this case there is a willing audience prepared to stay all night if necessary.

Using the raw footage shot by his brother Arthur, Sidney has edited the film with a sort of prologue, an artful collage, to set the scene: a long shot of Grady Stadium, closeups of faces in the gathering crowd, a mongrel dog scampering across the field, the McGill band members marching to their seats, the Cross Keys players and coaches arriving by school buses, the warmups, Rev. Beaumont delivering his pre-game sermon in the locker room. There is a buzz in the audience this night as the Mamas look for familiar faces in the crowd shots, some good-natured boos when they see the Cross Keys players embarking from the buses, much laughter as a waterboy chases the dog off the field. "Well, now, a little excited, are we?" Herman intones when the camera shows the boys in the end zone, about to make their grand entry, and then zooms in on a dark mass spreading across the crotch of one kid's uniform. Sidney Graves, in spite of his commitment to truth in film-making, has kindly ignored the impulse to show the face of Anterrius ("Mouse") Leonard in his opening-night agony. The crowd goes wild, just the same.

"All right, here we go now, first step on a long journey to glory," Tank says as, up on the screen, Mavis and Pac-Man, the Panthers' co-captains, walk to the middle of the field for the coin toss. When Shirelle's spotlight finds the two, seated on the stage, they raise their fists and the Mamas begin applauding. "Aw, me, boys, that ain't no way to get the season started," Tank says, to loud groans from the crowd, when the Indians' punt returner weaves his way to a fifty-yard touchdown run on the first punt of the game. "That's more like it now," he says, when Runt Armstrong takes in the ensuing kick-off and smokes up the middle for a seventy-five-yard return that ties the score. "Stand up there, Jerome, so we can see you." Runt rises and is high-fived by the teammates around him, to great cheers from the Mamas. "Time for 'Air Mavis,'" Tank says when Mavis begins to find his receivers, the spotlight finding Mavis, the Mamas beginning to chant, "*Ma*-vis, *Ma*-vis, *Ma*-vis!" "Let's give that young man a hand," Tank says when the game little Cross Keys quarterback goes down and is hauled away. With a wink: "Takes a lot of courage to play against the mighty McGill Panthers."

By the time the film is over, Tank hasn't missed a single player. Criticism for dropped or overthrown passes, missed tackles or broken assignments, fumbles or arm-tackling or foolish penalties—and there were plenty of such mistakes to go around during this opening game of the season—is for team meetings, not here, not on Film Night. What with all of the pauses and re-runs and asides by Tank, even a drum roll here and there, it's going to take nearly two hours to show a film of a forty-eight-minute game. "Son, how 'bout running that back one more time," is the emphasis here, Herman to Sidney, late in the game, when Mojo starts pounding away, time after time after time, at the Cross Keys defensive line. "Demetrius Anthony, stand up there, son, and point out yo' Mama and Daddy so we can see 'em." The spotlight plays on proud parents and a happy son, warmly applauded by everyone in the house, and soon the night is closing down on what has been a very fine day, indeed.

...

Standing outside on the front steps of the church, waiting for Mavis to come out so they can head home in the pickup, Billy Ray and Rima are making small talk with Tank when they see a middle-aged black couple approaching from the shadows. The man is a big one, well over six feet tall, dressed regally in a black double-breasted suit with a white-on-white tie; the woman is sleek and handsome, wearing silver hoop earrings and a tailored rust-colored dress.

"Doggone if you aren't getting good at this stuff, Herman," the man says to Tank. "You ought to buy yourself a bus and take your show on the road."

"Well, I've had a lot of practice at it after fifteen years," says Tank.

"Sidney's going to make a fine filmmaker one of these days. I know you're proud of him."

"Sure am. Much as I hate to admit it, they can't all be football players."

"And Arthur," the woman says. "Such a wonderful touch with the camera. I thought I'd die when he showed Anterrius's, well, *anxiety* before the game."

"That was a hoot, wasn't it?" Tank introduces the couple to Billy Ray and Rima. "This is Rashad's folks, y'all. Rashad, that's 'Streak' to me and you, Gun. This is Jabari and Janelle Lattimore. They're the ones that pay for all that film the boys shoot up every week." Jabari, he explains, is a lawyer in practice for himself; Janelle a doctor on staff at Grady Memorial Hospital. Billy Ray remembers now: their son is a good student who could have wound up in a private school, or maybe as one of Robert E. Lee's token black athletes, but he was about to graduate and simply wanted to finish high school with his friends. Tank continued: "I'm sure y'all know about Billy Ray helping out with the team."

"Rashad's told us all about that," says Jabari Lattimore. "I remember when 'Hunsinger the Gunslinger' was with the Packers. Looks like some of it's already rubbed off on Mavis. The boy isn't the same as last year, that's for sure."

Billy Ray puffs up and says, "We ain't done yet, but he's starting to come around. It helps to have somebody like your boy that can catch him."

Tank clears his throat and says, "Billy Ray and Miz Byrd are sort of looking out for Mavis while his mama's gone."

"Heard about that, too," says Streak's father.

"Poor woman," says Mrs. Lattimore.

"I just wanted to let you know, Billy Ray, that if anything comes up about all of this, just let me know."

"Everything's on the up-and-up, far as I can tell," says Billy Ray.

"That's the way I read it. But you never know."

Jabari Lattimore is pulling out his billfold to find a business card for Billy Ray when the five of them turn to see Mavis approach. With him is Shanikah. They are holding hands.

"We're gon' go out," Mavis says to Billy Ray and Rima. "I'll be home later."

"Hey, I don't know about this," says Billy Ray. "What time is it, anyway?" He checks Rima's wristwatch. "It's almost eleven o'clock, you know."

"We won't be long."

"It's a school night, you know. You gotta be up at six to get your work in."

"Hey, it's just for ice cream."

"Dammit, kid." Billy Ray sputters, thinks about apologizing to the Lattimores for cussing, looks at Rima. "What do you think?"

"Home before midnight?" she says.

Billy Ray looks betrayed. "That's damned late, if you ask me."

"Midnight, then." Mavis and Shanikah disappear into the shadows, as quickly as they came, headed off somewhere for the girl's car. Billy Ray's ears begin to burn when he hears Tank and the Lattimores begin chuckling and needling him about the futilities of parenting in these modern times.

TWENTY

Wrapped in dry ice, shipped from a meat-packing plant in Omaha, a crate of steaks arrives like clockwork at the doorstep of the gym at McGill High every Thursday morning. At first, the Mamas don't know what to make of this new deal. They miss the tradition and the camaraderie of their weekly soulfests—the ceremonial all-night cooking of the pig (even if their men did get carried away sometimes), the stirring of the beans and potato salad and cole slaw, the loud music and the matronly insistence that the boys stuff themselves until they collapse into a collective stupor—but the results tell them that this might be the best way to go. Fueled by the proteins and carbohydrates found in the steaks, and in baked potatoes sent over by Lorino's Grocery, calmed by a peaceful nap in the gym *sans* rap music, their opening-game jitters behind them, the young Panthers have settled into the long season.

At least nobody pees in his pants or throws up on the sidelines the following Friday night when they board a yellow city school bus for the ride to one of the outlying suburban towns and beat up on the Tucker Tigers, 48-17, with Mavis throwing three of his five touchdown passes to Rashad Lattimore. It's much the same on the third weekend of the season when the kid breaks out, completing twenty of thirty passes for six touchdowns in a 54-20 rout at home of St. Pius X, a small Catholic school known locally as

243

"Pi Hi," and the week after that when they pull out a 38-35 win up the road over the Decatur Bulldogs. Pig Thomas's skittish defensive players are still overly eager, as leaky as a fishing net, but Billy Ray's mantra is holding fast: *If they give up forty points, then we'll by-God have to score forty-one.* To be precise, they have outscored their first four opponents by an aggregate of 181 points to 94.

With such a suspect defense, they haven't cracked the top ten in the weekly rankings of metro-area high school teams published by the Atlanta *Journal-Constitution*, but "Air Mavis," as the papers are now referring to the offense, has begun to pick up a following. The game against little Pi Hi drew nearly 2,000 fans to Grady Stadium, about double the crowd for the opener, and inspired this headline: "The Little Train That Might." Assistant coaches from Georgia Tech, Georgia, Auburn, and a scattering of smaller colleges like Chattanooga and Western Carolina have begun to show up and express interest in Mavis, Rashad ("Streak") Lattimore, and Markese ("Tree") Fleetwood; maybe even "T-Bone," Melvin Williams, if he can lose some of that weight. Billy Ray likes to think that part of this interest is due to his radio show, which has evolved into a weekly ramble about high school football in Atlanta, with inevitable attention paid to the comings and goings of the McGill Panthers and their star quarterback. Something must be working, at any rate, for B. D. Spotswood's latest marketing survey shows that the ten-to-midnight slot on Sunday nights is now approaching the nine-to-ten-o'clock Sunday Night Gospel Hour in listenership. Out of either loyalty to Billy Ray or sheer curiosity about this team he is hearing about every Sunday night on his own radio station, B. D. has screwed up his courage to show up at Grady Stadium for both of the home games so far; with the hubcaps left on his Cadillac, and with the promise of a seat in the safety of the press box.

Billy Ray has been here before and he's loving it. Except that Mavis isn't his own blood and bone, this is becoming a replay of what it was like between him and Ricky. They're a long way from being father and son—Mavis is about to "yes-ma'am" Rima to distraction, and will refer to Billy Ray as "Gun" mostly when trying to impress his teammates—but the kid is a willing and apt pupil who seldom makes the same mistake twice. He's on a tight schedule during the week: rousing awake at daybreak, working on his legs at the Nautilus machine, shoveling in a heavy breakfast, walking the mile to school, taking charge of football practice in the afternoon, sitting down to a steak and potato for dinner, enduring an hour at the books with Rima, ending the day by talking football and studying college and NFL films that Billy Ray has taped.

Finally, after the Friday night game, there is the weekend: sleeping late to recover from his bruises, getting a rubdown from Rima if she's in the mood, joining Billy Ray to watch the Saturday college football games on the big television in the living room at The Ranch; all of that followed by a light workout on Sunday afternoon with Billy Ray and the receivers at the stadium. When she can sneak away from her daddy, Shanikah Jackson has taken to coming around the place in her car on Saturday or Sunday nights so the two of them can "go out" Billy Ray doesn't know exactly what that means and he doesn't ask, although he assumes that the boy is smart enough to use a condom if it comes to that—"going out" being a privilege the Gun has reluctantly granted in exchange for Mavis's full attention during the week.

...

It is his considered opinion that he and Mavis can accomplish more in a couple of leisurely hours at the stadium on Sunday afternoons than they can during a whole week of practices with the full squad. Most of the focus during the week is on preparing the team for that Friday's opponent, which is altogether necessary and good, but Billy Ray knows by now that nothing good is going to happen for this bunch if the passing game doesn't near perfection. He's leaving the blocking assignments and all of that to Tank and whatever defense can be mustered to Pig. His mandate remains the same, to push this passing game into full throttle, and he can best do that without having to waste time on anything else.

They gather at Grady Stadium as usual on the Sunday afternoon following their fourth straight win, the one they had to pull out of the fire in the last minutes against Decatur. There's nothing like catching a few touch-down passes to grab the attention of a teenager whose hormones are flow-ing like sap in the springtime, and this can explain why Mavis's main men are impatiently waiting when he and Billy Ray show up. All three of them are listed in the top ten, city-wide, in total receptions. Tree Fleetwood, the perfect tight end as a towering basketball center with sure hands, leads the entire city with twenty-seven catches. Streak Lattimore, the wide receiver with blistering speed, leads all receivers with eleven touchdown passes. There's no category for yards gained after a reception, but surely nobody in the city is close to Runt Armstrong, the quick little point guard on the bas-ketball team, whose assignment is to haul in Mavis's short outlet passes from his position in the slot and see how far he can run.

Billy Ray knows that Tank and Pig are already in the football office, grading the film of the Decatur game, trying to figure out some way to keep from giving up so many points, and that knowledge alone makes him even happier about being where he is at this precise moment: stretched out on the brown grass of mid-October on a perfect day, looking up at banks of puffy white cumulus clouds that look like snow-capped mountains, listening while four boys with their lives ahead of them talk about football and girls. They say that a middleaged man can go either of two ways when he hangs out with teenagers, feel either twice his age or half of it, and right now he feels that he, not Mavis Jackson, should be quarterbacking this team.

"No shit," Markese is saying to Runt, "poured water in your gas tank?"

"What I said."

"Motherfucker," says Streak.

"Said next time she catches me with that bitch she's gon' set the whole car on fire, man."

"God *damn!"*

"Mother!"

The boys ponder this, wonder if celebrity is worth the price, make the point that last year at this time the women of McGill High were laughing at them instead of stalking them, night and day, in the hallways and after games and even on the phone after midnight. "Drop one in the end zone and then see how much she cares," says Mavis, sounding like a man of some experience.

"You crazy, man?" Runt shoots a look at Billy Ray. "Then I got Coach all over my ass."

"Puttin' up with the bitch be better," says Markese.

"Panther Power!"

"Fuckin'-A."

This out of their system, they go to work. The boys are wearing shorts and T-shirts and sneakers, Billy Ray a pair of jeans and his Green Bay sweatshirt and Converses. While the three receivers do some stretching and lobbing a football among themselves, Billy Ray and Mavis take the other ball he has brought along, one of the two he lifted that day they popped in on Ginny at the big house in Crestwood to fetch the Alabama film and projector and stuff, and begin warming up like pitchers in a bullpen, increasing the velocity and the distance of their throws until Mavis seems ready for some serious throwing.

"Okay, sport," Billy Ray says to Mavis. "You know why that pass to Streak got picked off in the fourth quarter?"

"The one they scored on? The guy came out of nowhere."

"Naw he didn't. The ball had his name on it. You mailed it to him."

"Come on, man, the dude got lucky."

"Let's see what we've got." Billy Ray stands over the ball, spread-eagle, playing center. "Streak, flanker right. Runt, line up on his tail. Y'all haul ass ten yards, then Streak, you break for the sideline, and Runt, you come across the middle. You know the play."

Billy Ray bends over the ball, snaps it to Mavis, then turns to watch. The boys break away from the line as Mavis takes the snap, fakes a handoff to the imaginary Mojo, steps back into a pocket, watches Streak all the way until he pivots hard toward the right sideline, then completes a pass to him. Streak imagines faking a defensive back out of his jock strap, spins, and then sets fly toward the end zone. "Quick six!" Streak yelps when he comes back with the ball.

"Yeah," says Billy Ray. "For the bad guys."

Mavis says, "Shit, man, it was right on the numbers."

"Wrong numbers, kid." Billy Ray explains while he is handing Mavis the ball and telling the others to line up again. "We've got at least a dozen pass plays that work off this same set. If they're playing man-to-man and they're quick enough, they can cover everybody. Trick is, you've got to give 'em something to think about. Here's the trick." Mavis bends over the ball and snaps it to Billy Ray. Tree, lined up at tight end on the left side, breaks straight ahead downfield while Runt and Streak on the right side fire off the line and run ten yards before Runt breaks left, over the middle, and Streak heads for the sideline. While Billy Ray is faking to his fullback and moving back into his pocket, he looks first at Tree on his deep route down the left sideline and then, like an actor overplaying his role, follows Runt all the way until he makes his cut. He fakes a throw to Runt so convincingly that the kid finds himself bracing to make the catch, but then he stops and wheels and guns it to Streak. "The last guy you want to look at is the one you're gonna throw to," he says. What that pump fake to Runt has accomplished is to cause the man covering Streak to hesitate for a split second, he explains, which is all Streak will need to get clear. Mavis and the other three nod as though they've just been given the keys to the universe.

They go at it for another hour, Billy Ray now and then stepping in to show them another variation, all of them coming off of the same basic set, but mostly he lets Mavis learn it through repetition. Sometimes the throw is to Tree on the fly pattern in the end zone, sometimes to Runt across the middle, other times to Streak on the sideline. Nobody is working up a serious sweat or getting knocked on his butt. This is at three-quarters, not full-speed, like a training film. This is the way these plays are *supposed* to work; the way they have worked for twenty-five years, since the Dark Ages, when Billy Ray Hunsinger was running the show on this very same playing field for the Forrest Panthers. Over and over and over they go at it. "Again," says Billy Ray. "That'll work," he says. "Bingo!" is all he can say when even he buys the kid's pump fake. Finally, a good day's work done, they knock off and head for home.

...

The first thing they see as they turn the corner onto Rains Street is Ginny's red Blazer, parked in the grassy yard of the duplex beside Rima's black Ford pickup. Mavis cuts a look at Billy Ray when they see it and mumbles, "Uh-oh," under his breath. Billy Ray bumps over the curb and eases the station wagon onto the grass, parking beside the Blazer. "What the hell," he says, cutting the engine. From Rima's side of the duplex, they hear the two women laughing hysterically. Mavis jumps from the car and can't get inside The Ranch fast enough to take a shower. "Yo' problem, man," he says over his shoulder. "I'm outta here."

Billy Ray steps onto the front porch and peers through the screen door to see them sipping beer, seated across from each other at the kitchen table: Ginny in jeans and a T-shirt and sandals, Rima barefooted and wearing her ragged cutoff overalls, yukking it up like sorority sisters who haven't seen each other in years.

"'Hell, I can fix this danged *thang*,'" Rima is saying.

"How'd Florence King put it?" says Ginny. "'Give a man something to fix, he'll either drink it or break it.'"

"Or screw it."

Now they're completely out of control, bent over in laughter, banging their beer bottles on the rickety table. Sure that he has come upon them comparing notes about him, Billy Ray feels his face redden. He doesn't bother to knock, just eases the screen door open and steps into the front room. "Yeah, but if it ain't broke, don't fix it," he says. They look up, surprised to see him, and this sets them to cackling again.

There's only twelve years' difference between the two women, but seeing them together like this, for the first time, reminds him of how much they're alike. Forget the purple hair; with her sassy mouth and good looks, Rima could be Ginny's younger sister. Maybe that's why it's been so easy for him to work through all of this. Rima is the Ginny of twelve years ago, pre-baggage, the one who knew only the good times.

"What's so damned funny?" he says, still hovering in the front room, uncertain about whether to sit or go next door and take a shower, himself.

"Well, now," says Rima, "if it isn't Hubert Hubert his ownself."

"Lolita, I presume."

"You've met my mama." The two stifle giggles at this. "Oh, come on, sport. We aren't going to bite. Pull up a chair. I'll get you a Coke."

While Rima opens the refrigerator door and reaches in, he slides a chair to the table and takes a seat. Whatever the deal is here, he is woefully out of the loop. He has interrupted something and he would dearly love to know what. Instead of being tight-lipped, as she was when he left, Ginny has a new serenity about her that is frightening. "Hi," he says to her.

"Nice little *pied-à-terre*," Ginny says. "Every boy ought to have one."

"Gotta live somewhere."

"Whoever your slumlord is, he could go to jail for this."

"If you don't mind my asking"—Billy Ray hacks to clear his dry throat—"just what the hell's going on here?"

"It doesn't concern you, if that's what you're asking," Ginny says. "It's going to take a lot more money if I'm going to pursue this thing about the band playing 'Dixie.' Since Rima's an artist, I thought she might have something she'll donate for our art sale."

"Yeah, right."

"No, really. You wouldn't believe the legal fees."

"Art? Have you looked around this dump?"

"Better run that by Ham and Evelyn Sutton, hon."

"You mean they let you see that piece of crap?"

"Not really," Ginny says. "I guess I ought to be ashamed of myself, but I'm not. One day while I was visiting Evelyn the phone rang and I went to the bathroom and there it was. 'Eden Redux,' signed by Rima the Bird-Girl. How much did you say they paid, dear?"

"Two thousand. Cold cash."

"I don't think you know art when you see it, Billy. Dress it up, give it an ironic title, put an outrageous price tag on it, there's no telling what people will pay. These penises with the smiley faces, now . . ."

250

"Christ a-mitey," says Billy Ray. "You can't show those things in public. It's pornography, pure and simple."

Rima interrupts with feigned indignation. "I must beg your pardon, sir. It's 'erotica.' The human soul, unbared."

"Bullshit."

"We'd hold a private sale, anyway," Ginny says. "Right here. I've got an A-list of every yellow-dog liberal in Atlanta."

"Let me know when, so I can make other plans."

"Then you'd miss your biggest fans, Billy. The Ansley Park Ladies."

"Wrong," says Billy Ray. "They hide behind the radio. That's what rich people do. They aren't about to show up in public. Not for a stunt like this."

"But there's more. Show him, Rima. The *pièce de résistance*." Ginny nods to Rima, who steps into the front room and beckons for them to follow and drag their chairs in front of the inverted Ping-Pong table, still propped on the two chairs and covered with a bedsheet. When they are seated, she dramatically yanks the sheet away to reveal the result of all the posing and charcoal sketching that has gone on ever since Mavis moved in, most of it unbeknownst to Billy Ray. On a canvas that is nailed to the table with pushpins is an oil painting of Mavis, helmet off, standing on the sidelines at Grady Stadium during a game, the famous light standards in the background. The kid's ebony face with its hint of Cherokee cheekbones is streaked with rivulets of sweat, his eyes squinting in determined concentration, and beside him stands Billy Ray, in his purple-and-gold McGill sweatshirt and khakis, whispering advice to his pupil. The canvas is about four feet wide and two feet high, ready for framing.

"I'm calling it 'Black Prince,'" Rima says. "What do you think?"

Having seen it already, Ginny joins Rima as they turn their eyes toward Billy Ray, waiting for a reaction. He is clearly stunned at first. He leans backwards in his chair to get a longer view, cocks his head first to the right and then to the left, squinting, and finally he gets up and walks up to the painting in order to eyeball the details. The women await his judgment. From next door comes the shuddering of old plumbing as Mavis shuts down the shower.

"What's with the gray hair?" he says.

"That's it?"

"I ain't got no gray hair."

"It's just a little tinge at the temples," says Rima. "Just a hint of the man with the boy."

"Yeah, but hell, you make me out to look like some old fart."

"Check the mirror." Rima is exasperated. "It's not about you, anyway, bubba. It's about Mavis. How about it?"

"The truth?"

"I can handle it."

Billy Ray plays it out for as long as he can. Finally, with the women still waiting for him, he says, "I think you've got it, kid." Rima beams, does a little jig, then hugs him. Ginny stands up and reaches over to squeeze his hand and kiss him on the cheek. He says, "Too bad you weren't around five years ago."

...

A tour of the place seems in order, but that doesn't take five minutes. It *is* what it is, a flophouse for a middle-aged man on the lam and a virtually homeless teenaged boy, few surprises here. They look in on Mavis, sprawled out asleep in his room, and whisper about the orderliness of the room. Ginny finds the disheveled state of her husband's temporary bedroom not the least bit out of character, the ornate bed left behind by Walter and Robbie amusing, its unmade state not surprising. The kitchen, though, with a refrigerator full of steaks in the freezer, is spotless.

"He's starting to give me hell about leaving dirty dishes in the sink," Billy Ray is saying with a shrug. They settle into the overstuffed sofa in the front room, a repository of newspapers and magazines and VCR tapes, bubblegum wrappers and empty bags of Fritos on the floor, even socks and shoes he has discarded at the door. "Damned if I know where that comes from."

"I guess you learn to take care of what little you have," says Ginny. "By the way, what's the latest on his mother? Has he seen her since she left?"

"They've got her down in Macon, at one of those hospitals for druggies. She's in for at least ninety days, the first month in isolation. I've kept him so busy lately, he's quit asking about her."

"Will she ever get out? I mean, surely it isn't hopeless."

"Hell, Gin, I don't know. She can't be forty, but the one time I saw her I took her for sixty, at least. The lady was wasted."

"Looks like you're stuck here for a while, then, right?" Instinctively, she straightens a pile of newspapers on the floor at her feet, separating the New York *Times* from the Atlanta *Constitution*. "With Mavis, I mean."

"Until the season's over," he says. "Four games down, six to go. It'll be after Thanksgiving, if we make the city championship game."

"God, I forgot about that. Do y'all have a chance?"

"It's a long shot. I don't think so, but you never know when you're dealing with teenagers. Right now, this kid's looking like he's ready for the Cowboys."

"Then what? You'll be finished with him when the season ends. Right?"

"Not exactly. Some colleges are looking at him. I want to be kind of his agent on all of that."

. "But you can do that from the house. Right there in Crestwood."

"What I mean is, I can't just drop him, you know. Can't tell him to run along home, son, my work's done here. Back to the streets, kid."

"Maybe his mother'll be out by then. The eligibility rules won't mean anything anymore. Dammit, Billy, you know he can always move in with us until he graduates. I haven't touched Ricky's room since you saw it. I guess we haven't talked about that, have we?"

"No, we haven't, but that's not our decision. That's for Mavis to decide."

"I've got a novel idea. Why don't you ask him?"

"Like they say, I'm playing 'em one at a time."

They're still circling each other, each waiting for the other to bend, on the matter of how things stand between them. "This is pretty silly, you know," she says. "Fifteen miles apart, no more than thirty minutes. You here and me there."

"You want a date? Is that it?"

"Well, as a matter of fact, yeah. *Hell,* yeah. Why not?"

"It's the kid, again, I guess. Me and him, we're on a roll."

"Come on, Billy. He's doing fine. It looks to me like you could get away some Saturday night. We could cook steaks on the grill and, you know, whatever."

"Be okay with me if I never eat another steak."

"Hot dogs, then. Bring Mavis if you want. Yeah. We could have a regular cookout. How about that?"

"Sorry, babe." He wants a cigar, bad, but out of deference to Mavis he's not smoking inside the duplex these days. He wouldn't want him to wake up and hear them talking about him, anyway, so he points the way to the front porch. "I had a hell of a time last Saturday night," he tells her, lighting his cigar and idly watching two squirrels chasing each other in the yard. "I let him take the car so he could go out with some of his buddies. I figured it'd be okay, if he just went out with the guys on the team. Midnight came, no Mavis. One o'clock, no Mavis. I don't have to tell you what I was thinking. Came damned close to calling the cops. Anyway, he comes in at about two-thirty, like nothing's happened, says hello, pours a glass of milk out of the fridge, and then goes straight to bed. Never again. Whither thou goest, *I* goest, pal. The truth is, I'm afraid to let him out of my sight."

"Well, I certainly can't compete with that." Ginny has wrapped both arms around his waist from behind and is nuzzling her head against his back. It's been a while for both of them. Billy Ray turns and pulls her to him, slipping his hands into the rear pockets of her jeans, then chastely kissing her as though this were the first time. "Rima, now, that was another matter," she says. "I'm glad *that*'s over with."

He stiffens. "Glad *what*'s over?"

"My thinking you two had something going."

"Well. I can see how you might've gotten a little jealous."

"Jealous?" Now she breaks away from him and begins laughing, almost hysterically. "Billy, Billy, Billy. Don't you know? Rima likes girls. You mean to tell me you've been here all of this time and you didn't know?"

He tries to recover. "Well, hell, *sure*, I mean she's had some visitors, you know, looked sort of like *dykes*, maybe, but you never know about these art types. I mean, I—*Girls?*"

"A girl can tell, right off the bat."

"And she told you?"

"It's like she'd been dying to tell somebody."

"Well, I'll be goddam."

"Never underestimate the sisterhood, Billy. We girls stick together."

"Son of a *bitch!*" The blood has drained from his head and gone straight to his toes. "What a fucking waste!"

TWENTY-ONE

On the Saturday nearest the twentieth anniversary of Billy Ray's heroics on the field at Tuscaloosa, B. D. Spotswood outdoes himself. Great sheets of rain are whipping against the duplex at ten o'clock in the morning when Billy Ray stumbles out of bed to answer the insistent pounding at the front door. Standing on the porch is a deliveryman wearing a poncho and clutching a huge white box from a local bakery. "You 'Hunsinger the Gunslinger'?" the man says. "I used to be," says Billy Ray. "Happy whatever." He lets the man in and they clear space on the dinette table for the shallow package, which is four feet long and two feet wide. "Enjoy."

The commotion has awakened Mavis, who pads sleepily down the hall in bare feet to see what's up. What they discover is a sheet cake representing a football field, right down to the goalposts and ten-yard markers and red-and-white checkerboard end zones, with twenty-two little plastic football players, red jerseys for the Alabama Crimson Tide, gold for the North Alabama State Catamounts. Slightly larger than the other mannequins is a gold quarterback, wearing the number 13 on his back, with a football cocked in his right hand, and from the football five strands of thread radiate like clotheslines to five separate receivers wearing gold and "catching" the ball at various points all over the end zone. One for each touchdown the Gunslinger threw that day.

The phone rings. It is B. D. "Wiggle-Wiggle, War Damn Eagle, buddy!"

"When you gonna grow up, B. D.?"

"When we get even for that fifty-five to nothing score they ran up on us that time. Not a day sooner. I thought the Bear was gonna live forever."

"I wouldn't hold my breath. Only reason he lived so long was to make your life miserable."

"Bo Jackson's gonna take care of their asses this year. Bo knows! Go, Bo! War Eagle!"

...

Over the last couple of weeks, these interruptions have been coming to the duplex almost hourly, from sunup until close to midnight: phone calls, Western Union telegrams, FedEx letters, UPS packages, bronze teenaged honeys brazenly knocking on the door wondering if "he" is in, mail arriving in such torrents that it won't fit in the box, all of it directed to the attention of Mavis Jackson, c/o B. R. Hunsinger, 705-A Rains Street, Atlanta GA 30307. The McGill Panthers are 7-0 now, with no team of any consequence blocking their path to a perfect season, and it seems to Billy Ray that everybody wants a piece of the kid. He has had to borrow one of the laundry tables from Rima's apartment to bring some sort of order to the stacks of brochures and letters and promotional tapes that have been pouring in from colleges around the South—yes, to B. D.'s consternation, the hated Alabama Crimson Tide is among them—to be arranged in the order of Mavis's interest.

Through it all, the kid has kept his cool. He still wolfs down a big breakfast every morning, puts in fifteen minutes on the Nautilus machine, makes all of his classes, goes through the paces at practice, has his nightly steak-and-potato and thick milkshake to wash it down, and works on the books with Rima at night before talking for a while with Billy Ray, then going to bed with the Panthers' playbook. The Delilahs who keep coming around are flattering, tempting, some of them downright ravishing, but what he keeps hoping for is that Shanikah can shake her old man's unbending animosity toward football and boys who play it. He has gained nearly fifteen pounds in the two months since Billy Ray met him. The limp from the gunshot wound is gone now, but the memory of it has taught him to pay more heed to protecting his knee by simply getting rid of the ball quicker and going limp as a rag doll when he's hit.

The numbers he has begun to put up are phenomenal, better than anything the Gunslinger could have dreamed of for himself in his day and time: seventy-one percent completions, twenty-eight touchdowns against only six interceptions, well over a mile in passing yardage, only nine sacks in the seven games. Having taken a peek in one of the scrapbooks gathering mold in Herman Graves's office, Billy Ray has found to his chagrin that Mavis has already broken all of his records of that magical season in 1961 when he was *Parade* magazine's high school All-America quarterback. When he reluctantly passed that on to Mavis, the kid simply shrugged and smiled and said, "Well, they ran the ball a lot more back then," such humility sounding suspiciously like condescension and making him feel like crap.

Once, by popular demand but against his better parental instincts, Billy Ray took him along to appear on "Jock Talk" at WWJD. Never again. What with all of the phone calls lighting up the switchboard for the full two hours, Spider felt like one of those vaudeville comics trying to keep a dozen dishes spinning in the air. If it wasn't the young women cooing over the air to Mavis, it was the Ansley Park Ladies inviting him to dinner or wanting his size so they could knit him sweaters. Billy Ray would try to get some serious discussion going about how you go about calling audibles at the line of scrimmage when he would be dismissed by some old boy—*Yeah, but that was back in the old days; lemme talk to Mavis*—wanting to know what college he'd rather play for, if he was superstitious about wearing the number thirteen, who he liked among the pro quarterbacks, whether he reckoned Georgia was ever going to beat Tennessee. Sports agents called, and college coaches, and pro scouts, even a guy angling to make a deal with Mavis about representing him in the "not-too-distant future" in regards to commercial endorsements. Except for the opening and the close and the cuts for commercials, Billy Ray hardly got in a complete sentence. When they left, at almost one o'clock Monday morning, Mavis was wearing a satiny Auburn warmup jacket with his name on it, courtesy of Broadus Delaney Spotswood, who by now has convinced himself that only he has the full authority to offer Mavis a full four-year football scholarship to Auburn University.

...

In spite of having found his own way, Mavis still enjoys it when Billy Ray pulls out the cannister holding the film of the game between Alabama and North Alabama State on that distant Saturday two decades ago. It means everything to Billy Ray—they both know that—but there is still much to be learned from studying it, almost frame by frame, as one would constantly replay a training film or old movies showing a master at work: Ty Cobb dropping a bunt, Babe Ruth hitting a homer, Jackie Robinson stealing home. It's the same bad-legged quarterback, the same high-powered passing game, the same type of personnel being used all of these years later by McGill High. It seems to inspire Mavis, being reminded that anything is possible.

The kid has seen this thing so many times that he knows the script by heart. Alabama had lost its opening game that year, to Georgia in Athens, but they were on the way to a second straight national championship when they hosted little North Alabama State at homecoming in what promised to be a laugher. The mighty Crimson Tide was ahead by two touchdowns after only five minutes, hardly time enough for a Bama cheerleader to finish teasing her bouffant hairdo, which probably gave Bear Bryant the idea that this was going to be the romp he had anticipated when he scheduled this patsy in the first place. But then Hunsinger the Gunslinger went to work, completing passes at will, everywhere he chose, driving Bryant to distraction and setting up a thrilling denouement. Eschewing any pretenses of running the ball, working alone out of the shotgun formation, Billy Ray was king of his domain. He had the ball, he had time on his side, he had the Alabama defenders on their heels from chasing down receivers all afternoon. With the ball at Alabama's twenty, Bama leading 40-34, he called his last timeout with only fifty-six seconds left.

"Help yourself to the cake," Billy Ray is saying now to Mavis. He is standing at the projector, the kid stretched out on the sofa, as the rain continues to pour. "B. D. sent enough to feed the whole damn team."

"We could call 'em if it wasn't raining."

"They can eat their hearts out. Ain't got time for that." Billy Ray stuffs his mouth, wipes his lips with a bandanna. "Okay, kid, what next?"

Mavis knows what's next, but he goes along. "They still in man defense?"

"Biggest mistake the old man made all day. What do you see?"

"Their safety's so tired he can't stand up anymore. I've been watching."

"You got it. That's the one you're going after, then. Who you looking for?"

"Tight end, back of the end zone."

"Your biggest man against their tiredest back, right?"

"Like volleyball. Toss it up, let him get it."

"Bingo. Roll 'em."

Billy Ray gets the projector running again, at that precise point in the game, and they watch reverently as the Gunslinger takes the snap, pump-fakes a throw toward two receivers streaking down the left sideline, taking three defenders with them, then rifles a bullet to his tight end in the back of the end zone. The taller receiver, Stick Sims, goes up for the ball and it's no contest between him and the shorter Bama safety. Touchdown, Catamounts. A cut to the scoreboard after the extra-point kick shows N ALA ST 41, BAMA 40, with only thirty-one seconds left.

"Hell, we know the rest. Fuckin' onsides kick." That isn't what was planned. The North Alabama kicker screws up royally, taking his eyes off the ball and shanking what he hoped would be a boomer out of the end zone. Alabama recovers at its own forty-five, makes it to the twenty-five on two quick passes, calls time, lines up for a field goal, makes good on it with three seconds left on the clock. Final score, 43-41 Bama. Four thousand or so North Alabama fans swarm the field and try to take down the goalposts while the Alabama fans hang their heads in shame, lucky to be alive, and trudge out of the stadium. "Hard to tell who won that day," says Billy Ray. "Onsides kick. Can you believe it?"

...

While the film is rewinding, Billy Ray joins Mavis on the sofa and scoops up another slice of cake. "Another thing," he says. "If you're the underdog and you get into one of these games like this, the last thing you want to do is all of that jumping around and celebrating like it's the first time you ever saw the end zone."

"Gon' play hell telling Streak about that."

"That's your job, pardner. Smack him upside the head if he does it. You're the boss."

"Yeah, but hell, Gun, we're gon' be all pumped up."

"You weren't paying attention, son. Five touchdown passes we scored that day. Even on that last one to Stick in the end zone, the one that should've won it for us, you see what he did? Did he slam the ball to the ground, get on his knees and thank God, and then go running around yelling like some damn Watusi who's lost his mind? Hell, no. Didn't do no such thing. Handed the ball to the nearest ref, wiped his hands like he'd got 'em dirty, trotted off to the sidelines like he had some better things to do with his time."

"Stay cool. That it?"

"Tends to piss 'em off when you do that."

"Ta-*daaa*!" The door flies open and they see Rima, dripping wet, holding an armload of newspapers. At the A&P on Euclid Avenue, she has bought a half-dozen copies of the early "bulldog" edition of tomorrow's Sunday Atlanta *Journal & Constitution*, which she is now spilling all over the floor. She bends over to pull out a sports section to reveal what's above the fold on the first page: a big spread about the McGill Panthers, under a headline that simply reads AIR MAVIS!, with a full-color reproduction of her oil painting depicting Mavis and Billy Ray conferring on the sideline. "There's justice after all," she says to them and, to Billy Ray, "Blew your cover, bubba." He thinks of saying *You, too, bitch*, but decides to keep the peace.

He knew something might be up, the way this one sportswriter had been hanging around over the past couple of weeks, but Billy Ray didn't expect anything this grand. There might be some exaggerations here and there—the facilities at McGill aren't *that* bare, the kids aren't *that* poor, the defense isn't *that* bad—but all in all he couldn't have said it better himself. The piece covers just about everything, from what the writer could uncover about the personal travails of Mavis and Billy Ray to the unlikely possibility that McGill and mostly white suburban Robert E. Lee High might be headed on a collision course in the mythical metro championship game at the end of the regular season, but the main focus is on the unlikely relationship between this faded star and the black kid from the inner city. Just about everybody Billy Ray knows has been quoted: Herman Graves and Clarice Robbins at the school, his wife Ginny, B. D. Spotswood, Rev. Beaumont, Frankie Lorino, Mavis and Billy Ray himself, a couple of the Panthers; everyone, it seems, but Rima and Scottie Burns, which is probably just as well.

"You think the phone's ringing now, wait'll tomorrow morning," says Billy Ray. The three of them are sitting on the floor of the duplex now, reading the paper.

"Aw, man," says Mavis, "it ain't that bad."

"They owe me a hundred bucks for using my artwork," says Rima.

"I wasn't no damn alcoholic."

"Close, sport. Real close."

"Guy didn't have to use all that stuff about me falling off the convertible that day. I still say I slipped."

"Right," says Rima. "Live by the sword, die by the sword, I always say."

...

It's the phone, already. Ginny has also been to the grocery, has also picked up an early copy of the Sunday paper. "All in all, not bad," she says. "For one thing, it saves me a lot of time explaining where you've been all this time."

"Yeah, well," Billy Ray tells her, "we're sort of sitting around celebrating, ourselves."

"She's having all of the fun, Billy. Why can't it be me?"

"Just a minute." If it's going to take this turn, he'd better move to the bedroom. Rima and Mavis are still sprawled out on the living room floor, dissecting the story in the newspaper, listening in just the same. He tells Mavis to hang up when he picks up the other line, and soon he is on the Mickey Mouse phone, resuming the conversation. "Come on, Gin. None of this would've happened if you hadn't, if I hadn't moved into town. No McGill, no Mavis, no nothing."

"I know that." She sounds as though she's been crying. "Pretty ironic, don't you think?"

"There's that word again."

"I can't think of a better one."

"So how's Maggie with this? There's a lot of personal stuff in there, you know, stuff about her daddy that maybe she didn't know."

"Oh, hell, Billy, nothing gets by Maggie."

"She's okay, then."

"Fine. She doesn't look forward to having to choose between rooting for her daddy or her school, if it comes to that." In the background he hears a yelp from Maggie, something along the lines of how McGill sucks. "I stand corrected," says Ginny. "But anyway, let's say this game happens, McGill and Lee, will it be here or at Grady Stadium?"

"I think that's done with a coin toss."

"That's a flippant way to do business."

"I'll forget you said that."

"Well, how does this sound. If it's out here, we'll have a party at the house after the game, okay? Everybody welcome. Friends and foe alike."

"Whooaa. Hon, that's so damned far off. Probably won't happen, anyway."

"How about tonight, then? If this rain stops, we could do hot dogs on the grill. Beans, chips, slaw, the works. Just the four of us: you, Mavis, Maggie, and me. Watch some football, whatever. I want to get to know Mavis better, anyway. What do you say, ace?"

"Sorry, kid. Big night on TV. Florida State's playing Miami on ESPN."

"In case you forgot, believe it or not, we can pick up ESPN all the way out here in the boonies."

"You know the deal, Gin. No distractions. Me 'n' Mavis gotta study FSU's passing game. Make notes, chart routes, all of that."

"*Damn* football," she says. "Can't you tell when a girl's putting a move on you?" She slams the phone on him.

...

He knows he should've taken her up on it. Where he really belongs right now is back home, in the knowing arms of his wife, not sprawled out here like some guy passing through town. A halfway house, that's what this place is, a layover for wayward souls. By the end of the third quarter of the FSU game, from the Orange Bowl in Miami, he and Mavis have lost interest. The kid is asleep now, stretched out on the sofa, his face covered by the spiral notebook he was using to record offensive plays that might be worth a try. The girl is on the other side of the duplex, doing whatever it is she does, leaving him alone with himself, not the best company he can think of on a rainy Saturday night.

There's a few fifths of Jim Beam back there in the hall closet, the stuff he held back when he grandly announced he was quitting, but it hardly seems worth the effort to get up from the chair and go fetch it. How do they put it:

You may drink again, but you'll never enjoy it. Scottie says the boys at AA call it "stinkin' thinkin'," an odd phrase, right up there with "walk the walk and talk the talk," but he's too tired to spend much time pondering it. Had he gone out to the house, he might be buried beneath the covers by now, post-coital, hearing the hum of the heating unit and the soft flutter of Ginny's snoring, everything right in the world. Oh, well. He's got a job to do, many miles before he can sleep, might as well finish it. The job, not the whiskey.

At least half of the players he sees on the screen are black. He wonders where they come from, how they got there, what's next for them. Do they have parents and brothers and sisters sitting in the stands together, cozy little family units, proud as they can be, counting the days until the NFL draft brings the American Dream to the doorstep; or are they like most of them, semi-literates after four years in college, paid entertainers at the end of a gig, about to play out the string and go back to the streets as though nothing had happened? Glancing over at Mavis, asleep in a pair of cutoffs, he sees another young hotshot with all of that laid out ahead of him. It's not just the black kids, he reminds himself, reflecting on his own childhood as a gym rat, a street urchin who happened to be able to throw a football. Before you know it, you're stuffing yourself with the crusted remains of a ceremonial "birthday" cake and having trouble remembering what it's supposed to celebrate.

TWENTY-TWO

At sunrise on a foggy Saturday morning, past barns and pastures and Waffle Houses, B. D. Spotswood's dusty white Cadillac rumbles along I-85 on the way south and west out of Atlanta toward the Alabama line. Lest there be any doubt, B. D. has made sure everyone knows this chariot is bound for Auburn and the afternoon's game between the Auburn Tigers and the Georgia Bulldogs, the oldest football rivalry in the South. Hanging from the trunk is a striped tiger's tail. Every time he hits the horn to pass, here comes the first stanza of the Auburn fight song. Rippling in the breeze is an Auburn pennant, clipped to the antenna. The car's bumpers are decorated with orange-and-blue Auburn decals: *I'm a Dye-Hard Fan* (for the coach, Pat Dye), *Bo Knows* (for Bo Jackson), and one reading *Mama Wanted Me to Go to College but I Went to Alabama Instead*. There are also decals celebrating Radio WWJD, the McGill Panthers, and Air Mavis.

Although this will make the first time Mavis has ever been outside the state of Georgia or even metropolitan Atlanta, he is sleeping soundly in the wide back seat with a smile of contentment on his face. There is an Ace bandage wrapped tightly around his non-throwing wrist and a Band-Aid laid above his left eyebrow, from the thrashing he took last night in a 51-20 win over the Clarkston Angorras, McGill's ninth victim in a row, and it didn't help much when they had to be up and on the road before daybreak for the two-hour drive to Auburn. Dressed in a new pair of brown corduroy pants and a black wool crewneck sweater, courtesy of B. D. Spotswood, who wants his boy to make a good impression on the Auburn coaches, he is missing all of the fun Billy Ray is having with B. D. in the front seat.

Anything to break the boredom. "What would you guess is the best thing that ever came out of Auburn?" Billy Ray is saying.

"That's easy," says B. D. "Bo Jackson."

"Guess again."

"Pat Sullivan?"

"Naw, I-85."

B. D. straightens his orange blazer, grins and bears it. When Billy Ray sees a sign announcing an Auburn Agricultural Experiment Station coming up, he says, "Hey, slow down, you don't want to hit the hog." B. D. winces, runs his fingers along the fine crease on his new navy blue slacks, braces for more. "Got another one for you, boss. Auburn guy makes a move on a chick in a bar. She says, 'I might as well save you the time and money, bubba. I'm a lesbian.' Auburn guy doesn't blink. 'So,' he says. 'How's things in Beirut?'"

"I don't get it," says B. D., hitting the horn—*War Eagle, fly down the field, ever to conquer, never to yield*—and Billy Ray doesn't bother to explain.

"Take any Polish joke, make it an Auburn man, you 'bout got Auburn covered."

"I'm getting tired of this, Gun. We've had a bunch of astronauts, too, you know."

"Aw, the stories ain't *all* bad. This old boy from Auburn gets lost in London and asks this Brit, 'Can you tell me where Big Ben's at?' Brit says, 'My good man, here in England we never end a sentence with a preposition.' Auburn guy says, 'Let me put it another way, then. Can you tell me where Big Ben's at, you asshole?'"

"You gon' be out on the road hitch-thumbing if you don't watch it, Gun."

"No sweat getting rides around here. Just stand there scratching your ass and wait for a pickup."

...

The truth is, Billy Ray has always liked Auburn, the earnest underdog in the bitter intrastate rivalry between the state's two major universities. Auburn has always been cast as the "cow college," like Clemson in South Carolina, and Mississippi State and Texas A&M in their own states, the poor cousin to the rich state university. Auburn turns out farmers and engineers, the lordly University of Alabama doctors and lawyers, which has always put old Alabama Polytechnic Institute at a distinct disadvantage when it comes to influencing young football players about where they ought to go to college. Auburn won the national football championship in 1957 with a bunch of mean and hungry country boys from towns like Kansas and Grove Hill and Alexander City, Alabama, but then Bear Bryant took over at Alabama and nothing much worked for Auburn for a while after that. Auburn would wind up on probation for buying players, unable to go to a bowl game, but a slicker Bryant would keep sailing along. In his twenty-five seasons at Alabama until he died in 1983, Bryant lost only six games to Auburn, in the meantime winning a half-dozen national championships. Auburn's only consolation came when Alabama failed to win in a stretch of eight straight bowl games, prompting a story about a restaurant waitress asking Bryant how he wanted his soup: "Better make it a cup, darlin'. I can't handle a bowl."

The reason for this trip is that Mavis Jackson is one of only a dozen prime high school prospects who have been invited to visit Auburn for the Georgia game. They will be shepherded around campus by a gaggle of perky "Tigerettes," given a tour of the athletic dormitory and the practice fields, introduced to the coaches and maybe some of the players, fed lunch at the athletic dining hall, and then allowed to watch the game from the sidelines behind the Auburn bench. Billy Ray knows that Auburn is genuinely interested in recruiting Mavis, having spent many hours on the phone and in personal chats with their coaches, but B. D. is fairly convinced that it is he, a faithful alumnus, who is primarily responsible for their interest.

Having suffered long enough, B. D. isn't going to let Mavis Jackson get away. He has made sure his dues are current with the Auburn Alumni Association and has kept up a steady stream of advisories to the Auburn coaching staff about Mavis's progress, mailing newspaper clippings along with detailed handwritten accounts of each game as the Panthers roll along, assuring them that the kid has all of the right stuff. Out of his own deep pockets, he has paid young Sidney Graves to put together a highlight film of Mavis's season and mailed the tape to head coach Pat Dye. B. D. is also behind the "Air Mavis" movement, the man who financed the Air Mavis T-shirts, decals, and license plates being seen in certain parts of Atlanta these days. From all of these efforts he hopes to receive an upgrade of his season's tickets at Jordan-Hare Stadium, something better than the pair he now owns high in the nosebleed section of the end zone.

After crossing the Chattahoochee River and entering Alabama, they decide to make a restroom stop at the Alabama Welcome Station, decked out with an obelisk proclaiming We Dare Defend Our Rights. "We're in Alabama now, B. D.," says Billy Ray. "Don't forget to set your clock back. *Twenty years.*" B. D. ignores him this time as Billy Ray shakes Mavis awake: "Rise and shine, sport, you got a new world to conquer." Then the three of them stroll into the building, which is crawling with Auburn and Georgia fans alike, all wearing the colors.

There seems to be extra security in and around the rest stop, but they don't give it much thought until the three of them are standing side by side at the urinals. A Georgia fan, wearing all red, turns to an Auburn man and says, nonchalantly, "You know how you can tell a rich flamingo?" The Auburn man bites. "He's the one with a statue of an Auburn man in his yard." All hell breaks loose, the Georgia man barking like a dog and the Auburn man screaming "Waaar EEE-gulll!" at the top of his lungs, and it takes four of the troopers to separate them. Billy Ray has to pull B. D. from the fray and practically shove him into the Cadillac, leaving Mavis to won-

der what sort of madness possesses grown men to get on their knees and
bark like dogs.

...

Auburn, "Loveliest Village of the Plain," is a classic little college town
of about 20,000 souls whose population briefly expands by another 85,000
on football Saturdays. Certain of the parking lots around the stadium have
been small villages unto themselves since the gates were opened to let the
barbarians in on Thursday; vast oceans of tents and vans and recreational
vehicles festooned with Auburn pennants, temporary homes for the faithful,
all of whom are busy chugging beer and cooking barbecue and emitting primordial shouts and implorations to the football gods. It's a carnival, a tent
city, not unlike the scene in the infield before the Daytona 500 stock-car
race.

B. D. parks at the curb in front of Sewell Hall, the building where the
school's scholarship athletes are housed and fed, up on a hill above the stadium. Straightening his orange blazer, he leads Billy Ray and Mavis toward
the wide double doors. When he sees one of the assistant coaches approach,
he whispers, "Better let me take care of this." Hand outstretched in greet-
ing, he says to the coach, "B. D. Spotswood, WWJD radio, Austell, Georgia.
Auburn, class of 'sixty-five. War Eagle! Got Mavis Jackson here, just the
man y'all been waiting for."

The coach, Max Longstreet, gives B. D. a limp handshake and looks
right past him to Mavis and Billy Ray. "Hey, there, Gun, good to see you
again."

"What's up, Max?" says Billy Ray.

"Can't complain. Might rain, but it'll rain on both of us if it does." He
turns to Mavis. "Glad you could make it, Mavis. Welcome to Auburn."

"Thanks, coach. Good to be here."

"Hell of a game last night, Mavis."

"Thanks, coach. Good to be here."

"Tell you what, boys, we've got a busy day ahead for Mavis and the other prospects. Here's your tickets. Y'all take care of yourselves, now. See you after the game."

Wearing his favored long coat, Mavis is being led away by the coach, to be delivered to one of the smiling Tigerettes gathered inside the doors, when B. D. calls him back. "Better let me check you out, boy," he says. "You brush your teeth? Wash behind your ears?"

"What you talking about?"

"Comb your hair, or whatever y'all do with it?"

"Say what?" Mavis looks at Billy Ray for help.

"You want to be sure to call the coaches 'Sir' now, understand?"

"Hey, man. This ain't Sunday school."

"And lookie here"—he leans in to whisper—"don't do no running. If a *FUH-baw* comes your way, now, it might help to pick it up and th'ow it hard as you can, see. Let 'em see that arm, Mavis. Show 'em something. War Eagle! Just don't let 'em see you run. Okay? Got that?" Billy Ray rolls his eyes. It reminds him of the first time he and Ginny delivered Ricky to summer camp. B. D. takes Mavis's face in both hands, looks him in the eyes. "Go get 'em, boy. Wiggle-wiggle. War Damn Eagle!"

...

The book on Auburn fans is that they are among the most fanatical in the Southeastern Conference. It's always been that way, especially since Bear Bryant's arrival at Alabama in 'fifty-eight, when the Crimson Tide suddenly began to dominate the series between the two big cross-state rivals. The story goes that when Pat Dye, the current Auburn coach, decided to accept the job after being an assistant at Alabama for nine years, he went into Bryant's office to let him know about it. The Bear had one piece of advice: "Watch out for those alumni. They're crazy." He could have been speaking of B. D. Spotswood.

With a lot of time of their hands before the kickoff, Billy Ray and B. D. decide to see what's going on uptown, at Toomer's Corner, the intersection marking the heart of Auburn. At nine o'clock in the morning, with old grads beginning to converge from all over the state, the place is coming to life. The huge ancient oak there is still draped with toilet paper from the "rolling" it received after last Saturday's homecoming blowout of the East Carolina Pirates. From loudspeakers in the campus bookstore, where all manner of Auburn regalia can be bought, there comes the constant replaying of the radio tape recording the final four minutes of Auburn's most famous victory over Alabama, now fondly recalled as the Punt-Bama-Punt game, when Auburn blocked and ran into the end zone two consecutive punts to win, 17-16. Toomer's Corner is like a bazaar, set to the music of the Auburn fight song, and B. D. is in heaven.

The first sign that things might take a bad turn comes when B. D. can't resist buying a stupid-looking cap, something like a skullcap that fits over his bald head like a yarmulke, an eagle with wings that flap when the wearer pulls strings that are attached to the wings and concealed in his pockets. The second sign comes when Billy Ray observes that B. D. is nipping whiskey from a silver flask he is carrying in the inside breast pocket of his orange blazer. "Aw, hell, Gun, don't be such a *prune*," he says when Billy Ray tells him he didn't know he drank. "War Eagle!" By noon, when it's time to head for Jordan-Hare Stadium, Billy Ray is stuffing the trunk of the Cadillac with three hundred dollars' worth of Auburn junk B. D. has bought at the bookstore—pennants, boxer shorts, ashtrays, coffee mugs, his own copy of the "Punt-Bama-Punt" recording—while B. D. is freshening his flask from a bottle in the glove compartment.

...

Billy Ray takes it as a measure of Auburn's interest in recruiting Mavis that he and B. D., unlike the others who have delivered prospects to the game and are seated in the stands, have been given seats in the press box. This includes service at a buffet line offering barbecue, beans, slaw, and the works, plus access to the same statistical sheets and press guides and other services available to the working press. Having parked in a special VIP lot in the shadow of the stadium, they get on an elevator and are magically delivered to the press box level, and the minute the doors open B. D., resplendent in his Auburn colors and the stupid-looking eagle beanie, makes a beeline for the wide glass windows opening up to a view of the expansive stadium, slowly filling with 85,000 fans. It's more than he can stand. "Waarrr EEE-Gulllll!" he bellows, like a Rebel Yell signaling a charge of Confederate renegades. He is swarmed immediately by four security guards.

Warned about showing any further outbursts of partisanship in the hallowed press box, even if it's for Auburn, B. D. is shown to a table in a distant corner, handed a plate brimming with barbecue and beans, and told to shut up or be banished forever. Billy Ray gets in the buffet line, helps himself, sticks a press guide and the game-day stats under his arm, and joins B. D. to mollify him and try to keep him out of trouble. When he has finished eating, he sees someone beckoning him from another table. It is Max Longstreet from that morning, the retired assistant coach who is now in charge of recruiting.

"You're gonna have to baby-sit that old boy, Gun," says Max. "We can't have that stuff in the press box."

"I'll do my best, Max. This is a lot like Christmas morning for ol' B. D."

"Who the hell is he, anyway?"

Billy Ray gives him a capsule biography of B. D., of his abiding love of Auburn, the story behind his fervid interest in seeing that Mavis gets recruited by his alma mater. "He's a good old boy," says Billy Ray. "He just gets carried away sometimes. Loves *FUH-baw*, is all." They both glance over at B. D., who is humming the Auburn fight song, pulling the strings that make his eagle's wings flap.

"Look here, Gun, we want Mavis Jackson real bad. He's just what we need right now."

"With the history of his leg and all? Level with me, Max."

"Aw, hell, we got running backs up the ass. Bo Jackson's just the tip of the iceberg. We gotta diversify the offense, work in some passing."

"Mavis is your boy, then. I'm sort of handling all this."

"But he ain't worth probation, I can guarantee you that," says Max. "These damned alumni drive me crazy. Best teams we ever had, back in the late 'fifties, never went to a bowl game. This boy doing anything he ain't supposed to? Buying things for the kid?"

Billy Ray decides to lie, not mention the satin Auburn jacket or the clothes Mavis has on his back today or any of the other things like meals and other gratuities that have come up along the way. "Not having any family, things are a little bit special with Mavis, if you understand what I'm saying," he says to Max. "He's being more or less raised by committee."

"That's great, just *great!*" Max is not amused. "It was a 'committee' that gave a quarterback up in Huntsville an old fishing boat and a used air-conditioner that cost us a trip to the Cotton Bowl. Right after that, one of our own damned coaches wrote personal checks to the twins over in Gadsden that kept the National Champs home admiring their rings, instead of playing in the Sugar Bowl. Turned out the boys' daddy was a preacher, and an Alabama fan to boot."

"Aw," says Billy Ray, "ain't nothing like that going on, I promise."

"Just watch it, Gun. I'm keeping my eyes on that old codger. You better do the same."

...

The reason Billy Ray and B. D. Spotswood find themselves sitting on the top row of the end zone now, midway through the third quarter, is that B. D. lost his senses just before halftime when Bo Jackson hit the hole at right tackle, hurdled over a linebacker, reversed direction, and ran seventy-four yards unmolested for a touchdown that put Auburn ahead. B. D. couldn't just let it go at that. He began running around the press box, flapping his eagle wings and screaming "War Eagle" like a Comanche on the warpath, resulting in immediate banishment. The good news is that he had his regular season's tickets in his billfold. The bad news is that the seats are smack in the middle of a sea of Georgia fans wearing red sweaters, woofing like dogs, not pleased about finding this obnoxious Auburn drunk turn up in their midst.

"What's that on your head, bubba, a *buzzard*?"

"It's a War Eagle, you *chihuahua.*"

"Looks like a peace chicken to me."

"You don't know who you're messing with. I'm a radio *magnet* in Atlanta."

"*Maggot's* more like it."

"Oh, yeah?" says B. D. "I couldn't help noticing your Georgia ring while you were pickin' your nose, you creep."

With the rain beginning to come, Auburn in control of the game, Billy Ray figures the time is right to get the hell out of there. This might take some doing, since B. D. isn't rock-steady on his feet at this point and the elevator is no longer at their disposal. Careening down the spiral walkway like a runaway truck, muttering a "War Eagle!" to everybody he bumps into, B. D. manages to make it to solid ground with Billy Ray's guidance. They reach the parking lot just as another thunderous roar rocks the stadium. Billy Ray loads B. D. into the back seat of the Cadillac, slips in behind the steering wheel, and finds the game on the radio.

Like a beached whale, B. D. is snoring so loudly that Billy Ray has to turn up the volume to hear the rest of the game. It turns out that the roar he heard was to celebrate another electrifying run by Bo Jackson, the one that nails a 24-10 Auburn victory, and now Gun has to find an umbrella to go fetch Mavis from Sewell Hall so they can begin the drive back home to Atlanta. He finds one in the trunk, an orange-and-blue number the size of a pup tent, walks the two blocks up the hill in a steady rain, against a tide of human traffic, then retraces his steps with Mavis in tow.

...

It's eight o'clock, Atlanta time, before they manage to clear the traffic and make it to I-85. B. D. must have finished the bourbon while Billy Ray was gone to get Mavis at Sewell Hall, for now he is passed out in the back seat. "If I had a car like this, I wouldn't think twice about running down to New Orleans for lunch," Billy Ray is saying as he floorboards the huge white Cadillac and begins overtaking the caravan of Georgia fans headed back home. Mavis is beside him, riding shotgun, still on a high.

"Man, those guys are *giants*," the kid says. "Bo Jackson looks like Superman. I kept thinking about what ol' Runt would look like if he stood next to him."

"That's what the steaks and potatoes are for, amigo. That, and the weight room. You decide to come here, they'll have you up to one-ninety in no time flat. You actually get to meet Bo?"

"Naw, they'd gone to suit up when me and LaCherie got back."

"LaCherie? You rascal. Is there something I need to know about?"

"My Tigerette. Showed me around. Didn't have time to do nothing, though. Man, that place where the players live, it's like a fancy hotel."

"One thing you'll find out, kid. In the big-time, the tits are bigger, the lights are brighter, and the grass is greener. Hell, even the dirt's clean in the Southeastern Conference."

"I mean they're *big*, man. Big as elephants."

"Better lay off the elephants around here, that's Alabama's mascot," Billy Ray tells him. "Anyway, how about it, kid? You think you could play with these guys?"

"Yeah," says Mavis. "Hell, yeah. They ain't *that* tough. Bring 'em on."

"That's the stuff. I was talking to the coaches. I think it's yours if you want it."

"Be good to play close to Atlanta so my mama can see me. That'd be nice, wouldn't it?"

...

When they reach Austell, Billy Ray chooses to park the Cadillac in B. D.'s driveway, leaving him to sleep it off in the back seat rather than chance a confrontation with Mrs. Spotswood, and soon he and Mavis are bucking and chugging through the empty streets of Atlanta. It is nearing midnight when *Rosinante* finally delivers them to the bleak dungeon they have come to know, for better or for worse, as home. There is a welcome for them, of sorts. Rima has wrapped some orange-and-blue crepe paper around the porch railing, and tacked to the front door of the duplex a sheet of art paper with a crude version of Auburn's AU logo. *The girl never quits*, Billy Ray is thinking.

Then, once inside, he finds an envelope with his name on it, holding one of her business cards with a message scrawled on the back: *Mavis's Daddy Came By.*

TWENTY-THREE

The next morning has broken frosty but clear, the first truly cold day of the season. Picking up the newspapers, still in their plastic wraps on the porch, Billy Ray begins banging on Rima's front door. It takes five minutes before she finally appears in her pajamas, looking like death.

"Jose Cuervo, you ain't no friend of mine," she says when she lets him in.

"Tequila? You might as well main-line morphine."

"You know the drill. It seemed like a good idea at the time."

He tosses the thick Sunday papers on the floor and takes a seat in the living room while she puts on a pot of coffee, opens a beer for herself, and shuffles off down the hall to the bathroom. He sees that she has framed the oil painting of Mavis and affixed a price tag of $2,000, which tells him she would rather keep it for herself than sell it.

"Talk to me," he says when she returns.

"Brace yourself." She sits beside him on the sofa. "I'm over on your side watching the game on TV, see, trying to find Mavis on the sidelines at Auburn, when this guy starts knocking on the door. Big, tall, good-looking man in a bad suit. Says he's looking for you. I say you're out of town on business. He says, 'Where's my boy, then?' I say, 'And who might that be?'

279

and he says, 'Mavis Jackson. I'm his daddy. I've come to pick him up and take him home where he belongs.'"

"Oh, for Christ's sake. What'd you say?"

"I told him he was full of crap."

"And?"

"Says he'll be back today."

"That's great. Just fucking great." Billy Ray sinks back in the sofa, letting the air out of his lungs with a great *whoosh,* shaking his head. "What'd he look like?"

"I hate to tell you this, sport, but he's a dead ringer for Mavis."

...

Saturday had been a long day for Mavis, and Billy Ray figures the kid will sleep for as long as he'll let him. Back on his side of the duplex with the *AJC* sports section and a mug of Rima's coffee, he can't concentrate on newsprint for thinking about this development. Mavis's mother is one thing, a damaged woman who may or may not return whole, but this fellow claiming fatherhood is quite another. Is he one of those ne'er-do-well "uncles" over at the house in Fatback, or some other golddigger who suddenly sees a chance to cash in on the perceived riches awaiting a kid who might be on the verge of a career in college and the pros? Or is there really a bona fide father out there, absent for all of these years, finally showing up at the worst of all possible times, to claim what is his, just when the boy is about to realize a dream? Billy Ray figures that if anybody has ever filled the role of a father it is he, no matter how brief and tenuous his tenure, but he also understands the absolute power that blood can play. Every boy and every girl wants a real father, for better or for worse. He's an expert on that.

Pondering his next move, he recalls meeting Rashad Lattimore's father, the lawyer, outside the Rev's church after the first Film Night of the season. *If anything comes up, let me know.* Billy Ray finds his card in the pile of papers on the table in the living room and dials the number.

"We're all about ready to leave for church, Coach," Jabari Lattimore says when he is called to the phone. "What can I do for you?" Billy Ray tells him what he knows at this point. "You say he's coming by your place again today?"

"Said, and I quote, 'I've come to pick him up and take him home where he belongs,' unquote."

"Hmmm." Lattimore is thinking. "There's no father of record. We know that much. Checked into that before we let Mavis move in with you. Just the mother. We've got a copy of a birth certificate that says, 'Father UK.' Father Unknown."

"Well, hell, that oughta do it, then. Case closed. Am I right?"

"Not necessarily. There's common-law marriage to be considered. Seven years of living together would give him something to stand on, anyway."

"Mavis never said anything about a father being around. Ever. Just those 'uncles' he talks about."

"No phone calls, no letters, no contact of any kind?"

"Nothing."

"Tell you what"—there is a bustle in the background—"we're running late for church right now. Ought to be back a little after noon if Reverend Beaumont doesn't get carried away. I want you let me know if this fellow shows up again. Stall him if you can, and call me immediately."

...

Herman Graves ought to be told about this, too. There's no answer at the house, but when Billy Ray calls the football number at McGill High he gets Tank on the second ring.

"You getting paid overtime for working on a Sunday morning, are you?"

"Who you kidding?" says Tank. "Naw, I'm just watching some tapes of Robert E. Lee. I tell you, Gun, I never dreamed that boy they stole from us would turn out like this. He seemed kinda meek to me."

"That the tailback? What is it, Steed?"

"Dominique Steed. Runs like a bull. We're gon' have trouble trying to stop that one." Herman says Billy Ray has done the right thing to bring Jabari Lattimore into the Mavis situation, but he doesn't expect anything to come of it even if this man really is Mavis's father. He's guessing that somebody at Lee High probably hired the guy, just to mess with Mavis. "If anything was to come up, why, hell, Gun, we ought to get back at Lee for cheating. With Steed. They'll do about anything."

This is something that hasn't occurred to him. "How so? Maybe his folks just moved him to a better school. Any parent would do the same thing, wouldn't they? Christ, McGill's lost half its student body to white schools in the last couple of years."

"That boy's dumb as a post, Gun. They didn't move him out there so he could study nuclear physics. They *got* moved. The coach out there, this Swain fella, he fixed 'em up with a convenience store so their son can win a state championship for him."

"Yeah, but how come Mavis can't do that if everybody else can?"

"You've got to sit out a year before you can compete in sports if you move within the same district. The boy's illegal, Gun. Pure and simple."

"What kinda proof you got for all that?"

"Ask around. For starters, you could ask your wife."

...

Well, sure, why not? When Ginny answers, he starts her out not with the news about Mavis but with questions about Dominique Steed. That brings her up short. "If you want me to be a mole, Billy, you can forget it," she says. "Do your own scouting."

"Aw, hell, Gin, we've got game tapes. We can take care of ourselves. Jesus Christ. We're *coaches*."

"Well," she says, "I'll admit that I've got mixed feelings about the whole thing. I doubt that Dominique could find Africa on a map, but he's got a lot better chance of learning at Lee High than at McGill."

"Is he in any of your classes?"

"No way. The coaches are afraid I'll flunk him."

"You? The resident bleeding heart?"

"I'll ignore that. But, yeah, they know I'd flunk him if he didn't do the work. The truth is, I don't even know if he goes to classes. He's here to score touchdowns, period."

"And the coaches set his parents up in business so they could get him to play for Lee? That right?"

"You've just crossed the line, Billy. End of interview. Do your own sleuthing." She softens and says, "So how's Mavis?"

He tells her the latest. "He's putting on weight, getting stronger, playing at the top of his game, making his grades. He's got everything in order, and now this. This old boy sounds like he's fishing, to me, but this ain't no time for the kid to be getting his head turned around. If I find out that coach out there, what's-his-name—"

"Swain. Buck Swain."

"—yeah, Swain. If that sumbitch is behind this, me and him are gonna have at it."

"You know," Ginny says, "life's full of twists and turns, don't you think? He wouldn't even need a tailback if he had a quarterback worth a damn this year."

"Either way, I figure Mavis is gonna turn 'em upside down and backwards. I don't care how good this kid Steed is."

"You miss my point."

"I guess I do."

"His quarterback would be Ricky, hon. Ricky Hunsinger."

...

He hears the toilet flush, and soon sees Mavis walking barefooted down the hall, rubbing sleep from his eyes. The kid pauses at the refrigerator long enough to pour himself a glass of orange juice, then plops down beside Billy Ray on the sofa, and picks up the sports section. While he watches Mavis devour the pages devoted to coverage of the Auburn-Georgia game, heavy with florid descriptions of Bo Jackson's electrifying touchdown run, Billy Ray knows that he is looking at a young man who is on the verge of greatness himself and might not be aware of it. The bright eyes, the confident clenching of his jaw, the muscles rippling beneath his T-shirt, all of it seems to say that he can hardly be called a boy anymore. He's come a long way since those hot days in August; days of raising himself in that pig sty over in Fatback, of foraging for something to eat at Frankie Lorino's grocery, of hoping against all hope that his mother would be back any day now so they could resume a "normal" life, of throwing passes that no one could catch in front of crowds who couldn't care less. He's a man now, Billy Ray is thinking, stopping short of considering the dramatic changes in his own life during that same time.

"Sleep okay?"

"Great," Mavis says. "Wild dreams."

"How so?"

"Don't laugh."

"Promise."

"I know Bo's graduating, but I kept seeing me taking the snap, faking a handoff to him. He gets plowed, but he gets up and I toss that little lob to him behind the linebackers and he runs sixty yards with it every time. Over and over again. It's me and Bo. Jackson-to-Jackson. Touchdown, Auburn. War Eagle!"

"If it ain't Bo, it'll be somebody else."

"Yeah. Things could work out like that."

"Look here, Mavis"—if not now, when?—"we might have a situation here. There's a fella gonna be coming by today, claiming to be your father. We need to talk about this before he gets here, so we'll know which way to go with this thing."

Mavis casually looks up from the paper. "I told you, man, I ain't got no daddy." He goes back to reading.

"Everybody's got a daddy. How do you think babies get made?"

"Mama made a mistake one time, that's all."

"That could still make the guy your father, Mavis."

"A real daddy sticks around. This one didn't. Whoever the hell he is."

"I want you to think back a ways for me. You mean you don't ever remember a man being around the house? Christmas gifts? Somebody calling you 'son'? You know, a guy, a grownup, somebody your mama was sweet on? Anything like that at all?"

"Look, Gun, don't sweat it." It still seems odd to Billy Ray when he calls him that. "I've made it this far without a daddy. No reason I need one now. At least you stuck around. That makes you the closest thing I've got, if you want to be technical about it, but there ain't no fool gon' say you're my daddy. Little too pale, understand?"

"How about those uncles at the house?"

"'Uncles,' my ass. They're just a bunch of old drunks looking for a place to flop. That's Fatback for you."

"But maybe this guy's one of 'em's brother."

"I told you, Gun, quit worrying." Mavis gets up, stretches, sees that it's almost noon. "I need to wash up. Shanikah might be coming by after church. Don't run her off, okay?"

...

With only one game remaining in the regular season, and that against one of the weaker teams they'll play all year, they've decided to pass on the Sunday afternoon ritual with the receivers at Grady Stadium. By two o'clock in the afternoon, a bright sun warming things considerably, Billy Ray has finished perusing the sports pages and Mavis is in his room when, out on the lawn, there comes a great clatter. Peering through the window, he sees a maroon '70 Pontiac Chieftain with a Missouri tag pulling up beside the wagon and Rima's pickup. It could have been a thing of beauty if the money hadn't run out for a full restoration, but now it is tackied up with white sidewalls and mudflaps and a pair of fuzzy dice dangling from the interior rearview mirror. Emerging from the car is a tall black man in an ill-fitting green suit, carrying what appears to be an album of some sort. If this is the guy, Billy Ray is thinking as the man steps onto the porch, Rima was right. With his shaved head, high cheekbones, and erect bearing, he is a hint of what Mavis might look like in twenty years.

"You Mister Hunsinger?" the man says when Billy Ray opens the door.

"What you selling?"

"Leonard Jackson here. I'm Mavis's daddy."

"Yeah, and I'm his big brother."

"I ain't come to make no jokes, sir. Nossir."

"You got some kinda proof?"

"Yessir"—the man pats the scrapbook—"got my driver's license, got more right here. Got everything I need to get my boy back. Yessir. Anh-hanh."

"This better be good. Come on in. You've got five minutes."

Clutching the scrapbook, the man enters the living room tentatively, scanning the place, as though someone might jump him at any moment. Billy Ray isn't about to offer him anything except a seat in the worn yard-sale easy chair usually occupied by Mavis when they're watching football. The man sits on the edge of the chair without bothering to unbutton his coat. He places the scrapbook on the coffee table so that Billy Ray, now seated on the sofa, can see the legend MAVIS scrawled across the front.

"Okay, what's this all about?" Billy Ray isn't going to make this easy for Leonard Jackson, or whoever he is.

"First of all, I want to thank you for taking care of my son, Mister Hunsinger. I read all about it in the newspapers. Looks to me like you gone way beyond the call of duty."

"The boy didn't have any parents around, so I stepped in."

"I knows that, sir, and I appreciate it. His mama do, too."

"You've seen her?"

"Aw, sho. Seen Eugenia yesterday, down at the place in Macon. Terrible. Just terrible."

"Bullshit. She can't have visitors for another month."

"Lovin' husband, now, that's somepin' else."

"The question is," says Billy Ray, "where the hell's the loving husband been all these years? We're all dying to know."

"Don't blame you for that," the man tells him. "Been all over. Dee-troit, Chicago, Cincinnati, St. Louis. Name it, I been there. Had to go off to find employment suited to my talents, if you understand what I'm sayin'. Be workin' my fingers to the bone so I can make the rent, buy clothes and food for Eugenia and the boy, make sure they okay."

"Well, they weren't okay when I found 'em."

"That so? Humph. Sometimes checks get lost in the mail, you know. Happens."

"Not for eighteen straight years, they don't. Eighteen years times twelve months, that's a lot of money, pal."

"Got to be some kind of mixup somewhere. I'll be lookin' into that, all right. Sho' will. Anh-hanh."

Just when Billy Ray is starting to breathe easier, figuring he has an inept con man on his hands, easily dismissed, he and the man look up to see Mavis standing in the hallway. In spite of his bravado earlier, Mavis is staring at the visitor with eyes wide in what appears to be shock. "Lord, speak of the devil!" the man fairly shouts, leaping from the chair and rushing the boy. "Say hello to your daddy, son!" Mavis goes limp while the man clumsily embraces him, giving him nothing in return. If for only an instant, a chill comes over Billy Ray when the man and the boy are caught side by side in profile. Mavis still hasn't spoken when he enters the room and sits beside Billy Ray.

"So what've we got here?" Billy Ray says, patting the scrapbook, not sure he wants to hear.

The man speaks to Mavis. "Got some pictures of you 'n' me when you was just a baby, son. Here we go, yeah. First day, right out of the nest, Grady Hospital! Hunh? See there, got you holdin' the first football yo' daddy gave you. Anh-hanh." He's flipping pages now, giving a running commentary. "You and yo' mama at the house on Dixiana . . . Lookie here, son, here's that day I took you to the zoo . . . Here you are, wasn't even walkin' yet, took you out to see Hank Aaron play at the Atlanta stadium . . . First day at school

. . . Lookie here, we even saved the first tooth that fell out . . . Report cards. Humph. Wasn't doin' so hot first time around, was you, boy?"

Mavis has seen enough of the scrapbook. He looks at the man and says, "Where'd you get this?"

"Been carrying it around all these years, son. Just waitin' for this day."

"Have not. This is Mama's. She's been keeping it in her room ever since I was born."

"Aw, well, now, see, I *loaned* it to her."

"Bullshit. This is about all she had left."

"But look here, now, son, see, it's *ours*. All three of us. Family album, don't you see."

"Family, my ass." It is clear to Billy Ray that Mavis has made some sort of decision, but he can't quite read the look on the boy's face, which is somewhere between disappointment and disgust. "How come I don't see you in any of these pictures?"

"Somebody had to take 'em, you know."

"Yeah, right." Mavis looks the man hard in the eye. "You could be my daddy, all right. We look about the same. I'll admit that."

"There you go. I knew it. It's good to see you, son."

"But it really doesn't make any difference anymore, does it?"

"Well, I—"

"Tell you what"—suddenly, Billy Ray feels divinely inspired—"looks to me like it's a good time to celebrate. Mister Jackson, perhaps you would join me in a libation?"

"Say what?"

"A toast."

"Already had my breakfast."

"Not 'toast.' *A* toast. A little drink to celebrate this long-awaited reunion between father and son."

"Naw, they said I better not—"

"Oh, come on, Mister Jackson. This stuff's been aging for years. Waiting for the right moment." Now Mavis is staring at Billy Ray, about to interrupt, but Billy Ray stops him before he can speak. "Jim Beam, Mister Jackson. The finest."

"Jim Beam." Billy Ray knows a drinker when he sees one. The man's eyes water. His hand jerks when he wipes a tear. He licks his lips. "Oh, all right. But just a sip."

...

B. D. Spotswood on Saturday, this guy on Sunday. Billy Ray is starting to feel like a designated driver. This in itself is worth a month's worth of AA meetings, he is thinking, as he and Mavis drag "Leonard Jackson" out to his car. When they have him stuffed into the back seat, folded and crumpled like dirty laundry, Billy Ray finds the keys to the Pontiac in the man's pockets and tells Mavis to get the keys to the wagon and follow him.

It's getting toward dark when they reach the house in Fatback. Billy Ray wheels the Pontiac into the yard, and that brings the same two old men out on the porch to investigate. They seem startled at first, to see both Billy Ray and Mavis getting out of the two cars, looking pissed, as though to come up on the porch after them. But when they see Billy Ray open the back door of the Pontiac to reveal Leonard passed out drunk, they begin laughing.

"Fucked up again, didn't he?" one of them says.

"How 'bout a nightcap, Leonard?" says the other.

"Better get his ass back to St. Louis, what he better do."

"Y'all had your fun," says Billy Ray. "Now come on and help us out here. We got a sack of shit for you."

...

Later that night, before he leaves for Austell, Billy Ray has one more call to make. Buck Swain's wife answers the phone in Crestwood and says Coach Swain is watching film at his office and gives him the number.

Billy Ray gets the answering machine. "You want to hear this from me, Swain, or do you want to hear it on 'Jock Talk' tonight?"

Swain picks up. "What do you want, Hunsinger?"

"Nice try, asshole."

"What're you talking about?"

"How's this for irony?" Billy Ray likes that. "Your guy's passed out drunk, sleeping in his 'son's' bed."

This stops Swain, but only for a moment. "It ain't over, you dimwit. We know all about how that Dago's been paying the Jackson boy's rent. How do you like them apples, monkey-face?"

"Want to talk about the Steed family's business? Be my lawyer against your lawyer, you fetus."

"That's fine by me. Who's gonna believe a nigger-lover, anyway?"

"Now I've got you by the balls, Swain. How about we handle it this way: my guy against your guy. See you in a couple of weeks, creep." Billy Ray hangs up, wondering what he's gotten himself into.

TWENTY-FOUR

I know what you're thinking. This is just some more of that poor-mouthing that coaches do before a big game. Bear Bryant practically invented it. He'd go into a game against somebody like Chattanooga and say, Lord, I don't know what my little ol' boys are gonna do against this bunch. Them Moccasins look like Notre Dame to me. Too late to beg off, try to get out of it. Guess we're gonna have to play 'em anyway, do the best we can with what little we got, just hope our Mamas and Papas raised us right. Then he'd go out and beat 'em by forty points with his third team, boys that hadn't played all year.

I don't think nobody's gon' be accusing you of poor-mouthing, Gun. That Robert E. Lee team really does look like Notre Dame.

More like the Packers, if you ask me. We knew they'd take care of Clarkston the other night, but not by no fifty-three points.

Guess that's why they've been made an eighteen-point favorite.

Who says?

The gamblers. That's the word, anyway.

Bull. Anybody dumb enough to bet on a high school football game ain't got the sense to get out of the rain. The pros and college, now, I can understand that, but there's too much emotions involved with these kids. I mean,

hey, we had to win our first three games big-time before we even started get-
ting picked to win.

So you don't believe the eighteen points, then?

I'm just saying there ain't no telling what a bunch of teenaged boys are
gonna do on a given night.

Reckon you'd feel a lot better if y'all was playing at home, at Grady,
wouldn't you?

Sure, but that ain't the way the coin landed. We're gonna just have to
go with what we got. That big ol' stadium they got out there's gonna look
like the Rose Bowl to our boys. I been thinking I oughta take 'em out early
and measure the field to show 'em it's the same size as Grady. 'Course that
won't do much to get 'em ready for about ten thousand fans that'll show up
hoping they get to see the lions eat the Christians alive.

How 'bout Mavis? He ready for this?

All I can say is, he's looking forward to it.

Y'all planning anything special?

Wouldn't tell you if we did, hoss, but it won't be no surprise to tell you
we're gonna come out throwing from the git-go. That's what we do, you
know, everybody knows that. Just hope it ain't cold and raining. Tends to
screw up the passing game.

How y'all gon' stop that tailback they got, that Steed boy? Nobody else
can do it.

They named him right. That kid runs like a wild horse with turpentine
up his butt. You get any ideas between now and Saturday night, let me know.

I'll be there, Gun. Lotsa luck, now, you hear?

...

Line two, what's happening?

It's me, Gun—Scottie.

Hey, bubba.

Couple of questions. Number one, is Mavis going to sign with Auburn?
Two, do you plan to keep on coaching somewhere after this season's over?

That's easy, pal. If they'll name me head coach at Auburn, I'll promise to bring Mavis with me. I'm just kidding there. I don't know what the kid's gonna do, really. There's some more visits lined up for him at places like Miami and Nebraska, but I've got to tell you he liked it down there at Auburn and he'd like to play close to home. His mama's never seen him play football. He'd like it if she could.

How's she doing, by the way?

They won't tell us hardly nothing, Scottie, except that she had a little relapse a couple of weeks ago and it might be a while.

I'm probably talking out of school here, buddy, but don't you think you might be moving back home when the season's over?

You been talking to my wife, ain't you?

Maybe. Well, yeah, to tell the truth. She called this morning to invite me to the house after the Lee game. Says you'll be there, win or lose. But what I'm saying is, seems to me like things have changed a lot since last summer, you know.

No doubt about that. But, see, we've still got the problem of Mavis. Now I've got myself all tied up being his agent.

His daddy's more like it.

You said that, not me. Anyhow, this ain't no time for him to be moving back to Fatback like nothing ever happened. He's got another semester to go at McGill. Got to keep those grades up and graduate before he can start thinking about going to college to play football.

What I'm asking is, are you going to take him with you?

What, out to Crestwood?

Yeah.

I don't think that'd work, good buddy. There might be about a dozen folks of his kind out there. Wouldn't be fair to the boy. I mean, hell, he could stay at The Ranch, I reckon. Thing is, this is all a mute point—

Moot. M-O-O-T. Means arguable.

Whatever you say, professor. It don't mean anything unless me and Ginny can work things out. I don't see no gamblers making odds on that.

...

Hey, Gun, what's this I hear about a sign showing up in the Steeds'
front yard the other morning?

Say what?

Yeah. They woke up and there was this sign out in the yard. Had a
drawing of a player with the number thirty-four on his jersey. Instead of a
head, though, there was an Oreo cookie.

I don't know nothing about no sign. Who's this, anyway?

Just say I'm an interested party.

You sound damned interested to me. You live in Crestwood, right?

Yeah, I do, and I don't mind telling you that's a pretty low thing y'all
did. You oughta leave that boy alone, let him do his thing.

You're blaming McGill? This stuff about a yard sign is all news to me.

We don't appreciate it one damned bit, Hunsinger.

Whooaa, bubba, back up.

I don't know, playing the race card like that—

What's this Oreo cookie all about? Fill me in.

Come on, you know what that means. The boy's black on the outside but
white on the inside. Hell, this one can flat run with a football. We don't care
what color he is, as long as he can play. Come on, admit it. Somebody down
there put that sign up just to get Dominique messed up for the game.

Well, I don't mind saying that some of our boys weren't too happy about
him upping and leaving McGill to play for Lee. Ain't no secret that it left us
without a running game. Mavis can't run with that bad leg, and about all
we can do is send Mojo Anthony into the line now and then to keep 'em hon-
est. If we had this boy Steed to go along with Mavis, I don't see how any-
body could stop us.

I betcha it's more than that. My thinking is, they're jealous that he got
outside the Ring around the Congo. Like a runaway slave.

I beg your pardon?

You ain't heard that one? Ring around the Congo is what everybody out here calls the perimeter highway. Everything inside I-285 is black. Come on, everybody knows that.

Oh, crap. Who's playing the race card now? Maybe you'd like to throw in the N word while you're at it.

We don't use that out here no more, Hunsinger. That's how long you've been gone.

This what we call the New South? Just put it in code?

I don't care what you call it, Coach. You know what I mean, though.

One thing I do know is, you've lit up my phone line again. Hello? Yeah, it figures. Yellow-belly dropped the ball and ran. Line three, what you got to say to that?

...

Well, I declare. Ring around the Congo? That's just plain tacky.

One of my Ansley Park Ladies, right?

Eleanor Feingold, the one with the rowing machine.

Yes, ma'am. I been seeing y'all at the games, and we appreciate your support.

We'll be out there in Crestwood Saturday night, too. After hearing what that Neanderthal said, I just hope it's safe to go out there and root for Mavis.

Oh, I wouldn't pay that old boy no never-mind. They ain't that mean. They just talk a lot.

At least he could get his facts straight. Ring around the Congo, my foot! He ought to be advised that we live in Atlanta. Crestwood and Alpharetta and those places beyond the Perimeter, I don't know what to call them. They aren't Atlantans, that's for sure. We're rich and poor, black and white, Jewish and gentile, Atlanta to the bone. We're yellow-dog Democrats, too, not these turncoat Republicans speaking in tongues.

Come to think of it, Miz Eleanor, you might want to walk a little soft when you go out there for the game.

Hanh! We've bought our tickets and we're already making up signs. We've been coordinating things with Clarice and the other Touchdown Mamas so we can all sit together. If they want trouble, they'll get it.

Lord. And all I wanted to do was play a football game.

Well, they'd better watch it. Go Mavis!

...

Hello, Brother Gunn. How you doin' this fine evenin'?

What's up, Rev?

Red and yellow, black and white, they are precious in His sight. I didn't say that. The Lord said it. Means Jesus loves all the little children, not just a few of 'em. Understand where I'm comin' from?

Seems clear enough to me, Rev.

I know it does, Brother Gun, and that's what I'm callin' about. Seems like yesterday that I heard the Fal-coons were playin'. You remember that?

Afraid I do. Yes, sir.

Now look at you, Brother Gunn. Saved this boy's life is what you've done. Saved yours, too, while you were at it. Hallelujah!

Aw, come on now, Rev, you and me, we've talked about this already.

I know we did, brother. I just wanted to let some of those lost souls out there know that it don't hurt to love your neighbor. Don't hurt one bit, now, does it?

If I was a politician, I'd say it cost me the election.

Brother Steed's got a need. Understand what I'm sayin'?

Well, yeah, sure, but—

And Brother Jackson needs some action.

Rev, I swear—

We got to love one another, Brother Gunn.

You better call Coach Thomas and tell him that, preacher. Pig's got our boys thinking bad things about this Steed boy right now. Is it okay if they tear his head off Saturday night?

I think the Lord would go along with that, long as it ain't personal.

Oh, there ain't nothing personal about it, Rev. We just don't want nobody coming on our turf when they ain't been invited.

Why don't we bow our heads right now and take that up with the Lord—

Tell you what, Rev, how 'bout holding off 'til the pre-game prayer? We've got a lot of work to do this week and I don't want to see the boys getting their heads turned around.

The meek shall inherit the earth, you know.

Yeah, I heard about that, but we ain't looking for no inheritance right now. We're thinking about kicking some Lee butt.

But I'm the team chaplain, Brother Gunn. I've got a job to do.

With all due respect, Rev, I just don't know about this. It's a lot like war. You've got a platoon sergeant tellin' 'em to go kill the bastards, and then a chaplain comes along behind him sayin', Y'all love one another, now. Don't make much sense to me.

This isn't war, Brother Gunn.

The hell you say, Rev.

TWENTY-FIVE

No doubt there are better teams in the state of Georgia this year, especially in those rural redoubts like Valdosta where high school football is the only game in town, but this shootout between McGill and Robert E. Lee for a mythical metro Atlanta championship has reached historical, if not hysterical, proportions. Atlanta hasn't seen anything like it in a quarter of a century, in fact, not since the Gunslinger's senior year at old Forrest High, when nearly 10,000 fans crowded Grady Stadium to see him pass Murphy High dizzy and nail his selection as *Parade* magazine's All-American high school quarterback. With Georgia Tech and Georgia taking the week off to prepare for their season-ending civil war, and the woeful Falcons on the road, local fans have been able to focus on McGill and Robert E. Lee on this Saturday before Thanksgiving. Thanks to that, and special coverage all week by the Atlanta newspapers, the game is looking like a sellout at Lee's 8,000-seat Dixie Memorial Stadium. One of the local cable stations has even hired Herman Graves's son, Sidney, to televise it live for those who can't get in to see it in person.

The sportswriters and the sports talk-show hosts, not the least of them Billy Ray himself, have been madly chattering away about the duel between Mavis Jackson and Dominique Steed: their separate paths, their disparate talents, their bright futures. For better or for worse, though, it has become more than just a football game. It is David versus Goliath, In-town versus Suburbia, black versus white, the have-nots against the haves, the poor taking on the prosperous. There isn't much that hasn't been covered: McGill's endearing Touchdown Mamas and Lee's thousand-dollar-a-year members of Rebel Boosters Club, Inc.; the Panthers' raucous Film Nights in the basement of Rev. Beaumont's church; the "anonymous donors" who have kept McGill's football program afloat in its last year of existence; and, of course, the curious relationship between the broken old quarterback and the fatherless kid from Fatback.

Throughout all of this hullabaloo, in the week of practice leading up to the showdown, Herman and Billy Ray and Pig Thomas have done all they can to keep the boys focused on the game itself. They've lost four players to injury during the season, leaving them with only twenty-six able-bodied boys and forcing some of the better athletes to pull double duty on defense, and they can't afford to lose anybody else in practice. Thus, each afternoon, while the band practices its routines on the field at Grady Stadium, they watch an hour of Lee film in the cramped dressing room and then go outside in their sweats for another hour of work on timing and putting in some new plays. After supper each night at the duplex, with a tape running on the television set in the front room, Billy Ray and Mavis have been studying Lee's defensive unit until the kid knows every move they have ever made to meet every passing situation during the season. Mavis has come so far that Billy Ray has given him the ultimate authority of calling audibles from the line of scrimmage, which he has done ninety percent of the time in the last four games of the regular season. It's not so much the Panthers' offense that concerns them, anyway; it's stopping Dominique Steed, who has been averaging nearly seven yards every time he runs with the ball. They don't have to repeat the mantra that has served them well throughout the season. *If they score forty, we'll have to score forty-one.*

...

300

Startled motorists along I-85 can't believe what they are seeing at dusk on Saturday afternoon, which would be heavy-duty rush hour on any weekday. *The barbarians are coming!* Leading the way are two motorcycle cops, riding side by side, their blue lights blinking, holding at a pace of forty miles an hour, and strung out for a mile behind them is a caravan of vehicles, headlights ablaze, that looks like a circus troupe leaving town.

First in line is a black Ford pickup, its tag reading BIRDGIRL, driven by a young woman with purple hair. Next comes a dusty white Cadillac, WWJD for its license tag, driven by an obscenely fat white man wearing an orange blazer and an Auburn baseball cap. And then comes the bulk of the party: three white vans belonging to the First Calvary AME Revival Assembly, each rocking with black women who are singing and clapping and stomping; two yellow school buses holding members of a marching band in their braided purple-and-gold uniforms; another containing cheerleaders and majorettes who have opened the windows and are chanting at the passing cars; still another bus holding a load of pensive young football players, either scared out of their wits or deep in their own reveries. Bringing up the rear is a noisy procession of cars and pickups and vans, at least forty of them, all bearing streamers proclaiming PANTHER POWER! and AIR MAVIS! and STOMP LEE! Finally, there is a battered Chevy station wagon of uncertain vintage, GUN for a license tag, driven by a red-headed man who is smoking a cigar and conversing with the young black teenager riding at his side.

Both Tank and Billy Ray know that this is hostile territory the boys are entering, which is why they have ordered an early start. The pre-game meal was served at three o'clock, after which the players napped, briefly and fitfully, until they were stirred awake to begin the tedious process of being taped. Slipping into their uniform pants and jerseys around five, they loaded their pads and helmets onto the bus, and then they were off. They would arrive at the gamesite an hour-and-a-half before the kickoff, by design, in order to take a look around and get the feel of the place. The same goes for the Touchdown Mamas and the Mighty Marching Panthers band and the other parents and fans. Go, McGill! All for one, one for all. Might as well do this together.

Compared to their home field, Grady Stadium, stuck near downtown Atlanta amid the grime and clamor of the city, Dixie Memorial Stadium seems to them like something out of a painting. Lights on silvery towers are already turned on when they arrive in the gloaming. Groundskeepers are still preening the November-brown playing field, the smells of popcorn and hot dogs and pizzas permeating the air, while teenagers wipe the seats with towels and then let each one spring back into the upright position—*clap-clap-clap!*—like gunshots echoing through the empty stadium. The boys know that somewhere inside the cinderblock field house at one end zone, suiting up in their carpeted dressing quarters, the enemy awaits.

The McGill contingent has been directed to a far end of the huge asphalt parking lot, and now the players are trudging from their bus to follow their coaches through a tunnel opening up at midfield. Stiff from the half-hour ride from midtown, half-dressed in their purple pants and white jerseys, toting their helmets and shoulder pads in gym bags, they are silent, all eyes, as they stroll toward their bench on the opposite side of the field. Student managers trail behind, lugging kegs of Gatorade and armloads of towels and first-aid kits, like medics establishing a station on a battlefield. Behind them come the members of the Mighty Marching Panthers band, lugging their instrument cases, being shown to their seats on the visitors' side behind the McGill bench. The Mamas have stayed back in the parking lot, setting up a portable tent and laying out a spread of barbecue, fried chicken, iced tea, and all of the trimmings, open for business with the McGill fans who have followed.

"Listen up, boys." Tank, wearing his rumpled good-luck suit, stands before his intrepid band of players as they take seats on the long benches. They have been whispering among themselves, gawking, taking it all in: the lights, the 8,000 individual seats, the end zones painted in Confederate stars and bars, the flagpole atop the field house where wave Old Glory and the Confederate battle flag, the tiers of private boxes behind tinted glass that ring the top of the stadium on the home side. "I guess we could walk it off just to show you it's the same size as Grady and every other football field in town. Be a waste of time, if you ask me. See one, you've seen 'em all."

Pig Thomas jumps in. "We're gon' smear their noses in it! Make 'em eat shit!"

"Not now, Pig, later." Tank is trying hard to play the mellow grandfather. "No matter what happens tonight, I just want to say how proud I am of you boys. I been coaching for a long time and I don't think I've ever seen a bunch that's come as far as this one. Y'all ain't got no business in the world being where you're at right now, but you did it by working your butts off. Your folks know it, me and Pig and Gun know it, the whole city knows it, and now the whole damned world is about to find out." Suddenly, Tank's entire demeanor changes. His face flushes and there is fire in his eyes. "Find out *what?* Say *who?*"

One timid voice responds. "Panthers?"

"I can't hear you."

More, now: "Panthers, Panthers . . ."

"Say *what?*"

"Panthers, Panthers, kick their ass!!!"

"Anh-hanh, that's better."

" . . . wipe their butts in the grass . . . !!!"

...

Well, shit, they haven't even put on their pads yet. Billy Ray has been hoping this wouldn't happen, has talked with Tank about keeping the kids on an even keel, not getting them riled up until the time comes, but, hey, it's Tank's team, not his, so there you go. He knows he can't really blame Herman. The old boy's been slaving away for all of these years, seeing his best players get picked off by the likes of Robert E. Lee and whoever else wants them, soon to be pastured out as a principal at some other little poorass school nobody cares about, and now he's got a chance to go out in glory. This thing is big for Herman, maybe as big as any opportunity he's ever had, and you can't deny him that. It just isn't any way to win a football game, to

Billy Ray's way of thinking, especially against a juggernaut that is quite capable of sending these kids back home in ambulances. Their eyes are big now, more than an hour too soon, and they follow Tank and Pig toward the visitors' locker room in the fieldhouse.

Billy Ray hangs back, touches Mavis by the elbow, says, "Let's take a walk." They begin an aimless stroll around the field, as though this is their place and they're grading the work of the groundskeepers, checking for marshy over-watered spots, noting the pylons at the goal lines and the play clocks in the end zones, shielding their eyes from the glare of the lights, the teacher and his protege out for a walk. They know they are being watched by the early arrivals, Lee fans bringing blankets and picnic baskets, claiming the best seats on the home side, anxious to have a look at this kid they've been hearing about. From the other side of the field comes the disjointed jangle of the McGill band members tuning up, clarinet runs and trumpet flourishes and drumrolls, and from somewhere below the pressbox they hear a Rebel Yell, the Lee High mating call.

Billy Ray plucks a blade of grass and tosses it into the air, checking the wind, finds that there's hardly enough of it to worry about. "Nice layout, huh?" he says.

"It's okay. Gon' be a fast track tonight."

"You're fresh meat, you know. They're gonna be on your ass, big-time. Hope you're ready for that."

"Hey, Gun, when you've heard eighty-five thousand at Auburn, this ain't nothing."

"Be good to bear that in mind. Eight thousand folks won't amount to a fart."

Out of nervousness, perhaps, Mavis gets the giggles over that. "Hey, coach," he says, "who's playing, me or you?"

"I was just pointing it out, that's all."

"Just kidding. You've been here, right?"

"Plenty." For a moment, Billy Ray sees a vision of him throwing and catching with his son Ricky on some broiling summer afternoon, just the two of them. It seems like years ago. "A lot."

They hear their names being called—"Daddy!" and "Mavis!"—and turn to see Ginny and Maggie, madly waving at them from the other side of the fence on the Lee sideline. They wave back at them and sidle across the field. Maggie is in her Lee cheerleader's outfit, pleated short skirt and a red-white-and-blue knit sweater, but Ginny wears nothing that would signal an allegiance either way; just faded jeans and scuffed boots and a nylon jacket over a plain gray sweatshirt, her leaf-raking outfit.

"Where's Rima, hon?" says Ginny.

"Probably in the parking lot, pigging out on barbecue and fried chicken," Billy Ray tells her.

"Don't forget to tell her to come by the house, now. I made up some chili." She turns to Mavis and says, "You brought a change of clothes, did you?"

"Yes, ma'am. They're in the car."

"Go easy on us now, okay?"

"Mom!" Pretending to be offended, Maggie smiles at Mavis. "Consorting with the enemy. Go, Rebels!"

"I come to play," Mavis says, mock-seriously. "Gon' whup up on them Rebels."

"Yeah, sure. You're allowed to lose by one point, Mavis."

"We'll see about that."

Billy Ray says, "I know where you're gonna be, Mags, but what about Mom? It's a hell of a choice she's got to make." To Ginny: "What'll it be, babe, the good guys, or the bad guys? You with me, or *agin* me? There's a lot riding on your answer."

"Well," Ginny says, "good mother that I am, I thought I'd stick with my daughter in the first half. After that, we'll see. Mind your manners, play like gentlemen, I might come over on your side in the second half. I want to see your band embarrass ours, anyway. I can take just so much of hearing that damned 'Dixie.'" Billy Ray and Mavis have turned to leave for the locker room, time to get suited up, when Ginny calls her husband back. She looks around, drops her voice, and says in a near-whisper, "There's some bad vibes in this place, Billy."

"Aw, hell, we expected that."

"I mean *nasty* stuff. Racist crap."

"What's new? 'Dixie,' the Rebels, the Stars and Bars. They get off on it."

"It's more than that this time, hon. When we came through the gate, they stopped a couple of Lee kids who were trying to get in, wearing sheets, laughing, making Klan jokes."

"Just some punks full of that ol' Halloween spirit, far as I care."

"That's crap, Billy. These people are dead serious. That sign in Dominique's yard? Lee kids put it there. I've been hearing racist jokes all week at school. That guy on your show really started something with 'Ring around the Congo.' Look, I'm sorry. I just thought you ought to know these things." Suddenly she reaches over the fence, grabs Billy Ray by the nape of his neck, pulls him toward her, and kisses him hard on the mouth. "Do good, boys," she says, peeling away, laughing to see that her husband, the big bad Gunslinger, is blushing.

...

In the commodious visitors' locker room, carpeted and nearly half the size of the entire McGill gymnasium, the Panthers are making themselves at home, helping each other into shoulder pads, juking to the sounds of rap music coming from a boombox one of the kids has brought along, chewing gum to soothe their nerves. Under orders from Herman Graves, no one has erased the cartoonish drawing on the blackboard—a hooded Klansman saying "Boo!"—Tank's notion being that it might piss them off and somehow inspire them. At seven o'clock, in full regalia, they take the field for warmups.

There is a battle of the bands going on already, with the Mighty Marching Panthers playing "Sweet Georgia Brown" and the Lee band, nearly twice the size with more than a hundred pieces, doing "Dixie" as though it's the only tune in their repertoire. The place is filling up now, mainly with Lee students and parents, toting coolers and windbreakers and cameras, dwarfing the McGill fans huddled around their band in the smaller west-side stands. Billy Ray is standing with arms folded behind the Panthers' offensive unit, and when he sees the Auburn recruiter, Max Longstreet, he walks over to the fence on the McGill side to chat with him.

"You're off today, I see," he says.

"Yeah," the coach tells him. "Got Alabama next week at Legion Field. These boys ready for this?"

"Ain't gonna be easy." They hear chants of "Air ball!" and look up to see that Mavis has overthrown Streak on a fly pattern, the ball bouncing into a group of Lee players doing calisthenics in the end zone. Among them is Dominique Steed, wearing the number 34, who casually bats the ball away as though it were a fly at a picnic. "You can see what I mean."

"Anything I oughta watch for?"

"Our offensive line. If we can keep 'em off Mavis, we'll be all right."

"That's a big 'if.' He okay? How's the leg?"

"It's probably the best it's been all year. The time off helped. Depends on whether they go for it, try to tear him up."

"You know Swain. He'll try anything."

"That's what I hear. Oh, hey, Max, we're having a little get-together at my place after the game." How odd it sounds, *my place*, after only six months. "Gimme something to write on, I'll give you the address." Billy Ray is scribbling on the back of Longstreet's business card when he hears a gaggle of Lee students trying to start up a chant: "Two, four, six, eight, we don't want to integrate . . ." He shrugs his shoulders, and then jogs toward the locker room with his team.

...

At a few minutes before kickoff, Rev. Beaumont having finished his pre-game prayer and Pig Thomas getting cranked up by slamming his defensive players on their helmets, they hear a loud banging on the double doors leading onto the field and the sound of a deep ominous voice, like that of a warden who has come to fetch a condemned man on death row: "It's time, boys." Having seen enough games at Dixie Memorial Stadium in his days as the father of the quarterback-in-waiting, Billy Ray is not about to let these kids be subjected to the Lee Rebels' grand entrance. He opens the doors a crack, sees a white-haired man wearing a Rebels Booster pin on his blue blazer, and tells him, "We ain't ready." The man is taken aback and blurts, "But it's visitors first." Billy Ray says, "Fuck you." In all of his time, the Booster has never heard of such. He scurries away to the adjacent locker room. The Panthers have begun to crowd around the exit to the playing field, champing to go, but Billy Ray signals for them to back off. He steps outside, leaning against the doors to keep them closed, hoping that nobody can see or hear it.

He's thinking that Buck Swain must have suited up every kid at Robert E. Lee High School who can walk. There must be sixty of them, all in silver pants and red jerseys spangled with stars and blue-and-white trimming, and as a spotlight from the press box pans across the double doors of the Lee locker room, decorated with the stars-and-bars motif, the band breaks into "Dixie" and the doors blow open and the stampede of elephants begins. They are huge, bigger than anyone McGill has seen all year, and as they burst through the REBELS!!! paper banner held up by a corridor of cheerleaders, Maggie Hunsinger among them, they thunder onto the field with arms held high and voices bellowing a blood-curdling Rebel Yell. Not until the entire team has reached the benches on the other side of the field, and the noise of the crowd has diminished, does Billy Ray go back inside, put a hand on Mavis's helmet, and say so softly that the boys have to lean forward to hear him: "Stay cool. Show 'em what you've got." Then, for the first surprise of the night concocted by Tank and Billy Ray, the Panthers calmly trot—don't run—to their bench on the sideline.

For the entire two weeks of their preparation for this game, that's been the mantra: *stay cool*. Although it took a while for Pig Thomas to come around, he being of the mind that a football game is a controlled riot, the kids bought into Billy Ray's idea with great enthusiasm from the very first. "Look, these boys think you ain't nothing but a bunch of wild-ass niggers that eat out of garbage cans," Tank was saying nearly two weeks earlier, when they were beginning to focus on a game plan. "Don't give 'em any ammunition. I don't want any celebrations, any bitching at the referees, any hot-dogging. We're city dudes. We're cool. We've been where they ain't been before." He knows that the average play eats up only about five seconds on the clock, that all of the rest of the forty-eight minutes in a high school game is dead time, just getting up off the ground and preparing yourself for the next moment of mayhem. If you devote every ounce of your energy to those five-second bursts, when the ball is actually in play, then everything in between is time to rest and to *think*. "They won't know what hit 'em until it's too late." Now, with Mavis and Pac-Man strolling out to midfield for the coin toss, he can only hope he knows what he's talking about.

...

McGill loses the toss and Lee chooses to receive so they can put Dominique Steed to work immediately. This is no surprise to anyone, especially the McGill coaches, well aware that Steed averages better than six yards a carry and gets the ball close to twenty-five times a game. Running out of the Power I formation, a modern version of the old Single Wing, he simply hammers away at the tackles behind a wedge of blockers. Lee has no passing game to speak of, just an occasional outlet pass or a screen to a little scatback named Bryan O'Brien, allowing all of Pig's defenders to bunch up on the line of scrimmage and fling themselves at the wedge like kamikazes.

But to see it on film is one thing, to experience it from the sidelines quite another. This is brutal stuff. Starting from their own twenty-yard-line after Ali Allen's kickoff sails into the end zone, Lee begins pounding away at McGill's lighter defenders like a bulldozer carving out a new road. It's Steed right, Steed left, now and then a harmless little toss to O'Brien just to break the routine, and it winds up taking only six minutes for them to score the first touchdown, having moved the ball eighty yards on twelve plays. The Lee Rebels and their coaches and fans are delirious, dancing in jubilation to the joyous strains of "Dixie," rocking the stadium, about to bring the house down. From the huddle of McGill fans on the opposite side of the field comes silence.

Just when the Panthers are thinking it could get worse, it does. The ensuing kickoff is hauled in at the eight-yard-line by Jerome Armstrong, "Runt," who manages to squiggle back to the fifteen before he is plowed under by an avalanche of screaming Rebels. The ball flies out of the mass and is taken in midair by a Lee defender, who scoots into the end zone without being touched, taunting the Panthers sprawled in his wake, slamming the ball to the ground, dancing around like a madman, touching off a celebration more joyous than the first. Another extra-point kick makes it 14-0, Lee, with fewer than seven minutes gone in the game. The Panthers' defensive players are dog-tired already, begging for a break, and the offensive unit has yet to run a single play. It's a good thing that Billy Ray doesn't have to tell Mavis what to do, once the Panthers manage to handle the next kickoff without another disaster, because the kid wouldn't be able to hear him over the din of the crowd.

Now, finally, Mavis is getting his chance. Around his left wrist is a sequence of plays, printed on white paper covered with clear tape, decipherable only by him and Billy Ray, representing every play in his repertoire. Tank has recused himself, as usual, leaving the offense to them, and during the many hours over the past two weeks they have added some new stuff that they hope will cover just such crises as they now face. There's no way they are going to be able to go *mano a mano* with a superior force like this one, something they've known all along, so they've had to come up with ways to equalize Lee's size and numbers. Put simply, the way to do that is to keep the defense off balance; show them the expected but give them the unexpected; play head games with them; take advantage of their over-eagerness, much like a power pitcher might throw a soft sandlot curve to a brute digging in and preparing to put a fastball in orbit. It is, Billy Ray has told the kid time after time, the only way he made it through that long-ago day against Bear Bryant's mighty Crimson Tide.

Stay cool. Mavis brings the Panthers out of the huddle for their first offensive play of the game, stands behind T-Bone, looks over the defense, and sees exactly what he thought he would: a full seven-man rush, lots of heavy breathing and pawing, Lee's linemen eager to tear his head off, four defensive backs in man-to-man coverage of a like number of receivers spread from sideline to sideline. The play he has called is a simple feed to his fullback, Mojo, up the middle, but he doubts it will come to that. Crouching under center for the snap, none of his guys daring to move, he goes into a long count until, finally, the Lee nose guard can't wait any longer and crawls all over T-Bone. Offsides, five yards. *The fools.*

He goes under T-Bone again, same play, same long count, same result. Offsides, five yards, first down. The referees moving the chains for a first down at the thirty-five get entangled with Buck Swain, the Lee head coach, who has thrown his clipboard to the ground and is threatening bodily harm to his nose guard for jumping the gun on two plays in a row. At the line again, reading the same defense, Mavis audibles a play they haven't used all season long. *Hut-hut.* He takes the snap, backpeddles three steps, then throws a rope to Tree, his tight end, who has taken five steps straight ahead and turned. Tree takes the pass, his back to the defensive backs now surging toward him, and just as the first one is about to hit him he tosses a lateral to Runt, trailing behind him out of the backfield, and Runt doesn't stop until he has reached the end zone sixty-five yards away. The "flea-flicker," they call it. Piece of cake. Runt hands the ball to an official and walks off the field without a word. Ali Allen's point-after kick makes it 14-7.

Things settle down after that, as they always do once the first licks have been been exchanged, and soon it becomes the game everybody predicted: Dominique Steed's running against Mavis Jackson's passing. There doesn't seem to be much either defense can do to contain the two stars; just try to delay the inevitable. Time and again the ball is handed to Steed, and by the end of the first quarter Lee has gone up, 21-7, when their tailback ends another time-consuming drive with a dive from the goal line. What McGill must do now is give its bedraggled defensive unit a rest, and Mavis does that by putting together an eighty-yard drive that eats up most of the second quarter. Now and then he might keep the Lee defense honest with a feed to Mojo into the line or a little screen pass to Runt in the face of an all-out blitz, but mostly he is stepping back into the pocket and firing bullets to his receivers at points all over the field.

...

Years later, when they are old and gray, fifty thousand people will be telling their grandchildren that they were there at Dixie Memorial Stadium to witness the moment when everything turned during that famous game between little McGill and mighty Lee. By now the score is 24-14, Lee, after the Rebels settle for a field goal and Mavis hits "Tree," Markese Fleetwood, with a fade in the corner of the end zone. Mavis has been taking a severe beating from the Lee linemen and linebackers, and has already used all of his timeouts to recover from the poundings. Most of the licks have been delivered when the play is dead, leaving no doubt that a major part of Buck Swain's game plan is to knock Mavis Jackson out of the game. It has gotten so bad that Tank and Billy Ray, in spite of their instructions to the Panthers to lay off the referees, have been spending an inordinate amount of time and energy screaming at the officials after every flagrant foul against Mavis. But still the Rebels come, and still they get away with it.

The moment comes with about a minute left in the first half, Lee still ahead by ten points, when Mavis drills a perfect twenty-yard completion to Rashad Lattimore, "Streak," who steps out of bounds at the Lee forty, in front of the Rebels' bench. At the instant Mavis gets the pass off, he is mauled by a blitzing linebacker who isn't satisfied to merely put pressure on the quarterback. The kid has Mavis on the ground and now he is working on his left knee, like a wrestler whose intent is to break it, and he is still at it long after the play is dead. A hush falls over the entire stadium as Mavis writhes on his back, clutching his knee in great pain. The foul is so obvious this time that the officials call it—personal foul, roughing the passer, fifteen yards, first down McGill at the twenty-five—and now boos are heard even from the Lee side.

Running across the field as fast as he can on his wasted legs, Billy Ray is coming to Mavis's aid just as the linebacker who delivered the shot is reaching the Lee bench and being high-fived by a jubilant Buck Swain. Billy Ray is furious when he sees this. "How much you paying for a broken neck, you sonofabitch?" he screams at Swain, who retorts: "All's fair in love and war, Hunsinger!" The two go face-to-face and have to be separated by an official. Whatever else they have to say to each other is drowned out by the roar of the Lee fans, about a hundred of them now rushing toward the fence with malevolence in mind.

Quiet reigns on the other side of the stadium, where the McGill fans crane their necks and try to get an idea of how badly Mavis is hurt. Herman Graves waddles across the field, a couple of student managers following him with a stretcher, leaving Pig Thomas in charge of keeping the Panthers from running onto the field and starting a riot. Still dazed and groggy, Mavis tries to walk but can't. He is loaded onto the stretcher. Billy Ray holds the kid's helmet with one hand and walks beside the managers as they lug Mavis toward the field house in the end zone. There is dead silence throughout the stadium until an ominous voice is heard over the public-address system: "Your attention, please. Will a doctor please report to the visitors' locker room." A tumultuous cheer erupts from the Lee stands.

...

They have Mavis laid out on a high padded platform, the size of an operating table, in the center of the locker room. Dr. Janelle Lattimore, Streak's mom, has been checking the knee ever since she raced in from her seat in the stands. Glum is the word as she pokes around, cooing to Mavis, asking if this hurts and how about that and let's see if you can stand up and walk. And there's more. Not only is Mavis badly injured, they're now down by a score of 31-14, the result of a fumble of the first snap by a freshman quarterback that led to a thunderous run for another touchdown by Dominique Steed just as the half ends. Now what?

"Just tell me it's not the ACL," says Billy Ray, something of an expert on anterior cruciate ligaments and such, from personal experience.

"A bad sprain is all," says Janelle Lattimore. "That's the good news. The bad news is, it'll take a lot of rest."

"Hell, he's got all winter to rest."

"I don't know. He can't take another hit like that one."

"Well, shit." He catches himself. "Sorry. Come on. Give us some hope. Give us *something."*

"That's all I can say, coach. I suppose we could wrap it real good and take a chance. He's not going to be able to run, though, I can tell you that much."

"Hell, he never could run." Mavis is smiling up at him now, however faintly, and Billy Ray scratches the kid's head.

"It's taking a big chance, you know," she says.

"This kid was born taking chances, doc."

...

The odds of getting out of this mess are stacked heavily against McGill. Down by seventeen points with only twenty-four minutes of playing time remaining, against a team whose running game can eat up great gobs of time, like a whale swallowing entire schools of fish in one gulp, going with an immobile quarterback who can fall in a heap at any moment, Billy Ray knows it's time for extreme measures. The situation isn't all that much different from what he faced twenty years earlier, against Alabama, something that he and Mavis are quite aware of from the hours they have spent watching the film of that game. The bottom line is to score points, fast, a lot of them, without being scored upon.

The leg may not be there anymore, but the arm is. There's no reason to try fooling anybody for the rest of the way. Their game is to throw. And throw. And throw some more. From now on, Mavis will work out of the shotgun, all alone in the backfield except for having Mojo Anthony at his side as a bodyguard and a possible outlet. Surely Buck Swain, seeing no reason to guard against the run, will call for a three-man rush and drop everybody else back in pass coverage. That'll give him eight defenders to cover five eligible receivers. Given those odds, he'll probably stay in man-to-man, putting double coverage on the two most dangerous targets, Streak Lattimore and Runt Armstrong. The five-man offensive line should manage to hold easily enough against a three-man rush. Should Lee try an all-out blitz, just to keep Mavis honest; well, come on, suckers, let's see it.

Of what happens next, let the scouts and coaches and sportswriters speak of X's and O's, of masterful play-calling, of grit and determination, of how young Mavis Jackson proceeds to put on a clinic during the hour that follows. To the kid himself, born in adversity and raised to fend for himself on the mean streets of a forgotten corner of Atlanta, this is nothing more than an extension of life as he knows it. Football is life; life is a football game. Virtually alone in the backfield with the world watching his every move, standing upright to take the snap from T-Bone Williams, his eyes sweeping over the eleven players across the way who would do him harm, he has never felt so much in control of his destiny. If only his mama could see him now.

Hut-hut. The first touchdown comes easily enough. They are, indeed, in a three-man rush, sitting back in umbrella coverage to prevent the bomb, so the thing to do is play catch for a while with his tight end, Markese Fleetwood, who simply lopes ten yards and turns and takes a throw behind the linebackers for a first down. Four straight such completions to Tree sets up the defense for a post pattern to Rashad Lattimore, who streaks across the field like a bolt of lightning and hauls it in for the score. Ali Allen manages to deliver the ensuing kickoff to someone other than Dominique Steed, and for the first time in the game the defense forces Lee into a three-and-out series. Standing cool, plenty of time, Mavis begins to pick the defense apart with a series of jabs, eight yards here and fifteen there, waiting for them to do something about it. When they do, showing a blitz with second-and-three from the twenty, he rifles a shot to Tree at the goal line. The third quarter ends with Lee ahead, 31-27, McGill's Ali Allen having missed the point-after kick.

...

Now, with everything on the line in the fourth quarter, it has come down to what Billy Ray had promised Buck Swain over the phone on that day of their shouting match: my guy against your guy. Starting at their twenty after the kickoff has sailed into the end zone, the Rebels' power running game gets cranked up like Edwin Rommel's Panzers rumbling across North Africa. Pounding, pounding, pounding, Dominique Steed is banging away at Pig Thomas's intrepid defenders, four yards at right tackle, eight up the middle, another whack at the left side for a rare no gain. It takes them a full eight minutes to score, finally, and a two-point conversion makes it 39-27. Time is growing short for Mavis to catch up.

"How you feeling, kid?" Billy Ray is saying to Mavis when he limps to the sideline before the final push. The coach and the quarterback are so in sync by now that it hasn't been necessary for them to talk tactics. Mavis has the basic playlist taped to his wrist, sure, and Billy Ray has been signaling plays from the sideline all along, but for the most part it's been Mavis's game.

"I'll make it," Mavis says, being toweled off by a student manager, taking a swig of Gatorade. "Come this far. What's another four minutes?"

"Okay. The score's out of whack. Two-pointer killed us. Now we gotta have two touchdowns in four minutes. Okay?"

"We're going without a huddle."

"You got it. No-huddle, wear 'em out, score, then the onsides."

They get a break when the kickoff is short and Runt takes it back to the thirty-five. Even with the Lee crowd screaming, everybody on their feet, Mavis begins calling every play from the line of scrimmage. They can't afford the time to huddle, and they need to rush the defense in hopes of causing confusion. *Bing-bing-bing.* A complete pass, a tackle, a whistle, a referee spotting the ball, a linesman moving the chains, *hut-hut,* here he comes again. Saving its own timeouts, McGill will welcome any that Lee wants to call. No rest for the weary. The Rebel linebackers and defensive backs are beginning to drag now, like a patrol under fire from unseen snipers, pleading for a break from a coach who seems to have lost his senses under such a barrage. The touchdown comes when the two men covering Streak collide with each other at the goal line. The extra-point kick is good. The score is 39-34, and the clock, mounted atop the field house on a scoreboard the size of a billboard, flashes 1:51 remaining. McGill has no choice but to go for the onsides kick.

...

Billy Ray hates the onsides kick, and with good reason. It was a botched kickoff, one that might as well have been a planned onsides kick, the way it turned out, that cost him his chance to beat the Bear and Alabama at their own homecoming game. If Paul Bryant felt the odds were stacked against the passing game, then the onsides kick is pure folly. You have to kick the ball at least ten yards, into the teeth of eleven men who need only to catch it and hold on in the melee, and your only chance is to somehow take it away from them. Sheer luck is the only hope—a fortunate bounce, a bobble, an instant of panic by a defender—in a desperate ploy that works, oh, about once every ten times it is tried. For the entire two weeks of practice for this game, Billy Ray has pleaded with Herman to forget about it, it'll never work, but for one of the few times all time all season long, Herman has prevailed. They've got to have the ball, and this is the only way to get it. Unlike Billy Ray, Tank's history with the onsides kick is a positive one, the memory of a perfect execution that helped Grambling win its big game against Southern University back in 'sixty-five, that same year of the Gunslinger's loss to Alabama. Consequently, the Panthers have wrapped up practice every day of late with fifteen minutes' work on a scheme that Tank swears can't fail.

Desperate times call for desperate measures, and that time has come. While the Panthers huddle behind the ball, teed up at the forty-yard-line, Billy Ray grabs the head linesman by the elbow to explain what he can expect. Maybe the Lee coaches have had moles staked out during McGill's practices at Grady Stadium, maybe not, but Buck Swain nevertheless has brought his most sure-handed athletes into the game to go up against what is, essentially, McGill's starting basketball team. The two lines face each other, ten yards apart, and when the referee sees that each side is ready he blows his whistle and drops his arm. Not a single person in the entire stadium is seated as Ali Allen slowly approaches the ball for the most important kick of his young life. It is a soft squib that floats dangerously close to the left sideline, seeming to hang in the dank night air like a wounded duck. All at once, twenty-two frantic teenagers are converging on the ball just beyond midfield, slamming into each other, scrambling, grunting, clawing, when suddenly the tallest man on the field, Markese Fleetwood, rises up out of the mass and pulls it in as though he has claimed a rebound. There is an audible gasp coming from the Lee stands, pandemonium from the hardy band of McGill fans. McGill has it at the Lee forty-eight, first down and ten to go.

Now is the time to strike, to shove the dagger in the heart. The Lee defenders are in disarray now, bone-tired and stunned by this turn of events, and Mavis knows it. Still in the no-huddle offense, standing in shotgun like a commander on a battlefield, he begins pecking away at the secondary with quick flicks, safe and sure passes, to Runt and to Streak and even an outlet toss to Mojo, drifting out of the backfield. Across the field, Buck Swain and his coaches are yelling, pointing, cursing, slamming caps to the ground. There seems to be no way to stop the onslaught. Lee's timeouts are gone and the clock is moving when Mavis hits Rashad Lattimore on an out pattern at the seven-yard-line. Streak steps out of bounds immediately to stop the clock. Suddenly, although down by five points, everything has swung in McGill's favor: first-and-goal, seventeen seconds to go, one timeout left. Only a touchdown will do. Unless time runs out, they will have four cracks to get it.

Mavis will save the timeout in case he needs it. He doubts that it will come to that. On first down he goes for the jugular, hoping to hit Runt on the fly beneath the goal posts, but at the last instant a hand comes out of nowhere to bat the pass away. Lee is still rushing only three men, leaving eight to cover the truncated end zone, and for a moment Mavis thinks of a pump-fake to get the attention of the defensive backs and then a draw to Mojo up the middle, but abandons it as a bad idea that might not work and surely will eat up the scant time left on the clock. Instead, he tries a quick shot to Rashad Lattimore in the right corner of the end zone, something that has always worked, but Streak is bumped at the line and doesn't reach his mark in time, the pass tumbling harmlessly onto the track surrounding the field.

On third down, time running out, he tries the bread-and-butter, flooding the left corner of the end zone with four receivers, lobbing a fade, sort of a controlled Hail Mary intended for Tree, but again a hand rises from the masses and again the ball bounds away. Mavis calls for his last timeout. It's come to this: fourth down, still seven yards to go, two seconds left, the entire season down to one more play. In spite of the circumstances, the entire stadium has gone eerily quiet as Mavis limps toward his sideline, meeting Billy Ray halfway.

"Okay, what've we got left?"

"I'm taking it in," Mavis says.

"The hell you say."

"I've got 'em right where I want 'em."

"*What?* Jesus, kid, you can't even *walk*, for Christ's sake."

"See you at the house."

...

Like a statue, some kind of bronze god, Mavis stands alone at the twelve-yard line, hands held together at his chest to take the snap, eyes narrowing to take it all in: receivers spread from sideline-to-sideline, Mojo crouched beside him in a three-point stance, the orange pylons at either end of the goal line, play clock reading :02, the end zone flooded with red jerseys and silver helmets, a sea of hands that would deny him. He lifts his left leg, the bad one, the signal to snap the ball, and when it flies toward him from between T-Bone Williams's legs the receivers spring away from the line, sprinting for the back of the end zone. The play clock blinks :01 and then :00.

Arm cocked, looking, looking, looking, defenders locked onto his receivers like Siamese twins, he sees a highway open up ahead of him, a red carpet, a yellow brick road, as though the Red Sea has parted, and he tucks the ball under his right arm and takes off, straight ahead, with only little Mojo Anthony leading the way, a bodyguard, an arrant bowling ball. Startled, the Lee players are spinning around, snorting and charging him now, a race to see who gets there first. He hears no screams, feels no pain, thinks only of how fine it is to have the wings of an angel, as he plants the good leg on firm ground, only six feet away now, and flings himself into the air, both hands extended, clutching the ball, a precious golden egg bearing new life. Glory! He has seen the elephant and heard the owl. Nothing can harm him now.

TWENTY-SIX

By the time they arrive, the house is lit up like a roadhouse and Billy Ray has to park the wagon on the street a block away. Vehicles of every description are there, from B. D.'s Cadillac to one of the church vans to Rima's pickup, and through the picture window they can see that a party is in full bravado. His knee now locked up, his white jersey soiled with blood and grass stains, Mavis hobbles along behind Billy Ray, equipment bag in one hand, as they enter the foyer to cheers from the crowd: Ginny and Maggie, Tank and Pig, Scottie and Rima, Frankie Lorino, Rev. Beaumont and several of the Touchdown Mamas, B. D. and the Auburn coach Max Longstreet, Jabari and Janelle Lattimore, even a couple of the Ansley Park ladies who must have invited themselves.

Billy Ray leads Mavis up the stairs and down the hall to Ricky's room. He finds that Ginny has dusted, turned on the bedside lamp, fluffed the pillows, laid out a set of clean towels. Going through the equipment bag, Mavis tosses his helmet and pads into a corner, finds a clean change of clothes, and sits on the bed while Billy Ray helps him pull the uniform pants over his swollen knee. "Not exactly the Holiday Inn," Billy Ray says, conscious of the oil painting of Ricky hanging above the bed, then smiling and rumpling Mavis's damp wiry hair with his hand. "Grab a shower and come on downstairs. Don't want to keep your fans waiting."

Quickly washing off the grime and brushing his hair, changing into a fresh pair of jeans and a Green Bay sweatshirt, Billy Ray comes down the stairs to join the crowd. Most of them have gathered around the pool table in The Gun Room, where Ginny has laid out a large tureen of chili, a platter of cornbread, a carved ham, and loaves of white bread. They are standing or sitting where they can, admiring the trophies and talking excitedly about the game and the season. He ladles a bowl of chili for himself, grabs a spoon and a hank of cornbread, and goes into the living room to see what's up with Maggie. His daughter has changed out of her cheerleader's outfit into jeans and one of his old shirts. She has been crying, and is being consoled by the women.

"I just hope they fire the old sonofabitch," she is saying.

"Maybe now they will, hon," says Ginny, rubbing the nape of Maggie's neck and holding her close.

"What'd you do, babe?" Billy Ray says. "Somebody's gonna have to fill me in here."

"I *quit,* Daddy. When they hurt Mavis, that did it. I've never been so mad in my whole life. And then he congratulates the boy who did it, that *thug,* Sammy Tubbs. It was *disgusting.* I'll never, never, *never* go back."

"Quit in the middle of the game? How'd you pull that off?"

"You were a little busy, Daddy." She laughs, sniffles, laughs again. "I just walked away at the half and went over on the other side to sit with Mom."

Rima says, "I presume you told 'em where they could put their megaphone."

Ginny jumps in. "You missed all the fun, Billy. As soon as Mavis scored, Buck Swain ran into the end zone and whacked one of his players on the helmet. Knocked the poor kid to the ground. Then the McGill kids started trying to tear down the goal posts, and that's when they turned on the fire hoses. All they needed was some German shepherds and it would've been Birmingham all over again."

...

Back later for a refill of chili in The Gun Room, where all of the men have fled, Billy Ray figures this is just like old times: men, among themselves, talking football. Ginny has even done some cleaning up here, in his private sanctuary, vacuuming the shag carpet, dusting, bringing the windows of the glass trophy cases to a shine. The last he saw, she hated the place. But, then, many things have happened since he left.

"Lookie here now, Gun, I've been having these *hallucidations*," B. D. Spotswood is saying, dabbing at some chili on his shirt.

"Yeah, you dreamed I'd shut up." Billy Ray winks at the other men in the room, flopped back, collegial, as though it were a locker room.

"Aw, naw, now, Gun, you know that ain't so. It's shooting pool with you, right here in The Gun Room. How's about it? Just one game of eight-ball, Gun. Then I figure I can go ahead and die."

"Well, pardner, I don't want you doing that. Not until you've paid me what you owe me."

Tank has a glow about him. "Unless I miss my guess, Gun, you might not be long for your radio show. The athletic association's gon' be all over Swain for the way he handled himself tonight. You could probably be the next coach at Lee if you want it."

"You'd get my vote, Gun," says Max Longstreet. "That's unless you might want to come along to Auburn with Mavis. I don't think I've ever seen a kid turn around like he did this year."

"I don't know," says Billy Ray. "I ain't going nowhere without Tank here. I can say that right now. Anyway, I think this is probably it for me and coaching. This boy, this team, this season. I probably ought to stop right here while I'm ahead."

...

There is a rumbling in the living room, where Mavis has arrived from upstairs, now wearing jeans and a sweatshirt. He is being welcomed as a hero, surrounded by the women, who can't keep their hands off of him. Rima and Ginny embrace him, the Ansley Park ladies introduce themselves, and

Bernice, the Touchdown Mama from Manuel's, nearly squeezes the life out of him with a bear hug. He follows the smell of chili to The Gun Room and is closely followed by Janelle Lattimore.

"How's the knee, son?" says Max Longstreet. "Auburn's gonna be wanting to have a look at it, you know, before we can talk scholarship."

"Aw, it's okay," Mavis tells him. "Just kinda tightened up on me, is all. It's okay."

"All that work we did on the leg might be paying off," says Billy Ray. "I don't think it would've stood up to what it went through tonight."

"Ice," says Dr. Lattimore. "We ought to put a bag of ice on it right now."

"Heat, or ice?" says Billy Ray. "I never could remember which comes next. It's been a couple of hours since they worked it over."

"Hey, give the kid a break." It's Scottie Burns. "He's young. It'll come around. Let's let him celebrate for a while. Mavis, that's about the damnedest run I've ever seen. Congratulations."

"Thanks," says Mavis, who seems embarrassed by all of this attention, would really prefer to be somewhere else. "Like I was telling Mojo, he just cleared a road and I black-topped it."

"Say, now," says Rev. Beaumont, "this looks like the right time. Why don't we all hold hands and thank the Lord for all of these many blessings?"

"Aw, let's save it, Rev," says Billy Ray.

...

Rima has slipped outside without anyone noticing, and now she is pushing through the front door with much clamor, hoisting a large object wrapped in brown wrapping paper and carrying it into The Gun Room. Ginny and some of the others follow her to see what she's up to. Rima places the package on the pool table and begins peeling off the wrapping paper. "Ta-*daaa*!" she says with a flourish, revealing the oil painting of Billy Ray and Mavis on the sideline during a game, now in a gilt frame.

Ginny has seen it only as a work-in-progress and then in the newspaper, and now she is speechless. "My God," she says, running her hands over the surface. "After what happened tonight, it ought to go in a museum."

"Au contraire," Rima says. "It's yours."

"But all of the time you put into it. Don't do this, Rima. Sell it. Really."

"I insist. This is where it belongs."

Billy Ray says, "How about payment-in-kind, then, kid? Six months rent for the painting. How's that sound?"

"Got yourself a deal, bubba," she tells him.

...

At midnight, when Maggie has gone to bed and the guests have left, Billy Ray and Ginny are picking up around the house and loading the dishwasher when Mavis comes in and says, "You got the keys to the wagon, Gun?"

"Hey, I forgot. I had to park down the street. Thanks."

"Naw, I thought I might go out for a while."

Hunched over the dishwasher, Billy Ray and Ginny stiffen. *"Out?"* says Billy Ray. "Christ, kid, it's midnight. Where you going this time of night?"

"Downtown, is all. Some of the guys were gonna get together. Little Five Points, maybe."

"You really ought to take care of the leg, son."

"Come on, Gun, it's just the guys. You know how that is."

"Yeah, well, the last time you did that you damned-near got your butt shot off. Great God-amitey, Mavis. It's getting cold. It's late. It's dangerous out there. You ought to know about that better'n anybody. Come on. The bed's ready. We'll put something on the knee. Hell, you can go out and celebrate tomorrow."

"Aw, shit." Mavis catches himself and apologizes to Ginny. "Just for a while. I promise."

Ginny cuts in. "I'm with Mavis, Billy. He's a big boy and he deserves this. Let him have his moment."

"You, too? Don't you remember?"

"That was another time, hon. Come on. Give him the keys. He'll be fine."

...

Upstairs, rummaging around for a pair of pajamas in the bureau, he hears Mavis start the station wagon down the street with a great roar, can't remember whether he fixed the headlight that got knocked out of line that time he wrecked, or even if there's enough gas in the tank for a round trip downtown. He thinks of running downstairs to hail Mavis, tell him about these things, but he's distracted by the sight of his own wife coming out of the bathroom in a sheer negligee. He grins, feels he might even have blushed. It's been a while.

"Feeling pretty good about yourself, are you?" Ginny says.

"Why not? We won, and I'm home. I tell you, Gin, this kid—"

"Later, stud. In the morning." She has slid under the covers and is shaking her blonde hair so it fans out over the pillowcase. "Come on, get in bed, it's cold. *Now* what are you doing?"

"I'm looking for my pajamas."

"Hurry up, will you?"

"I know they're in here somewhere."

"Listen to me, Billy," she says. "Listen close. If I'm not having sex in the next five minutes, I'm going to die. You wouldn't want *that* on your record, would you?"

...

Somewhere in the shank of the night, he jolts awake, uncertain at first of where he is. The digital clock at bedside reads 3:10. Ginny is dead asleep, a contented mess, snoring softly. Trying not to wake her, he gets out of bed and slips into the jeans and sweatshirt he left in a pile on the floor, fishes a robe and slippers from the closet, then looks through the curtains onto the street below. If the station wagon is anywhere out there, he can't see it.

To make sure, he walks down the hall and looks in on Ricky's room. It's exactly the way he saw it late in the night, Mavis's helmet and shoulder pads and dirty uniform tossed in one corner, bed made up but not slept in. A chill runs up his back, raising the hairs on his neck, reminding him of another boy, another time, another automobile trip. Fumbling in the dark for the handrail, he pads downstairs, finds the light switch in the kitchen, and decides to start a pot of coffee.

While the coffee is brewing, he goes into The Gun Room. An ashen light filters through the sheer white curtains. He parts them for a view of the backyard, seeing in silhouette the fallen limb and the grotto and the tire still hanging from the big oak. Turning to the pool table, he remembers that B. D. never did get in his game of eight-ball, nor did they ever get around to deciding where to hang Rima's painting. It is still lying on the table, waiting for a home. He thinks he might hang it over the bed in Ricky's room, with the one of Ricky at thirteen, or maybe somewhere here in The Gun Room. Yeah, he thinks, that would bring everything full circle: the Gunslinger, from his first sandlot uniform as a ten-year-old to this vision of him thirty-two years later, virtually a lifetime in football, ashes to ashes.

No. That means death, and he doesn't want to think about it. A black teenager, on the streets in a wasted old car in the middle of the night, one of the headlights probably out, giving some cop reason enough to pull him over. God knows what's happening down there. *You the owner of a 'sixty-two Chevrolet station wagon, Georgia license tag G-U-N? Well, sir, I'm afraid I've got some bad news. . . .* He can't bear the thought. Twice in a lifetime, that's too much. What the hell do these kids *do* this time of night, anyway? Everybody ought to be in bed by midnight, not tooling around town, looking for trouble, asking for it, really. He can guess the headline in Sunday's paper already: Air Mavis Bombs Lee for Title. He cringes to think of a followup story in Monday morning's *Constitution:* Prep Star Killed in

Accident. Or worse, in case some old geezer with a morbid sense of humor happens to be working the copy desk: Athlete Dies Young.

...

The waiting is getting to him. It's three-thirty now. He goes into the kitchen to pour a cup of coffee, stirs in gobs of sugar, then remembers the old cop who's been moonlighting for games at Grady Stadium before working the graveyard shift for the downtown area; the same guy, it turns out, who gave him his DUI that time. Bruner, he thinks. Gary? No, George. George Bruner. He looks up the Atlanta Police Department in the phone book, dials the number on the wall phone in the kitchen.

"Zone Two. Sergeant Bruner."

"Hey, Sarge. Billy Ray Hunsinger."

"Gun." The cop seems surprised to hear him. "I was just sitting here with the Sunday paper, reading about the game. Y'all flat put it to 'em last night. That kid of yours must've played a hell of a game."

"Well, the boy's missing, Sarge. That's what I'm calling about." Billy Ray fills him in, describing the car and the license tag, making some guesses about where Mavis might be. "I hate to ask. You got any reports about the car?"

"I can tell you no without looking it up, Gun. I'd know that heap anywhere. Remember?"

"Yeah, yeah, yeah. That was a long time ago. Nothing, you say?"

"Well, we're a little bit behind, but nothing's come in yet. It's like a war zone out there after midnight on weekends. I don't even want to think what it's like at Grady emergency right now. Shootings, stabbings, you name it. Queers come in, screaming, got little mice up their assholes. People are stacked up there like cordwood."

"Maybe I should call Grady, then."

"I wouldn't bother. We'd hear about it first." The sergeant tries to calm Billy Ray. "I'll get on the radio and put out an APB for you if you want me to, but I wouldn't worry about it if I was you, Gun. Boys will be boys, you know. Give me your number. I'll call you if I hear anything."

...

Thanks a lot, Sarge. With nothing to do but wait, he turns off the light in the kitchen. He finds the stump of a cigar left in an ashtray in the Gun Room, lights up, then decides to step outside into the night air. After these months of living downtown, he's forgotten how quiet it is out here this time of night: no sirens, no barking dogs, no people shouting at each other. Like Mavis said one time, it's like Disney World, a perfect place of law and order and manicured lawns and clean sidewalks and gaslights on each corner.

The lights, in fact, cast an eerie glow all over Crestwood, shut down tightly since the last guests left before midnight. If anyone is still up at this hour in never-never land, making love or fighting or worrying themselves to death about where the next million will come from, they're keeping quiet about it. He sits on the doorstoop, relights his cigar, settles in to wait it out. He feels foolish, a middle-aged man in a robe and slippers, waiting up for a teenager much older than his years, but he can't help it. He catches himself humming, *I've grown accustomed to his face, da-da-dah da-da-dah*, something like that, embarrassed to think it, presumes nobody is peeking through curtains to see him like this.

The coffee has grown cold and the cigar keeps going out. He has just closed the Zippo and sucked the butt back to life when he thinks he hears a gunshot. It can't be; not here, not in the middle of the night, not in Crestwood. No way. They don't do that sort of thing out here. He stops breathing, holds still, cups both hands behind his ears and leans forward in the direction of the sound. There it is again, *bang-bang-bang*, three shots in a row this time. Billy Ray rises from the stoop and looks wildly over the rooftops, up and down the streets, trying to zero in on the commotion. *Bang-bang. Sputter-sputter. Cough-cough.* And now he knows. It's the death rattle of a 'sixty-two Chevy station wagon, lurching home on its last legs, gasping and belching, coming 'round the bend. Of this he is sure: it's the sweetest sound he's ever heard.

ABOUT THE AUTHOR

PAUL HEMPHILL has traveled many miles in an eclectic career spanning four decades: failed minor-league baseball player, sportswriter, newspaper columnist, magazine writer, editor, teacher, radio commentator, and author of ten non-fiction books and four novels including *Long Gone*.

Son of a Birmingham trucker, graduate of Auburn University, a Nieman Fellow at Harvard, and a Pulitzer nominee for his memoir *Leaving Birmingham,* he is married to Susan Percy, executive editor of *Georgia Trend* magazine. They live in Atlanta, where he teaches writing at Emory University while working on another novel.

His website is www.paulhemphill.net.